D0597132

REMEDIES

REMEDIES

KATE LEDGER

AMY EINHORN BOOKS

Published by G. P. Putnam's Sons
a member of
Penguin Group (USA) Inc.
New York

AMY EINHORN BOOKS
Published by G. P. Putnam's Sons
Publishers Since 1838
Published by the Penguin Group
Penguin Group (USA) Inc., 375 Hudson Street, New York, New York 10014, USA • Penguin Group
(Canada), 90 Eglinton Avenue East, Suite 700, Toronto, Ontario M4P 2Y3, Canada (a division of
Pearson Canada Inc.) • Penguin Books Ltd, 80 Strand, London WC2R 0RL, England • Penguin
Ireland, 25 St Stephen's Green, Dublin 2, Ireland (a division of Penguin Books Ltd) • Penguin Group
(Australia), 250 Camberwell Road, Camberwell, Victoria 3124, Australia (a division of Pearson
Australia Group Pty Ltd) • Penguin Books India Pvt Ltd, 11 Community Centre, Panchsheel Park,
New Delhi–110 017, India • Penguin Group (NZ), 67 Apollo Drive, Rosedale, North Shore 0632,
New Zealand (a division of Pearson New Zealand Ltd) • Penguin Books (South Africa) (Pty) Ltd,
24 Sturdee Avenue, Rosebank, Johannesburg 2196, South Africa

Penguin Books Ltd, Registered Offices: 80 Strand, London WC2R 0RL, England

Library of Congress Cataloging-in-Publication Data

Ledger, Kate.
Remedies / Kate Ledger.
p.   cm.
ISBN 978-0-399-15589-5
1. Physicians—Fiction.   2. Medicine—Research—Fiction.   3. Physicians—Family relationships—
Fiction.   I. Title.
PS3612.E3422R46   2009   2009012943
813'.6—dc22

Printed in the United States of America
1   3   5   7   9   10   8   6   4   2

Book design by Chris Welch

This is a work of fiction. Names, characters, places, and incidents either are the product
of the author's imagination or are used fictitiously, and any resemblance to actual persons, living or
dead, businesses, companies, events, or locales is entirely coincidental.

While the author has made every effort to provide accurate telephone numbers and Internet addresses
at the time of publication, neither the publisher nor the author assumes any responsibility for errors,
or for changes that occur after publication. Further, the publisher does not have any control over and
does not assume any responsibility for author or third-party websites or their content.

For Jonny

Cast away our sins and transgressions
and make us a new heart.

•A KOL NIDRE MEDITATION

Ah, love, let us be true
To one another! for the world, which seems
To lie before us like a land of dreams,
So various, so beautiful, so new,
Hath really neither joy, nor love, nor light,
Nor certitude, nor peace, nor help for pain;
And we are here as on a darkling plain
Swept with confused alarms of struggle and flight,
Where ignorant armies clash by night.

•MATTHEW ARNOLD, *"Dover Beach"*

PART ONE

S imon Bear knew he probably shouldn't have hired the young nurse with the bouncy ponytail, a slender woman whose clavicle bones protruded like bicycle handlebars at the base of her throat. He had no need for additional staff, and she'd only just completed her nursing degree. Emily would have said without hesitation that he was making a tactical error by extending his practice and putting another person on the payroll. A *lamentable* business mistake was what she would have called it. But he'd gone ahead and hired the nurse, whose name was Julie. He'd done it on impulse, and he hadn't mentioned the decision to his wife.

This Julie—Julie McKinley, even her name rang like the head cheerleader from a high school squad—was due to start today. The even-toned sky suspended over Baltimore had only just begun to lighten with the dawn, and he rose with a hard-on. Emily remained on her side in a prawn-like curl, twirled into private space, breathing deeply. The night mask she wore over her eyes was askew, the elastic riding up in her hair. She had plugs in her ears. He sprang from bed with purpose, brain buzzing with phrases, bits of prepared speech, things he intended to tell Julie McKinley, and he found himself jerking off in the bathroom, his mind skittering, his hand moving like a machine. The hard-on was physiological, he knew, early morning blood rush to the spongy tissue of the *corpora cavernosa* generated by a thalamic cascade of irrepressible hormones. He honored the physiology with cylindrical fingers and his palm. To finish, his mind reached for an image, and settled on pink, the pansy-petal bloom of an areola, Emily's nipple crowning the small mound of her freckled breast. It was an image so old in his mind, finding it was like recovering a worn photograph, unimaginative and dull, and yet so achingly familiar, he felt almost ashamed. Beneath the areola, he imagined the flutter of her breath, intent and inviting, the first time he'd ever undressed her, unsure and eager. His hands, his mouth, moved over that new geography, breasts and hipbone, the dip of a sandbar in between. He'd fumbled, ventured here and there, tried to discern from her movements and the sound of her breathing if he was pleasing her. And he was! He'd surprised himself, Little Engine That Could! He'd brought her to consonantless moans, to cataclysmic writhing. He shuddered as he came, more from relief than pleasure, and thought, *Well, that's that.* Showering and dressing with zealous speed, he found himself humming something without words, and he was eager to be downstairs, in his office, to greet his new hire.

If Simon had asked, and he hadn't, Emily would have provided a long list of reasons why not to hire a nurse just out of school, the investment of time, the risk of mistakes, but he'd done it. It was a gut thing. Julie McKinley had taken a tour of the practice and he'd found himself won over. She was the bright recipient of some big nursing school honor and she came with a recommendation from a dean at a university, but what interested him most was her energy and her excitement, even the way she'd inspected the exam rooms, gobbling up the details with her eyes and nodding, nodding, nodding. There was none of that sullen, hardened, know-it-all efficiency in her manner, the result of *too much* work experience, an attitude he'd encountered in so many nurses. As Simon would have said to Emily, work experience was something a person comes by in the process of working; it was Julie's *character* he'd found hireable and a necessary change for the office, and character was something that couldn't be trained. The moment he'd offered Julie the job, jumping up from the chair in his office, his hand shooting forward from the sleeve of his white coat, congratulatory guffaws spilling from his mouth, he'd felt like patting himself on the back.

Anyway, negative outcomes tended not to fit into his worldview. As a matter of personal policy, he refused to sweat the small stuff. He bounded down the hallway, floorboards creaking under the lush wool knots of the Persian runners that Emily had chosen for the house, negotiating their purchase from a rug dealer in D.C. who hadn't even wanted to sell them. He'd been certain he'd seen the dealer's fingers tremble handing over the receipt. Emily was skilled in that way, making things happen quickly, with quiet finesse, and he felt a weird giddiness to have made a decision without even telling her.

On his way to the stairs, as a matter of habit, he poked his head into Jamie's bedroom to peek at his daughter, almost fourteen, a sleeping tangle of limbs and newly knobby joints. A silver thread of drool dangled from the corner of her mouth, pooling onto her pillow. It was the second week in July, and she was not supposed to be home, having sent herself off in a surprising burst of authoritative maturity to summer camp in Connecticut. He lingered in the doorway, just looking.

She'd come to him in March with the camp brochure and application in hand, having procured the information from the back pages of *The New York Times Magazine*. "They sent this to you?" he asked, blinking at the glossy literature. "You called them?" She didn't have many friends, and this seemed a hopeful turn for a kid who could spend weekend afternoons reading in her bedroom. But that was like her, forceful since the day she could stand on her own, able to make a plan and act on it. Her will had always been a marvel. At age five, she practically taught herself to ride a two-wheel bicycle, refusing to let him hold on to the back of the

seat even as she tottered into the trunk of a tree. As he saw it, his responsibility as her father was not to question any of the decisions she made;
instead, it was to enable her to make the grand gestures to shape her
life. Without even reading the text, he'd nodded at the brochure description of team activities and outdoor appreciation and written the check to
Camp Minnehaha.

What came as a surprise was that she didn't last in Connecticut more
than two weeks before the camp called saying they were sorry but it wasn't
working out and they were sending her home. Crossed wires was what
it was, he'd determined. Summer camps were simpleminded businesses
at the core, and they didn't really know child development. First, they'd
gotten their hackles up because she'd borrowed a knife from the mess
hall. Her punishment was a kind of probation, and they didn't let her
attend evening activities with all the other campers. In response, she'd
managed to distress the staff by threatening to go on a hunger strike.
Of course she wasn't serious! She was thirteen, for chrissake, and it was
likely she had some secret stash of food on the side and was just trying
to make a public point that they'd punished her unjustly. But she scared
them, all right. She skipped meals for two days straight, a protest that sent
tremors of intrigue and rebellion among the other campers. Minnehaha
did not have a sense of humor, it turned out. Instead of quelling what was
undoubtedly an imaginary insurrection, the directors gave her the boot.

Jamie didn't show one ounce of regret. What she said was the brochure
had turned out to be one long lie about camaraderie and outdoor skill-
building. She was a kid with long, straight dark hair, broom-fringe bangs
that lifted and whipped when she turned, a smart girl, but maybe a little
too cynical, he thought, a little too humorless for her own good. If she
could just lighten up a bit, take things a little more in stride, everything
might be easier for her. Emily put up an argument that the camp owed
it to Jamie to resolve the issue, if not to give her a second chance, and
after all, it was the director's word against hers regarding the knife, and

it was a matter of perspective whether it was borrowed or stolen. What a waste of money, she added. But those were the practical arguments again. *Always with the practicalities when so much of life demanded trusting your instincts.* When he peeked in on Jamie from the doorway, he was glad she was back home. He enjoyed this part of his routine, and marveled that Jamie might not even be aware that he'd been poking his head into her bedroom just about every morning since she was a baby.

The light outside had shifted to slate blue. In the kitchen, he grabbed an apple from a wooden bowl and began eating as he headed down the back-hall stairs to his private practice in the basement. Rotating the fruit in his hand, he gnawed at the white flesh, winnowing it down to the core as he descended in the dark. By the time he had reached the large mahogany door that separated the house from his office, he had chewed into the core itself, swallowing seeds and stem and the tiny leaves on its nether parts. He was a man who ate the entire fruit. *All or nothing* was what he planned to tell Julie McKinley. His philosophy. At forty-eight years of age, he was better than he'd ever been. He had energy in spades, happened to be one of those fortunate people who require little sleep, the result of good genes, probably, the dictates of a remarkable pineal gland in the brain leading a seamless biorhythm of extremes. He was also a man committed to caring. He considered himself a rare breed of doctor, refusing even to read magazine articles about crises in medicine, slashed reimbursement, all that crap. Those doctors who complained they couldn't earn as much as they used to—crybabies, all of them. Any doctor whining about money should have chosen another livelihood. The proof of his worth was in his busy waiting room, where patients willingly endured his overbooked schedule and wheedled to be fit in between other appointments. Proof was in the flood of e-mails and pink phone messages from people wanting to get in touch with him. He'd explained part of this to Julie when she'd visited the practice, nodding agreeably. And there was so much more to tell her. He entered his office, placed himself at his desk amid piles of paper, strewn notes and half-read, earmarked medical journals. Julie McKinley was due in at seven thirty. It wasn't quite six.

He'd already told her the proud history of the house. In the posh Guilford neighborhood within the city limits of Baltimore, it sat on a rise of land, just half a block from the famous, tulip-studded expanse of Sherwood Gardens. Several other impressive mansions surrounded the public park, but none as eye-catching as his family's stone mansion with its tabernacle windows—like heavy-lidded eyes rimmed with leaded glass—and the dramatic, Spanish tile–crowned turret in front. Built in 1892, the mansion was even registered on the national list of historic sites; the plaque by the front door attested to its status.

He had taken latitude in honoring its history. He and Emily had been obligated to receive permission from the city's historical society to build the rising curved driveway and the slate paths around the house, but he'd maintained motifs, evident in old photographs from the city's archives, of the landscaping from the beginning of the twentieth century. He'd hired a gardener to trim the topiary bushes into conical spirals. A rambling walkway led to a Japanese footbridge and pointed the direction into a shaded plateau of flat lawn. There, with a slight intervention of modernity, a latticed gazebo that Simon had built with his own hands provided a picnic space for the family. The grounds, including the gazebo—his own design and construction, not quite finished but still undeniably functional, with a two-tiered platform, and a roof and three walls of the hexagon—had been on the city's garden-visit tour.

He had also told Julie McKinley that he'd been fortunate that the wing on the north side of the estate had been added in the 1940s. Seventeen years ago, in 1990, when he parted ways with Guilford Medical Associates (they'd requested his resignation—it came down to a matter of differences of personal style—but they continued to respect him, hell, they still sent patients to him), the fact of the late addition had provided a legal loophole to establish a business on the residential estate. He was able to build a three-suite medical practice on the north side of the building. Patients with appointments to see him parked along the street and, spotting the tasteful little gray-and-gold sign stuck in the ground with the emblem of a grizzly and Simon's name and title in small capital letters, followed the slate path to the clinic entrance, which was level with the basement. His office, with his desk and his books and his diplomas, was situated at the front corner of the house, and its short windows, offering more light than view, faced to the north and the west.

Waiting for Julie McKinley, he answered patients' e-mails, jumping up each time he thought he heard the sound of a car. From the window, he saw Rick Grove heading down the block, briefcase in hand, pointed little head tucked down, walking toward his shiny black BMW. The Groves lived in an angular stucco house with Grecian-style bas-relief trim, a structure Simon had always—to Emily—referred to as The Sarcophagus. He called the Groves' shiny car the Hearse. Rick, whom Simon had always considered a conversation hog, taught Russian literature and language at American University, and his wife, Janet, was an art museum trustee who organized charities. The two families socialized as a matter of course because Emily had long ago hit it off with Janet, though the women's friendship remained something he'd never understood. He remembered he was supposed to call the Groves to ask if they wanted a pair of tickets to the Lyric Opera House for a weekend in September when Emily was due to speak at a conference. Lingering at the window, he watched as Rick got into The Hearse and sped off. Then he returned to his desk to answer a patient's e-mail question about an antibiotic. When a motor idled on the street and went quiet, he jumped to his feet. He peeked through the curtains and then rushed down the hall to the waiting room, where he flung open the front door of the clinic. There she was, emerging from her car in pale purple scrubs, the color of an Easter egg, hoisting a blue backpack over one shoulder. *Why get into it with Emily?* One couldn't always be expected to explain the people who were necessary to get things done. The morning was bright, dappled with affirming sunshine, and he squinted as the young woman turned toward the house.

"You're an early bird," he called out, holding open the door and waving her inside.

"Yeah, to a fault, almost," she acknowledged, stepping past him. "I'm always afraid to be late. I wind up leaving too much time to get places." If she was pretty, and he wasn't sure she was, it wasn't in a conventional way. Her face had a small, fragile look, the features within it batlike and hopeful: mascara-fringed little eyes, a slim nose, a tiny mouth. And then below her neck, those startling clavical bones.

"Come in, come in!" he said, though she'd already entered. "We have a place for your things."

He led her around the corner of the reception area to a walk-in closet reserved for the staff. As he stood next to her, he realized for the first time how little she was, only about a head taller than Jamie. He felt a rush of pride—and relief—as he realized he didn't want to sleep with her. Sex was certainly not the reason he'd hired her. If the topic had come up with Emily, he could have said with grave honesty that he wasn't attracted to Julie McKinley, but Emily wasn't jealous of other women in that way.

Julie tucked her backpack onto a waist-high shelf in the closet. Her body was concertedly, even unreasonably thin, her cheeks feathered over with a chalky foundation meant to hide the pitting from adolescent acne. All of the details suggested, endearingly, he thought, a person intent on trying hard. He'd gathered that about her from the interview, as she sat with her shoulders squared in the chair opposite his desk, wearing a dark blue suit with a skirt and a choker of pearls too large to be real. The assessment had made him all the more eager to explain how he'd started the practice from scratch and had built a reputation in the most respectable way possible: by word of mouth. Wives now brought their husbands to see him, neighbors passed his name along to their friends, and physicians referred their mothers-in-law. He had produced evidence,

displaying for Julie the file he kept of gushing, grateful cards patients had
sent to the office. On his wall and on his bookshelves were gifts they'd
brought back from their vacations, a silk fan from China, a fertility statue
from Mozambique, a pyramid-shaped bottle—still unopened—of agave
tequila from Mexico. He ate free at every Dora's Café in town because
he'd suspected—correctly, it turned out, and in contradiction of an emi-
nent doctor in town—that the general "weird" feeling that one of Dora's
aunts was having wasn't simply nerves or indigestion but a slowly evolving stroke. He was respected by the medical community, by internists
like himself, and by the specialists to whom he referred his most difficult
cases. Twice, he'd been on the list of *Baltimore Magazine*'s Top Docs. The
glossy clips were mounted and framed and hung side by side in each of
the three exam suites.

Throughout the interview, he'd hoped she was impressed by his practice and that word would get back to the dean. Then he'd noticed the
pearls and had realized he wanted to help her. "If I get this job," she'd
gushed, "it'll be the best day of my life." She'd grown up in Towson, just
across the county line from Baltimore, with a single mother who worked
several jobs to keep the family afloat. To put herself through nursing
school she'd waited tables and tended other people's children, and she'd
taken more time than most students to finish the coursework, but her
grades were solid and she'd won the Torrence Nursing Award, the most
promising graduate in her class. All her life, she'd been waiting to move
out and live on her own, have a salary and a steady job and the means
to make significant decisions about her life. If he hired her, she stated, it
would be the day she proved she was going to make something of herself. "*Have* made something of myself," she restated. The phrase caught
him off guard, and for a second he thought he might laugh, just at the
guileless way she continued to nod. Emily would have rolled her eyes
at that point—the young nurse had no idea how to present herself. But
Simon had the opposite response to Julie's honesty. What Julie wanted

was a mentor, someone to guide her to the next phase of her career. It was within his power to be that, and so he offered her a job. The impulse made him feel as expansive as a wide-winged bird. He was not far from trying to press a wad of bills into her hand.

Now, standing in the waiting room, she looked around, taking it all in with the look of a person marveling over an inheritance. "Such an incredible space," she commented. "It's so awesome how the waiting room doesn't look like a waiting room. It's like—like a czar's salon."

He was amazed by how much she reminded him of his daughter. But he looked appreciatively at the deep russets and forest hues of the walls and drapery, the chairs edged with gold, the cushions trimmed with elegant paisleys, and the detailed woodwork that had been added at great expense and trimmed with light blue and gold paint. "That's my wife's brilliance," Simon said with unreserved enthusiasm, glad for the opportunity to mention Emily. "She's smart about these things. Most doctors don't sink a lot of money into the waiting room, but where do patients spend the most time?"

"Who did the ceiling?"

Simon looked up. Above them, a painter's fine detail work had created an overarching canopy of branches, small leaves fluttering, and beyond them, sky.

"Can't remember the guy's name," Simon said. "Local artist. The ceiling was my idea. I have to admit, trees wasn't what I had in mind."

"It's peaceful."

"I wanted a replica of the Sistine Chapel," Simon confided. "We went to Florence when we were first married, and the ceiling just blew me away, the creation of man, God about to touch Adam's hand. A bunch of rosy angels watching. You know that outstretched arm? It seemed like something that would be unusual, absolutely bold. My wife said, 'Whoa.' A million reasons, no. She didn't think it sent the right message." Actually, Emily had argued against the painting because she said it would give the impression (to patients) that Simon thought he *was* God. Nothing could be further from the truth, he argued. If anything, he thought the painting, in a medical setting, suggested that everyone was ultimately equal, all created by the same divine touch, every last human indebted to a higher power, God or something else. More than a decade ago, they'd gone around and around on it.

"And besides that, my wife said, 'What are two Jews doing with the Sistine Chapel on their ceiling?' I said, 'It's *art.*' It's not a religious thing. Anyway, we're not even that religious," he added guardedly, then wondered aloud, "You Jewish?"

He knew she wasn't—the name McKinley, for chrissake—but he often asked when he met someone new and sometimes found himself taken by surprise. (Years ago, he'd had a receptionist named Candice who'd grown up in the county and who admitted to him that he was the first Jew she'd ever met. It blew his mind. Baltimore! Where'd she been? He hadn't been able to forget that fact about her, or let it go. "So *now* what do you think of us?" he'd chided Candice after she'd worked in the office for a month. He badgered, "Are we what you thought?" Her face blanched, but he wouldn't relent. "I gotta know if I'm doing right by my people," he teased. Finally, she waved him off, saying, "I meant the *other* kind of Jews. You know what I mean." He tried, but he'd never been able to needle an explanation out of her, and eventually she left the office for another job.)

"We're Jewish, but not that Jewish," he continued with a wave of his hand. "We belong to a temple on Park Heights. It's Reform. Mostly a social thing when you get down to it. We go only on High Holy Days." He looked up at the ceiling again. "Anyway, we hired an artist to paint this natural scene, as museumlike as he could. Complements the furniture in an interesting way, I think," he said, his hands on his hips as he considered the space above, still able to imagine the painting that hadn't happened.

But Julie McKinley was looking downward. "Cool fish," she said.

"The pond was my idea," he bragged. Between the large paisley-covered chairs, a section of the waiting area was carved to include a fountain, ringed with stones, and a small waterfall. Below, in the water, four lank orange and white fish sidled alongside one another, still, but seemingly listening, as if they awaited a command. "My wife was skeptical but I wanted the biggest one we could build in this space. My wife's a genius about public relations, partner of a company in Bethesda, you heard of Frith International? Even she had to agree the indoor pond was an inspired idea. I wanted it for the calming effect, but it turned out to be a great way to make the practice stand out in patients' minds."

"They're like goldfish, but big."

"Japanese koi," Simon corrected. The water rippled as a pipe-thick fish slunk sideways and then resumed its motionless vigil. Julie stepped to the edge of the rocks and watched. "Certain varieties of them cost thousands of dollars. I collect them."

Suddenly impatient, Simon turned and walked back to the reception desk. "Let's get you oriented," he said. "We open in twenty minutes."

"You can show me where you keep supplies so I don't have to keep asking all day," she suggested, and he heard Emily's voice in his head again, reprimanding.

They walked down the hall, passing exam suites A, B and C, to his office. Why had he asked her to come early? It wasn't to preview the filing system. He wanted to describe to her how he thought about things. In truth, he considered his own history as someone who'd *made something of himself,* even though his parents were educated and hardly down-and-out. He'd fashioned a career according to his own vision. His father, Charles Bear, had made a pretty penny in real estate. After returning from a tour of duty with the Marines in the early 1960s, in which he was responsible for rescuing a hijacked passenger vessel in the Atlantic, Charles had invested in a small area of land and built a putt-putt range south of

Baltimore. Small, recreational and unassuming. The unassuming part was the key to his success because the county government overlooked him, the developers left him alone. For years, like a frontier squatter, Charles had purchased plots of land adjacent to the range, quietly expanding until he owned a vast valley in Montgomery County. Then he established a golf course and a country club, which he'd managed into the mid-1990s, until he sold it and moved with Simon's mother, Lucille, to Florida. She was college-educated, though she'd been a homemaker all the years Simon was growing up.

He'd been aware for all of his life that his parents represented a successful unit, that Charles's strategizing had ensured money was a non-issue, that Lucille's duty to her husband had given the marriage a rare, if idiosyncratic, integrity. But he'd known since he was small that he was different from them. Charles had made his life about getting—and what was the quote? Simon read it in college and the words stuck as they hit grave understanding: "Getting and spending, we lay waste our powers." His mother's domesticity was a ritual of obsequiousness, an impotent, underachieving method of serving his father. Neither of his parents had set out, as he had, to improve the world and to save lives. Now *there* was putting one's powers to use. Even as a teenager, Simon had been drawn to the idea of healing other people, easing their hardships. He'd committed himself to that goal. And then, years ago, when he and Emily had been beset by their own tragedy, he'd stayed the course. At that moment, everything might have changed for him. Another doctor, another kind of man, a father who'd lost a son, might have given up on a life that was burdened by other people's problems. Caleb had been all of six weeks, a pale and squirming starfish, and the fact of his death had been a sucker punch in the belly. But Simon had rededicated himself to his ideals, continued to see patients, persisted in his effort to do *good,* trying to help. He'd overcome Caleb's death the best way he knew how, by investing in what was noble and right about his career.

"This is no ordinary private practice," he informed Julie McKinley. "In a ten-mile radius of my office, you can find excellent physicians of all kinds, but no one thinks about medicine the way I do. That is, really *thinks* about it. People don't consider all the changes that can make things better, easier, more effective. I think about the world that way. I've made dozens of innovations."

Julie McKinley bobbed her head.

The pieces of Simon's prepared speech flowed to him. He had so much to impart, there were so many facets to it, but it all came down to one thing. "My mission is to point patients toward whatever will help them. Period. That's most of what you need to know. I've found terrible flaws in how most physicians practice," he stated. "And I'll be damned if I repeat those mistakes with my own patients."

Julie's small eyes squinted at him. "What do you mean 'flaws'?"

"Ha. Good question," Simon answered, perhaps a little too loudly as Julie McKinley jolted a tiny bit in surprise, and then resumed her agreeable nodding. "Most doctors wouldn't even acknowledge that flaws exist. But I've thought about things. I've considered what happens in the doctor's office. I've discovered some of what we do could use a little tweaking."

"Like?" Julie said.

He led Julie back down the hall to a cabinet. "Every patient leaves with one of these." He handed her a blue folder, the kind with interior pockets. On the cover was a profile of a foraging grizzly embossed in gold foil.

"Oh, Bear, I get it." She fingered the illustration. "Pretty."

She really was like a child. But he would not change his mind now. If Emily were to challenge him, he'd assure her that he'd take responsibility for Julie. He'd make the decision work. "Every patient gets a write-up of what happens during the appointment," he explained. "When I first started practicing medicine, I found patients saying yes, yes, yes, while I was talking with them, but after they got home, they didn't understand, or plain couldn't remember all of what we'd said. They'd asked a question but only held on to part of the answer. Or they'd say, 'Yeah, the doctor says it's my iliotibial band,' and they'd have nothing in front of them to help them look it up. So, no more. Patients leave with the information they came in for right in their hands. Even little questions. And not like a scrap of paper like some doctors who scribble on a paper towel or whatever's handy. Sometimes the nursing staff complains about the extra paperwork, but that's how I have a top practice."

"It's a good idea," Julie acknowledged.

"That's how I see my job. To come up with good ideas. I was warned against casually handing out records to patients. A doctor I met on a plane years ago told me it'd open me up to all kinds of litigious problems. 'Certain kinds of patients are bloodthirsty,' he said. 'Records that float around are bound to work against the doctor in the end.' But I don't see it that way. People who're treated well—pampered by a doctor who's visibly doing everything on their behalf—aren't inclined to sue. People sue when they feel their needs aren't being taken seriously. When they feel small. Suing is the very primitive urge to be heard. The typical interaction between a patient and a doctor—guess how long? It was in a prestigious medical journal. Seven minutes. If you can believe it," he emphasized. "That's reimbursement, overbooked schedules, whatever. But doctors who spend four minutes longer with patients get sued twenty percent less."

"Maybe they're less rushed," Julie suggested. "Four minutes longer and they make fewer hasty judgments. In nursing school, we—"

"No," Simon interrupted. "It's not the work, it's the tenor of the interaction. It's that patients have the perception, in eleven minutes versus seven, that a different sort of encounter has taken place. Four more minutes and they feel somebody's taken the time to listen. I'm not worried about giving patients precious documents. I've been giving patients write-ups of their appointments for almost a decade, and I haven't been sued yet."

They both turned their heads as a key jiggled in the front door of the practice. Simon stepped forward and pulled it open as Rita Golodkin, rotund and huffing, wearing a purple dress with splashes of color, tried to snatch back the key ring that swung away from her.

"Everyone's early today," Simon said with obvious pleasure.

"You startled me," Rita said, stepping into the office. She was older than Simon, motherly, with a dandelion halo of pewter-colored hair. Large hipped, she brought to mind the shape of a Russian nesting doll. She mopped her bright and jowly face with a paper napkin. "What're you doing in?"

"Julie's first day. I'm orienting her to the ways of our world," Simon said.

"Our little world," Rita echoed, depositing a large purse on the reception desk. "Well, welcome. He'll talk your ear off. But he's also the nicest person you'll ever work for. Biggest heart ever. He really cares."

"Rita's been here almost as long as the practice has been open," Simon said. "Seventeen years. She even served as a subject when I developed the Boardwalk Diet. Did you hear about that? It was in the paper."

"It worked," Rita attested. "He had a lot of critics, but it was a good plan."

"It required the right kind of patient," Simon said. "See? That's another problem with medicine. People think a treatment is only good if it works for all people. But each person is different, and you can't write off potentially helpful treatments just because they're not right for everybody."

"What's the Boardwalk Diet?" Julie asked.

"Watch out," Rita warned, jesting. "You'll get him started."

"The theory behind that diet," Simon explained, "was that some people have what I call problem foods. That's foods—or food groups—they can't resist. The source of their excessive, unwanted weight."

"Mine was chocolate," Rita confessed. "Sweets in general, but chocolate in particular. You couldn't keep me away from it. I had truffles in my nightstand, Hershey bars next to the shower. Sometimes I had chocolate before breakfast, and I couldn't stop myself, either. If I ate one chocolate doughnut, I wanted all of them."

Julie looked back and forth between them as though she wasn't sure if they were pulling her leg, but Simon recalled the background of his inspiration.

"One summer when I was a teenager, I worked in a fudge shop in Atlantic City," he explained. "You know, on the Boardwalk. At the shop, you were allowed to eat as much fudge as you wanted, no holds barred. So I did. The first week, stuffed myself silly with fudge, practically made myself sick, and you know what? I was around it all summer, and I never wanted another taste of it. Still don't care for fudge very much. Anyway, that was the idea behind the diet. I got to thinking about foods and people's indulgences, and I realized that if you put people on a regimen where they're forced to eat to the point of discomfort, where the very problem foods bring up negative associations and negative physical feelings, that they'd actually lose the desire to overindulge and you could eliminate some of the most troubling sources."

"So, chocolate?" Julie turned to Rita.

"I did the whole regimen," Rita said proudly. "Lots and lots of chocolate. Boxes of it. It was sublime for about a day, and then I couldn't stand it. I had to keep eating, truffle after truffle, and I wasn't allowed any other food. Nothing but chocolate. So I hit my limit. Even threw up chocolate. And now, I don't eat it at all. Don't want it. If I smell it, I want to get away from it."

"But that's sad," Julie blurted. "Like bingeing and purging? That doesn't sound healthy at all."

"For some people, it's a start!" Simon said, taken aback. "What's *not* healthy is lying to yourself that that one diet or another's going to work.

Not everyone can maintain resolve on a weight-loss plan. Sometimes there has to be an internal mechanism—like negative motivation—to support a behavioral change." He softened some, as he seemed to consider it again. "The Boardwalk Diet clearly isn't for everyone. They do something similar for alcoholics, kind of a negative associa-tion thing to make people lose the urge for drinking, but I got to thinking—what about weight loss? What can we do here? That's just my point. We have to be thinking constantly about what can help people."

Rita smoothed both hands down the sides of her color-splashed dress. "I'm much thinner than I was," she said. "It's a good plan."

"I never heard of that diet," Julie said numbly.

"Of course, there were skeptics. They let me have it. There were letters in the paper. People were threatened. Some of them wanted my license suspended. You gotta expect that when you're making changes, rethink-ing the way things are done."

Rita sat down at the desk and snapped a headset over her head. "It worked for me," she said.

"Julie's very happy to be here," Simon told everyone suddenly. He had a plan to offer. "We have to make sure we keep her happy."

"Did he mention," Rita said, "that he's earlier than anyone in the morning, and after that he isn't on time for one single thing for the rest of the day?"

"Don't let anyone here try to convince you my lateness is a problem," Simon said to Julie. "They'll complain that we're behind schedule, and they'll complain that things aren't in order, but I know what I'm doing. Couldn't have been here for seventeen years if I didn't know what I was doing."

"There's a method to the madness," Julie said. He was relieved to see the return of the nod, so he did not address her comment. It was not madness to be driven, to be enthusiastic, to have ideas when real insights were in short supply.

"I was thinking," Simon said to Rita, "Julie could follow me around for a few days until she gets the hang of things. Then we shove her out of the nest, and she'll fly on her own."

Julie nodded to this plan and her eyes looked to Simon. She said, "I won't disappoint you, I promise." He could smell it on her, the drive to perform. It was right there on the cardboardlike ketonic scent of her breath. He felt a rush of sympathy—and nurturing—for her all over again, as she appeared to picture a literal nudge from the nest, that first scramble through empty air.

He'd forgotten the gratification of having someone observe him while he worked, the pleasure of performing for an audience. Several years ago, he'd been on the list as a rotation site for medical students. A third-year—Winton Harbanger—had shadowed him for a month as Simon made diagnoses and ordered tests and described how to *listen* to patients. Winton had been curious, to the point of annoyance, about the economics of "hanging out a shingle," as he put it. Question after question about reimbursement and insurance—Simon didn't care about those details. He had no idea what had happened to Winton Harbanger in the end, if he had a shingle swinging over a doorstep somewhere, but the gratification of performing, explaining himself, being the authority had been real. Julie followed him into the exam rooms as he realized he should call the student affairs office to make sure his practice was still on the list. He knew there was ludicrousness to his energy, that some of his gestures constituted acting. He talked louder than usual, lingered with the patients, cracked jokes that showed how well he knew them and their families. He found himself striking poses as he listened to their complaints, pausing with his chin on his hand like a person sitting for a photograph, or placing his pen in various positions against his head. Emily, who'd once coached him in public speaking, would have been amused if she'd seen him. "No, no, no," she'd said, sinking her face into her hands. "You look like you're pointing out where the thinking's taking place." He couldn't stop. Julie's presence in the exam suites, just the fact of her watching, made him feel robust, completely refreshed.

They established a pattern: He entered the exam suites with her, introduced her personally to his patients, and then he left so that she could take their vitals on her own. He waited for her in the hallway outside his office, and they conferred before reentering the room together. He acted the instructor, the illuminator, the didact. "The next one's Ed Penzy," he said. "Just watch, he'll come in for something small, a wart or something, and then just as I'm leaving the room, he'll say, 'Oh, by the way, I've been having these chest pains that make it really hard for me to breathe.'"

"What do you do?" Julie asked.

"I wind up sending him for a bunch of tests. But he's proof positive that if you're a good doctor, you don't rush out of the room too fast."

Or, whispering in the hallway: "The next one's April Frock. Epileptic. Twenty at the time of her first seizure but never knew it. Thought she was having an allergic reaction to Chinese food, can you imagine? When she kept having these dizzy, fainting spells, a neurologist stuck her on medication and never even told her what the meds were for. *I* was the one who told her. Once she knew what she was up against, everything changed for her. Now she's real positive about her condition, and she can drive and everything. We have to keep tinkering with her meds, though, to get the right levels in her system."

Julie hugged the papers to her chest, listened and nodded. Yes, he was sure he'd done the right thing to hire her. It was an infusion of something to the practice, a jolt of something that had been missing. In late morning, Maxi Bailey was waiting in exam suite B, and he recognized instantly another opportunity to show off. "She's a tough case," he whispered to Julie in the hallway. "One of my toughest. She was in a car accident several years back. Haven't seen her in a while. She's one of those patients most doctors hate to treat because she wasn't getting better. I'm not afraid, though. I don't scare off easy."

The truth was, he took pleasure in treating those patients, the chronic pain sufferers, who mystified and frustrated other physicians. They were patients whose pain continued for months—even years—on end, even though there was often no sign anywhere in their bodies of what was causing the trouble and no surefire method to stop it. You could break it down, to try to think about what was happening. The mechanics of acute pain—the pain of injured tissue—were fairly straightforward: First, a trauma. The awareness of pain alerted the body about the presence of a problem. The free, branching tips of pain cells, long silvery bundles of thin, highly specialized nociceptive fibers, took note of an assault on the skin or deep in the tissues of the body. Electrical charges shifted across the membrane of a neuron, the depolarized end firing a message through the length of the cell, like a flare shooting from a troubled ship. The alarm sped to nerve clusters, the dorsal root ganglia, lined up outside the junctures of the spine. There, operating like a gate, the pain message was processed with brute labels: "Significant!" "Worth noting!" "Get right on this one!" and was admitted to the main circuit, the spinal cord.

Onward to the brain! The pain message bounded up the lateral spino-thalamic tract to the limbic system and the cortex. Long dendritic fingers at the end of one cell released chemical messengers that swam across synaptic oceans into the receptive docking points of adjacent cells. And at that point, Simon well knew, the route became complicated, infinitely convoluted and impossible to trace. The chemical response met and mingled with emotions and memory, conjuring past fears and instilling new worries, that could not only make sense of the injury but heighten the sensation. The very first message of pain could be answered by a motor reaction, descending from the brain, like one telling the arm to pull the finger away from the hot handle of a pot, but it also etched a path of experience, a way to make sense of the world.

But chronic pain, the kind that outlasted its function, was another story. Sometimes there was an injury that started the pain response, but sometimes there was no inciting event at all. In any case, something more happened. Injured cells released agents of inflammation, distress-signaling molecules—serotonin, bradykinin, prostaglandins, growth factors, and cytokines—that somehow altered the nociceptive nerve endings. The machinery itself became changed so that the life of the injury did not end. You couldn't find a doctor the whole world over who could tell you what changed in the system, but even as the original damage appeared to heal, the effect in the nerves continued to thrive. Viciously, the pain cells continued shooting off messages of pain, an alarm continuing to sound. As they coopted messages from surrounding cells, the undamaged skin around the injured site suddenly became painful. The nerves became even more sensitive than before, responding as though they were confused about their function. The effects could be so terrible that people suffering from this hyperalgesia would cry even to have their bedsheets brush against their skin. For these patients, there was no clear pathology for any doctor to treat. By then, the pain message obscured the source. For these patients, there was only the mysteriously bushwhacked path—a sensation lost somewhere in the neurons, in the synapses, in the gateway to the spinal cord, in the brain—its course becoming more unclear. The pain became its own disease.

What Simon found amazing was that most physicians, accustomed to addressing a problem and fixing it, couldn't stand the mystery. They hated not being able to pinpoint where the pain was or to measure its severity with any known tool. With only the patient's description of sensations to guide them, there was only to take aim in the shadows for an unknown, unseen, untraceable foe. Simon welcomed the challenge. Chronic pain patients turned up often in Simon's office. They sought him out, and he did not turn them away. The key to treating them, Simon had come to believe, was assuring them. They were scared most of all of being told that nothing could be done, that there were no easy answers, that the pain was all in their heads. Whatever they described to him, he treated. It was a game for him: find some form of relief for each person. He believed there was always another treatment to suggest, another dose of medication to alter, something new to try—just as long as he kept thinking, devising something new they hadn't tried.

Once, after boasting a little too complacently about his ability to help, Gabi, the physician's assistant, had accused him of being intoxicated by their gratitude. Gabi was long-limbed, from Jamaica, and bossy, with an oval forehead, a slender nose and a mouth capable—it seemed to Simon— of a hundred expressions of impatience and displeasure. She grumbled about Americans, their culture of entitlement, their self-importance, their get-it-done-yesterday attitude and their *rudeness* to one another, and she told him that he loved the pain as much as he loved the patient. He couldn't deny she was right. He was aware of the way they looked at him when they were in its grip, the way they listened to his suggestions, the way they hung on his advice. Desperation made their attentiveness acute. They were hopeful, vulnerable, eager, angry at the world and at fate, and they came to him for answers. He did what he could to find solutions, and he didn't begrudge anybody any kinds of drugs for any reason. He was not afraid of their needs. He prescribed for them the best that was available.

In suite B, Maxi Bailey sat on a chair next to the exam table and lifted a head of greasy blond hair with dark roots. She was only thirty-eight, with bone structure that suggested she'd once been a wholesome type of pretty, but her looks had taken on a decade's worth of wear, as worry lines marred her cheeks and creased her brow. Her shoulders pressed forward, and her chin turned downward so that the prongs of her tinted bangs hung into her face. She regarded Simon as he entered, large brown eyes turned down at the outer corners, resulting in a grave and doubtful look, like a greyhound.

"Maxi, good to see you again," Simon greeted her. "It's been a while,"

he added without pausing for a response. Maxi Bailey smiled weakly. Julie
stood at his elbow as he asked Maxi about her son, who he remembered
was a few years older than Jamie.

The greyhound eyes lifted, but the shoulders remained hunched.
"Sam? He's fine. Lifeguarding at a pool this summer. And my older one's
leaving for college."

"Your husband—don't tell me, let's see if I can remember—still at
Black and Decker?"

A small smile. "They promoted him this year," she said, "so he's been
busy."

"And how about you?" he inquired finally, with a tone he hoped
sounded more intimate, more gentle. He sat on a stool, rolled close
to where she sat and stretched his arm out so that it rested beside her.
"What's what?"

"I've run out of doctors to see," she said slowly, her shoulders curled
protectively. She held her body still and braced, as though she imagined
mere blinks of her eyes could cause shockwaves through her body. "It's
still my back. I don't know what else to do."

"Still hurts." He didn't ask. He stated it, knowingly.

She glanced at him, then back at her hands, limp in her lap. "Worse,
even. It feels like it's down my arms."

"When was the accident again? You were rear-ended, right?"

"Four years ago."

"That's a good while," he said with sympathy. He saw his pain patients
as victims of the nervous system's infinite complexity, which was capable
of horrific misinformation. Maxi's car was butted at forty-five miles an
hour, the chassis tweaked, the trunk crumpled like an accordion. As she
jolted with the impact, her spine jarred against itself. All along her vertebrae, the adjacent muscles had been bruised, and the pain nerves sounded
the distress signal. But what then? The bruises healed, the tissue returned
to normal. But four years later, her nervous system continued to rail.

"It's gotten so bad I can barely function," she said. "I can't sit for long before I have spasms. The worst you could ever imagine. Like a snake writhing through my spine. Like fire or something. Shocks go down from my shoulders. I never know how long it's going to last. Some days it's so bad I can't get off the couch. When it hits, the pain's so bad I can barely see. And then for hours after one of these—I don't know what to call them—episodes, my arms are sometimes buzzing and sometimes numb like I can't lift them. I can't stand in line at the supermarket. I can't even do the smallest house chores."

He shook his head with understanding, but there was no way to understand, to know what someone else's skin felt. Each patient's pain was so individual, so intensely private. What was clearest was that there were never adequate words for the sensations. His patients groped among adjectives: *searing, wrenching, pounding, jamming, twisting, aching, burning, prickling, buzzing, throbbing.* Certain words, like a pain that *buzzed,* could tell him about the nature of the problem and sometimes direct him to a particular spot on the body. Often they came up with associations involving tools—*a knife slicing* or *a vise tightening* or *a screwdriver jabbing*—but they were only approximating to give a rough picture of what they endured. He would never say it to a patient, but he'd occasionally had the thought that the inability to describe the pain gave it a sacred quality, too. When you lacked words to make others understand your truths, you stood apart from the jabbering masses. You alone possessed proof of your unique and involuted humanness, and through that, contact with something divine.

But such notions didn't help patients, whose own lives had become unrecognizable.

Noticing that her eyes were tearing, Simon placed his hand on her knee. Then he rolled back on the stool and looked at Julie. "Once it was a simple problem, but the body changes, trying to accommodate the damage," Simon explained. He asked Maxi, "Do you have support at home?"

The greyhound eyes blinked. "My husband believes I hurt," she said, "but he thinks I have a low tolerance." Simon imagined the husband, whom he'd never met, a business-minded guy scared out of his wits about what was happening to his wife. Doctor after doctor and no answers. Simon had seen it happen before; it wasn't just the suffering, it was the mystery that tormented. One person's inexplicable and indescribable pain was like another companion. It moved in. It took a place at the table, demanded to be addressed. It was an intruder that could rip a marriage apart. "He thinks I should buck up. Or like it's a bad case of PMS, and I'm *choosing* to stay inside and sit on the couch because I don't feel like doing anything. But it's nothing like that." She smirked. "I gave birth to two kids—with no epidural or anything—and this is worse than any labor."

When she'd last seen Simon, he'd given her the names of two doctors she could see, a spine surgeon he knew at Johns Hopkins and a rehabilitation specialist. He hardly was surprised to hear now that her journey had taken her to sixteen other doctors and treatment centers as well. The X-rays she'd had showed nothing, not even the mildest inflammation of arthritis. The CT scans were normal. The spine surgeon had told her that her back was in perfect alignment, all the vertebrae perfectly stacked up like checkers, adding that he wished his own back looked as good. There was no fracture along her spine, no tumor, no signs of infection. Simon peered in Maxi's chart, reading the surgeon's notes.

"It would've been easier if he'd found something," Maxi said, "even a bulge in the disks between the vertebrae pressing on a nerve. Then they'd have had some reason to want to operate—just *do* something. I wanted to know, couldn't they just go in and cut the damaged nerves so that I wouldn't feel pain?"

"No, no!" Simon interjected. "You don't want to go cutting nerves. Even when surgeries are successful at first, the pain can come back. And different too: sudden, inexplicable aches, searing pain, cold, heaviness, burning, and weird unpleasant sensations that are almost impossible to describe. They spent the better part of the twentieth century slicing away nerves to treat chronic pain. They wanted the treatment to be surgical. Everybody thought if you interrupted the pain pathway, snipped the wiring, you'd stop the message from traveling to the brain. But the body stores memories of the pain—nobody knows how exactly. The truth is you can continue to feel it whether the nerve is intact or not."

During the course of seeing doctors, she had been on antidepressants, which were commonly used to stem pain, and steroid injections to quell inflammation. She'd done physical therapy, acupuncture, acupressure, hypnosis, meditation relaxation. A chiropractor had gone through the steps of realigning her back. "My husband drove me all the way down to North Carolina, and I entered a study at a university. They gave me shots of Botox in my back, thinking that it might stop muscle spasms, if that's what I was having."

"I've never heard of that, but it'd make sense, I guess, the way that stuff works," Simon reasoned. "Did it help?"

"Not really."

After that, she'd driven with her husband to a big teaching hospital in New York City, where the pain doctors had recommended something called prolotherapy, injecting irritants into her back, intending to break down ligaments and tendons that would then repair themselves in a natural and fortifying healing process. Stronger connective tissue, their theory stated, meant less pain. But that hadn't worked either. She'd stopped short of having a spinal cord stimulator implanted in her back. Simon turned to Julie. "You've heard of that, right? There are wires connected to a battery that sends electrical impulses to the electrodes. Electricity. The idea is that one impulse overrides another."

"Pain's so complex," Julie commented. "I guess you need a lot of ways to approach it."

"Nobody's been able to do anything for me," Maxi Bailey said, glancing at Julie and wiping at red-rimmed eyes. "It's like my body's betraying me—and everyone around me's betraying me, too. I can tell what doctors think when they see my chart. They think I'm difficult. I'm imagining it. Or exaggerating it. And that I must be one of those people with some deep-rooted psychiatric problem who doesn't really want to get better. They think I just want attention. You know me, I was an active person before. I liked rollerblading. We used to go, the whole family, to Lake Montibello, and do the loop around. I liked gardening, spending time with my sons. But since this happened, I spend most of my time trying to prove to people that I really feel as bad as I feel." Her voice cracked. "I don't want my sons to know me like this." Her head wilted down. Simon stared at her palms turned up helplessly on her lap. "I can't go to their swim meets, can't meet with their teachers. I missed the school science fair this year because I couldn't get in the car to drive. I'd like to hug them, but I don't even really want to be touched because I don't know what's going to set it off. There have been times"—now she would not look up—"where the pain's been so bad, and I've just felt so alone, so cut off from everybody, and such a burden that I've thought maybe it would be better if I were just—" A tear fell into her lap, and she looked at it a moment before her hand went to it, negating it by rubbing it into her pants. "I've wished I were dead."

"It's taken over your identity," Simon pronounced. "It's not just that you have the pain or that you live with it. Now the pain *is* you." He looked at her, the downturned eyes, the shoulders curled like a fiddlehead fern. He had never touched a patient in a way that might be misconstrued, but he was aware suddenly of the strangest urge to take her face in his hands and press his cheek to hers. What he felt for them—all of these patients—was inexplicably like love. "Are you on meds?" he asked.

She nodded. "OxyContin. I got it from a pain clinic. But I only take it now and then. I don't want to get hooked."

Simon believed in opioids. He prescribed them frequently, sometimes in magnanimous doses. He hated the skepticism about addiction. He believed the studies that showed opioids were the best therapy for chronic pain. Those studies were reason enough to use them. "There's no point in suffering," he stated. As Maxi Bailey lifted her head and looked at him, he found himself enunciating and poking the exam table with his index finger. "Your pain isn't helping you get better. Your body doesn't benefit from feeling it. Nothing about it heals you. It's the opposite, in fact, if you just ignore it—if you live just trying to get by—it can do damage. It can change the nervous system, tamper with it, screw it up. The nerves become like strings of an instrument that's overplayed. After a while, it's just not making music anymore. And the problem is, when this happens, nerves don't just go back to the way they were before. They deliver amplified messages, and what you feel is heightened, a kind of distorted sensitivity. And all of this changes you, too."

"Yeah, I feel changed," she acknowledged.

"It's been a long haul for you," he said. "I can say this: I'm *sure* there's a cure somewhere for you. I believe every biological process that goes awry has an antidote. It might be different for every person, or might work differently for each person at another time in their lives, but I believe we live on a planet that contains complementary compounds for the systems that exist. Somewhere in the world we have the remedies we need. We just need to find them. You haven't tried slowly raising the dose of opioids, so why not give it a shot?"

"I don't know," she said hesitantly. "I don't want to become a junkie."

"See?" Simon said, mostly for Julie's benefit, as he could hear himself speaking louder than was necessary. "That's the kind of prejudice that keeps patients from healing! There's a lot of misconceptions about narcotics. What you're calling addiction happens in less than five percent of patients." He stood up and lifted his prescription pad from his right-hand pocket. "You need permission not to hurt anymore?" he asked her as he scribbled. "*I* give you permission. I'm telling you your pain is not good for your health."

Maxi stared at the leaf of paper he held out. His words seemed to have perked her up, and she wavered as though she were trying to overcome her skepticism.

"Look, it's a drug," he conceded. "It's got side effects. You might feel like your thinking's a little fuzzy. So what? You won't do quantum mechanics right now, but you'll be better disposed to your body mechanics. Take back your life!"

"I don't know." She shook her head. "I'll have to go to the drugstore, you know?"

"Are you embarrassed to have the prescription filled—you don't want the drugstore guys to think you're up to something? I'll give you the name of a pharmacy. It'll be in your folder—the one you take home with you. It's a guy I know and trust in Glenburnie. He's a little off the beaten path so you don't have to worry about running into people you know, and he won't give you a hard time about your medication. Only you know your pain, Maxi. You've got to determine what will make you better."

Finally she reached for the prescription with trembling fingers and folded it once without reading it. When she looked to him again, there were tears standing in her eyes. They were different tears, though, and he felt billowing satisfaction as he stood, smoothed his coat and tucked the prescription pad back into his pocket. He told her he'd keep up with her to find out how the dosage was working and that she could e-mail him with any questions. "You have the right to reclaim your life," he reminded her. Julie, hugging the chart to her chest, followed him to the door. "You must never give up on yourself," he commanded.

Maxi Bailey thanked him in a voice barely more than a whisper.

By evening, he felt he had arrived at the closing scene of a play that he wished was not about to end. The sun outside was low, and the windows glowed with golden light. Like a host at the end of a dinner party, Simon personally escorted the last patient to the door. The nurses, Joyce and Melinda, each of whom had children who needed to be picked up from school or day care, had long since departed. Gabi peeled off her cardigan, preparing to head out into the humid July night. She hung it in the closet, muttering about the intensity of the air-conditioning in America, did it have to be a refrigerator indoors, after all? Rita Golodkin, who typically stayed late finishing the appointment write-ups to go in the bear-embossed folders, rapped at her computer keyboard, tuned in to Simon's dictation on a headset. Julie stood by his side, like favored progeny, waiting for the signal that she, too, was dismissed. A perfect day, as far as he was concerned. If he'd had to explain it to Emily, he would have said, well, there weren't even words for it.

"So whaddya think?" Simon asked Julie.

"Busy," she said. "Everything went fast." A piece of hair, fallen from her ponytail, curved around the edge of her small face. She looked tired, but intent not to show it.

"It's not always this hectic," he said apologetically.

There was a silence. Then Julie burst out, "You offered that woman such a high dose of narcotics." Her face startled him. It was pinched in accusation, hard, with feral eyes. Her nose and chin seemed to jut forward.

"Which?"

"That woman, Mrs. Bailey."

"Don't tell me you're one of those," he sneered.

"One of what?"

"Those people who get on a high horse about narcotics. Gimme a break. The brain has its own opioid receptors. Endogenous receptors on the surface of brain cells. They found them. Right here in Baltimore, they discovered them. Little molecules attached to the cell membranes that are waiting to receive opioids, and when they do, they're capable of making a person feel better. It's hard to begrudge a person what their brain is wired to receive."

"But it's just a drug," Julie countered. "In nursing school, we learned it's like giving a patient a Band-Aid. It's just covering up the pain. If she doesn't figure out the source of the problem, she's just going to need more drugs. And that if you help a person find other ways to handle the problem, counseling, or rehabilitation therapy—"

"She can't do *anything* if she can't get off her couch," Simon retorted. Julie's mouth snapped shut. He turned, heading down the hall toward his office. "My job is to treat my patients. I can't just sit back and watch, can I?"

"Don't you know," Rita announced, without even pausing in her typing, "there's a reason patients call him Dr. Feelgood. He's their biggest supporter."

Suddenly, he didn't want to talk medicine or Maxi Bailey or his mission to relieve suffering. It'd been a remarkably successful day, easy, lively, smart, and he didn't want his buzz killed with her doubts. He looked at the young nurse, the Torrence Award winner for the most promising career, when he heard the phone ringing down the hall in his office. He hurried toward it, but once he was standing at his desk, decided not to answer it. Julie had followed him as far as the doorway, and she looked like she was getting ready to leave. He remembered something that she didn't know about him, and he believed it was a detail that explained more. "You know anything about wines?" he asked.

"Um—" she stammered. "Not really."

"Promise not to spill the beans," he insisted. Emily was still at work, probably wouldn't be home for another hour, depending on traffic from Bethesda. He couldn't remember if tonight was one of the nights she went to the gym. At the back of his office was the dark mahogany door leading into the basement of the house. He motioned for her to follow him, as he twisted a skeleton key that jutted from the door. When Julie hesitated, he added, "Not to worry. I don't bite. I can ask Rita to come too, if you'd prefer."

"It's okay," Julie said, following him into the house. She stepped onto a floor laid with ruddy Mexican tiles. The ceiling was lower than in the office, and the room had a basement's damp coolness, lovely on the cheeks, the backs of the hands.

"This door's part of the original house," he pointed out. "The office, this entire side, was the addition. You can tell the construction's slightly different."

"It's amazing how you can forget that there's a whole house attached," Julie said.

"It's an extraordinary estate. Did I tell you it was once owned by a director of the Peabody Conservatory? In the Twenties. He and his family lived here for a bunch of years. All kinds of famous people visited him here, honored him." Simon had never found time to dig up the archives at the conservatory, but when he and Emily had first considered buying the house, delirious about the prospect of owning such a large piece of property, the previous owners described at length the luminaries who'd crossed the doorstep at one time or another. "There were all kinds of parties," Simon told Julie. "Happy people and lots of music. Caruso sang in front of the fireplace. One year, Rachmaninoff played an impromptu concert on the piano for the director's birthday. It's true. When we bought the house, the previous owners considered taking the piano with them, but I insisted it stay with the house, so we paid extra to have it." Austere black body, gleaming curves, it sat in the large living room upstairs, though nobody played. He'd thought about taking lessons himself, but he'd never found the time. At one point, he'd even tried signing Jamie up for lessons. "Don't even bother," she'd stated. "I'll never practice."

Even Emily had agreed with him, lessons for Jamie might be a good idea. "You might find you like it," she'd suggested to Jamie.

"Not interested," Jamie said, and they'd all dropped the topic. But it was a magnificent instrument, wired with its strings and padded hammers as its gargantuan viscera, and somewhere in that body, the memory of the music that had been played upon it. The history of the house so enthralled him—what boisterous, glorious noise had once filled the place!—he'd always felt having the piano was like owning a piece of that time.

All along the length of the basement, large shelves broke the space like the aisles of a grocery. He glanced sideways at the meticulous storage: life's overspill. For Emily, it was where items went that were too expensive to throw away but had proved irrelevant to daily life. For him, it was where the items waited to be put into use again. Lorraine, the housekeeper, had taken pains to keep the flotsam organized (or at least hidden away) in tidy plastic boxes. There was scuba equipment, acquired after a vacation to St. Bart's, when they had rented and Simon had reasoned it would ultimately be cheaper if they bought what they needed. They each owned a set of golf clubs. Emily's had been purchased used, in a pink golf bag, and she'd probably been out on a course twice during their entire marriage. Two enormous Tupperware bins contained the remains—fertilizers, pots, misters—from the days of raising orchids. There were collections: Roman coins; vintage records; old pocketwatches in velvet boxes waiting to be repaired, with tools whose tips were smaller than the end of a grain of rice. There were boxes with the yet-unused hardware and the wood pieces for the garden gazebo. Emily so disliked the abundance of abandoned material, she seldom came into the basement, and he was confident he could store his most recent purchases without her coming across them.

"Look." Simon pointed toward the corner, where a large sheet draped over a many-haunched mass, the shape of an enormous caterpillar.

"What is it?" Julie asked.

Picking up the edge of the drape, he revealed a row of rosy wooden barrels, three of them, ringed with silver bands. Next to the barrels were several wooden crates, still unopened. On the floor stood a large stainless-steel tank, shaped like a jug, that came almost as high as Julie's waist. He had purchased three impressive-looking machines with pistons and ratchets and hinged arms.

"I ordered it all off the Internet," he said. "It's a kit for brewing your own wine."

Wine-making was something altogether different from anything he'd attempted in the past. It wasn't seasonal like his ventures into scuba or skiing, though he was still waiting for the grapes. It didn't require a slew of unobtainable parts, like the watch repairs, or dangerous tools, like the woodworking.

"It's not that hard to do," Simon said. "I got books, and I bought all the best equipment available. I was a chemistry undergrad, and I've always been kind of a test-tube tinkerer. Making wine's not all that different from chem lab. You can do all kinds of creative things when you're blending flavors to make a great wine. The whole process is really only a few basic steps."

"Hunh," Julie responded.

"See here." He stepped up to the stainless-steel tank. "This's what's known as the primary fermenter. You get your juice, you add your yeast—and there are different kinds of yeast, too. Did you know that? There's this Champagne yeast I read about. I got some kind of French yeast. Different kinds of yeast give different yields."

"Geez, that thing's huge. How much are you making?"

"I'm thinking of starting with upwards of fifty gallons."

"Of wine?" Her mouth gaped.

Simon nodded vigorously. "Sounds like a lot, I know. But the next smaller size wasn't in stock, and I didn't want to have to wait around. So I just bought the bigger one and I figured, why start out small and wish in two years that I had bigger, better equipment?" He stepped back and gazed at it. "It's big, all right."

She couldn't be expected to understand because of her age, of course, and her background. What would she know about wine-making? It would be an impressive task, not impossible, but certainly enterprising, especially for the people he knew, like the Groves and the Ebberlys.

The inspiration to brew had descended upon him after dinner, one night three months earlier, when all three couples had dined at La Bouche, an upscale French bistro in Federal Hill. It was an evening of frustrations and disappointments, though nothing in particular had happened. At a crowded table in a far corner, Rick and Janet Grove sat across from him and Emily. Betsy and Ted Ebberly sat apart from each other at either end of the table. Simon remained privately disdainful of Janet Grove, who had once been a smoker. At one point, years ago, she'd come to him for medical advice about her inflammatory bowel, and he'd intended to refer her elsewhere. It was his policy—no smokers, all his patients were duly warned—and he believed as a matter of principle he should stick to his word. He'd tried to make the case with Emily that physicians were the ones who had to take a stand against the scourge of smoking. "She's my *friend,*" Emily had seethed, until he relented. To everyone's relief, Janet had managed to quit since then, but Simon still felt the chafing of having been forcibly compromised.

She had a narrow mouth with high cheekbones and tousled hair that was miraculously still blond as wheat. Emily, he thought, treated her with a little too much fawning, a little too much eager attention, and it was all the more apparent when he saw his wife interact with Betsy Ebberly. Emily maintained a friendship with Betsy, too, but she was cooler toward Betsy, he'd noticed, more distant and polite.

"I'm against it," Janet was saying, and he realized she was talking about a show at the Contemporary Art Museum where she was a trustee. "Call me old school, but as I see it, we're still in that phase of trying to attract and inspire. You know, bring people in. We're still in need of underwriters. This is just asking for trouble."

"Is this that exhibit about fanaticism? The one you described before that's so controversial?" Betsy asked. Freshly plump, in roseate sweaters, she had soft hair that spilled onto her shoulders as if she hadn't quite figured out how to control it, and a habit of squinting as if she were trying to see through a mist. She was the guidance counselor at a high school, and Simon wondered if professional snobbery was another reason Emily didn't engage her seriously. Janet was well connected, influential, even elitist in her associations. Betsy, on the other hand, didn't thrive on lofty ambitions or public attention, high-strung business mavericks or the manipulative press. Her career involved having conversations with maladjusted teenagers about their hormone-affected social lives, delivering advice and ideas that probably went unappreciated. The modest salary she earned was constantly in jeopardy from the school district. She was a saint, if you thought about it! Snubbing Betsy was an oversight on Emily's part, he decided ruefully. Here was a caring, attentive and sincere woman—who gave without expecting back and who deeply deserved the highest order of respect.

"What's the exhibit?" Simon said loudly to Janet. "Sounds to me like bad art."

"It originated in the Netherlands," Janet explained. "*From on Deep,* it's called, portraits of so-called extremists. There's a painting, it's very haunting, of suicide bombers, done by the brother of a suicide bomber. There's a photo of that woman, what's her name, the abortion protester, the famous one?"

"Avery Scott?" Emily suggested. "Even Frith steered clear of any company that had anything to do with her."

"There's a portrait of her," Janet continued, "in the hospital, from when she had breast cancer, getting chemo. It's a view from inside, instead of as a spectator from the outside."

"So the point," Betsy filled in, squinting pensively, "is humanity. Across the board. Even people we don't really understand."

"But can you imagine the public response to this one?" Janet demanded. "It's like shooting ourselves in the foot." There was something about the angle of her wrist, he noticed, or maybe it was her fingers, that made it seem she was holding a cigarette even when she wasn't.

"The best thing to do," Emily said plainly, "is to get the show and present it appropriately." She made her point in the calmest of voices, with a finger touching the edge of a wineglass, and Simon was again taken with the way she pressed for common sense. As if the answer were obvious, and you'd be an idiot to have any other perspective. "Don't present it as if you're already apologizing. You package it for your membership. If it's truly about humanity, stand behind its humanity."

"I don't get it." Simon leaned toward Janet, challenging. "What do you mean 'insiders'? If you're immersed in something, even if it's bombing people, how can you comment on it like an insider? Once a person's looking at something, actually analyzing it, aren't they already an outsider?"

"Ah," said Rick Grove appreciatively, lacing his hands behind his head. He looked, Simon thought, like he'd wanted to point out the absurdity himself but hadn't dared. "Fascinating conundrum."

Janet defended, "It's not like a foreign journalist coming in to take pictures. I understand its merit, but to embroil the museum? Not now."

"I always think about these things in terms of the kids I deal with," Betsy said. "It seems we're always worrying about sanitizing the wrong things. And if there's something that prompts discussion, real talking, it's usually worth withstanding the fire. I agree with Emily. You go for it and make sure your audience understands your message and your position clearly, whatever that position is."

"A-always d-dangerous for a m-museum," Ted Ebberly commented as everyone waited patiently for him to work his way through the sentence. "R-remember that one in N-nebraska that never recovered from the d-display of t-torn American f-flags?" Ted was a neuroscientist at the medical school, one of those stupefying fact-gatherers who retained everything he read. In his round, olive-toned head with its thick eyebrows, the straight-across lips like an Incan statue, he had details and figures on the most arcane topics in a way that made Simon feel amateurish. The marvel of his stutter was that it tended to dissipate during the length of an evening. ("You're a neurological phenomenon. Someone should study you," Simon had once announced at a dinner gathering, after Ted's speech pattern had normalized. "You just need time to warm up. Once you get going, you know how to bring it home." Emily had purpled at the frankness of his comment, but Betsy had jumped to the rescue: "It's true! He's the perfect gauge of a party. As soon as the stammer disappears, you know everyone's having a good time." She'd saved Simon from the arrows in Emily's glare, but she'd also shown everyone how she wanted nothing more from Ted than what he was. Betsy Ebberly, he was convinced, was the nicest person he'd ever known.) "That m-museum l-lost its lease, just because it accepted the show," Ted reminded everyone, "and ev-ev-eventually had to close down."

They abandoned Janet's predicament, but it was not long before the conversation at the table had turned to hobbies, and there was concurrence at the table that they'd all reached an age of reckoning in which hobbies—however once passion-stirring and preoccupying—had become mere dalliances. It began as Betsy Ebberly announced that she'd signed up for an adult extension course in French and was studying a second language for the first time in her life.

"I'll never be fluent," she conceded, "but it's fun."

"Well, you're not alone," said Rick with a knowing air. "Just recently, I realized I'll probably never make the senior tour." Everyone at the table laughed. He'd been a compulsive golfer for as long as anyone could remember.

"Ha!" chided Janet. "Like it just dawned on him. For years he's been trying to get his handicap lower than the number of children he has." Ted Ebberly whistled. The Groves had bred five.

"But you're still able to compete. You haven't slipped," Emily said, and Simon marveled again how she was able to come up with a placating comment every time. "You're still in tournaments, aren't you?"

"Yes," Rick acknowledged, "but my fantasies are tempered."

Betsy reflected, "It's a lovely thing, being at this stage of life. The pressure's off. We are what we are already. We can explore whatever interests for sheer enjoyment."

"Right," Janet agreed. "You can relax on the course. Your goal now can be to have a good time."

Simon felt his neck growing hot. "That's a cop-out if I ever heard one," he blurted, in a voice too loud, too aggressive for the conversation. Under the table he felt a kick from the toe of one of Emily's pointy shoes. But the truth seemed obvious, and Simon couldn't just sit there and let them spout off about what was and wasn't possible. Rick might have been happily tenured ("a specialist in long books," Simon often kidded), but if that was the limit of his vision of himself, then Simon was disgusted to hear it.

"I've come to terms with it," Rick said. "I'm good, but I'll never be quite that good. I can accept it."

"What's changed?" Simon demanded. "Nothing's changed. Success is about desire! State of mind! There's no time limit."

"Well, wishing something into being isn't quite the same as having the talent. You have to have the talent," Rick said. "I humbly admit: I don't got it."

"I agree," Emily said genially. "Most of us could come up with the resolve if we had the talent to begin with."

"If you really wanted to make the tour," Simon said, pointing his finger at Rick Grove, "if you really, really wanted to make it, you'd quit your job and commit the rest of the time you had to playing golf. It's that simple."

"Well," Rick said, leaning forward, glancing at Janet. "I've got a family. There're practicalities to consider. Also, I have a career I care about."

"So, really," Simon concluded, "what's standing in your way is you."

Fortunately, the hors d'oeuvres arrived just then. As a communal plate of foie gras was passed around, conversation turned to vacations. The

Groves were heading back to France—a conference of Pushkin scholars and an art tour—followed by a holiday. They were making a special trip to one region south of Bourgogne famous for a particular kind of wine.

"There's nothing in this country that even comes close to the wine they make," Janet stated. "They just consider themselves farmers with a family tradition, but they've actually tapped into something of superior quality, even for France."

"It's phenomenal wine," Rick said. "Rich, flavorful, almost as intense as a Barolo, but with even more complexity. And of course you can't get it in this country because the international distributors don't deal with them."

Emily, masterful controller of conversations, guilty-as-charged for fawning too much on the Groves, announced, "I adore Barolos."

"Did you know," Rick informed everyone, "that white-wine glasses are intentionally smaller and thinner and when you hold them, you're supposed to touch the stem, and not the vessel part of the glass, with your hand? That's to keep the wine cold. Red-wine glasses are fuller and rounder to get more air in them, and you're meant to hold the body of the glass itself and warm it in the palm of your hand."

Betsy laughed and insisted she couldn't tell the difference between a cabernet and a merlot, and Rick began to list the names of Californias from all along the coast, wineries they'd visited, and years that were worth springing for. Simon, put off by the discussion of golf, found himself attacking the foie gras with unusual vigor, but he glanced up to see Emily rooting through her purse for a pen and a piece of paper to write down the wines Rick recommended.

At his side, his wife wore a navy suit with snappy white stitching around the collar and cuffs. He knew it was high style—she was an excellent dresser—but the outfit looked to him like an unfinished sartorial enterprise. He didn't like it, and he felt miffed she hadn't asked his opinion of it, the way she used to when they went out. She was still beautiful to him, he realized with a pang. If he were just meeting her for the first time, he'd have the same impression of her face he'd had when they'd first met: There was perfection in the particular assemblage and proportion of features. It was a primitive sort of perfection, not pinup girl, or bunny, the kind of creature who would be taken for defenseless food by a creature in the wild. Instead it was, and had always been, the kind of perfection of the fittest, the face of a creature meant to survive. She was tall enough to appear imposing, but even more, there was an alertness, a spark under the skin, that intimidated. She did not seem to gaze long at any one thing. In the length of an exhalation, the sharp, dark eyes went quickly from looking amused to looking bored. She was assessing, constantly appraising, not quite imperious, but aware of the details and forming an opinion about everything. When she smiled, revealing just the right number of opalescent half-ovals and not at all too much gum, you felt you had earned something. Even the slightly arched nose, that staid and somewhat Semitic ornament, had a way of looking judgmental, made you want to do right. Made you want not to have fucked up, ever. You wanted her to respond with approval. Her looks were the kind that promised the propagation of a better species. When he'd met her, he could have delivered a thesis on the role of such physical features in a Darwinian picture of evolution.

At forty-seven, she still emanated that striking keenness. So he was taken aback by her complacency at the table at La Bouche. He felt betrayed by the concession that they were all up in age and that things were more or less over. He refused to believe that the tracks of their lives had been laid, the direction set, and there was nothing left to do but modulate the speed at which they raced toward the end.

That night when they had returned home Simon had descended to the clinic in the basement. He sat in his office in front of the computer. Several patients had written to him with questions or simply to update him about their conditions, and he wrote back to all of them. But then he was curious. With a search engine, he looked up wine-making. It wasn't particularly difficult, he discovered. There were kits with simple components, plastic fermenters, rubber stoppers, hydrometers, entanglements of siphon tubing. But why go to all the trouble if all you were going to make was a crappy wine? He surfed until he found the best, most expensive components he could find, hard oak, air-dried casks that had been toasted over open fires by able French craftsmen, assembled by expert coopers in tiny villages that specialized in wine barrels as an art form. He found a checklist of necessary items and scrolled through the list, ordering one by one. There were individually blown glass tubes, computerized jet filters, premium electric transfer pumps that could move 122-degree liquid for the racking process. *Click, click, click.* In no time, he'd ordered nearly five thousand dollars' worth of wine-making equipment—and then he found himself on the phone to France, trying to wangle even better air-dried oak casks from an individual vintner. How hard could it be? People with a lot less intellect and fewer resources could brew wine—why not he?

He ordered several books on wine-making, but what caught his eye were the contests. They were held in Sonoma and attended by wine-tasters from all over the world. There were ribbons for the most sophisticated varietals. He read through the instructions and was moved by the simplicity of the process. You could have your wine in four weeks if you wanted, or you could wait longer and allow the fermentation to continue for an entire year—or several. Patience was all.

It was past two in the morning when he was finished making purchases. Logging off the Internet, he crossed back to the silent house, bounding upstairs. He passed Jamie's bedroom, its door open the width of a hand, her night-light illuminating a small yellow ring of light. He had a mind to poke his head into the room, but he decided against the risk of waking her. In their bedroom, Emily was already asleep, her face dewy with moisturizer, one hand above her head, one across her chest.

What he wanted was to wake her and tell her about the wine kit, but he decided that he'd wait. He decided he'd show her when the kit arrived, surprise her. What he imagined was a family project, Emily selecting the type of wine they would make (they could make a Barolo, for chrissake; it couldn't be too hard to figure out how to order—what were they called?—Nebbiolo grapes from northern Italy), and Jamie designing the wine label. He'd give Jamie the text, and she'd design the lettering and whatever artwork went with it. He kept the secret as the equipment slowly arrived, and now he was waiting only for the season to do its work on the fruit.

"You went to town," Julie said, surveying the equipment.

"French white oak casks! They're better than kiln-dried American casks. You wouldn't believe how hard they were to get. Handmade, too. Beautiful, aren't they?"

Simon pried open a wooden crate and reached into the wispy haylike packing. "See this here—" He pulled out a handheld tool with a rubber grip and a small viewing window. "It's a refractometer. Hold it up to your eyes, and it tells you how much sugar you have in your sample. That part there's a prism. You hold it in natural light, and the way the juice bends the light, you can tell how ripe your grapes are."

"So what's the secret?" Julie wanted to know.

"It's a surprise," Simon said. "For my wife. My staff knows—Melinda, Joyce and Gabi—they helped me haul everything in here. But Emily doesn't know yet. She's going to have her very own wine."

The shipment of grapes he'd ordered would arrive at the end of August. Bright, ruby grapes—the picture of them brought jewels to mind—four hundred pounds of Barbera grapes from Piedmont (he hadn't managed to find the Nebbiolos, but an Italian clerk had assured him that he'd enjoy the Barberas even more and that the wine-making process would be quicker). He'd purchased an automatic, motorized crusher-stemmer with aluminum fluted rollers that would break the grape skins and expose the juice and then channel the fluid through a screen. The stems, capable of imparting harsh tannins and excessive acidity, would be expelled through a chute, and nobody would ever have to touch them. Emily would resist, at first. He could hear her protests about the expense or the mess or the extravagance, but he'd change her mind. It was such an elegant project, and the results would impress their friends. (How great it would be to serve a bottle of their very own wine and challenge Rick Grove to guess where it was from!) Emily wouldn't possibly object after the fermentation was under way.

"She'll love it," Julie said.

"Really?" he replied with genuine hope. He was not ashamed of the reason he'd hired Julie, which came clear to him just then. Julie McKinley, who looked like a child only vaguely older than his own daughter and whose unsophisticated aspirations reminded him of himself. What he needed, what he longed for, were only a few words of sincere encouragement. Some reason to continue hoping. It was impossible to explain that, no matter what he did, he was no longer capable of impressing his wife, or engaging her, or altering her chilliness toward him. He wished he could go back in time. Back to—when? He barely remembered what it was like to live without her disdain. For so many years, he'd been striving, every action aimed to make amends, and nothing he did was ever quite right. Yet he was eager to believe Julie. He looked at the three pregnant-bellied wine barrels with their expertly crafted staves from some unpronounceable town in central France, awed by the care that had gone into their creation.

"Oh," sighed Julie, her eyes wide, one hand pressed to her chest as she took in that he was doing it all for the love of his wife. She was a romantic, this hungry, hungry girl, that was why he'd hired her. The gesture with her thin, dramatic leaflike hand said yes, there was still time to live a different life than the one he was living. He turned from the handmade casks. His heart rose against his ribs; he could almost feel the blood cresting his aorta. "Oh," she said again, and he looked at her as she sighed, "Who wouldn't?"

And then, not knowing what he was intending or why he was doing it, he reached for her wrist, the one not making the approving gesture. It was happiness that propelled him, simple as that. His fingers encircled the narrow radiocarpal joint, bony as a door hinge, and she went still under his touch. Her eyes widened, but she didn't pull away. Surprising even himself, he leaned over and kissed her.

PART TWO

E mily wasn't aware of him until she had stumbled against his body. She was preoccupied by the shortcomings of her purse. Emerging from the tawny-stoned Bethesda office building with her head down, she groped inside her bag for a pair of sunglasses and a slender oval ring of keys. Later she would think it was unlike her to walk that way, unpoised and unprepared. She'd been reared on excellent posture, chin lifted, shoulders set, like a person geared up for a fight. It had been her father's mantra: You can't take advantage of opportunities if you don't see them walking toward you.

She had paused, one shoulder propping open the tinted glass doors, feeling for the glasses and thinking that if the traffic went smoothly, she might still make it to the gym when she got home. Outside, the sun was low-slung, and even the parking meters shone with a bourbon glow. The evening security guard, a man named Elmer or Albert, she hadn't heard it clearly the first time and it was no longer appropriate to ask, hollered a genial "g'night." He gave an exuberant wave, and she looked back and nodded politely in his direction, and wondered, as she did every evening, at the persistence of his good nature. Some people were rosy to the bone.

It was a confounding purse, the size of a Sunday *Times,* slightly triangulated. The exterior was a buttery blue-black leather, with an overhanging flap. Its edges were banded with horsehair piping. Over her shoulder, the flat, smart strap widened like a man's tie and then, descending, narrowed again with architectural flair. Two years earlier, it had been a forty-fifth birthday present from Simon, straight from the private collection of the Parisian designer Marac. Some grateful patient had worked with the designer during New York Fashion Week, getting first dibs to bid on the most prized items, and Simon had finagled a deal.

Several times she'd been stopped on the street as women complimented the geometric detail, the imaginative lines. These were women who understood fine accessories. Marac knew what he was doing. For all its good looks, though, it wasn't *functional.* An interior wall divided the main space into four unreasonable and almost useless compartments. If she sought her keys, or sunglasses, she had to scrabble like a mole past a vertical pile of personal items, which slid and shifted so that she was perpetually digging blind.

Still peering after her hand, which had been swallowed by the bag, she stepped past the glass door onto the crimson sidewalk and slammed right into the shoulder of a man. Her face smacked against his bicep and underarm, jarring her chin. Her nose pressed into his rayon shirt. A leisure shirt, she thought at once, and not well-ironed. Not the type of shirt worn by the men she took meetings with. Soft material and the kind of khaki that she'd always considered a bland, unassertive color. The strap of her purse slipped off her shoulder, and the bag landed like a body against the cement.

"Whoa there," the man said, grabbing her upper arm as if to steady her. "Y'okay?"

She shook off the stun of the collision, one hand touching her jaw. She was appalled to have smelled him, an intimate mixture of a piney deodorant and a warm body smell like graham cracker. "Ex*cuse* me," she said without hiding her annoyance, extricating her arm. In his opposite hand, he held a white shopping bag, she noticed as she bent down for her purse. The overhanging flap of Marac's design mercifully had kept the contents from scattering. She lifted the strap to her shoulder and inspected the underside of the bag. Tiny scrapes, like short claw marks, marred the leather.

"Sure you're all right?"

"I'm fine," she said. So the purse was ruined. Not ruined exactly, but would require attention, some kind of maintenance. Simon would insist on having it repaired because he was so proud of having given her a gift that fit her taste and because it had cost so much money in the first place.

The man placed his hand on her upper arm again, just above her elbow.

"Emily?"

The heat that rose up her neck touched both sides of her face. Only one person in her life had ever said her name quite that way, lingering on the "m," or tripping on it, drawing the "e" out too long with too much air, too much emphasis, too much space in the throat. As if her name were "Hemily." Every cell in her body seemed to hold its breath, waiting—trembling, even—and in a moment, she thought, she'd see she'd been wrong, but what a funny mistake to have made. After all these years. But even before she lifted her eyes, she knew she was not mistaken.

"William Garth," she pronounced, sounding more than she meant to like a prim, old schoolteacher.

"Wow. You look—wow." His head shook, incredulous.

His face was thinner than she remembered, the cheekbones more pronounced. He'd shaved his head to combat a receding hairline, and the stubble across his scalp shone with silver. The slimmed angles of his face made his mouth look larger, but the lips were the same, lush, slightly turned up at the corners. There was the thumb-sized scar, a waxy-looking patch on the left side of his jawbone where a beard would never grow. It was the result of a childhood dog bite—she remembered that story at once. He was a man who had never liked dogs. His eyes, even with the creases at the outer corners, were exactly the same. Nobody, not even her husband, had ever looked at her with such—what was it?—admiration? bemusement?—even when she was on her worst behavior. She would have recognized those eyes anywhere.

"I know, I know." Grinning, he mussed a hand over his balded scalp. "I woke up one morning with a few gray hairs and a couple of wrinkles. How'd it happen? I've no clue."

She'd wondered about him over the years, though not often. He'd sauntered into her consciousness at the oddest times, like when she took a knife to the fat bottom of a tapered candle, paring it to fit in a socket of the Tiffany candlesticks. Always then, so strange, standing over the trash as the wax bits shot off the base, she'd think of Will and his Swiss Army knife, the magicianlike way he handled tools. It wasn't often that she and Simon needed candles, but if she trimmed them, there was Will in her thoughts. She wasn't prepared for this encounter on the street. If she'd been looking where she was going, if she'd seen him walking toward her, she'd have made an effort not to run into him. She would have liked to plan what she would say, how she would act. Things had ended so awkwardly, so many years before.

"That bad, huh?" He was smiling.

"I—" she stammered. "I'm in shock."

"You look the same," he said earnestly. And there was that look in his eyes again. "Really, the same."

"That's a lie," she countered with a laugh, "but I'll take it."

"Really," he persuaded, "wonderful."

The signs of aging in his face pleased her. The intentionally shaved head seemed particularly touching. (Simon, with his full jaw and leonine forehead, seemed to defy the tugging and wrangling of time. His face continued to look like sanded wood; his hairline hadn't even thinned. His mother's side of the family had never wrinkled, even those relatives who'd lived into their eighties. "Genetic good fortune," he boasted.) She was surprised to feel her heart pounding. She coughed and tugged at the lapel of her suit jacket, straightening herself and composing a smile for him. "I'm on my way home."

"It's late." He sounded impressed.

"I'm a senior partner of Frith International," she said, amazed by what had come out of her mouth. She added, because the Will she had known had never heard of anything, "We're one of the three most influential public relations firms in the country." She realized she wanted him to know something: She had more confidence, more wherewithal, than when they'd known each other. She'd been so fragile and timid back then, so scared of everything and wistful for the right things to happen. But she'd hit her stride. She'd made a name for herself as one of the best in the business, specializing as a professional troubleshooter. She'd saved countless companies billions of dollars as she managed their missteps and resurrected their reputations.

"So?" she asked, lifting her chin. "Are you still—?" With her index fingers at either side of her face, she mimed a camera, punctuating with clicks of her tongue. She didn't intend to sound condescending, but when he cleared his throat she suspected she might have. What had taken hold of her? She was not acting like herself.

"As much as I can," he answered, with a nod. "I got into some other stuff, too. I'm in town for a conference. Otherwise, I'm in Philly. Was. In Philly. I mean, I'm still in Philly." Then he blurted, "I'm staying at a hotel."

"Here?" She pictured the Radisson, a small room with gold-tasseled curtains and a television set.

"Well, yes, a hotel here. Near Dupont Circle. But also in Philly. It's a long story." She waited, but he didn't offer it, just a small smile. Did he look sad? His eyes had that tender look again. He was six years older than she was—he'd been almost thirty when they'd met, and could it be? Already past fifty—and what she remembered most vividly was the way he once made her feel like he was the young one and she was the grown-up. "How's your father?" he asked finally.

She adjusted the bag on her shoulder as her father's face appeared in her mind. "Passed away. Nine, no, let's see, ten years ago now." Will looked like he was waiting for more, so she added, "Heart attack."

"Sorry to hear it. I liked him."

Emily laughed out loud. And she surprised herself again, saying bluntly, "He didn't like you."

Will looked down, still smiling, and shifted his feet. She was abusing him. Hadn't seen him in almost a lifetime, and she was rude. She didn't mean to be! Well, served him right. He shouldn't have surprised her like this on the street. A little warning and she would have been more collected, and kinder.

"I guess he had his reasons," Will said.

"Well, all of that's done now."

"Yes."

"Well."

He cleared his throat again, still smiling. And there was still that look in his eyes. Yes, all of that was done, but at one point she'd been unable to imagine that she'd end up with anyone other than Will, the way he'd adored her, the way she'd loved his attention. Worshipful attention, like a fairy tale. But he'd been so frustrating, too. Unabashedly eager, and silly, really. He was from a small mining town in Pennsylvania. He didn't know that Firenze was Florence or that *Gone With the Wind* had been a book first. He pronounced words terribly, *ek-cetera* and *nuk-u-lar*. When she'd met him, he'd never heard of sushi. In an otherwise pleasant conversation, there'd be a lull, a missed beat, and his ignorance would be revealed. He'd simply weather the moment with a smile and then his eyes would widen at what he didn't know, and he'd laugh at himself, and even repeat the story later in front of someone else—"I didn't know it was a book, did you?" Back then, you always had to feel sorry for him, and a little bit embarrassed, though it occurred to her years later—possibly as she was paring the bottom of a candle—that maybe she should have marveled at his utter inability to be pretentious. At the time, she'd felt piercingly aware of all their differences.

"It's funny, you know," Will said, "I didn't get your father, I mean, really *get him,* until about two years ago. My daughter, the younger one, just turned nineteen, but two years ago there was this guy hanging around, wanting her, I guess, and all I could think of for seven months or whatever was how he wasn't good enough for her and how much I wanted to wring his neck." He laughed as he dramatized, with the hand that wasn't holding the white shopping bag, a single-handed strangulation.

Will had two daughters? She tried to picture them: fresh-faced young women with those full lips, those wide-eyed laughs. They would have his ease, that twinkling way of walking through the world. Maybe they would have all kinds of earthy politics and practices, like veganism and meditation. She glanced at his hand; no ring. But men didn't always wear rings. She was struck by the familiarity of his fingers, which were long and slender. Once, at a party, he'd done a coy peeling trick with an orange and his Swiss Army knife, twisting and carving so that when he finally unveiled the fruit, he'd crafted an orange gingerbread-shaped man with the peel. The stem of the orange, extracted from the center of the sections, protruded just where the gingerbread man's penis ought to be. The huddle of admirers laughed, but she found the trick crass and childish. The attention he got embarrassed her, and she refused the slice of orange that was handed to her. Could he have turned out to be a good father? she wondered. All those facts about the world he didn't know. Simon had always amazed her with his stores of knowledge. If you ate an apple, he could tell you growing techniques in New Zealand, and which kinds made the best pies, and that minute traces of cyanide existed in the seeds. His confidence in his own opinion thrilled and amazed her. And she wasn't the only one. People told her constantly: Your husband is a brilliant man. Your husband saved my father's life. When Simon entered a room, people turned, their eyes following him expectantly.

"You didn't like the boyfriend?"

"I just acted like—a father," he explained, shrugging, smiling at himself. "You think you know love, and then you have children and it's an entirely different thing. There should be other words you can use, an entirely different vocabulary, for the things you feel for your kids. You got any?"

"A daughter," she said. She had one child. No need to explain about Caleb or to describe what they'd been through. You didn't dish up such details to a person who was ostensibly a stranger, even though, once upon a time, he was the one person who might have known her better than she'd known herself. And she, who was masterful about how details were meted for public consumption, knew what not to say. She suddenly remembered an expression he'd once used, from his German grandmother, for when you started a conversation and then were obligated to finish it. "You cackled," he would say, "now lay the egg." Anyway, he was asking her about the present. So, yes, one child. He shouldn't have surprised her on the street. It was rude of him. It was an ambush. She wouldn't mention, either, that the one daughter was supposed to be at camp for the summer, but instead was home, skulking around the house like a storm cloud that had seeped inside. A mass that brewed and billowed and hated her mother. "She's thirteen," she added.

"Ah, thirteen," he said. "That's a great age."

"Great age," she echoed, prattling despite herself. "She was an honor student this past year. Both semesters. She won a prize for a study of butterfly migration."

"And you're married?"

"Oh, yes."

"Happily?" Really, it was just like him, she thought, to ask questions as though some filter in his brain had gone missing. A person was prodded for a testimonial, right up front. "Wait," he said, before she'd even mustered a response, "I know. That's not a thing a person answers in the street. That's a real question. Listen, I know you're heading home, and you've probably had a really long day. Can I persuade you to stop for a moment, just for tea or something? Just to catch up?"

"Catch up on the last twenty-four years in the next twenty minutes?"

"Well," he acknowledged, and there was that smile again, "whatever's possible. Promise I won't keep you. I have to get back to the conference anyway."

She tried to imagine "tea" with him, an awkward question-and-answer session with grating clanks of china ("tea," when anyone else would suggest getting together for coffee). What would she say, "I don't know how it happened, but somehow I became a partner in the company," because she didn't owe him any explanation? Or, "It wasn't what I imagined when I was young, but I found out that it's the thing I'm good at," which, at least, was honest. Undoubtedly, he'd be disappointed in the way she'd turned out. Back then, he'd been so disinterested in the real world. All he cared about, it seemed, was some vague notion about art. What he *felt*. What she felt. What people felt, as if you could know. The words "building equity" used to make him roll his eyes and guffaw. If anybody mentioned "financial security," his face adopted that dumb smile, and he shrugged. When she'd known him, he'd had no plans. He wanted to photograph, but he didn't have goals, like going full-time with a magazine or winning awards or having shows in galleries. He was simply interested in doing what he was doing, the hell with a list of ambitions. Back then, she thought him impractical, deluded and immature. What words would he have now for her silver Sebring convertible, with the vanity license plates that Simon had bought for her reading "NTCIP8"? ("Don't you get it?

Anticipate!" Simon had crowed when the plates arrived in the mail and she'd stared at them with her brow furrowed. "Applies to your work, and to the driver behind you on the road!") She knew she wasn't defined by a vanity plate, but there it was, with its truncated warning, coming and going.

"Tomorrow, noon, is the closing session," Will said. "But I've got other things to do in town, and I can stay another day," he suggested, "if Thursday afternoon will work better."

"You were never one to care about the time," she said, hoping to sound breezy, like she was making a joke, but it didn't come off, and she regretted it instantly. Anyway, it wasn't true. Back then, they'd stayed in bed for days, naked, phoning for takeout, as *she* was the one who made excuses to friends, lied, called into the office sick, coughing into the phone to impress her father's secretary. She'd been the one laughing and wailing, "Don't go, don't go," tugging him by the arm and wrestling him back onto the bed when he made a move to start the day. But the Will standing in front of her just smiled—that old smile, bright and admiring—and she was embarrassed all over again.

"Thursday would be fine," she decided. At first she thought she would suggest he come up to her office, meet her on the twenty-first floor. She was about to explain that he needed to take the second bank of elevators, past the lobby and the security guard there, which would put him right in front of Frith's glossy reception area. She knew if she pointed toward the doors, he would turn to look and she would have the opportunity to peer again at the scar on his jaw. But then she wasn't sure she wanted him to see the posh interior of Frith, the columns in the reception area, her stately corner office with its view of the tops of trees that must have been as far away as Rockville. Instead she suggested, "Why not near where you're staying?" She named a modest café, for which she would not have to make apologies. "Two thirty, does that work for you?" Middle of the afternoon would give her the chance to keep it brief.

"Oh, okay," he agreed. "Thursday." Then he sounded like a kid again—too eager, no filter. "How about I walk you to your car?"

"Thursday," she insisted, smiling, and she hoped she sounded pleasant and not condescending, but she was eager to get away. It was just like before. He wanted too much. "We can catch up on everything at once. It's nice to see you. Really."

"Okay. Thursday."

She turned quickly and left him standing there, and she didn't look back because she was certain she'd find him staring after her as she departed. In the garage, she leaned on the elevator button, which was already lit. A woman in a pale pink linen suit stood with her. They nodded at each other, though Emily was lost in thoughts about Will. What felt exhilarating about seeing him, she realized, was suddenly touching that former time in her life. In the expression of his eyes, she felt her old self—her young self—handed to her, before all of the complications. But the fact of Will, his eagerness, his insistence on making plans, his desire to *catch up,* was overwhelming. She dreaded Thursday. She would plan how to compose herself for tea with him. For certain, she'd have her eye on her watch the whole time. Perhaps she'd find a way to cancel.

The woman in the pink suit leaned over a few inches. "What an incredible bag. May I ask where you got it?"

"It's Marac," Emily answered, glancing down at it. "His private collection."

"I've been looking for something just like it."

"It was a gift."

Emily adjusted the purse strap on her shoulder. Breaking up with Will had been the first determined choice of her life, and choosing Simon had been the next one. She'd known at once that she and Simon were much more similar to each other, more suited for a life together, with ambitions in sync. And hadn't they done just fine? Nearly two and a half decades had passed since she and Will had parted, and people respected her; they

valued her opinion when it came to brand name recognition and reputation management. She knew she came across more aloof, even colder
than she meant to, yet somehow, it was a way of being that had fostered
her career. It turned out to be necessary, too, for the kind of resolve it
took for a person to get on with life after—well, why go there? She did all
she could not to think about Caleb. More than enough time had passed
since then, and she'd never been one of those *poor me* types anyway.
She'd been to that place where it felt like her core had been plowed raw,
clawed apart, as if inside her rib cage were shapeless heaps of terrain. In
that loss of sense and order, there also had been panic. Every moment
had threatened the terror of a knock-down wave, where she'd lose the
sense of which direction was up. She fought it. Instead of letting it take
her down, she forced herself to keep her bearings. She moved on. And if
there were one person in the world who would take interest in the missed
opportunity for sentimentality it was Will Garth. As she walked toward
her car, her pulse surged in a way that made her temples feel hollow. She
dipped her hand into her purse, feeling a rush of certainty, and also relief,
as her fingers closed fast around her keys.

The sun had slipped from sight by the time she pulled into the circular
drive at home, but slate-blue daylight stretched on. From the illuminated
windows along the north side of the house, she surmised Simon was still
in his office. The cars belonging to the staff had departed, but she knew
he would be at his desk. In the very beginning of their marriage, she'd
been surprised by all the time Simon gave to his patients. He was attentive to them, no doubt about that. She'd supported his fervor, accepting
the long evenings he was absent from the house, enduring phone calls
that jarred them awake during the night, as if it were part of her role,
too. He was needed. People were desperate for his assistance. Will might
once have thought that she cared about financial security above all else,

but what had mattered to her was a life that made sense. Photographs were, well, gratuitous. Health and healing were essential. The very fact of Simon's work had humbled her. A good doctor, someone who could make a good diagnosis or even just hold a hand at the right moment, could change a person's life.

But after twenty-two years, she saw his work differently. All his ardor for medicine, and the virtue of it, seemed less of a marvel and more of a detail, Emily thought, looking toward the upper windows of the house. A detail in a life strewn with details. The reverence she'd once felt was tapped out, and she felt instead the functional weight of his job and an emptiness about the idea of heroism altogether. Simon's attention to his work had given her the space over the years to grow into her own career, and the autonomy had turned out to be a necessary condition for professional success, but it also took him out of the fray. Never mind that he was down a single flight of stairs from the kitchen. If he had a list of calls to make or e-mails to answer, he might not come upstairs for another two hours, and she had to manage on her own.

What had changed this summer, Emily realized, slowly gathering her bag from the front seat, was that his absence from the house had a new consequence: It thrust her in Jamie's path. When Jamie had turned thirteen last fall, they'd finally done away with babysitters. There had been strings of them, culled from Craigslist and from the bulletin boards of Goucher College, as well as occasional housekeepers and teenaged children of neighbors who met Jamie off the school bus and stayed through dinnertime. The babysitters and others (it was embarrassing to acknowledge, but it was true) were gentle buffers for the smooth functioning of a household. Everyone's behavior became more chipper when someone from outside the family was around—at least everyone put on a good face. Lately, it seemed, Jamie had become even more caustic and more accusatory, and now that the babysitters were done with, there was nobody to shield Emily. Now every interaction between them went insidiously, irrevocably awry.

The desire returned to head straight to the gym. Hiding out at the gym, that's what life had become. She eyed the dashboard clock and realized with dismay that she'd never make the evening spinning class. Not only was Fitness Galaxy her refuge, she had come to crave the bold rush of adrenaline in the darkened room of the late spinning session, the twenty-something-year-old instructor rising onto the pedals of the stationary bike, barking encouragement. Emily was capable of exerting long past the aching twangs of muscles, lengthening and stretching themselves, to the point that she felt all the mechanics of her limbs, the hinges and sockets of her joints, the swelling blood vessels alongside them. In those moments, she climbed beyond the grin-and-bear-it of her everyday motions. Breathing hard, sweat winging from the tips of her hair, her vision gone ragged, she welcomed the frenzy. The closest she could imagine to a religious experience, like those monks who starved or those worshippers who fainted, it was the feeling of being lost, slightly delirious, and then unburdened. She forgot her obligations to other people, and her frustrations. To get to that point, you had to push through discomfort and overcome it. But once you mastered that moment, the trancelike lightness enveloped your entire body. It was ironic, really. You pedaled and pedaled and went nowhere in spinning class, and somehow it could take you to a place you felt free.

No such luck tonight, though. Running into Will had made her late, and spinning class was going on without her. She grabbed her bag and trudged up the winding front steps. Jamie was probably upstairs, with the bedroom door shut tight. She'd always been a solitary kid, preferring to read a book than play with other children, but maybe it was time for her to start getting out, phoning some friends. Where were all her little friends this summer? Emily took a breath for resolve, her single goal to get through the night without losing her temper, retorting, criticizing or inciting more hostility. She had once expected that she'd be skilled at this stage of parenting, which involved reasoning and persuading, communicating with a person who could communicate back; that expectation had turned out to be wrong. She struggled, or she misspoke, or she held back when she had more to say. She offered idiotic advice when she feared that saying nothing demeaned her. Every day she found herself embroiled in conflict and every day wished she were better at parenting.

As she stepped into the dark entryway, she was startled by the apparent calm inside the house, and then, the sound of the phone, trilling through the rooms. She rested her keys in the crystal bowl on the sideboard, alert for Simon's bounding steps coming up the stairs or Jamie's tiptoeing creaks across the floorboards above her. There was no movement from anywhere, and the ringing continued. She trotted to the kitchen, grabbed for the cordless and exhaled a quick hello.

"Emily?" A woman's voice.

"Ah, Lucille," Emily answered, recognizing Simon's mother at once.

When Emily had first started dating Simon, his parents seemed to like her. This thrilled Simon, though Emily was accustomed to winning over almost everybody. In time, as she began to sort out all the odd tensions, it became clear to her that his parents' appreciation of her was limited, and their interest in him negligible. Lucille and Charles Bear had cultivated their own private world in the suburbs of Baltimore and, in retirement, had moved to Fort Lauderdale to live among a handful of similarly transplanted friends. There they played bridge with couples they knew they could beat and talked politics with people who didn't challenge their opinions, but they prized, above everything else, their insularity. They sent occasional postcards, particularly Lucille, who enjoyed writing letters. Simon pored over the few clipped sentences with informative updates, parsing for hidden meanings, wondering obsessively, "What do you think she meant by *holidays* when she could have written *Hanukkah*?" Emily had long recognized the truth about postcards: They were one-way missives that didn't anticipate or require a response.

"I tried to reach Simon," Lucille said.

"He's still downstairs. I just got in myself." Emily flicked on the lights in the kitchen, all tidy, even the polished little jars along the granite counter, in order of descending size. Yet something felt off, and she shifted the phone, venturing, "Everything all right?"

"It's nothing, really. It's Charles. A little mishap with the car is all."

"Mishap?" Emily was picturing Lucille, a tiny woman with expertly teased and dyed black hair, and that flawless, ageless skin.

"A great big nothing," Lucille reassured. "He's fine. They want to look him over, but he's fine. I figured I should call to let you know."

She felt her pulse quickening. "I don't understand."

"Really, there's nothing to tell."

Emily put the story together quickly: The car was totaled, but the dog that had bounded into the street had survived unscathed. Charles, driving alone, had swerved into a telephone pole. An ambulance had taken him to the hospital, Lucille reported, but he was fine. She said it over and over. *Fine.*

There was no emergency, Emily determined, but her mouth had gone dry just the same. Ten years earlier, her father's assistant had called to say that Al St. Bern had been rushed by ambulance to the hospital, but that they'd got to him too late. He was already dead. The assistant had little information at the time, but he didn't need to utter the word "suicide" for Emily to know exactly what had transpired. (Later, the coroner pronounced death had come from a mixture of pills and drinks that had stopped the heart. It appeared accidental, but Emily knew better.) At the time of her father's death, she'd hung up the phone, feeling stunned, but also distant and immune, as she sifted through the decisions she faced. Her sister, Aileen, traveling somewhere in Peru, was unreachable, and their mother was dead by then. Their father had been such a complex figure, abject mourning wasn't Emily's first response. Moreover, she was still putting behind her the fact of having lost Caleb. She'd experienced about as much feeling as a person could bear; she didn't have room to take on more. As a matter of necessity—her own necessity—which needed not to dwell where there was nothing to be gained, she insisted that she and Simon forge ahead with their plans for the evening. They already had a babysitter for Jamie, who was three, and they were expected at a cocktail party at another physician's home. Even if she'd been able to figure out what to do—travel to New York? stay home and cry? make phone calls?—she explained to Simon, there was nobody to do it for.

"Nothing hurts him," Lucille repeated. The more his mother said it, the more she underscored that she was calling out of a sense of obligation rather than need. "The hospital admitted him because they're being cautious. Because of his age, they say. He broke a rib, but he's fine. He just wants to go home. We're in a room. Private. It's very nice. We just have to wait is all."

"I'm so sorry. You must be shaken up," Emily responded with compassion. She meant it, but she also intended to make Lucille at least a little self-conscious about being so miserly with information. "Anything we can do for you from here?"

Lucille didn't seem to take note. "We just have to wait," she said. "It's a very nice hospital. The doctors have been very nice."

"Simon's not upstairs yet," Emily said. "Let me go down to get him." Then, through the phone, she heard other voices in muffled tones, and she could tell Lucille was distracted. She couldn't make out any words.

"The nurse just came in," Lucille announced, "so gotta go. Just wanted to let you know."

"Wait—" Emily pleaded, scrounging for a pen. Phone number? Hospital?

"No worries. Everything's under control." Lucille hung up.

Emily stared at the phone a moment, then reset it in its cradle on the wall. Don't make a big deal about it; that was the message. The clock read seven twenty. Charles was fine. Simon would be relieved there was nothing for them to do but wait for Lucille's update. She imagined he was still calling patients and sending e-mails, and her reasoning was simply practical: No point in interrupting him. He'd be upstairs shortly. In the refrigerator, she found a foil-covered casserole that the housekeeper, Lorraine, had made for them. Green beans, it seemed. Or was that asparagus? It was hard to tell. She was picking at it with a fork when she heard a noise upstairs, then the sound of something hitting the ground, clattering like metal.

"Jamie?" she called up the kitchen stairs.

A door opened. "It's nothing," Jamie's voice called back. "Forget about it." The door shut again.

Emily craned her neck. "What's going on?"

The door opened again. "Nothing," Jamie called downstairs, then, "Just a bowl. Nothing broken." The door shut again.

It was the abrupt shutting noise that prompted her to head upstairs. She worried about her daughter, who seemed so disgruntled and so out of step with the world. It was strange with a child. You could see the changes that would help them, and you could give advice, but just the act of opening your mouth turned out to be a violation of the highest order. She'd put her foot in it the very day Jamie had arrived home from camp.

"You must not have wanted to be there," Emily had pointed out. She'd said it gently, as matter-of-factly as she could. She didn't mean to accuse, but rather to voice what seemed obvious, in case the idea might be useful to Jamie. It certainly helped Emily, at least to fathom what might be going on. What Jamie had done seemed like sheer stupidity. Threatening a hunger strike, of all things. In proximity of other teenagers, such utterances went over like jokes about bombs in the airport. But what was at stake, really? As Jamie told it, she'd only wanted to finish a craft project that was half done, but nobody listened to her explanation about the knife and nobody cared. Hardly grounds for a protest, Emily thought. But after Jamie skipped her fourth meal in a row, the camp directors were swift and resolute. They made the phone call home. And no, they wouldn't put her on a train. Simon had to drive to Connecticut alone on Sunday evening to gather Jamie, not even a little emaciated, and bring her home.

Simon had tried to argue with the directors. Emily, who'd had a critical meeting first thing the next morning with the director of an Italian company, couldn't make the trip, but she didn't have to witness the scene to know exactly how it went. First came his logical appeal, in which he reiterated Jamie's side of the story. Then he resorted to yelling at the directors for their incompetence and their bone-headed policies and their lack of sensitivity to children. Once he'd returned home, Simon continued to believe the whole event was a misunderstanding—Jamie wasn't stealing, she was just borrowing. Miscommunications happened, and there was nothing to do but "suck it up," as he put it, and get on with the summer. But Emily just didn't get it, and she couldn't tell if she and Simon should be worried—what did all of this mean? If Jamie had stolen something of value, for instance, or taken items from other campers, Emily might have understood her daughter to be jealous or insecure. But arts and crafts seemed like a paltry payoff.

But Jamie insisted otherwise: "I was working on something."

"Well," Emily probed, "you must've thought on some level that there'd be consequences. If they found out?" She searched her daughter's face for clues, but Jamie, under the crisp edge of her bangs, produced an expression as bare as a stone. How was it possible for any parent to ferret out what a child hid beneath the surface?

"I told you," Jamie said. "I wasn't thinking that far ahead." Then came real disgust. "Why don't you listen? It's like you have some kind of image of how things are, and that's all you're willing to see."

Even when Emily kept her theories and suggestions to herself and uttered only the most Pollyanna comments, she still came out the villain. When she suggested that Jamie figure out an alternative activity for the summer, anything, a morning program at the Aquarium, for instance, where she could learn about fish or even sharks, Jamie retorted, "So you can assure your friends—ooh, the Aquarium, I'm so proud?" Jamie's acerbic moods wearied Emily, but even more, they made her sad. Other people—Betsy Ebberly, for instance, who always, infuriatingly, inserted her guidance-counselor knowledge of children, giving advice and platitudes so that it was almost impossible to be friends with her—assured her that "stealing" sounded like the spontaneous, poor decision-making typical of underprocessed, adolescent thinking patterns. And the angry moods were age-appropriate, too. Betsy added, in words too cavalier for Emily, such family tensions were par for the course: "It's the price of being mother to a girl." But Emily knew otherwise. She was well aware how deep the strife between her and Jamie ran. She wanted to be close with her daughter, but the strain in their relationship was years old. By now, Emily felt damn near powerless to change it.

She pushed open the door to Jamie's room. "Jamie?" No answer. She glanced at the unmade bed, the walls crowded with posters of *South Park* and that sour-looking Avril Lavigne and Simon Cowell, of all people, on the wall and even on the ceiling. On the slanted corner of the room, Jamie had tacked a collection of bumper stickers, the majority of which Simon had bought for her, as if they shared some private joke. Most were appalling, and old-and-jaded sounding, one-dollar-ninety-five-cent banalities. She half-believed that Jamie didn't understand most of them. DON'T VOTE. IT ONLY ENCOURAGES THEM, read one. I ♥ MY ATTITUDE PROBLEM. PINK SHEEP OF THE FAMILY. And, in glaring neon, MEAN PEOPLE SUCK. The last was a generic message, she knew, but somehow she felt it was directed at her.

She did not often think about Caleb, but now and then she found herself wondering if her relationship with him would have been tender. He was a difficult baby, colicky and hard to please. It was unfair to speculate—she felt like she was betraying Jamie even to imagine what he would have been like, but sometimes she imagined that if his colic had ended, she would have hit her stride as mother, and—what? Would they all have lived happily ever after? Each interaction with Jamie managed to show her the dead end of her power. She wanted to help Jamie, but she couldn't get her daughter's *compliance*. And then, when she put her foot down for something larger, like a principle or a necessary lesson Jamie should learn, she was the one who suffered consequences. Years back, she'd gotten into a scrape with Jamie over a toy, some hideous, hard-plastic pony thing with pink hair. They went back and forth, Jamie constructing one argument after the next—*but I've never had one, but I like horses, but Daddy would buy it for me.* He was a father who believed in big, expensive presents and was unstoppable in his excesses. But Emily couldn't bring herself to spoil Jamie. First of all, even the child knew materialistic doting was a kind of apology. And what was the message anyway? Jamie begged for the pony, but Emily held back, insisting that Jamie could wait until her birthday. "You don't want me to love you," Jamie had accused finally, folding her body into a dark sulk. It was a comment that hadn't even made sense, but Emily had never forgotten it.

"You in here?" She tried the door of the bathroom, and was surprised as she twisted the doorknob to find it unlocked. The light was on.

Her daughter stood in front of the sink wearing nothing but a long T-shirt. Blue-green, tattered around the collar from age, the shirt was an adult size that still dwarfed Jamie's frame. Simon had given it to her years ago after having made a large donation to an ocean conservation organization. The faded stencil showed a finned creature leaping above the waves as the arching print below read, MY LIFE'S PORPOISE. "Why would I want this?" Jamie had demanded at the breakfast table when Simon handed it over. It was clear to everyone, especially Jamie, the shirt was a give-away he was passing along. "You're my porpoise," he told her, grinning. They had both stared at him, trying to gauge his sincerity against his blatant love of the pun. Standing in the bathroom, Emily's first thought was about the now-ratty gift, which had obviously meant something to Jamie, who'd incorporated it into her wardrobe as a nightshirt. A nightshirt? Was it later than she thought? But something in her clenched at once at the chalky pallor of Jamie's skin, slightly gray under the eyes, though the tip of her daughter's nose was pink.

"Hey!" Jamie exclaimed, scowling.

Emily stood for a second trying to figure out the scene, aware from the hush that she had walked in on something of significance. On the floor lay a stainless-steel mixing bowl from the kitchen and a scattering of ice, knocked over. Her brain was trying to make sense of the array of items that didn't seem to belong on the bathroom floor. She was also struggling to think of the most diplomatic way to be parental, but all that came clear was the one fact she knew. "The door was open," she said.

She looked from the floor to Jamie's face, framed by her long, straight hair. The overall shape of her face was round, with narrow, chocolate eyes and astounding lashes. It occurred to her that the familiar mousy brown had disappeared, and even the color of Jamie's hair was slowly becoming darker and more defiant-looking. A fleeting memory of Caleb flickered through her mind, the feathery fringe on his head in those first weeks—how it had amazed her, that ducklike softness—so fine, you almost couldn't feel it with your fingertips. She checked herself, swallowing, feeling her insides churning, not sure what had unsettled her, the intrusion of memory or the sense that Jamie was already angry. She steadied herself again, not wanting to ignite a feud. "Need a towel?" she offered.

But Jamie quickly rebuffed her. "I got it."

You don't want me to love you.

But I do, she thought back, *if you'll just stop fighting.* She couldn't think of anything more to say. "Did you eat?"

"Does *anybody* eat in this house?" Jamie replied. "It's more like food magically appears and then disappears."

Emily was about to say something rational and reasonable and chastising, something about the demands of the jobs that made them able to buy food in the first place, when she noticed a capless bottle of rubbing alcohol on the edge of the sink. Her curiosity won out. "What exactly are you doing?"

"What's this, an interrogation? I knocked over a bowl. I'll clean it up. What's the big deal?"

Then she happened to notice the way Jamie was holding the edge of the long T-shirt, tenting the fabric away from her body. She took three steps toward Jamie and, with a single gesture, lifted the hem of the shirt. A large red welt encircled the top of Jamie's navel. At the center of the welt, a narrow, silver stud with a ball on either end staked a translucent web of skin. The sight of the injured skin around Jamie's freshly pierced navel sickened Emily, the raised and whitened ridge surrounding the stud, the offended bull's-eye of inflammation. Emily swallowed against a moment of feeling ill.

Jamie wavered for a second, ever so slightly leaning away from her mother to avoid being touched. Though Emily said nothing, Jamie's eyes narrowed. "I'm not taking it out."

Brisk clouds moved in. A dozen arguments crowded her mind, reshaping themselves, dissolving and re-forming. The piercing was too sexual. It was too declarative. It made her look like a child who'd already rejected parenting. Emily shook her head. "I can't even look at it," she said finally.

"So don't," Jamie replied. "It's *my* body."

Yours, Emily thought. She swallowed again. She was not a stupid woman, and she didn't need a Betsy Ebberly to help her interpret. There was nothing innocent in the piercing, a small act of violence, intended to engage a battle. *How primitive.* Even the dropped bowl had been intentional, a trumpet call to the troops. Perhaps another mother would have taken a stand. That mother would have insisted Jamie remove the jewelry. That mother would have lectured. Once, a very long time ago, she'd read a parenting magazine that recommended every disciplinary injunction begin with, "I love you, and . . ." like a mantra. "I love you, and you're not allowed to stay out until eleven." Or, "I love you, and you must finish your homework." "I love you's" until they didn't mean anything anymore, functioning like a public relations campaign. Her jaw tightened. The experience of parenting had become one of constant abuse—three months ago, she'd been surprised by Jamie's insistence on signing up for camp, as Jamie shunned suggestions and packed up by herself as though she were fleeing. Then Jamie bestowed another surprise, suddenly sent home, as if nobody would care. Now this: primal torture performed in the bathroom. What did Jamie expect her to do? Each encounter was like a jolt to the senses. *You're the one,* she thought, *who doesn't want to be loved by* me. She turned, composed, and left the bathroom. A few steps down the hallway, she turned back again as a thought occurred to her. Evenly she said, "I hope at least whatever you used was clean."

She walked down the hall to her bedroom, but as she sat on the corner of her bed, her hands shook like a woman with palsy. Jamie had come into the world watching Emily and testing her, and Emily continued to fail. Now Jamie was trying to anger her, and the only thing to do was to refuse to succumb. What she couldn't stop was the sensation in her rattling hands.

She'd been an awkward mother when Caleb was born, unsure from the start she had the necessary nurturing instincts. It was one thing to be pregnant, all ripe with anticipation. It was another to look at a newborn in a bassinet next to your hospital bed and realize the moment had come to perform. He was on the small side, barely six pounds, which all the maternity nurses found humorous, considering that she and Simon were so tall. His eyes were wide set, the pumpkin-seed shape of them pleasant to her. They reminded her vaguely of her sister, Aileen, and they were so filled with the copper brown of his irises that you almost couldn't see any white around them. Old soul eyes, she thought. They looked like they were already familiar with everything, even the details of her own face, though everyone said he couldn't possibly focus yet. *Here we are,* they seemed to say, with consuming intensity, *me and you*. It was a moment, she knew, to feel an overspilling of love and attachment. To feel the desire to give with a kind of joyful craziness. Instead, she felt slightly sick to her stomach. Maybe she'd made a big mistake having a child. Maybe she wasn't cut out to be a mother. Had her own mother, who loved a clean house above all things, ever enjoyed parenting? The sensation of doubt was so alarming that she fought against it, smiling for the nurses and forcing herself to cradle Caleb without moving until her arms cramped and her wrists ached.

He was a difficult baby, and she struggled. She felt frustrated most of the time, and worn-out tired, and all she could do was hope something would kick in that felt like maternal euphoria. She yearned for a heart-swelling sense of pleasure, a sense of pride, a shred of the competence she felt when she was at work. But mostly her ears were filled with the sound of his unhappiness as he cried, urging her to do something. Every moment, to do something, and every moment to figure out what that something was. At the very least, she longed for time to pass more quickly to put the phase of unending crying behind her. At four weeks, between all the jags of colic, amid all the fretful hours he refused to be calmed, he began to smile, a tiny, lopsided upcurling of his lips. That tiny smile and the eyes that locked onto hers, *me and you,* and she experienced a glimmer of relief. Within two weeks of that moment, he was gone. Barely sick one day, and then—it was incomprehensible. Whatever in her being that had been available to the world, exposed to its elements, testing and trying, pulled back like a finger touched to flame. There was anguish initially, the feeling that she couldn't breathe. The air caught in her lungs. Her eyelashes hurt. The follicles of hair in her scalp ached. The surfaces of her eyes felt turned inside out. Her body seemed slow and cowlike. There was a period of insomnia to endure, in which she was always tired yet never able to sleep more than an hour or two at a stretch. But even as she lay awake in the night, she couldn't hold a clear thought in her head. *I am—sad? I am—broken?*

Then reason kicked in, and a voice that seemed like clarity. Enough pitiful, pointless lazing. Enough suffering, when it couldn't do anything to change what had happened. Even the pediatricians had missed the diagnosis. It was time to get on with it. She had a job. She had to function, as did Simon. There would be punishment, she was certain, some cosmic retribution for her self-interest, but she craved normalcy. When she woke up one morning less than a year after his death with a strange sense of change happening in her abdomen, a kind of acidy bloating with pressure, she thought, *There's my punishment: cancer.* Ovarian. Uterine. Her stomach churned. Some deep organ was already rippling with ferocious cells. There would be all kinds of tests, and time in the hospital. She would be given glimpses of her innards on X-rays and suffer long, quiet periods of waiting. A terminal diagnosis would not have surprised her in the least. At the doctor's, she was given a blood test, but she wasn't prepared for the call the next morning conveying instead (in an absurdly singsong voice) that she was pregnant.

"Are you sure?" she burbled. Since she wasn't dying, she forced herself to take a deep breath. She was a practical person, a problem solver, and she would handle this, too. She gathered herself for the course ahead, though she knew she wasn't ready to have another child.

Now, staring at her trembling hands, she felt the urge to hold them under water. Like a machine, she went to the sink of the master bath. Cupping the flow that streamed from the faucet, she scooped handfuls of water against her face. Restorative drops fell from her chin, and she stared at herself. She'd been hypervigilant when Jamie was born, always watching for signs of distress or illness, trying to guard against disaster. Fortunately, Jamie turned out to be an easier baby than Caleb had been. As she grew, the sense of urgency and imminent danger that Emily felt wore off. Anyway, it was physically, humanly impossible to maintain that level of attention, especially when you were merely protecting against your own worries. But things became complicated just the same. Jamie was a defiant toddler, sharp-tongued and unwilling to behave. The terrible twos felt like they lasted for many multiples of two. Emily felt helpless and often annoyed, unable to control the child or make things right. She became guarded and apprehensive and afraid of being accosted. Jamie wasn't fooled. It was like being with a dog that you knew was able to smell your fears. At every turn, Jamie fought back, trying to incite her. Emily, holding her ground, became unable to spoil her daughter.

"Of course, it's challenging. It's the hardest job there is, and nobody ever warns you beforehand," said the ever-reassuring Betsy Ebberly, who knew about Caleb, but who seemed to have no clue that a person could find herself one day, like Emily, with the will to mother all but drummed out of her.

Looking into the mirror at the water dripping off her chin, she felt sad for the ways her face had changed. Her eyes, which someone had once told her were merry, had lost their stars. A wrinkle of consternation had etched itself vertically into her forehead. Even her lips seemed to turn downward. Had they always been shaped in a pout, or was the damage she'd suffered becoming visible? Something white and hot rose in her field of vision, and before she composed a clear thought, she grabbed a hairbrush that was sitting on the edge of the counter. Bristles upward, she brought the backside down, hard, against the edge of the cream and gray granite countertop. There was a popping *thwack* as the brush broke, its porcupine head spinning in the air like a bottle cap. A semicircular piece of the countertop chipped off and scuttled across the tiled floor to a corner, as if it were afraid. The sound of what she had done startled her, and she stared at the counter edge in horror. The gap in the granite grinned back at her.

She dropped the handle of the hairbrush into the trash and dried her face, now cool. Her hands were steady; she was no longer angry. What was there to do about any of it, the piercing, the fighting? Nothing. Noticing water rings on the countertop, Emily rubbed at them with her towel. If they could go back to the beginning of Jamie's life, start over from scratch, she might be able to do a better job. She would keep her mouth shut more, let Jamie lead, find a way to be more gentle. Jamie knew she was second-born, of course, though Caleb's name seldom came up for any reason. Things were what they were now. Emily patted a puddle of melted goop from the bottom of the soap dish and peeled cellophane from a fresh bar. She looped two fresh new cream-colored hand towels through the silver rings on either side of the double sink and sifted new petals into the bowl of potpourri. She ran the shower to steam the mirrors. With a swath of toilet paper, she mopped stray hairs from the eggshell tiles of the floor. She picked up the piece of granite, and she fitted it back into the edge of the countertop. Superglue would hold it in place. You wouldn't even notice it. Looking up, she found Simon standing behind her, framed in the doorway, and she jumped.

"I didn't hear you come upstairs," she said. She closed the checker-sized chip of countertop in her fist, blocking the gap with her body.

"Long day." He looked tired, but his eyes shone with a happy, satisfied gleam. He so thoroughly enjoyed being useful, sometimes she thought he might be in the grip of something like an addiction. "Many patients, many problems."

Many problems, she thought. Would he consider Jamie's home-piercing salon a "problem"? She decided not to mention it. He was masterful at being unencumbered by problems, championing the rationales of "What's the big deal?" and "If it makes her happy." It wasn't fair. All of his blithe doting made her feel all the more like the bad guy. She thought about telling him about Will, running into him in the street after twenty-four years, but decided not to.

"Your mother called," she said instead, remembering, as he turned and headed into the bedroom. "Charles apparently banged up the car."

Simon sat on the bed, taking off his shoes. He shook his head. "I was telling them the last time we were down there that he shouldn't be driving. What time did you get home?"

"He's fine, apparently," Emily continued. "The car's banged up, and they're checking him over at the hospital, but he's fine." She could still hear Lucille's dismissive voice reiterating, *He's fine*. "Lorraine left a casserole in the fridge. You can nuke it."

Simon looked surprised. "They took him to the hospital? Did he hit his head?"

"Lucille just said he's fine. The nurse was there. She had to go."

He was shaking his head. "Where's the number? I'll call them."

"No number. She kept saying he was fine. They had everything under control, that's what she said. I don't think she wanted us involved, to be honest. Like before, remember?"

Simon ran his fingers through his hair, which he did when he was frustrated. "When you said he banged up the car, I thought you were talking fender-bender. I thought maybe he cracked a headlight. But they're looking him over at the hospital?"

"He was trying not to hit a dog," she explained. "Don't get huffy at me. I'm telling you everything I know. And Lucille said she'd call back. Otherwise, there was nothing to tell."

He pressed, "What hospital? That's no bang-up, you realize. That's a car accident."

"She said 'mishap.' Really, you're making this much more than it is. You were downstairs, Simon," she said, chastising. "I was waiting for you to come up."

But Simon had already turned down the hall. She heard him sit at the computer in the library, already online to figure out the possible Fort Lauderdale hospitals. Then she heard him calling operators. Technically, Charles was his stepfather. Charles had adopted Simon as a baby—Emily had heard the story just once from Lucille, how Charles had married her even though she was a ruined woman. (It was absurd how Lucille had clung to the idea of being ruined, but that was a notion from another generation.)

"What's the number for the main operator?" Simon asked the person on the other end of the phone.

Emily came to the door of the library and stood with her arms crossed. "She said she's got everything under control," Emily interrupted. She felt certain about what Lucille had communicated. "Shouldn't we respect that?"

"You do?" Simon was saying into the receiver, ignoring her. "Very good. Can you tell me what room number please? This is his family physician"—she winced as he lied—"from Baltimore. Yes, thanks, you can transfer me."

Emily left as his call was connected to the private room. She could hear him grilling Lucille with questions, his tone growing increasingly impatient. Of course Lucille didn't know Charles's blood counts, couldn't report oxygen readings, couldn't even remember which rib was broken. Simon's voice rose until he began to sound like he was talking to a very stupid child. "What do you mean you don't know what kind of break it was? I don't understand. Hit his head? Well, did they do a CT? What do you mean you don't know what tests they've done so far?"

For someone who made frequent speeches about empowering his patients, Simon sounded unduly reproachful, she thought. Lucille and Charles were staunch, independent people, boastfully self-reliant. When they'd moved to Fort Lauderdale, they'd refused help, even to pack their belongings. They hated to be the object of anyone's fussing. She heard a door close down the hall as Jamie made some mysterious movement from one room to the next, and Emily listened but didn't move. The image of the taut skin around her navel returned, along with a wave of revulsion. *Have your revolution,* she thought. She looked back at Simon and then returned to the bedroom, sat in front of the vanity and reached for the cream to remove the makeup from her eyes, the foundation from across her cheeks. Then, carefully, in small circles, she began applying moisturizer to her face. Her skin was so dry, the ginger-scented cream seemed to disappear instantly. Will had said she looked the same as she always had, but he must have been saying it to be polite. All those lines, so weathered-looking. Finally, Simon entered the bedroom.

"They have no information," he said, annoyed. "They don't know what they're doing. They're like sheep, and they're letting the system herd them around." His fingers raked his hair again as he got worked up. "I knew he was driving badly the last time we visited. That bastard never listens to anything I say."

"This is a molehill you're turning into a mountain." With a pinky-tip, she worked the moisturizer into a small circle at the edge of her eye. "You've got to let them do their thing."

"He wrapped his car around a *pole*. He could have died."

"But he didn't," she said, with a grim smile. "He's hardly dead at all." She continued smoothing cream across her forehead, but she felt herself flush. He was standing in the middle of the room with his mouth agape. "What?" she asked innocently.

"You're not taking this seriously."

"All I said was, we should respect their space."

Then he made a decision. "We should all go down there. As a family. To support them and help them figure out what's what. Nobody should be in the hospital without an advocate. I'm a doctor, for chrissake."

"Jamie won't want to go," Emily said slowly. "And I have meetings I really shouldn't miss." Oh, horrible hospitals, the movement of the carts, the beds, everything on wheels, nothing anchored down. She hated waiting around so long it felt like you were hanging on each other, like you were breathing in the air you'd only just breathed out. She was not one for blood and gore, for weepy scenes or melodrama. She'd had quite enough of hospitals for a lifetime, she felt. And in the back of her mind, she realized, if they made the trip to Florida, she would not see Will on Thursday. He would return to Philadelphia and they would have no cause to meet. She recognized suddenly, with a tingle of alarm, that she was curious. Who was the woman he'd married finally? What had he named his daughters?

"Three years ago," she pointed out to Simon, "I had to remind you to call him when he had his prostate biopsy."

"This is different."

The timing was terrible, but Simon would need her in Florida simply to mediate. His parents didn't understand his forcefulness. In fact, they were visibly put off by his declarations, his conviction of his own importance. He, too, didn't understand what would help them. Ultimately, however, you couldn't argue with someone intent on going to great lengths in order to help. Instead, if you understood your role and your particular skills, you chipped in. You did whatever you could to facilitate the goodwill. Not to help, it seemed, would be heartless.

They made their way to Baltimore/Washington International Airport the next morning just after dawn. Was it proof of whose will was stronger, she wondered as she looked out the massive windows of the airport, or was it something else, a shared sense that death had been near, nearer than was comfortable, nearer than they cared to believe? There was no way to prepare mentally for a hospital visit. She had already visualized Charles's injuries, contusions, bruises, puckered stitches, lost teeth, sunken lips, jaundice, the shock of sudden age that comes with trauma. She knew she was right about how best to help Lucille and Charles—to stay away—and yet she would never be able to persuade Simon. The best thing to do, in fact the only thing, was to make the trip all together, keep it short and under control. She canceled her meetings for Wednesday and Thursday. She had no idea how to reach Will to let him know she wouldn't be able to meet, and she regretted that he would get the impression she had either gotten cold feet or simply didn't care.

Standing at check-in, noting that their tickets were grouped two and one, Simon overheard that a seat in first class had come available. Before Emily could say anything, he cajoled the ticketing agent into an upgrade for the single seat. "There really is a difference," he said, holding out the boarding pass for Emily to take. Any other person, it seemed, would have tried to arrange having three seats together, even asking other people to move out of their row, but he found a way to turn the seating on a plane into a theatrical gesture. She realized resisting would only sound stupid, if she tried to explain that first class felt like she was being exiled. In his typical unconcerned way, he said he'd enjoy sitting with Jamie in the back of the plane. Emily took another glance at Jamie, who glowered. Emily reached out and, without a word, accepted the boarding pass.

Jamie had been surprisingly nonresistant to the idea of the last-minute trip and had packed an overnight bag quickly and without a word. But in the airport her attitude was belligerent again. Like a grudging pet, she trailed a step behind them as they moved toward the line to board. Emily first looked for signs that she was suffering from the freshly pierced navel and was about to ask her how it was healing, but Jamie's scowls were so forbidding, Emily decided not to mention it. Pushed away, that was what she was. Jamie had made the declaration: It wasn't Emily's body to worry about.

"Remember," Emily leaned into her as they took their places, "this trip is about doing what we can for Charles. And Lucille." The reminder seemed as much for herself as for Jamie.

"Yeah, so?" Jamie shrugged.

She had a thought to say something about how things could take a turn quickly, people—however you felt about them—could be gone before you said boo and it was worth at least realizing that. That it was important to make an effort. But Jamie's insolence made her start and what came out was, "So stop glooming around, and try to look like you care."

Jamie released a long, thin stream of air. They watched a far window, where a jet had just taxied up to another gate, and the accordion walkway stretched out to meet it. Simon, apparently oblivious of Jamie's mood, recounted the story (for the billionth time) of the flight when he'd had to administer insulin at thirty-five thousand feet to a passenger who'd gone into diabetic shock. The airline had sent him a fruit basket. By the time they were on the plane, she was glad for the peace and the distance of her solo seat. She settled herself and looked out the window. The man in the seat next to her had an amplitude of fat in dimensions Simon might refer to as morbidly obese, and he was making low noises in his throat. He slumped low with his legs stretched out and mixed his own Bloody Mary. He wore long, carefully trimmed sideburns and large princess-cut diamond stud earrings in each ear.

"I'll take another-a these," he urged the stewardess, waggling the empty baby-sized bottle of vodka between two thick fingers.

For a split second, Emily and the stewardess locked commiserating gazes. Though the woman's expression remained pleasant, Emily was certain she read the annoyance that flickered deep in the retinas of the woman's eyes. It was the stuff and substance of Emily's livelihood to understand such moments, how people presented themselves and how they were being received. Quite often, multimillion-dollar reputations were at stake. Right now, she was in charge of a case involving the Bandy nut company, accused of using water potentially contaminated with pesticide residue. Protests had ensued, some senators had called for bans of Bandy products. Boycotts of peanut products raged in several states. Frith had been consulted to navigate relations between the company and the public and to win back the confidence of nut consumers by restoring trust in the Bandy brand name. She had approved a plan for the project: There would be committees to establish scientific, point-by-point rebuttals to the charges. Laboratory tests would prove the contamination was negligible. Her deputies would consult with a federally funded environmental agency. She herself would call for a task force to investigate pesticides as a broader problem facing the food industry. They'd learned from the mistakes of other companies. You had to face these crises with your head up, whether you were culpable or not. Attitude was everything. If you appeared to be making a noble effort, people were inclined to assume the best.

It was not a career she'd ever anticipated. She'd once strived to do something artistic in the footsteps of her famous father. Everyone— whether they knew him or had only heard of him—regarded Al St. Bern as a creative genius. He represented near-royalty of the American kind, self-made, bold, eccentric in a way necessary to make things happen. His empire had germinated in 1949 in a cramped shoe store and repair shop on the Lower East Side. He was Alvin Bernstein then, and his store carried a respectable collection of both popular and designer footwear. What the place was famous for, though, was the mannequin in the window, a doe-faced, elegant female figure with lifted, lithe hands, her bearing almost too elegant for the strong smell of epoxy and shoe polish that pervaded the store. The cleverness of the mannequin was that she was privileged to wear a new ball gown each week, and a new pair of fine shoes with each one. People stopped at the window of the little shop just to see her latest attire. The family referred to her as Queen Esther. When the delivery arrived, on loan from Brettelheim's on Seventh or Zeiselman's on Broadway in exchange for a sign in the window, she or Aileen would alert their parents: "Queen Esther's dress is here," and then hover as Al or Judith tore away the wrapping to see what she would wear the following week. "She's a practical woman at her core," Al would repeat to his daughters or any customers who commented on her outfit, "but the right shoes make her fit for a king."

All those years, even Emily perceived their station in life was only temporary; they were en route to larger fortune and greater fame. In 1970, when Emily was ten and Aileen sixteen, Al Bernstein moved the shop to a site just off Park Avenue, a bright store with a large, honey-colored showroom and velvet-cushioned seats for people to sit on as they sampled sizes of immodestly expensive shoes. Remaking the store, he also remade the family. He relieved his wife of her bookkeeping duties and set her out to do volunteer work and participate in civic projects, as he imagined a socialite would. A woman named Pearl was hired to take orders and keep track of the paperwork. He shortened the family name to Bern—and then changed it again to St. Bern. They moved to the Upper East Side, quit B'nai Yisrael shul, left the Hadassah group, dropped out of Sunday morning Hebrew school classes, stopped ordering from the kosher butcher and, almost overnight, shed all signs of being Jewish.

"We're *what?*" a teenaged Aileen had shrieked. She had entered a stage of life in which she hated anything and everything phony.

"Unitarian," Al St. Bern declared. "It fits us better."

Emily had asked Aileen in private what the change was about since they didn't go to synagogue anymore and they didn't belong to a Unitarian church. "Because there are no Jews in New York's social elite," Aileen spat. The new identity might have meant a beginning for Al, but it staggered Emily. It was not clear where to side, with the erratic or with the anger, but Emily perceived the rift for the first time: Aileen was drifting from the family.

The new boutique advertised special imports from Paris and Argentina. Its location made it a popular shopping destination for wealthy women, actresses and politicians' wives. But in 1974, the year Emily turned fourteen (by then Aileen was away from home, a sophomore at Wellesley), he sold the store and launched his ultimate empire: St. Bern Design. High heels, open toes, closed toes, sling backs, pumps, mini boots, thong sandals, moccasins with heels. He hobnobbed with the editors of *Vogue* and *Cosmopolitan*. He slept in the stairwells of downtown office buildings, so that in the morning he could push his designs with executives at Chanel. Not until she moved away did Emily consider that he'd been in the grip of a kind of mania during those years, that there might have been something odd, erotic and unwholesome in his obsession with footwear and his craze for upward mobility. There were down times, too. He would yell abusively at anyone in his path, or retreat into his office and refuse to eat, hardly showing his face for days at a time.

But in their Upper East Side apartment, shoes were joy. Shoes were life. He drew them on an easel like a painter, working in black ink, sketching each shoe from several angles. Then he added watercolor or pastel or oil paint. Each sketch had notes for the men at the shop in New Jersey, scribbled in ink up and down the sides, detailing creative inspiration and reading almost like poetry: "straps fit like a bangle of jewels," "small heel holds her aloft but not in jeopardy." Then he carried his artwork rolled up under his arm and had a car drive him to the Jersey shop to have prototypes made. In the years he was designing, shoes were everywhere in her parents' East Side home, on the sofa, on the dining room table, on the kitchen counter. Emily once asked whether they could have the prototypes made in their sizes, but they were tall girls and apparently it wasn't economical for the company to make a size nine or nine-and-a-half to test out a style.

The fervor for St. Bern Design grabbed the fashion world. St. Bern himself was a gift to style writers: gabby, eager to be accessible and capable of giving fearless, well-parsed sound bites. He socialized with celebrities, persuading them to wear his lines. Everywhere Emily went, to parties, openings or shows, as soon as people found out whose daughter she was, they gushed about her father's visionary designs as well as his flair for self-promotion. By the time she was a student at Barnard, she knew that a normal life—a quiet existence with a workaday job out of the limelight—was tantamount to failure. The problem was, she couldn't figure out how to distinguish herself. The impulse to create bubbled up inside her, but what? How? She took several art classes, but never possessed any flair for drawing and was not admitted to the upper level art courses. Aileen, by then, had said to hell with them all and after graduating college had joined the Peace Corps, an angry humanitarian digging irrigation ditches in Indonesia. But Emily believed in her father's sense of ambition. She just didn't know what to do with herself.

More than anything, she hoped to join her father's empire. Whatever it was she needed—artistic talent, creative inspiration—she believed she could learn if she had the right mentor. If she could place herself under his tutelage, she could develop the skills to follow his direction. On the day after graduation ceremonies, with a cobbled-together degree in art education, she asked her father if she could join his design team. At Judith's insistence, he agreed to make her an administrative assistant to the deputy designer. "You'll work your way up," promised her mother, surprisingly optimistic for a frustrated woman who'd been excused from the business world to be what seemed, even to Emily, an unrewarded and unrespected figurehead.

In the brightly lit office, Emily set up her own easel with a broad and hopeful sketchpad. She bought black ink pens. "I want an assignment," she told her father. He set her to the task of designing a line of shoes for young women new to the working world, just like herself. "Young," he declared, "and fresh—but also earnest, demure and smart." She created a shoe, a simple black pump, and brought her father the illustration.

"Look," he said, pulling a two-year-old catalog from a drawer. He thumbed to page 12 and pointed out an out-seasoned black pump with many of the same features as her sketch. Even she had to agree, the shoe in the book had a more aristocratic look. "It's not about functionality," he instructed. "Not at first. It's about attitude. This shoe," he pointed to her sketch, "doesn't say anything. Our women"—that was how he'd come to speak about his clientele—"know that shoes speak worlds. Make the shoe speak."

For two years, she struggled in his office like a tourist trying to piece together the syntax of a foreign language without a dictionary or a sympathetic guide. "A shoe is an extension of the personality," he would say. "Shoes are about intrigue and possibility." Nothing he said prompted ideas; none of the cryptic directions made her see anything new in the stretch of an arch, the angle of a buckle. Instead, something else happened. Her mind began to freeze. She stared at the easel and drew a heel. Then she erased the heel. She drew a toe. There was a blank page in front of her and a winter in her head. She doodled and crumpled paper while answering the phones.

Then, one day as the company was gearing up to produce a spring catalog, she was instructed to wheel boxes of new shoes from the basement for a photo shoot. On the set, she noticed Will, the photographer's assistant. What she noticed about him, in truth, was that he had noticed her. Distracted, flustered, grinning like an idiot, he nearly crashed a studio light over the set displaying the spring open-toe selections.

She hadn't meant to fall in love, but being with him felt new to her and intoxicating. They ate bratwurst—which seemed like the unhealthiest and most base of all foods—on a bench in Central Park. They picked through knickknacks in pawn shops, and rode the subway to the end of the lines. One time, in a Salvation Army store, he bought her a pretty watch that didn't work. The band was like nothing she'd ever seen, double tortoise-shell tubes bound with silver hinges, and the face, an oval, like a Dali painting. "I can have a new battery put in it," she said, admiring it on her wrist. He just shrugged. He was easygoing, willing for things to happen to him, happy to sit back and simply feel what was happening. Within the cramped, cool walls of his East Village basement apartment, she encountered the antidote to all the pressures of trying to prove herself. His creative yearning was nothing like her father's. It came out of a free place, a desire to explore, and for the first time in her life, she felt buoyed by a kind of happy, childlike energy. One lazy afternoon when they were still naked, she lifted his camera to her face and aimed it at him. Surprised by its weight in her hands, she said, "Tell me what to look for. What do I do?" He reclined on the bed with his half-smile and shrugged. "Just see what you see." She wasted a whole roll of film just snapping pictures of him, his face, that look in his eyes, that gnawed and healed patch on the side of his jaw. They weren't good pictures, she knew—they didn't *say* anything—but it was a powerful experience to isolate each part of him with the lens of the camera.

She loved him in all of the fragments: his nimble-moving fingers, his simple laugh, the patience and admiration that lit up his eyes. It was the totality of him that didn't add up.

So she tried to take charge. "Look, Daddy." She sneaked samples of Will's work from wax-paper folders in his apartment and smuggled them to her father's office. Will's photos of people—a pregnant woman on the subway, hugging her belly as though she were trying to protect her unborn fetus from the riffraff around her; a policeman eating a hotdog as if he imagined it needed to be overpowered; a woman in a fur coat sauntering alone into the cinema, the look on her face testifying to her loneliness—each one was a world you could disappear into. The sampling enthralled the design team, suddenly taken by the concept of projecting glamour shoes into real-world grittiness. Al St. Bern outlined the proposal himself: He wanted Will to photograph an upcoming ad series to run in full-page installations in *The New York Times*. Though she shouldn't have been, she was surprised when Will declined. "It's just not for me," he explained. But turning down the job was the end of being in Al St. Bern's good graces.

"That young man's got a troubled relationship with money," her father announced. "Can't figure out how to earn it."

She began to see it, too. What Will lacked was a sense of direction, a drive to compete. Suddenly it bothered her that he didn't have a clear goal in sight for his life. He didn't even have a savings account. Even though she wasn't sure what she wanted yet, she knew she'd eventually know how to succeed.

Then Will said, "Let's go to India."

What was India to her? No colors, no shades of light, no faces she needed to see that she couldn't see right there in New York. The idea sounded to her like more of his immaturity, his love of the impractical. But when she hesitated, Will misinterpreted and suggested they get married. Get married first, he said, and go to India on a honeymoon. She could still recall his face during their breakup, the way it blanched and then composed itself again around the wound, but she closed herself like a fist. "It just won't work," she told him.

It turned out to be a healthy break, too, because it terminated many delusions she'd had about herself. Shortly after breaking off with Will, she quit her father's business. Using one of his contacts, she became an intern at a public relations firm. Public relations involved managing events, but you dealt with things as they were, instead of issuing them from the mysterious, inaccessible recesses of your consciousness. You made people understand what you needed them to see. When her mother died suddenly of a brain hemorrhage during the next year, Emily had already secured a full-time job with another firm and was about to be promoted again. She wasn't as good at the unreserved enthusiasm of basic promotions, but she turned out to be particularly resourceful in crisis management. Public relations involved fighting back when you were cornered. It involved having a sense of conviction about the world and a game plan to turn it around. It wasn't creative. It didn't require brilliance, ingenuity or poetry. She understood decorum, was well-spoken, liked parties. She could banter with just about anybody, steering a conversation like an expert equestrian with just the right hold on the reins.

And then, at a party thrown by a college friend, she met Simon Bear, who seemed to her to be everything Will was not. He was a doctor, part of a group practice in Baltimore. She liked his face at once, broad and striking and full of expression, looking right into her eyes as he talked to her. He got so excited, in fact, that he spilled his drink all over his wrist and arm, taking her cocktail napkin right out of her hand to blot the streaks of rum and Coke. There was none of that shy nodding, that awkward self-effacement. Everything about him was like an uncoiling spring of optimism, even a lock of his dark hair that popped forward as he spoke, as if it wouldn't be held back. Sheer ambition had gotten him from his modest upbringing to medical school. He was unreserved in his critiques of other people (as she was) and in his ideas about how to improve the world. He was awed by her and, she sensed, a little afraid of her too, and she liked the way it felt when he wanted desperately to please her. A fit between two individuals, she realized, was only part electricity. That was necessary, of course, but you could find attraction a million places. The rest involved having a rational sense of what you needed from another person in order to grapple with life, and Simon Bear's vigor and hope were capable of propelling her toward the kind of life she wanted to live. Some of his notions were as odd-sounding as her father's, but most of them were undeniably interesting and teeming with both the expectation of success and, breathtakingly, the goal of altruism, which, it seemed at the time, trumped everything.

The airplane chugged as it headed into its descent. Emily looked toward the window where the sun shone blindingly off the Atlantic horizon. Given the opportunity, she could speak emphatically about her job, but deep down she believed that anyone with a clear head, a bright smile and a basic command of decorum could be a mogul in public relations, just like anyone with a shopping list and the right number of chairs could pull off a reasonable dinner party. She tried to imagine how she would have explained herself to Will if they had been able to keep their Thursday meeting. Her finesse in PR had helped her achieve the kind of respect and social presence she'd longed for in her youth. But even in smaller ways, her talents had come in handy, like at the beginning of their marriage, when Simon was fired from the group practice. She had not let him become consumed by worry, and she'd helped him reestablish a reputation to build a thriving private practice. (Simon bragged about her; he thought she was brilliant and marveled at what she was capable of.

"I'm the doctor, she's the spin doctor," was what he invariably said when they were introduced together, a line that always prompted a chuckle and made her grin sheepishly.) Her prowess had come in handy, too, in subtler ways, perhaps. After Caleb, she'd made sure people didn't know them simply as the couple who'd lost a child as she'd navigated their professional and social steps. Right away, she'd connected Simon with influential people so that he could spread the word about his Boardwalk Diet. (It hadn't been received well, though Simon, himself, had been spoken of in some circles as a brilliant proactive clinician, possibly ahead of his time.) Socially, she'd been quick to smooth their interactions with friends, putting everyone at ease with emphatic, directive comments. *Thank you, you're kind to ask, we're doing so much better now,* which made the asker feel good, or *It was hard at first, but we're doing everything we can to move ahead,* which emphasized that they'd turned a corner. Art may have eluded her, but success had come to her when she'd acknowledged her best skill and put it to use. She'd gone on to use that skill like a knife, carving a life with it.

The hospital where Charles was recovering was called Landesmont Memorial, and it wasn't easy to find with the free map from the rental car agency. Their path was rerouted by orange detour arrows at every construction site on the highway and then down the palm-tree-studded side streets. Simon refused to accelerate even a single mile per hour over the speed limit, and not too long after leaving the Fort Lauderdale airport, they were lost. Emily stared out the window of the front passenger seat, knowing that if she said anything—anything—they'd fight. When Jamie asked for the map, Emily passed it to the backseat and sat with her lips pressed together.

They passed one strip mall after the next, pastel-colored, with endless parking lots.

"Left on Seventeenth Street," Jamie was saying. "It's on Seven*teenth*."

"We already passed Seventeenth," Simon said.

Emily could hear the map in the backseat being rotated sideways. She wouldn't have guessed her daughter knew how to read a map, and she felt pleased to note Jamie's skill at the same time that she smarted with another reminder of how distant they had become.

"Okay," Jamie suggested, "then how about East Davie?"

"Closed," Simon said.

"Well, the map ends," Jamie said, exasperated. "I can't tell you what to do, the map ends."

"I'll just try to turn around somewhere," Simon said with what Emily thought was surprising patience. "Do you see Las Olas? How about Broward Avenue?"

"Dad," Jamie said. "We're off the map."

And so they were, Emily thought wryly, off the map. The whole family. She put her best face forward with the rest of the world, but it didn't work at home. What she knew for certain was you couldn't force love out of people. Either it flowed toward you from them or it didn't. "Why don't we call?" she interrupted finally. "I have my cell. I'll phone Information at the hospital and get directions from this intersection."

"Not at all," Simon objected. "Jamie's doing a fine job. Okay. Southwest Fourth. What about now? Are we back on the map?"

"Left on East Davie," Jamie said, "and then right on Third."

Let them have their confederacy, Emily thought, determined not to extend herself in any more unwanted intervention. By the time they pulled into the hospital parking garage, it was nearly eleven.

"More construction," she commented when they approached the entrance of the hospital. The double glass doors were blocked by a wall of pressboard, spray-painted with arrows pointing to the side of the building. "They seem to be redoing all of Florida."

Inside Landesmont Memorial Hospital, the maze of temporary walls continued, and they turned one way and then backtracked before locating the reception area. Simon approached the desk with great strides. "I'm looking for Charles Bear," Emily heard him say to the receptionist. He leaned so far over the reception desk, he looked as though he might hurdle it. "I'm a doctor."

"Is one of your patients admitted?" The receptionist reached for a list marked with neon pink and yellow highlighter.

"It's his father," Emily clarified at Simon's side, sensing the way Simon's neck muscles tightened. He liked to handle things his own way, especially in medical settings. What he didn't realize was that the receptionist might have two separate lists. Or that they might be treated better, in fact, being family. She was only trying to help. "What?" Emily said to Simon's glare, neither expecting, nor getting, a response.

"Everyone visiting?" the receptionist asked, smiling, reaching for rectangular guest pass stickers, which she informed them were to be worn at all times in the hospital. "Bear, you said?" She ran a finger with a French manicured fingernail down the second page of her neon list, then across. "Fourth floor. Room 417." With the same finger, she directed them to the elevators, down the temporary hallway to the right, through the makeshift corridors.

In 417, Charles looked remarkably well. His cheeks were pink and only a mild shiner darkened the feathery skin beneath his right eye. The bed in his private room was propped up, and he sat tall against the pillows with the sheet pulled to his waist. An IV drip dangled above his head, like a hovering jellyfish, Emily thought, its shiny tail trailing to his inner arm. When she, Simon and Jamie entered the room, they found Lucille sitting at his bedside, reading aloud to him from a newspaper. She wore a sleeveless pink tank top that glowed against her flabby tan arms, and tilted her dyed-black head to see through bifocals. As she read, Charles surfed through muted channels on the television mounted near the ceiling. His hair, Emily noticed, was impeccably combed and the quiet between them, even with the hospital bed and the IV pole, struck her as something Norman Rockwell might have captured in a painting, a kind of pastoral, all-American illness. Lucille had been right. They had everything under control.

Simon didn't seem to perceive this. "There's almost nobody working this floor," he exclaimed as they stepped into the room. "What kind of hospital is this? Where's the nursing staff?"

"Here you are," Lucille said, putting the paper down and standing to kiss him on the cheek. "They're supposed to discharge him today, whenever the doctor comes around. I told you, you didn't need to come all this way."

"What did they say this morning?" Simon asked, as Emily felt herself bristle at his forcefulness. "Did they round?"

"Hello, Lucille." Emily pressed her cheek against her mother-in-law's. "Hello, Charles. How *are* you? What a terrible thing to have gone through." The fluorescent bulbs above the bed gave off a depressing yellow sheen, and the heavy smell of sleep hung in the air, unmoving. She felt the urge to rush to the window and fling open the curtains, let the light in, but she refrained.

"We brought this," Jamie announced, holding up the plant wrapped in vermilion foil they'd bought in the airport.

"Here, Jamie." Emily pointed to the windowsill. "Do you remember what happened?" She addressed the question to Charles, but Lucille took part in the answer. Charles let her. This surprised Emily, and moved her. Somehow their separate stories—two completely different experiences from two distinct locations—spun into one narrative. Lucille told of how she'd been waiting at the apartment for Charles to get home. He'd been driving down the street at a perfectly reasonable speed. The dog bounded from between two parked cars, and with only an instant to react, he'd steered toward the opposite sidewalk. A mailman witnessed the accident and called 911. The paramedics took six minutes and eighteen seconds to arrive from the time of the call. Charles phoned her from the ambulance, and he berated their driving the whole way to the hospital. A neighbor drove her to the emergency room, and she stayed with him through the night. "It wasn't on a leash," she concluded.

"Next time I won't be so charitable," Charles said.

"Oh, Charles." Lucille patted the sheet that covered his leg.

"I want to know what the doctors said," Simon said.

"They said he looks good," Lucille replied. "The X-ray showed a broken rib, but nothing else. He's stable, and he's feeling good so they say he'll probably go home this afternoon." She looked at Charles as he flipped again through the channels of the television. "I think they were trying to cover their asses, if you'll pardon my French," she added in a whisper.

"Are you comfortable?" Emily asked gently, politely. It seemed to her the most important questions had not been asked yet. "Does anything hurt?"

"No problems," Charles said. "That's what I keep saying."

"You're allowed to complain, you know," Simon said with an uneasy chuckle.

"I don't hurt. I'm a little stiff, kind of like I was lifting weights or something. But nothing hurts."

"You don't have to be macho, Dad." Simon was shaking his head. "It was an accident."

"Nobody will think less of you," Emily added helpfully.

"They offered him morphine. That's what's in the bag." Lucille pointed at the IV. "But he hasn't needed it once." She sounded almost proud. "He's got a button he can use if he wants some, but he doesn't need it."

Charles did look good—vibrant and fleshed out, certainly not as haggard as Emily had imagined. Even his eyes were clear. "Doesn't hurt at all in your chest, where you got hit?" Emily asked. "It's amazing."

"They asked him if he feels numb, but he doesn't feel numb either, do you, Charles? No numbness at all."

Simon, at that point, had helped himself to a clipboard that was tucked in the bottom of the bed. "Why'd he have a chest CT?" he wanted to know. It didn't seem right to Emily for him to be digging into the records.

"They're just being thorough." Lucille waved her hand. "They don't want to leave any stone unturned."

"They must've been concerned about something if they ordered a CT," Simon said. "Didn't you ask what it was for?"

"I feel fine, damn it. How many times do I have to say it?"

"Dr. Smitts said there was a tiny hazy area on the X-ray," Lucille explained. "Nothing serious, he said, but Charles should have the test so they could have a peek."

Lucille patted Charles again. Emily found herself unable to look away from where the age-spotted hand rested on his leg with so much quiet kindness.

But Simon shook a finger at his mother. "This is why we had to come," he said. "You need a network around when you're dealing with health issues. You need to be able to ask all the questions—not just the right questions—*all* the questions." Emily looked at him. He looked notably tall and explosively broad next to the hospital bed. His nostrils flared as he lectured. "And it helps if your network includes a doctor, too." He strode to the door and poked his head into the hallway. "Where is everybody in this hospital?"

Within an hour of stepping off the elevator on the fourth floor, Simon had immersed himself in Charles's care. Graciousness didn't occur to him, and Emily didn't even have a chance to run interference. He badgered the staff to take Charles's blood pressure twice in a single hour, and he insisted on checking the thermometer himself, as if the technician couldn't read. He went around introducing himself to the nurses on the floor, and shortly after, he was using their names as if he worked with them: "Matthew, can someone call down to radiology to see if the CT's been read yet?" In particular, he couldn't get off the topic that his father wasn't experiencing the appropriate amount of pain. "It's just not proportionate," he insisted.

"Yes," Emily reasoned in a voice she hoped would help calm him, "but he says he feels fine. Haven't you always said that listening to the patient is—"

"He broke a rib. Do you have any idea how painful that is? I've had a world-class athlete in my office crying, *bawling* over a broken rib you could barely see on a chest X-ray. Just a hairline fracture and he couldn't stand up. All the surrounding muscles are affected. That guy couldn't take a breath. I'm not making up that it's a painful injury. It just is."

"Maybe his pain tolerance is higher than other people's. Being a veteran and all." Charles had served in the Marines on a special mission deployed by battleship in the early 1960s. It wasn't a typical tour of duty for a marine, as she understood. When he enlisted, the Korean War was over; troops had not yet been sent to Vietnam. He'd participated in some kind of seafaring brigade that fought "pirates," as Charles had once explained, "before they were called terrorists." He claimed to have helped rescue a hijacked Portuguese passenger liner in the South Atlantic and to have been among the troops providing reinforcement at Gitmo when Castro threatened to overtake the base. She believed his stories might be somewhat exaggerated—pirates?—and she didn't know anything about the injury that had sent him back to the States and forced his military retirement. Simon had once said Charles had been shot in the ass, but she hadn't been certain whether her husband was being facetious.

About the apparent lack of pain, Simon was adamant. "We can't just brush this off," he insisted. "He could have some bleeding in the brain, for all we know."

He procured the names of the consulting doctors in orthopedics and neurology, and he requested the nursing staff check Charles's pain medication machine, to see if it might be malfunctioning, somehow delivering morphine without revealing the dosing on the digital display. He asked the nurses for the physicians' rounding schedule. Emily suggested that maybe they should just wait like everybody else for Dr. Smitts to round. This struck Simon as possibly the most terrible idea in the world. "In the hospital it's the squeaky wheel that gets oiled," he responded. "Believe me, I know."

The worst came when Simon informed them he wanted to review his father's complete medical chart himself. At that, the nurse's eyes widened. She was young and prissy-looking, with a pattern of ducks on her scrubs. The nurse said she wasn't allowed to give the charts to family members. It was a violation of patient confidentiality, she said, and a legal issue for the hospital. She said she could arrange for someone from hospital administration to come to the floor to review the chart with him. "But I'm a doctor," he answered, as if that were code to employ another set of rules.

"Maybe you should head down to the cafeteria and get a drink," Emily said finally. "Some coffee? You're very wound up."

"Something's strange," Simon insisted.

"Maybe a walk will help you sort it out."

He paced outside the room, on the lookout for Dr. Smitts. Emily sat politely in the stale-smelling Room 417 with Lucille and Charles and Jamie, chatting about the weather, comparing the heat in Baltimore to the heat in Fort Lauderdale and speculating about Jamie's plans for the rest of the summer (they'd made the trip to *visit,* after all). She caught another glimpse of Simon every few minutes when his Ping-Pong course took him past the open door again, and she began to feel despair that he wouldn't listen to her. Charles was clearly fine and ready to be discharged. The trip had been excessive after all. What Charles needed most of all was to go home and have everybody leave him alone.

Emily had not known Simon before his medical career, his training, his title. Secretly, she believed that he was not one of those people who became a doctor because he was a natural, intuitive helper. Instinctive healers understood nuances in human actions, sometimes extracting themselves from the center of the stage simply to let events unfold. She believed that Simon was smart, but that he'd learned to be a helper because such skills were necessary in order to be a successful doctor. He'd cultivated the right kind of personality. Did this make him a fraud at the core? she sometimes wondered. He had a way of overcompensating that made her embarrassed for him. You could see it in almost everything he touched. When he'd planned to grow a whole array of orchids, he'd insisted on cultivating them from the bulb. "If you buy them grown," he stated, "it's not raising them. You're just sort of babysitting them. What's the point?" A simple trip to the Baltimore Museum of Art one afternoon had given him the idea to hire a metalsmith to build a sculpture garden in their own backyard. All of the energy, the loftiness of his ideas, that had intrigued and inspired her (and that had once reminded her of her father) seemed to be based not on actual talent or creative genius, but on impulse, something flighty and hopeful and not well informed, as if he were propelled by sentiment that he didn't know how to manage.

A solid fifteen minutes passed without a sighting of her husband. But just as Emily stood and peered into the hallway, Simon trapped Dr. Smitts emerging from the elevator. She watched Simon gesticulating with wild hands, his white oxford shirt untucked on one side. Dr. Smitts listened, apparently agreeing. He was a bland-faced doctor, pale as a sand dune, clutching a folder. *Hold your ground,* Emily was thinking. As she approached them, she heard Simon suggesting an additional test.

"Isn't a brain CT in order, considering everything?"

"Not necessarily," Dr. Smitts was saying. "We ordered the chest CT to rule out pulmonary contusion, any kind of bruising on the lung, which would be possible, considering his broken rib. Plus his oxygen was low, which concerned me a little. But he's got no chest pain, so I think there's no sign of a contusion."

"It could develop twenty-four hours after the accident," Simon argued.

"I think we're in the clear. No hemothorax, no pneumothorax."

"Which means what—?" Emily asked.

"No bleeding in the chest cavity. No fluid in the lung cavity," Dr. Smitts explained. "The CT was normal."

"But what about his head?" Simon asked.

"We don't usually do brain CTs unless there's a clear sign he hit his head and we're concerned about bleeding."

"I'd say a brain CT is in order."

"I'd agree if he had head pain, but he doesn't."

"Is it possible there's something, a brain lesion maybe, that's keeping him from feeling pain sensations?"

"Possible, of course, but highly unlikely. I can't explain what your father's experiencing, but I'll tell you he's a fortunate man."

Simon would not be deterred. "Did it occur to anyone to check for signs that he might have blacked out *before* the accident? I mean, did anyone talk to the mailman who called 911? Anybody confirm there was a dog in the first place?"

At that moment she felt with a shock wave that his whole take on the accident, on Charles's well-being, was out of control. Just then, Emily wanted to go home. They'd made the trip. They'd proved they cared. It was clear to Emily that Charles and Lucille wanted as little fanfare as possible. No doubt her father-in-law was embarrassed to have been in an accident in the first place. Now, what an indignity to have his judgment called into question, to be told that he couldn't possibly feel the way he felt because this or that test showed some result. Who were these doctors? Emily listened, her heart raging like a knocking fist, as Simon argued for the need for additional tests, a brain CT, an electrical nerve stimulation test, something to explain the impossible absence of pain sensations. Charles's healing called for privacy, for normalcy, for the opportunity to shrug it off and get on with life—not the kind of helping that Simon was trying to impose. Couldn't Simon see that? Leaving was how they could *contribute*.

"The neurologist would know better than I about those tests," Dr. Smitts was saying with deferential, agreeable diction. "But pain is highly subjective. It can be highly influenced by emotions and environment. That's what makes it difficult to define and treat."

"I'm just concerned that something else might be going on here," Simon urged. "He broke a rib. Anyone can tell you that's a helluva painful injury."

"I agree, your father's absence of pain, in light of his injuries, is unusual."

"Warranting a closer look," Simon said.

Emily listened for a moment, then interjected, "I don't understand. Whatever happened to 'if it ain't broke'? Nobody's listening to Charles. Can't anybody listen to what he says he needs? He keeps telling everyone he's feeling okay."

"He shouldn't be." Simon turned to her, loud and didactic. "He's got a significant break. Even if there's nothing that can be done about it. It hurts, understand? So either he's faking it, and there's a pain issue to be addressed, or there's some underlying problem keeping him from feeling it."

"Darling," Emily said, as delicately as she could in front of the slow-blinking doctor, "I think it's possible you might be too involved."

"Yes," Simon agreed, much to Emily's surprise. "That's possible. But isn't that my responsibility as his son?"

She hit a breaking point. She could not bring herself to stay even one night. All the posturing and the arguing and the indeterminacy. The numbers seemed to mean nothing, all the tests they'd conducted. It was impossible to know whom to believe or how to feel certain about any of the results. And Simon. The way he wouldn't listen. What it reminded her of, what she preferred not to think of, was the night they'd rushed Caleb to the emergency room. She returned to Room 417 to sit with Lucille and Charles, as Jamie asked for a dollar for a vending machine. She watched Jamie hesitate in the doorway, uncertain which way to turn. All she could think of was that night and how they'd been so lost. So many tests—so many questions—that amounted to nothing. Made you think that medicine was just a lot of lucky guesswork and that having faith in the doctors was just that—faith. You put yourself in their hands and you hoped everything they found was simple and that they didn't encounter any surprises.

At first she and Simon had clung to Caleb, holding his hands, caressing his head, as the doctor examined him in the ER. Then the staff suggested they leave the room, as the equipment careened around the corner for a spinal tap. Simon wanted to stay, but she felt she'd crumple if she was forced to watch a single needle enter that tiny body. All her senses were on edge and yet she felt unable to focus, unable to talk. She sat, trembling, in the waiting room. What kept coming back to her was that knowing look that had been in Caleb's eyes when he was only hours old. *Me and you.* Rocking her body, she clasped her hands together—she couldn't remember what Jews did with their hands, whether you were supposed to put them together or not—and whispered a single word, *please,* into her knit fingers. The results of the spinal tap showed a raging infection. Meningitis, they said. There was even a rash on his body. There were antibiotics and IV fluids, and everyone seemed to be moving as swiftly as possible. Then there was nothing anybody could do.

No, she did not want to spend another second in a hospital. And whatever Simon was trying to prove, she didn't want any part of his overblown quest for pathologies when it was clear there was nothing wrong with Charles other than a broken bone. Twenty minutes and a single phone call later, Emily had arranged tickets for herself and Jamie to return that evening to Baltimore. Simon didn't want a ticket, and she didn't book one for him. Instead, Simon insisted that he should stay over in Fort Lauderdale, just in case, and in fact he'd managed to sway Dr. Smitts, who'd gone ahead and recommended Charles have the nerve test because the indications were, indeed, baffling. "I'd feel terrible if I didn't recommend it and then it turned out there were some sort of lesion," Dr. Smitts reasoned.

Lucille looked pale at the word "lesion." "Maybe one more night, just to be safe."

That's what it was, Emily thought. You looked for as many problems as possible just so you could say to yourself that you'd left no stone unturned. Because how could you go on otherwise? No, she didn't want to spend another second there. She wanted to go home.

"Our flight's at nine thirty," Emily told him, as they stood in the hallway outside Room 417. She slipped her cell phone back into her purse.

"You know," Simon pointed out, "it's possible that if he's not feeling pain—and I'm not convinced he's telling the truth—but if he's not, he could injure himself more just getting in and out of bed. He could jar that broken rib right out of place and possibly puncture a lung this time. The truth is, a little pain would probably serve him well. It'd keep him from moving around like a person who doesn't have an injury."

"I'm sure we can probably take a cab to the airport," Emily said. She felt like she might have a headache coming on, a pinching behind her eyes. "A cab would be simplest." The air of the hospital was thick. She was looking forward to leaning back in her seat on the plane. She wished Simon would stop being righteous. She wished he would stop talking so loudly.

"No cab," Simon said, reaching into the front pocket of his slacks and jiggling his keys. "That's ridiculous. I'll drive you."

"The airport's in the opposite direction," she protested, "and it was hard enough getting here with all the detours."

"Visiting hours don't end for a while," Simon persisted. "I'll drive you and Jamie and then I'll swing back here and take my mother home."

He followed her into Room 417.

"Well, one thing's certain. You look great," Emily said to Charles. The nurse, this one wearing scrubs dotted with clouds, adjusted a tray table across the bed that was set with the hospital dinner offerings.

"I think he does, too," Lucille said with satisfaction. "It's remarkable."

"And I think it's a miracle to high heaven that you're not in pain," Emily proclaimed. "A blessing. You should cherish every moment of it. You're a very, very lucky man. Don't let anybody tell you otherwise."

"I'd enjoy it more if they'd let me go home," Charles said.

"Well, just one more night," she said. "Jamie and I are heading back tonight. Our flight's soon." The nurse began peeling plastic wrap from the bowls. Beads of condensation ran down the strips of plastic onto the tray.

"I want to stay, too," Jamie blurted from her side of the room. "Can I stay?"

She looked at Jamie. Every time, it was like being pinched, she thought. Not just with clamping fingers, but with a grip that twisted, too, intending to make her hurt. And Simon continued to be the favorite, no matter how he behaved. "We're going to get out of the way," Emily said.

"I'm staying," Simon explained to Lucille. "I can help you tomorrow once you're home."

"It would be perfectly simple to get a cab," Emily said.

"I'm starved." Simon rocked on his heels, ignoring her. Apparently, all that overbearing energy had left him with an appetite. "You starved? Catch a little something to eat before hitting the airport?"

"I'm not going to miss this flight," Emily insisted.

"Miss the flight?" Simon cawed. "It's not even seven. You've got hours."

Jamie piped up, "I'm hungry."

"Yes," Simon said, as if they'd settled the matter, and it was the two of them against her again. "Let's eat."

Emily sighed because the larger battle was that she was leaving on a flight, and she'd already achieved that victory. They said their good-byes and walked across the Landesmont parking lot to an Italian restaurant on the corner. Either the dinner rush was over or hadn't yet begun, but they were the only patrons as they seated themselves at a table.

"We're in a bit of a hurry," Emily informed the waiter, an acne-blotched teenager with his hair parted down the middle. He wore a black apron around his waist.

"Gotcha," he said with his pen poised.

Emily ordered a chicken Caesar salad, which she knew would be quick to prepare, but Simon ordered a baked filet of flounder with a salad and a side of butternut squash—he always made a point of ordering a variety of colors when eating out. Jamie insisted on gnocchi, even though Emily warned her that gnocchi was a lot of starch for one plate.

"But I like it," Jamie said.

"She should get what she likes," Simon interjected. "And don't worry about the time. There's plenty of time."

Jamie dished up a complacent grin, her little eyes glittering, and Emily sat back. There was a mosaic above their table, a replica of something Italian, made of splinters of tile and mirror, and what popped into Emily's head was a morning long ago in Baltimore that she'd all but forgotten. It was just days after she'd discovered she was pregnant for the first time, and she was giddy with the new secret that she and Simon shared. They were so awed with what they'd managed to do, they giggled and used every expression they could think of to describe her new state. "Now that you're with child," Simon said with drama, "we should make the little room into a baby room." He had already announced he wanted to build a crib from scratch.

"Now that I'm in the family way," she said.

"Gravid," he said, jumping onto the bed, straddling her and placing two hands on her still-flat belly. "Parturient."

"Knocked up."

One of those mornings early on, when Simon was at work, an errand had taken her to Charles Street, just past the famous Washington Monument. As she walked past a chic art gallery and an expensive custom-furniture store, she happened to avert her eyes from the dazzling sun. Right up to the edges of the sidewalk, the street glittered with the bright flints of glass embedded everywhere in the asphalt, green and blue shards winking, twinkling at her. In city folklore it was known as "glassphalt," a failed engineering experiment to keep the expanding and contracting road from cracking during weather changes. But at that moment it seemed one of the prettiest sights she'd ever set eyes on. She felt a swelling sense of wonder, a bloom deep down of pride. *Expecting,* she thought, intending to tell Simon later, overcome with something eerily like fulfillment. All the old longings, she realized, every yearning that had eluded her in her father's office, had been answered. She felt marvelous conspiracy with Simon, and great personal accomplishment. In the simple act of walking down Charles Street, observing all that accidental beauty, she happened to be in the process of adding something to the world. Her body had taken charge of the task. She was creating.

She looked at the mosaic on the wall. She'd never even mentioned that moment to Simon. Now, as she sat in the restaurant, she thought, with a sorrow that felt biting, it had been one of the few moments in her life when she was truly happy. What had happened to her? "You'll put a hole in that," she said, alarmed, as Jamie idly poked a fork into the weave of a cloth napkin, and she remembered again about the piercing. No one ever warned you how hard it was going to be, having children. And you could never guess how much destruction they would do to you, inadvertently, or with your own abetment. You could never imagine how desperately you would want to protect yourself. She wondered whether Jamie was still wearing the stud in her navel, but she decided again not to ask.

She placed a napkin on her lap. "Maybe when you get home, you can come up with an idea for the summer," she suggested. "You know, plan B."

Jamie shrugged. "I've got things," she said. She brushed her bangs out of her face, combing her fingers through them. For the tiniest moment, she seemed to steal a peek at her father as if for backup, and then Emily couldn't let up. How they excluded her! The vision returned to Emily of Jamie standing defiantly in the bathroom, and she felt anger wash over her. Did Jamie think she didn't care at all?

"Are you ever going to tell us," she asked pointedly, "what happened at camp? I mean, what could have been so wrong with that place?"

"I told you." Jamie blinked. "I had this project, and I wanted to finish it. That's all. But it was dumb, everything about it."

"Dumb?" Emily echoed. "One week, and you'd sized it up? I find that hard to believe."

"Like we were supposed to compete all the time. Everything. Like which cabin could clean up the fastest. Or who could be the first person to dive down to the bottom of the pool and pick up all these rings that they'd thrown in there." She sat hunched over the table, tooling with the fork and twisting the edge of the napkin between the tines.

"So you weren't winning?" Emily prompted. "Is that what this is about? Because it sounds fun to me."

"It was just so fake," Jamie complained, and Emily was reminded all of a sudden of her sister, Aileen. Someone like Betsy Ebberly could claim all the moodiness was a teenage phase, but Emily knew for certain some children always felt disdain for their parents and were capable of rejecting them completely.

"You gotta hand it to her," Simon said, folding his hands on the table. "Life is short."

Emily looked at him. "That's the message she should get?"

"The message is we take her word for it. And there's no point in suffering."

"It's camp," Emily reminded everyone, "it's not suffering."

The waiter brought their meal, two dishes on one arm, one in the opposite hand. As quickly as everything had arrived, the grilled chicken on her salad turned out to be overdone, even hardened at the edges.

"The flounder's great. Anyone want a taste? Just great," Simon said, scooping up tricolored forkfuls.

She ate part of the salad, decided she'd had enough and pushed her plate away. The waiter swooped by and removed it. She opened the Marac bag, fished around until she located a compact and began to refresh her lipstick. "They might need a little breathing space, you know," she said into the mirror. "Whether they're in the hospital or at home."

"It's not like I'm a guest," he retorted. "I'm family."

"I'm just saying."

"He totaled the car," Simon reminded her. "He's doing fine right now. But they don't know what tomorrow will be like. He might be really bruised. She might need help getting him home."

She put her compact and lipstick away and took a breath. It had to be said. "What you're doing isn't going to make them any different. You're not going to win them over."

She half expected Simon to answer, but he didn't. The same muscle tightened in his neck. He glanced at Jamie, who was hunched over her gnocchi digging into the mound of glistening potato knobs. *Hunger strike,* Emily thought. *Indeed.*

With a mimed pen, Emily signaled the waiter for the check. He brought it and Emily inspected it. She slid her credit card into the leather folder. When he brought it back, she added a perfunctory tip and scribbled her name before returning the card to her wallet. It was midnight black leather with a circular magnetic clasp that snapped shut with a sound like a kiss.

———

"Seatbelts," Simon called out as they got into the car. He got on the highway toward the airport and established himself in the middle lane. Traffic passed them on both sides. Emily stared out the passenger window. She glanced at her watch, realizing that it was impossible to tell the hour by the brushed metal color that had overcome the sky.

"Ten to eight," Simon said, not even looking at her. "We've got plenty of time."

She wasn't thinking about making the plane, however. She was thinking about the color of the light, neither here nor there, the way it hung suspended in the unnatural, awkward length of the summer evenings. By midsummer, the sun seemed to take forever to set every night. The days felt impossibly long, like guests who had worn out their welcome. Afterward, night came on quickly.

Finally, Simon exited. The ramp led to a light, and a green sign with the outline of a plane pointed the direction of the airport. Sitting at the light, Simon reached for the radio. It crackled to life with static. As he searched, it jumped through the bands from one station to the next. Emily suddenly wondered whether she'd gotten her credit card back from the waiter. She couldn't remember. She was fumbling through her purse when a shadow rose in the corner of her vision. Before she even looked up, she sensed a face just outside her window. A boy, standing in the midst of lanes of traffic where you least expected a person to appear, practically pressed against the glass.

"Oh!" She started, yanking her purse to her chest. She looked at him, her mouth open, as if she'd temporarily lost control of her features. He couldn't have been older than eight or nine, narrowed eyes, long lashes that curled. His hair was covered with a bright bandana, and he wore a puffy, sleeveless winter vest over a white T-shirt, even though, Emily realized at once with a terror that was inexplicable to her, the weather was hot enough for no shirt at all.

"Get away!" She hit the power button, locking an already locked door. The boy was shorter than the height of the car. When he leaned his face into the window, a flower of steam appeared next to her head on the glass.

"Clean your windows?" he asked, lifting a dripping squeegee.

She answered by banging the power-lock button again, turning her gaze ahead, refusing to look at the window.

Simon dropped one hand from the steering wheel, ducked his head and hunched forward to see. "What's that?" he asked.

"He scared me!" Emily said. Her heart was still thundering, shaking her chest.

"He just wants to do the windshield," Simon said.

Everything that happened next seemed to take place in slow motion.

Emily glanced at the boy. At first he looked amused by her, but then his face transformed. The grin dissolved, as if he'd only worn it on the skin, and it had just been reabsorbed by the muscles underneath. The stare in his eyes hardened. It was a look of such complete hatred, such unveiled contempt. All her body seemed to know how to do was to clutch her purse into her chest with her whole arm, to cover herself with it like a shield. She understood: He hated her. A boy in the street. A little boy hated her. What had she done to deserve such hatred? She'd been holding a purse, that was her offense. It wasn't even a purse she liked. It was an overblown gift from her husband—and it wasn't even functional. She didn't deserve his contempt, but he wanted her to know his hatred, to feel it. She couldn't move. His glare made her feel small and pathetic. And then, without turning her head an inch, Emily became aware that Simon was shifting sideways, raising one buttock in his seat. He was reaching into his rear pocket for his wallet, which he pulled out and waved at the boy.

"What are you doing?" Emily said. Her voice came out with force but no fullness, like a hiss of steam.

Simon leaned across Emily's lap, looking into the boy's face. "Go ahead," he mouthed widely, waving the wallet again. "Do the window."

The boy nodded at Simon and got to work. He lifted the sponge end of his squeegee, and sudsy water bled down the windshield. He scrubbed quickly, efficiently, oozing soap bubbles across the glass. Then he flipped the tool. But as the rubber blade cut clean trails across the window, it seemed to Emily he didn't take his eyes off her face.

"See?" Simon said triumphantly, looking at the pane in front of them. "It needed washing. We couldn't see before, but now we can."

Then the boy finished. He walked around the front of the car to Simon's side. Simon opened his wallet, fished out a bill and folded it lengthwise, holding it between his index and middle fingers. Emily didn't move. Her hands continued to tremble. She stared forward through the changed windshield, vaguely aware of her husband's familiar hand holding the creased bill like an elegant origami swan, the dull shine of his wedding band as he passed the money out the window. She felt like she would always remember the expression on the boy's face. She didn't turn her head to see him snatch the bill and stow it in a pocket of the puffy vest. When she dared to look again, he had turned his back on the car. Then the light changed, and Simon shifted into gear and continued toward the airport, hitting the button to roll up his window.

"I can't believe you did that," she breathed.

"The windows were dirty," he said with a half-laugh.

"You should have defended me!" she said.

"From what? A squeegee?"

"He *scared* me."

"C'mon." Simon waved her off. "He's just a kid trying to earn a few bucks. What's the big deal?"

They slowed in the traffic glutting the lanes of Departing Flights. Simon flipped on his blinker and shifted, angling toward the drop-off point for American Airlines. Long ago, shortly after Caleb died, there had been a dog, a standard poodle, that Simon had wanted to buy from a breeder. He had the idea it would be easier to get over the shock of it all if they had something else to love. On the screened-in terrace of the breeder's house, just as Simon was about to write a check, the puppy had defecated on the rug. It occurred to Emily to inquire how they should go about the process of housetraining. The breeder nodded, and in a single swift motion, grabbed the dog by the back of the neck. The dog straightened its front legs, bracing against the braided rug, rearing back and whimpering in resistance, as the breeder forced its nose directly into the pile of shit. "No other way it's gonna learn," the man said. They left the farm with the dog, but without another word. They'd lived with it for six years—its presence replacing nothing, making no amends; it was a dog, after all—until it developed a tumor and had to be put to sleep. But now, sitting in the car, she felt how the force of that breeder's hand must have felt on the back of its neck, and she felt herself unable to look at Simon. Then she remembered Will. *Happily?* he had asked, and the word jarred and stung, with painful reverb like a banged funnybone. *Happily?*

Just then, Jamie leaned forward from the backseat. "*You gave him twenty dollars!*" she belted, almost laughing.

"Seat belt, please," Simon called out. "We haven't come to a stop."

"You gave him *what*?" Emily asked in a voice that still didn't sound like her own.

"I can't believe you gave him twenty dollars," Jamie said again. "Look at that." She pointed to smudges on the windshield. "He didn't even do a good job."

Simon waved them both off. "It was a tip. I was just helping him out. What's wrong with that?"

Then Emily understood. She understood more than she wanted to, and more than her heart could bear. Simon could help and help, but the helping was sometimes just a distraction, just a fluttering flag to catch your eye, to keep you from noticing anger—yes, anger!—that surged and churned beneath the surface. And you would never be able to address what was underneath because the grandiose gestures of giving made the anger easy to deny. A person could only wait and wonder at all the good-will, while the rest of the world smiled and approved its various disguises. *Happily?* It was then that the noise inside her gave out and what followed was a silence, vast and cloudless. She knew before Simon pulled to a stop. Whatever had kept her marriage aloft had begun its slow exhalation, and what was left in her hand was like the string of a deflated balloon.

"Twenty dollars," Jamie repeated, flabbergasted, sitting back in the seat, and it wasn't clear if it was the size of the bill that amazed her or the inexplicable, impulsive largesse for a boy on the street.

But nobody was asking. "Not everyone's had all the advantages you have," Simon answered her in the rearview mirror. "You should always remember that."

For Emily, there were no explanations and no good deeds left. It had been this way for as long as she could remember: He had all kinds of kindness in reserve for people he hardly knew—for strangers. But all of that kindness had been at her expense. They pulled up curbside at Departing Flights. She stared at the ribs of dirt that wavered across the windshield, between the wide streaks where the glass had gone clear.

PART THREE

S imon, returning from the airport, had only one aspiration for the evening. He hoped that by nine, when visiting hours terminated, he'd find the scans read, the pathology revealed, his father labeled with a diagnosis. *No pain at all? Impossible.* He knew his father's determined privacy, the clenched jaw of his reserve, but he hardly imagined Charles would go to such lengths to play the role of hero. *It was an insult. Anyone could tell you the agony of a broken rib.* He'd had a patient, a Jake M-something, a long time back, who'd tumbled down concrete front steps on an icy morning, breaking both his nose and a rib. The man had an intimidating build, like a beer keg, and he didn't care about his nose, which had still been shapeless as a zucchini when Simon saw him a week after the accident. But he was in such pain from the broken rib, Simon couldn't put a hand against his chest without him whimpering. That Jake was left taking shallow inhalations, mere teaspoons of air, because it hurt that much to breathe and, in fact, wound up with a case of pneumonia two weeks later because he refused to try to draw deeply into his lungs.

Simon wound his way through the labyrinth of pressboard walls in the hospital's construction zone, the shrill scent of spackle tingling in his nose. *No pain? Does he think I'm a fool?* He was confident the CT would bear evidence of a neurological compression or lesion, even a minute mass that would explain it all. A man couldn't be so invulnerable to wounds. Furthermore, it was *insensitive* of Charles to act like everyone else was making an unnecessary fuss. The least the old man could do, Simon thought as he found himself in a wrong corridor and had to stop and double back past the elevators again, was express a little appreciation that Simon had made the trip. A simple thank-you would do. Simon had corralled his entire family, dragged everyone to Florida, for chrissake, just to be supportive. But this was how it had always been. Simon had been waiting for some sign of appreciation for years. By now, it seemed, his father owed it to him to have a tumor.

Simon let himself be guided through the temporary corridors by pieces of paper taped to the walls, computer-printed signs pointing to the main throughway. Neon *x*'s and arrows in spray paint on the pressboard provided additional instructions. In the maze seemed to be implicit promise about the shape of the future space—hospitals all over were ever becoming more grand, more like shiny hotels—and this one would have a lobby with marble columns. He knew as well as anybody that medicine was as much about the experience of being treated as it was about the treatment, and he knew that each institution was struggling to keep up. But the construction only revealed to him that the place was as contrived as any other, and he believed his father would be sent home simply for saying nothing hurt. "Some hospital," he muttered to the sleepy-looking security guard, who sat placidly at a curved desk and played with a pen, as Simon paced in front of the elevator. "It's like a third-world country in here."

"Sixteen-million-dollar renovation," the guard responded, sounding as though the people who passed through were generally dumb and he'd grown bored hearing their complaints. "Can't get better without them having to take it apart first."

"They should hurry up and get it over with," Simon said. Dinging sweetly, the elevator appeared, and he stepped into it, remembering, just as the doors began to close, that it never served anybody to be an ass. "'Nice night."

"You too."

When he reached the fourth floor, he found the nursing station deserted, the halls resounding with echoes. Dr. Smitts was nowhere to be found. Likewise, his parents did not greet him when he entered the room. With faces lifted toward the mounted flat-screen TV, they'd fallen under the spell of disaster reportage. A shooting spree in a local convenience store. The clerk had been killed, along with a child who'd come in to buy a slushie. They shook their heads at the tragedy. They *tsk*ed at a report about a train wreck in India, in which two hundred had been maimed and injured. Lucille rested a hand on the sheet covering her husband's leg as they watched brush fires raging out of control in California. Aerial views revealed the creeping fire line, an orange-rimmed wave. They watched a recurring loop of film: a little prop plane dumping a billowing trail of chemicals, the firefighters disembarking from an emergency vehicle, homeowners being escorted down hills, some of them carrying belongings tied with string, the kind used for binding cardboard recycling. The reporter-on-the-ground, a young hopeful journalist in a necktie that fluttered above a flame-retardant vest, shouted against the wind. The loop replayed; Simon couldn't take his eyes off the string, binding clothes and books and boxes of jewelry into tiny parcels. All the things they'd amassed in their lives—millions of dollars' worth—reduced to a bound package that could be toted in one hand down the hill. Life was simple when you got to the core of it. Poignantly simple.

"What're you watching this for?" Simon broke in. "This isn't going to help him relax."

"Started naturally," said Charles, nodding toward the television. "Drought's been going on so long, the hillsides are practically kindling. That's millions of dollars of loss there."

"Those poor people," Lucille murmured. Simon's eyes went again to the string. So little holding together so much.

"It's how nature cleans up after itself," Charles informed. "Sets its own fires to clear the debris. If humans never interfered, the forests would be destroyed anyway. The real problem is, you got people building homes that aren't designed to be in a fire-prone environment in the first place. They don't think. That's why we have a government spending billions of taxpayers' dollars to get in there and save the property."

He's showing me up, is what he's doing, pretending nothing has happened. His display is an act. He's trying to put me in my place, Simon thought.

Charles was bald, except for a fringe of frost-colored hair that wound around the back of his head. The crown of his skull shone pinkly, with coffee-and-milk-colored liver spots that seemed to deepen in intensity when he went up in arms on a particular topic. Arthritis had stiffened and slowed the carriage of his body, but his trunk and his limbs were still lean as a dancer's. He owed his thinness to an abstemious diet—no sweets, no red meat, no alcohol. His hands, even in age, had retained their powerful angularity, the hard backs of the knuckles, the crusading joints of the thumbs, which Simon knew by heart without even having to look at them. Charles prided himself on being disciplined and principled, but he was also regimented to the point, Simon thought, of being cruel. Why, the old man cared more about his regimens than he cared about the people around him! He was righteous, money-conscious, with an old man's politics that were often party-line conservative but occasionally tended toward libertarian. As if he were too good for the government, too. You couldn't have a conversation of substance with him without wanting to tear out your hair. You had to remind yourself his views were informed by television, talk radio, and the guy who sold him his daily paper. It was important to know when to stop listening to him.

"Fires are burning hotter than they did only twenty years ago," Charles continued. "It's because people are mucking up what's fundamentally a natural process."

On the television, the hills were colorless heaps of shadows. Shadows upon shadows. They watched the footage of the prop plane in its course above the flames again.

"Time for me to take you home, Mom," Simon said finally, taking control. "We'll come back first thing in the morning."

"Is it time?" she murmured, still watching.

Simon waited, but neither of them moved.

"Got late fast, didn't it?" Charles said with a sigh. When Lucille patted his leg, he murmured, "Go on, now. I'm fine here."

She reassured him. "You won't have trouble sleeping. You've had enough excitement for a whole month."

"If they have enough sense to leave me alone," Charles replied dryly, "I'm sure I'll sleep."

"Can he ask the nurses?" Lucille wanted to know. "Can he request nobody wake him? He's feeling fine, after all. He doesn't need them taking his temperature or whatever all they do in the middle of the night. He gets cranky if he doesn't get enough sleep. Trust me, I know him."

Simon tried not to sound as exasperated as he felt. "Can't he just let them do their job?" He turned to Charles. "If they need your temperature, just let them take it."

"But every few hours?" Lucille protested.

"If he's feeling as fine as he says he does," Simon retorted, "he won't care. And you'll be more help to him tomorrow if *you're* well rested."

Lucille gave up the fight. She bent over the bed. Reflexively, Simon looked away as they kissed. He was ready to leave. "C'mon."

"I'll be back first thing," she said to Charles, leaning into his face with intimacy. "You speak up during the night if you've had enough."

As she followed him to the elevator, their shoes on the polished floor shucked like clucking tongues, *tuk, tuk, tuk,* like reprimands. "I'll carry that." He took his mother's purse out of her hands, cradled it like a foot-ball against his forearm. The purse was white, some kind of shiny patent leather, like a kid would have as part of some dress-up costume.

"I'm not an invalid," she protested hotly, though she didn't take it back. "I can still manage my own handbag."

"Indulge me," he said, steering her through a revolving door at the end of the maze of newly crafted walls. In the garage, he held the door for her as she got into the rental car and shut it like a gentleman on a date. She sat hunched, small in the seat and, he thought, gnomelike, as he walked around the car to the driver's side. Her skin was faintly translucent, peri-winkle under the surface when you looked closely, but her cheeks were still mostly unwrinkled. Her mouth sealed in a fine line as she watched him. She saved her best expressions for her husband.

"Jamie's gotten taller," she commented when he got in. "Almost wouldn't recognize her."

He buckled himself. As patiently as possible, he said, "In two years, yes." If you waited that long to take interest in your own grandchild, of course you wouldn't recognize her.

"Are you sure a hotel wouldn't be more comfortable?" his mother asked as he started the car. "We don't even have a room for you. Just the couch. I can't imagine how you'll sleep on it."

It dawned on him, in all the years since he'd moved away from home, he'd almost never found himself alone with his mother, just the two of them. His relationship with her—from first memory—was wedged by the presence of Charles. When Charles was in the room, Lucille trained her attentions on her husband like a spotlight; Simon floated out of sight. At dinnertime throughout his childhood, Lucille had filled Charles's plate first, heaping generous portions of the best of the meal, the whitest, heartiest piece of breast meat, the slice of bread second to the heel. She then would pass the platter to Charles, who served a plate for her. Simon, waiting, received his helping last. Lucille commented on the freshness of the meat or the process of preparing it; Charles complimented Lucille's fine touch in the kitchen. Then Charles described his day, and Lucille listened. They didn't suffer spoiled children or obstreperous behavior, and they did not engage him during mealtime. They insisted on formalities, acute politeness, children being seen and not heard. One time, so frustrated by the chains of his invisibility, Simon had reached over and plucked a petal from the centerpiece, placed it in his nostril and blew it clear across the table. He received the belt for his untoward manners during an otherwise pleasant meal and was sent to his room with no dinner at all for abusing his mother's flowers.

He glanced sideways at her, sitting in the car. She'd always been a petite woman, and he was aware of the impression that she was getting smaller. He felt he shouldn't be surprised, but he did feel alarm to note how quickly the changes had crept up on her. How long would she live? he wondered. Another five years, another ten? Would her death come as a shock or would he watch a slow decline, a sucking away, like quicksand? His biological father—whom he'd never known—must have been tall because Simon was nearly six feet with broad shoulders. The times he'd dared to ask about the man, Lucille deftly changed the subject, and he couldn't broach the topic in front of Charles. The story of how Charles had adopted Simon had been narrated privately by his mother with almost no alterations, so rigidly it was almost liturgy. And always she underscored his debt of gratitude, as if, as a baby, he'd had anything to do with any of it.

And then his wondering was followed by a strange thought: Would he miss her once she was gone? He could hardly fathom it. Months went by when he didn't see her. He didn't even think of her if she didn't call. What he suspected was that the feeling when she died would be less of an acute distress and more of a slow, protracted anxiety, something more along the lines of, *Well, this is it, we're next.* "We" being him, Emily, and everyone they knew, the Groves, the Ebberlys, but it wouldn't be connected to *missing* her. He'd never had that kind of relationship with either of his parents. In fact, the first time Emily had seen the new condo, she'd pointed out its inhospitable limits. One bedroom, one modest bathroom. An adjoined living room and dining room with a blond carpet whose shifted plush revealed the tracks of the last person who had dared to cross the room. At the dining room table, two chairs, and none for guests. Folding chairs hung on a hook in the hall closet. Beyond the living room, a spacious balcony with an aqua-painted wrought-iron railing overlooked the courtyard. There was a table on the balcony, covered by an umbrella, but only two seats for anyone to enjoy the view.

"That's because there's just the two of them," Simon had explained when Emily pointed this out. "It's streamlined and efficient and inherently practical."

"They could've afforded a three-bedroom."

"He's an ascetic," Simon said. "It's his way of showing off. He still wants everyone to know how hard he's had it his whole life. Just so that it's clear he's toughed it out and isn't indulgent."

But Emily had insisted otherwise: "They don't want anyone else in their space."

He liked his explanation better and grumbled that Emily had no right to her certainty. She couldn't possibly know them better than he did. "Why do you insist on defending them?" she challenged angrily. "She's clung to him her whole life because she's terrified of what she'd do without him. She has no sense of self. She validates his existence, and he lives on her fawning. It's the emperor with no clothes. She'd never give an honest opinion, even if she could formulate one, and he's perfectly happy with that. They don't need anybody else around wrecking such a perfect arrangement. Including you." Simon retorted that Emily had no right to be judgmental. She called him obtuse. He said she didn't understand. No, *he* didn't understand.

"I'm fine with the couch," he assured his mother. He steered onto the highway, and they passed chain link that enclosed a gutted foundation for a building underway. "So much construction going on down here," he said, changing the subject.

"We're getting a new shopping center right near our complex. A Publix and a Chinese restaurant and possibly even a cinema. Traffic's already a problem. I've written to the city planning committee. There ought to be speed bumps on the road in front of the complex."

He'd forgotten about the letter-writing, and his throat tightened to think of it again. It had annoyed him his entire youth: her thrice-folded missives, "LB" in looping, interlocked script at the top of the page, underneath which she wrote out her directions or questions or remonstrations or reproofs. Every letter closed with a flourishing phrase, "Ever so sincerely yours," sounding like it hardly meant to be intrusive and couldn't possibly cause any offense. Though she was no southerner, her letters (at least the closing line) had always sounded to Simon as though they were meant to be read in the voice of a debutante, inquiring about the catering for the coming-out ball—practiced, carefully rehearsed sincerity that had been taught in a class. She'd sent him to school with letters. Letters for the principal, letters for the French teacher, letters for the football coach. Somehow, he'd never been ballsy enough to throw away the envelopes he was expected to deliver. He'd stood there while the recipients read their mail, watching their eyes dart back and forth across her spindly print. The recipients would say, "Ah," or "Hm," and fold the paper, reinsert it into the envelope and then respond to Simon, "Tell your mother . . ." And he'd endured it. How strange. What was wrong with him back then? Why did he stand for it? For some reason, it hadn't ever occurred to him that he could have put an end to it, simply refusing to be the mailman. Or he could have pretended to deliver letters and concocted responses for her benefit. He hadn't, of course. He'd played the role of dutiful messenger. Only as an adult did he realize he could have rebelled. It had never dawned on him that, as the resident carrier pigeon, he was actually more empowered than, say, a kid whose mother made *phone calls*.

"I didn't realize you were still doing that," Simon said. "Writing letters." Really. He felt sorry for her, with all her pretend politeness. He felt sorry for her relationship with her husband, if it was true, as Emily had said, that Lucille couldn't express her own opinion except in the letters she sent to strangers. "People don't have time to read letters anymore. They don't have time for anything that's not right in front of their faces."

"Sure they do. People read plenty."

"People read e-mail. That's the way to go. These days."

She began looking for something in her bag. "I don't need all the technology. When I have something to say, I send a letter."

"Does anybody ever respond, *ever?*" he asked irritably.

"Certainly," she said, snapping her bag closed. "I got a letter back from the manager of our local supermarket that they're going to fix the wheels on all their carts so that they're easier for older people to push. Because that's who shops there. I pointed that out to him. I got one back from a dentist I'd like to switch to saying that he's intending to add several insurance carriers, and he'd be happy to look into ours. People care to hear how they can improve."

They approached the exit and he snapped the turn signal and moved into the right lane. "He's in for it tomorrow, you know. Just watch. His whole system's stunned. His body doesn't know what to make of what happened, but he'll be feeling it tomorrow."

"I hope it's not too terrible," she said, looking out the window.

He could tell by her jaw that the lines of her face were arranged in worry. "What he's experiencing is called stress-induced analgesia, I'm sure of it," Simon continued. "It's part of the fight-or-flight response. No pain because the brain is otherwise occupied. The effects can last hours after an injury, but it wears off. Even if they discharge him tomorrow, he'll be hurting. You'll see. It's lucky I was able to come down, just to give you another pair of hands." At a light, they sat in silence. "No, I don't mind the couch. Not one bit."

They entered a stuffy apartment. Simon flicked on the light to find himself before the blond carpet that stretched like a windswept beach. "I suppose you want me to take my shoes off," he said, standing a foot inside the doorway, as if to show her it was too late to avoid perturbations in the duff.

"Oh yes," she said. "Otherwise I have to vacuum."

He sighed, bent over and undid his laces. "Why don't you just hire somebody? We have somebody. She comes every week. She cooks, too."

"I've never liked the idea of other people cleaning up my mess," she said crisply. "And you never know who you're going to get. Some of them steal."

"I never even see ours," Simon admitted. "I know she comes because I hear the vacuum sometimes, all the way down in my office. She could be robbing us blind, for all I know."

"Who needs that? I don't need that." There was the tinkling of metal hangers, like chimes, as Lucille reached into the closet to hang her sweater.

Eager for air, Simon walked to the glass doors. "I'll open up the door to the balcony. Get some fresh breeze through here. It's cooled down outside."

"I'd rather have the air on."

He didn't want air-conditioning. He wanted to feel the outdoors coming in, something penetrating the cocoon of the apartment. And he was as stubborn as a child who needed to have his own way. "It'll be better once the door's open."

He slid wide the glass door leading to the terrace and stepped outside.

The balcony overlooked the condominium courtyard. Sunk in the center was a luminous kidney-shaped pool, limpid and holy-looking, glowing blue with submerged lights. The lightly wet night air touched his skin with tenderness. All he wanted from his mother was for her to acknowledge that he passed muster. That he'd turned out all right. That she was proud of him. Was that so much to ask? He was a good doctor whose patients were grateful. He wished he'd brought the file with their thank-you letters for her to read. He printed their e-mails. She believed in correspondence; let her read what he'd received. He considered calling Emily when she got home and having her FedEx the entire file to him. It was a thick file and would have to fit in a box. They'd arrive by the afternoon. Charles would be home by then, and he could see them also. *Dear Dr. Bear, I just wanted to let you know how much you meant to my family through our cancer scare. You were the first person to suggest the problem might be something serious . . .* And *Dear Dr. Bear, Happy holidays to you and your family. Thank you so much for making Franny's last Thanksgiving a peaceful one . . .* And also *Dear Dr. Bear, Thank you for checking up on me these last few months and making sure that I was taking my medication.* Several of them he could recite by heart.

Then he thought how annoyed Emily would be to be suddenly burdened with the task of FedExing files to Florida. "You're not going to win them over," she'd say. And he didn't want her trooping through the basement, encountering the wine casks when he wasn't there to present them to her. The truth was, though, if she ever came to the office, she typically insisted on walking around the house, refusing to enter the basement where she would have to walk past the storage bin marked simply "Baby" that held photos of Caleb and a few tiny, stray stuffed things that had once sat in his crib. The woman had hardly been all the way downstairs in her own house in sixteen years. Then, in lieu of having his file of letters, the hanging folder he'd entitled "Kind Words," a treasury of cards and commendations, he told his mother about his plans to make wine.

"I got a kit. It's a surprise for Emily."

He might as well have told her he had plans to send messages into space to coordinate the date and time for his own extraterrestrial abduction.

"Why wouldn't you just buy her a nice bottle and be done with it?" she asked.

But he didn't care for his mother to understand. She was not a woman with imagination. On the plane to Fort Lauderdale, in a confidential conversation as they'd hunkered down in the last row near the toilets, he'd managed to enlist Jamie's help, convincing her to participate in the first fermentation. Jamie was sullen, earphones in her ears, the cords trickling like a wiretap down the front of her sweatshirt to a CD player tucked in the front double-handed pocket. She wore the hood up, looking like an angry elf. The engines whirred, and a middle-aged stewardess performed the seat-belt demonstration, double-pointing toward the exits and jiggling an oxygen mask in a mime of what it would look like dangling during a moment of crisis. Simon felt strangely energized by this impromptu trip, purposeful. He'd gifted Emily with the seat in first class, though he was certain he'd seen her grimace when she learned their seats were near the bathroom.

"Guess what," he'd said, nudging his daughter in the side.

"What." She twisted out of range of his elbow.

"You know what a vintner is?"

She rolled her eyes, plucked the earphones from her ears. "Are you going to quiz me the whole flight? 'Cause I'm not in the mood."

He started over. "How would you like to try making our own family wine? I've got this kit—"

"Is this going to be like the other kits? Like the car?" she said when he looked like he didn't remember. "Remember? I told all my friends we were going to build our own antique car from scratch. I told everyone. Nobody believed me, and I said yes, it's true, and then it didn't happen. They called me Scorch Shorts for an entire year."

"Scorch Shorts?"

"Liar, liar, pants on fire."

"It turned out to be much harder to get the parts than I'd anticipated. One of the companies had even gone out of business. Anyway, this is different. I've got all the components. We're all ready."

"So?"

"You want in?" He waggled his eyebrows at her, pretending to sell the idea.

"Why me?"

Because, he wanted to say. *Because of your mother. Because it's not too late to change the way things are.* Instead, unable to hide a note of irritation, he demanded, "You wanna help or not?"

"Am I going to have to crush grapes with my feet? That's just gross."

"No, I've got a machine for that. Much more civilized."

"Do I get to drink whatever we make?"

He considered this. "You get to taste. Sure. The way you'd get sips of wine at Passover, or something like that. You can't kick back with a glass, but you can taste."

"Can I have my friends over for a wine tasting?" She was a wheeler and dealer. It delighted him to negotiate with her.

"One, maybe, yeah. For sips. It's a surprise for your mother. She doesn't know anything about it. Don't tell her. I want to present her with a wine we've made in our own house. She'll be amazed."

Jamie fitted the earphones back in her ears. Then she asked, "Where are the grapes?"

"Being shipped. An enormous amount of them," he bragged. "And they're fantastic quality. It takes about fifty pounds of grapes to make just five gallons of wine, and I thought we'd start big. I thought we'd start with fifty gallons."

A passenger angled by their row, heading for the bathroom. Simon looked up, but he'd lost Jamie's interest already. She'd tuned out.

"Hey," he said, nudging her again. Scatological humor had once greatly amused her. They'd rolled off the chairs in the living room giggling over jokes about diarrhea and poop and turds. Once upon a time, they'd sung rousing rounds, *Great green gobs of greasy grimy gopher guts, mutilated monkey meat, little dirty birdie feet.* They'd sung it until Emily, who was naturally squeamish, stomped her feet, told them to quit it, she'd had enough. "Know what the hole in a barrel is called?" Jamie looked at him, unblinking. "A bung hole."

She looked at him as though she were regarding slime. "Ugh," she said, turning toward the window and turning up the volume on her music. But she hadn't said no to the project, to being his ally, and this was enough to consider a victory. All he wanted was a project they could do together. No, that wasn't exactly true. He wanted a project they could do together whose end result would impress his wife; he wanted Emily to look at him again with the faintest hint of desire in her eyes. It didn't matter that his mother couldn't fathom the worth of the endeavor or that Jamie would participate only grudgingly.

On the far side of the kitchen galley, Lucille filled a tea kettle at the sink. Her wrist wobbled under the weight of the kettle.

"Let me get that for you," he said. "Are you sure you want tea? It's so hot out. And you should turn off the air since we have the door open. It's very inefficient."

"My house," she insisted brightly. "I make the tea."

He said nothing, leaning over the galley, and then decided, in the uncommon absence of his father, to take aim at her least favorite topic. "So, Mom, don't you think it's time I know?"

"What's that?"

"About my father? My real father?"

She looked at him with bald disappointment and sighed. "This again?"

"Again? I know nothing."

"There's nothing to know."

"Jamie's going to be asking any one of these days. What am I supposed to say?"

She took a deep breath through her nose. "We've been over it. You've heard it all."

"I don't know the first thing about the guy. And you know, biology's key. Certain types of colon cancers are more prevalent in Ashkenazi Jews. Also some birth defects she might be worried about when she's ready to have kids. She should know *something,* don't you think?"

Lucille placed two cups on the counter. They were actual teacups, like a dainty china set. "I don't know anything about his genes," she said.

"That's all the tea you're having? I could finish that cup in one swallow. I'll take a mug instead," he insisted. She turned to find him a mug. "Well, for starters, his name was Lawrence Blumberg?" The name was on his birth certificate. A guy who sounded like an accountant. But who was he?

Lucille sighed. A moment later, almost in echo, the kettle let out a petulant hoot, and she busied herself pouring.

"I was very lucky to have met Charles," she began. He slumped. It was the same rehearsed version he'd heard long ago. She aimed the hot water over the tea bags, pouring with tediously slow motion, he thought, and replacing the kettle just as slowly. When she returned to the galley, she settled her teacup on a saucer and pushed the mug across the counter in his direction. Not quite in front of him, he noticed. She said, "You and I were lucky beyond our stars that he was willing to adopt a child that wasn't his."

"So you've said." He could practically mouth the story along with her. It began with the dance.

"We met at a dance. It was the summer, and he was about to leave for duty. I'd made mistakes, that's for sure. I was walking around several weeks pregnant, my whole life upside down, and I hadn't told a soul. In fact, I was determined to ignore it for as long as I could—"

"But what had happened? Who was he? The guy, I mean. Was he your boyfriend?"

Her eyes fluttered as though she had caught something in them. "Just an older boy from the neighborhood. He lived nearby. All the kids, we all knew each other."

"Did he—force you?" It was the first time in his life the idea had occurred to him, and he felt horrified for a moment until he thought he saw her coloring change slightly—was she blushing?

"Oh no. Not like that," she said quickly.

"So you knew him from the neighborhood," he prodded. When she didn't say more, he scolded with exasperation, "Didn't you think I'd have to know someday?"

"It wasn't like it is today," she protested. "It was still the Fifties. People cared if you were pregnant and not married. I was lucky to meet a man who could see past all that. When I met your father—Charles, that is—I didn't think I had a chance. With anyone." The skin around her eyes was so fragile-looking, so complex, that for a moment, he was stunned by it. For a moment, he forgot to be annoyed by having heard the story so many times before, and he thought about the vessels pulsing beneath the surface of her skin, feeding the fascia, and the groupings of those tissues that created all the expressions her face was capable of. "I believed I was doomed to spend my life alone. I couldn't see how I could possibly keep a baby—not by myself, that's for sure—and who would want me after all the mess I'd made?"

He pushed his tea away and sat back in the chair. "Did this Lawrence know?"

"I was going to tell him, sure. The weekend I was prepared to, though, he died with his cousin in an accident." She took a sip of tea. Again he had the feeling that the story, the one she'd told so many times, was suspect. All the details came up short. Something heartfelt was missing at their core.

"On a motorcycle, right? Racing around." He'd heard that much before. That his father had died in an accident. He'd always imagined the guy on the motorcycle, he realized, but never imagined the young Lucille, finding out. "That must have been awful," he ventured.

"Oh, sure."

Oddly, he felt pleased to hear it. He'd never imagined his mother distraught. The way she told it, he'd presumed that the circumstances of his own origin involved a convoluted series of transactions, as if she'd negotiated a raw deal with the Blumberg guy and then managed to wrangle a better one with Charles.

"Were you in love?" he asked, feeling cautious.

"What did I know about love?" she scoffed. "We hardly knew each other. Two kids, you know? We didn't know what we were doing."

"Well, did you go to his family? Did anybody know?"

"I didn't think anyone would believe me. And I couldn't prove anything. They had money, and I figured they'd think I was just some kind of gold digger. And then I met Charles at a dance," she said, smiling at the memory, and Simon rolled his eyes as she started in on the story of the dance again. "My friend Shelly made me go. I didn't want to, but she insisted. He was tall and so strong-looking, like a sports star. He liked my hair. I used to wash it in egg to make it shine. When he left on duty, I really believed I'd never see him again. But he kept in touch. He couldn't get me out of his mind, that's what he said. Me. I could hardly believe it. We corresponded the whole time he was at sea. And when he was injured in the service, I was able to be there for him when he came back. I was the one who took him home from the hospital. I had to tell him that I wasn't the person he thought I was, but he didn't care. I got the chance of having my life steered right. Charles saved us. He really did. Saved us and provided for us. Made us a family. We should always be grateful to him for that," she added pointedly, "in case you're inclined to forget."

He was astounded that this Lawrence Blumberg could be so efficiently erased. "Did he tell you not to talk about, you know, before?"

"He didn't have to," she sniffed. "It's ancient history."

"*My* history," Simon said.

Her eyes fluttered indignantly. "That man's *gone*," she argued. "Almost fifty years now."

He sat staring at her face, the lines, the ginkgo-leaf skin. He had come to Florida because he imagined that he would help. He imagined becoming useful to them. But he realized that Emily had been right. His motives hadn't been pure. He'd wanted more from them. Whatever caring was going to take place, he wanted to be there for it for some reason. And right now, he wanted the story of his origin, perhaps even an inkling of life before Charles entered the scene, but he couldn't get it from her.

"The point is, I met Charles, and he saved us, you and me. I'd made a mistake, and he helped fix it. We moved on. And when you do that, move on, I mean, it's best to leave the past behind. Wouldn't you agree?" She took a sip of her tea. He couldn't tell, but he damn well suspected that she was saying, cryptically, something about Caleb. She was reminding him that there were sources of pain too difficult to carry with you. When he didn't respond, she added, "So you understand, people move on."

Then, quickly, she pushed her cup and saucer away from her, and she stood. He didn't watch her as she headed down the hallway. There was the sound of a closet door opening and then closing. When she returned, she had a pale green folded blanket and a pillow cradled in her arms.

"More blankets in the hall closet, if you need them," she informed him. "I'm tired. It's time for bed."

Long after she'd retired to her room, Simon lay awake, his feet jutting upward on the armrest, the blood draining from them, wondering about Charles and how she loved him. Did that love have anything to do with Charles, in particular, or did it spring from her sense of gratitude? It looked the same from the outside, and only she would know the difference, if, in fact, there was a difference to know.

She hadn't been kidding. It was not a comfortable couch.

They escorted Charles home from the hospital the following afternoon in the glaring sunshine. There had been no diagnosis. It was like the stupefying end of a foreign film where you were left hanging. The scans showed no compression anywhere. There wasn't a hint of a tumor to be found. Simon had begun to inquire about other tests, but Dr. Smitts had put up his hand. "There are mysteries we can only wonder at," he said, and pronounced that it was time for Charles to go home.

Simon drove them from Landesmont to the condo. Lucille sat with Charles in the backseat, holding his hand. When they arrived, Charles stepped gingerly from the rental car, but waved off assistance as he teetered toward the entry hall of the building. It was a building for old people that had a smell, Simon thought. Despite its cheery pastel color, a beauty-salon pink with aquamarine trim, it smelled like boiled barley, he decided. It smelled like the oily inside of a hat. The doorman, wearing a costumelike suit with epaulets, looked even older than the residents. Charles greeted him with a salute. Lucille trailed a step behind, holding her head high.

"How's everything, Mr. Bear? Heard about that accident."

"I saved a dog's life," Charles said triumphantly.

"That's the way to do it. And you're feeling all right?"

"Couldn't be better."

"Give a call if you need anything."

"Will do."

Charles and Lucille appeared no more flustered or out of sorts than a couple that had just returned from the local bridge game. Simon, holding the paper shopping bag with the clothes his father had been wearing

in the accident, said hello to the doorman, accompanied by a grave dip
of his head. He hoped the gesture, if not his tone, would reveal there
was more gravitas to this slow trek through the lobby. He'd had to fight
his mother to let him carry the bag of clothes. She would have carried
them herself. *They're incapable of accepting help,* Simon told himself. *It
has nothing to do with me. It's that they fear death. If they accept my help,
they accept that they're capable of dying. As long as they refuse assistance,
they can keep up the illusion their lives will go on forever.*

"Can I help you into bed or would you prefer to be set up at the
couch?" Simon asked as they entered the apartment.

"Lunch first," Lucille called out.

"He could have lunch in bed," Simon suggested.

"The table is fine," Charles insisted. "We're not going to make this
into a big to-do. I feel fine. I don't need bed."

"But Dr. Smitts said—"

"Simon, get yourself a chair from the closet if you're going to sit and
have lunch," Lucille instructed.

After the meal, Simon said, "Now's the time to rest," but his father
puttered around the apartment. He wanted to finish fixing the door of
the entertainment center, which he'd been working on just before the accident. "Did you not hear them at the hospital?" Simon demanded.

Finally, Lucille pulled him aside by the elbow. "He's doing fine," she
said. "Just leave him be."

But when he saw Charles going for the toolbox, he suggested, "Why
don't you just instruct me and let me do the work?" He put out his hands
in a gesture he knew looked clownish. He felt like a clown. He proffered
himself to his father. "Just use me. I'll be the hired help."

Charles sighed and lowered himself onto the sofa. Simon sat cross-
legged in front of the entertainment center, with the toolbox open at his
side. Above him on the shelves surrounding the television, the carefully
arranged display reminded him of props. *Webster's* dictionary, a *Time*

magazine three-volume history of the United States, a *National Geo-graphic* atlas of the world, and a copy of *The Seven Habits of Highly Effec-tive People* (which Simon doubted either of his parents had read), all of them possessing a secretive air in their upright, affected poses.

Above the volumes, from silver frames, a pair of unsmiling Russian im-migrants stared into the room, the man in a shapeless dark coat and the woman in a long peasant skirt, yellowed and fading portraits that looked like they'd been rubbed against stone. Simon knew almost nothing about Charles's grandparents except that they'd emigrated from Russia as a young couple with a young daughter at the end of the nineteenth cen-tury. Industrious and hopeful, they'd fled the pogroms, their little village burned to the ground, neighbors and relatives killed as they hid. With just sacks of clothes, they'd disembarked at Ellis Island, where they'd guilelessly traded in their rubles for what they believed was American paper currency but were actually gum wrappers. The moment they real-ized they'd been had, Charles had often said, was the beginning of a fam-ily legacy of distrust in the government.

"It wasn't the government that got them," Simon had pointed out. "It was some shyster working at a money exchange window who realized he could make some extra cash."

"The window was on the island," Charles said. "That shyster repre-sented the country."

Twenty-some years later, the immigrant grandparents wound up rais-ing a very young Charles after his mother died in a building fire in New Jersey. They distrusted the government, refused to put their money in banks and held disdain for everything modern and, Simon believed, pleasurable. As the details had emerged, they'd refused to believe the radio accounts of events unfolding in Europe. They were skeptical about the government's motives for the war. When they witnessed firsthand the photographs of the American liberation, they disavowed God. They'd seen it themselves, but here was proof for the rest of the world. No God worth believing in would allow such a thing to happen. You could see it in their faces, Simon thought, peering into the yellowed photograph. These were people who depended on nothing beyond themselves. The more insular they were, the better their defense against the universe. Charles, who was in his twenties when they finally died, had grown up in their spartan apartment with no toys (or so he said) and an abundance of chores. His understanding of their love was the fact that they had taken him in.

"What are we doing with this bookshelf?" Simon asked, rooting through the tools. "Looks fine to me."

"Your mother wanted me to adjust the hinges. Doors aren't straight. See that?"

"Easy as cake." He selected a Phillips screwdriver and set to work inside the low cabinet door. "I'll keep tightening. You tell me when they're even," he said, happily unscrewing. "Did I tell you I hired a new nurse?"

"You're not doing this right, see? You have to loosen both sides at the same time."

Simon shifted his weight onto his other knee and leaned into the cabinet. "Trust me, I know what I'm doing." He was thinking about Julie. "She's just starting off, a new graduate. Which is the best way to train people. Fresh. She's very motivated, and she's already won prizes. She's very determined, and she wants a mentor who'll take a real interest in her career, not just whether she's clocking in and clocking out."

He bragged about her, still complimenting himself on the decision. What he did not mention was that kiss. It had happened quickly. After he'd dared to bare his soul, telling her about how he was planning to surprise Emily with a bottle of her own Barolo. He'd been describing the kit and the casks, the wholesome, nesty smell of the wood surrounding them. Julie had responded with warm and rapt appreciation for his romantic spirit. She'd made an incredible gesture with her hand, pressing it against her heart, and he'd felt such a swell of emotion, standing in front of the barrels, envisioning Emily's response to a bottle of wine, that he'd managed not to contain himself. Julie McKinley had been standing there, looking at the casks, and he'd simply reached for her.

The gesture had been a gentle one. No pulling or groping. His frame, broad across the shoulders, turned in front of her, a kite moving in an arc. She couldn't have been any taller than five-three. He angled, swooped like a swift, and kissed her. Their lips met warmly, without wetness, an almost chaste kiss, like a boy would kiss a beloved babysitter, with exuberance, knowing and not knowing what he was doing. She smelled like powder, like the end of a bath. He backed away with embarrassment. He hadn't intended anything; he wasn't even attracted to her. Those features had a fundamentally cold look, and the body, in his opinion, was too thin. Her expression appeared somewhat less surprised, as if she were aware of a certain effect she had on men, but he apologized.

"Hm," he had said, stumbling. "I'm sorry."

"It's okay," she reassured him.

"I didn't mean to. I mean, I didn't plan to."

She produced a small smile. "I know."

"It won't happen again. I love my wife. I really do."

She blinked. "Okay," she said, as if she were fine with the decision, either way.

He astounded himself. He had never cheated on Emily. All the years they'd been together, he'd been wanting and waiting for Emily. Other women did not interest him. Their bodies were in front of him in the office, their bra straps down, their legs wide as they asked him to look at this mole or that patch of skin on the curve of their buttocks. He was between their thighs doing Pap smears, and their bodies failed to look sexual to him. They were puppets, dolls. Their bodies were machines. And in fact the idea of being aroused near them slightly repulsed him. But this? What was this? He had not expected it to happen. He wasn't sure what had compelled him, and he had gone back to the office with her and he'd quickly put out of his mind that it had happened. He hadn't planned it. It just as easily might not have happened. Anyway, she said it was okay. She didn't seem offended.

"Listen," Charles was reprimanding, pointing at the cabinet doors, "if you just tighten, they're still going to be crooked. You have to loosen both sides."

"Just trust me," Simon insisted, twisting and twisting at the tiny screws. When he stood, opening and closing the doors, he'd managed to readjust them. The upper corners of the doors appeared aligned, but now the bottoms were too close together. "I can fix this," he said, attacking an upper hinge again.

"I'm telling you, you have to take them off and start again."

"I can do it with some simple tightening. Trust me, you're not supposed to have to take the whole thing apart."

The peasant in the shabby black coat and his stony-faced wife gazed over them. Their expressions looked as though they concurred with Charles: The doors would have to be removed and the hinges rescrewed in tandem. It was the cabinet that screwed you back. It was possible, Simon realized, that marrying Lucille might have been less an act of heroism and more a way for Charles to escape their dark and burdened world. What would Lucille say to that?

"How's that?" Simon asked, twirling the screwdriver. "Close enough, I think. If they're uneven, you can barely tell."

"Don't ask me. Ask Lucille. I would've taken them off."

"Yeah, but this way was easier. What'd your grandparents say when you told them you were getting married?" Simon asked, looking into the photograph.

"What do you mean, what'd they say?"

"Did they approve?" It was the closest Simon had ever come to asking Charles about his past.

"I never crossed them. Ever. Now"—he stood up from the couch—"I'm going to sit on the balcony and read my paper."

It dawned on Simon then that Charles might not know anything about the Larry his mother had known. But if Charles did know, and had known for years, then he and Lucille shared yet another bond that had long excluded Simon. Simon stood, watching Charles lumber toward the balcony. "You don't need to be a stoic, you know."

Charles folded his paper under his arm. "I don't know what you're talking about."

"You don't need to pretend this wasn't a major event. You're not young, for chrissake. You can't take your body for granted anymore."

Charles gave a brisk, phlegmy cough. "All I can say is what I know, and I know I feel okay. I don't need your diagnosis. Got it?" He slid open the glass door, which made a wet-sounding shushing noise.

Simon suggested, "I'll go down to the pharmacy and fill your prescriptions. Just in case you need them, you'll have them on hand."

Charles pooh-poohed with his free hand. "I wouldn't waste the money."

"Dad, you're allowed to lean on other people besides Mom. In fact, if you think about it, it isn't fair to make her the only person responsible for you."

"I'm sure I'll hear from her if she's got a problem with it."

Simon repacked the toolbox, testing the doors and squinting to verify their realignment. With satisfaction, he returned the box to its nook under the sink. He saw that Lucille, too, was seated out on the two-chair balcony with a flat folder that seemed to contain stationery. *He's obsessed with death,* Simon thought. *By refusing my help, he forces me to think about it too. He forces me to think about Caleb. This is how he controls me.*

"A lot of good it did," Charles had once said, "your being a doctor." The words shot back to him, like a torpedo darkly through an ocean of sixteen years. A lot of good, indeed. Caleb had been born on a Tuesday in the lucid, wide-eyed hours of an afternoon. Emily's water had broken that morning just after she arrived in Bethesda, having insisted on working right up until her due date. She'd driven herself back home to Baltimore, contractions and all, entering the house through the north side door, standing in the waiting room with the rest of the patients.

"You're sure?" he'd asked her, after Rita had pulled him out of an appointment. "We should go to the hospital." He'd refused to take a Lamaze class, which he'd considered a crutch for those unfamiliar with bodily fluids and biological processes, and he was beginning to regret the decision.

"No chance," she breathed, as a new round of tightening began to wrench her abdomen. "I'm not getting back in that car."

"You want to deliver here?"

"I want it over with," she seethed.

"Then we should go to the hospital."

"No chance, no how."

"Well, honey," he said, feeling desperation creep up on him along with a clammy sweat.

"*Do* something," she gasped, as the contraction took hold, and he realized they were late in the game.

From a stash in a locked cabinet, he found her an injection of morphine to make her more comfortable, but he knew it would only take the edge off the pain. Suddenly, he was panicked. He hadn't delivered a baby in years, not since his residency, and he struggled to remember how to catch a newborn. She lay on the exam table, telling him that she wanted to push, she couldn't keep from pushing. And yet the baby who was Caleb descended and then retreated and then descended and retreated, and Simon grew increasingly desperate as he began to recall a whole list of possible complications that could trip up what was supposed to be nature's most inevitable event. It was the first time in his life he'd felt the strain of knowing too much information.

"Call 911," he shouted to Rita.

The ambulance arrived, and a ponytailed paramedic named Tony guided Simon's son through the birth canal, unlooping a twice-wound purple cord from the baby's neck.

Later, they called Lucille and Charles from the hospital and recounted the story. "A lot of good it did," Charles commented wryly, "your being a doctor."

Simon heard the remark but dismissed it in the roar of his ecstatic mood. He had a healthy baby boy. A boy. His wife, barely torn, heroic, tender and tired, now rested. He would never forget the stunned look in her shining eyes, the way she gripped his hand from the bed, finishers in a great race. The baby, wheeled in from the nursery, had perfect lips and a nose as geometric as a cat's. Under rice-paper eyelids, his eyes moved inside newly dry dreams. Then his mouth opened and released a shriek worthy of a barn animal.

He and Emily could not speak of Caleb's death. Back then, when he looked at her, suddenly, at breakfast, or emerging from the bathroom holding a jar of cream, he used to think she might be about to say something. The longer she said nothing, the more he dreaded what she might say. They bickered instead over the inane, insensitive commentary other people provided. "You're lucky you're young," said a neighbor. "You can try again if you want to." And a friend (who would consequently be dumped) said, "It's got to be easier now than when they're older and they've developed a little personality."

"The nerve," Emily fumed.

"They mean well," he reasoned. He meant to keep her from being hurt. She was intent on proving to people that they were okay, they were getting through it. And so they began to act as though they were getting through it.

But people knew, and they had opinions. He was certain of their accusations, even if no one would dare to be explicit. He and Emily weren't merely an unfortunate couple who'd lost a child. They were the victims of the worst of ironies. Caleb died despite having a father who was a doctor. Simon had failed. There was nothing to do but try not to dwell on it every minute, follow Emily's strong, forge-ahead lead. He made every effort to move energetically, optimistically into an unburdened future. He suspected she was suffering even more than he was—wasn't that the burden of mothers?—but her anguish wasn't evident on the surface and she would not discuss it. He didn't intrude. The way he explained it to himself, he was respecting her space. He came across her in the kitchen, throwing nipples and bottles, unused diapers, packages of unopened booties, into a black trash bag.

"Most of this stuff could be donated," he suggested.

"Be my guest," she said, tossing in the last package of nipples and tying the drawstring of the bag in a knot. Then she left.

He reopened the bag and made two piles: one to give away, the other to hide away. The diapers were taken by one of his patients who knew of a new baby elsewhere in town. The other pile contained a few tiny items of clothing, a bib, the ice-blue newborn hat Caleb had worn in the hospital nursery, and a small collection of photos they'd taken during his short life. They'd only managed to arrange a few of the snapshots into albums. He stacked the prints and the books in a Tupperware tub and took them down to the basement.

Their silence eased the acuteness of the misery, but did not erase it. The effort to forget pressed on them. They made love infrequently, but with purpose, charging ahead like climbers roped together, pushing onward through a whiteout of mutual sadness. When they spoke, they fretted about the private practice at the house, but patients continued to come to him, and many seemed not to know about his personal life. Then Emily was pregnant again, and, at last, they had a tangible reason to try to be happy.

Though Charles and Lucille had retreated to the balcony, Simon could hear their occasional comments to each other, the rustle of the newspaper and the clink of glasses on the terrace table. Treading in silent, shoe-less prints across the carpet, he wandered down the hallway and into his parents' bathroom. He found himself in front of the sink, and without thinking, yanked open the medicine cabinet. Calcium supplements. Vi-sine. Multivitamins. An eyeglass repair kit. Nail clippers. Thermometer. Oil of Olay. Fleet enemas. Band-Aids. Hair gel. Mylanta. Rolaids. Advil. Motrin. Tylenol. Aspirin. He couldn't have said what he was looking for along the glass shelves or what he hoped to find. In the hospital, holding Charles's chart, he'd felt a power over his father he'd never felt before. In the summation of his father's condition, the test results, the remarks from the consulting physicians, he'd felt Charles's secrets laid bare. In the authorized trespass of medicine, he'd gained access where he'd always been forbidden, and the titrations—the white blood count, the hemato-crit, the platelet count—had prompted a tenderness he'd almost never felt for Charles.

Their bedroom down the hall looked similar to the bedroom they'd had in his childhood. He felt a moment of childish familiarity to see the old green and blue quilt taut over the bed. Lucille had arranged upon it an array of multicolored pillows, like a hotel suite. Simon opened the dresser drawer to see Charles's neatly folded boxers, his mother's care-ful hand having pressed the corners square. He paused to listen for the heaving swish of the glass door to the balcony sliding in its metal track, but he heard nothing. Sitting on the bed, he inched open the drawer of the bedside table. There he found a comb, shoehorn, matches, two watches—one with a leather band, one with metal, both showing the in-correct time.

Then, in the back of the drawer, his hand landed on a small plastic Ziploc, crammed with a jumble of two-inch vials—he estimated at least twenty—each containing what appeared to be about a milliliter dose of clear liquid. A second plastic bag contained a stash of individually wrapped sterile syringes. Popping open the Ziploc, he inspected a single vial, marked with a number. The label said merely, "Active ingredient, sulmenamine . . . 2%" and below it, BOEKER. He didn't recognize the generic drug name, and in fact felt embarrassed not to recognize a drug. But a person couldn't be expected to know all of them, he reminded himself. His father was taking injections of some sort. Simon felt his throat tightening. He'd pored over his father's medical chart at the hospital and had seen no mention of this particular drug. Certainly Charles and Lucille had failed to mention it. He didn't hear the terrace door, or his father's steps on the airy carpet, and he started when Charles appeared in the bedroom doorway.

"Now, what's this?" Charles asked.

"I should be asking you. What's *this*?" Simon held up the vial between his thumb and forefinger.

"Mine, is what it is." He moved into the room, his long dancerlike arms reaching for the vial.

"I didn't see it when you were in the hospital. What's it for?"

"Anyone ever remind you to mind your own business?"

"This *is* my business!" Simon said, nearly shouting. "I came here to help."

"What's going on here?" Lucille appeared behind Charles, her voice heavy with disapproval. "Simon. How dare you raise your voice at your father like that?" She stepped into the room for a better view, and when she saw Simon next to the nightstand scolded, "Now, really."

Charles leveled his eyes on Simon's face. The eyes were light blue, the rims pink; the directness of the stare made Simon tremble. It was not usual for his father to look into his face. "He's been snooping," Charles stated.

"Are you?" she asked. "Are you, Simon?"

"What is this?" Simon demanded, holding the vial between pincer fingers.

"No manners," Charles said with a dismissive wave of his hand, and he was done looking at Simon. "In our house for a day and he's going through our drawers. Give him an inch and he takes a mile."

"Can't you tell me what it is?"

"Medication," his mother said, holding out her hand. "For his arthritis. I'll take it. Right here, Simon."

Simon held his ground. "I've never heard of this stuff. Is his regular doctor prescribing it? What is it?"

"Simon." Her open palm jutted forward.

"Why didn't you tell anyone at the hospital?" he persisted.

"It's my own damn business."

"Don't you get it? This could have been dangerous, not telling anyone at the hospital. You don't know drug interactions. You don't know what's contraindicated. I don't even recognize this. What is it?"

"You can tell him, Charles."

"Hell if I will. He's not my doctor."

"No, I'm your son, and I'm trying to help. But you're beyond help, aren't you?"

"You just don't know when to butt out."

"It's hard to butt out when a person you care about crashes a car. When he doesn't have a clue how to take care of himself, yes, it's hard to butt out. What's this medication for?"

"Just give it back. It's nothing."

"Why are you taking it?"

"I'm not having this conversation."

"Dad, what's the medicine for?"

"I don't have to put up with this." With mincing, ginger steps, Charles turned past him, heading for the bathroom. "I'm getting ready for a nap now, if you don't mind. I'll thank you to stay out of my things."

"The medicine, please. Simon."

Simon deposited the vial onto his mother's outstretched palm. She slipped it into the pocket of her sweater. He followed her to the kitchen, her turned back making clear that she was done with the interaction. She rededicated herself to an artful, systematic arrangement of the lunch dishes within the spines of the dishwasher shelf.

He stared at her curved back, the distal, disinterested hunch of her neck. "You didn't tell anyone at the hospital."

"We didn't think of it."

"Who knows, some kind of drug interaction, and you could've really harmed him. How'd you like that on your head?"

"I didn't mean to. He's just—you know how he is."

"I know, but you should've known better."

She turned to him, a dishrag bunched in her hands. "I think you should go, Simon. He needs peace and quiet, and I can take care of him."

"I can help."

"When's your flight?"

"Not till late."

She put her hand on his arm with an apologetic, patronizing nod. Her touch on his sleeve did not feel like kindness but, rather, like punctuation. "Maybe best to make it earlier."

Gunning the gas so hard the tires screeched, he sped out of the condo complex minutes later, heading for the nearest Publix, a strip mall and a half away. Bounced from his own parents' house. As he slammed the brakes in an undersized parking spot, he did not feel like himself. His thoughts whirred, and he hardly knew whether to laugh or kick the bumper of the car. One detail gave him satisfaction. In a final gesture (of spite, he couldn't deny it) as he'd prepared to depart, he managed to steal a single vial of the mysterious drug from the hidden cache in the nightstand. Charles had disappeared into the bathroom. Lucille had stepped out onto the balcony with a watering can. Simon tiptoed back into the bedroom, and absconded with a single vial. One missing dose would probably go unnoticed, he figured. And one would be sufficient for him to put an end to the mystery.

Inside the supermarket, the pharmacist focused on the task of measuring a dispensation of white capsules and didn't look up. "Be right with you," he said. He was older, balding, with a mustache befitting a barbershop quartet. When he approached the counter, Simon could tell the guy had a smarmy manner before he opened his mouth.

"What can I do you for?" he asked.

"What is this, do you know?" He held up the vial, trying not to show his exasperation. "Sulmenamine?"

"Is it yours?"

"My father's, actually. I found it in his things."

The pharmacist took the vial and squinted at the label. "Probably I can't tell you anything because of patient confidentiality."

"All I want to know is, what kind of drug is it? I've never heard of it. Is it for arthritis?"

"Don't know it off the top of my head, but I can look it up." He moved to the computer and tapped with two fingers. "Nope, nope, nope," he murmured at the screen.

"I was just wondering if it's a prescription you've filled recently."

"Not in the computer, not in the database. And no, I can tell you this," he said, pecking at keys, "it isn't a drug we've ever filled here. Might be new on the market and we just haven't seen it yet. I usually have information ahead of time, though. Hold on a sec."

The pharmacist took the vial to the back of the pharmacy. Around a corner, he appeared to consult with someone else. Simon leaned to the right for a better glimpse. The second pharmacist in a white coat was gaunt with old age. The pearl-colored tuft of hair on his head had the swooping architecture of a meringue. Simon watched him turning the vial over in a cramped hand. He made his way slowly to the front counter.

"This yours?" he asked, lifting the vial.

"Do you know this drug?" Simon asked.

"I know the name. It's an old one. Old old, like before my time. Like early twentieth century. It was used for syncope. Fainting, you know? Probably mostly in women. Fell out of use. That happens with drugs. They find something better, or they just realize it's ineffective."

"Fainting?" Simon echoed.

"I'm not sure how it was administered. I doubt it was by injection."

"We don't treat syncope," Simon said, adding, "I'm a physician. There's no treatment for it."

"They did back then. Or tried to anyway. I don't think they made much headway with this drug or it would've lasted. Where'd you get it?"

"My dad's."

"Your dad's, eh?" the old man said. "Can't ask him about it?"

Simon ran his hand through his hair, thinking. His father was taking a drug for vasovagal syncope? But his mother had said clearly that the medication was for arthritis. Hadn't she said arthritis? Something for arthritis had been in the chart. Was the drug in the vial for some other condition? Lies upon lies. A heat prickled over him. How were they so generally polite but so private that you couldn't know them at all? Emily had been right. He should have realized how well she interpreted their actions, and he should have paid attention. He'd been a bother to them always, and he was still a bother. Even worse, what they had with each other underscored everything that was wrong with his life. He longed for that rare dependence with his own wife. They proved to him what he was lacking.

"What's the company?" the old pharmacist asked, squinting at the vial. "Boeker? They're in Delaware, I think."

"Thanks," he mumbled.

The pharmacist handed the vial across the counter. "Don't know how he got it. I do know it wasn't sold here or in any pharmacy."

He handed it back to Simon. The vial fit in the center of Simon's fist, which he tucked into the pocket of his pants. He left the Publix without another word.

The two-day hiatus jammed up his Friday schedule. The waiting room was thick with anxiety, patients waiting and checking their watches, and there were not enough chairs. They perched themselves on the rocks around the koi pond. They complained to Rita about how long they'd been in the office for a scheduled appointment. Gabi and Joyce moved with exasperated gestures. They were in each other's way in the hallway, reaching over each other to get into cabinets. Julie McKinley followed Simon breathlessly through the office. He was so preoccupied, he found himself unable to enjoy her attention, despite his determination not to regret having hired her. The word "lamentable" clung to him like plastic underwater that he could not kick away.

He had only spoken to Emily once since he'd left his parents' apartment. In the airport, wandering around for four hours as he waited for his flight, he'd phoned her to let her know he was on his way.

"I get in at eleven thirty," he said.

"How's Charles?" She sounded interested. He imagined she had already begun her before-bed rituals, the moisturizer, the pumice for her heels. In fact, he thought he could hear the scraping of an emery board in the background, and he pictured the tilt of her head as she held the phone against her shoulder. Despite the coolness in her voice, he wished he were home.

"Are you in bed already?"

"Don't be ridiculous. It's early. Was he still feeling okay today?"

"He's the same."

"Well, that's good, isn't it?"

A rhetorical question, he decided. He couldn't tell for certain, but he thought her voice sounded like a machine slightly overwound. He longed to tell her that he'd been right not to leave Florida early, that he'd uncovered mysteries about his father's condition because of the fact that he'd stayed. *So what,* she would probably say, reprimanding. *They didn't want us in their space in the first place, so they weren't up front about every detail. They don't owe anybody anything.* Vaguely, he hoped she might meet him at the airport, but he thought it might be too much to ask because the flight was so late.

"Jamie didn't want to eat dinner with me," she reported suddenly. "I even brought home that Boston Market chicken she likes. She just camped out in her room."

"That's her way, isn't it?" He meant it supportively. He wished Emily were less held back as a mother, less concerned with practical details. She meant well, but he believed she'd reap more if she were more carefree. Nagging never got anywhere with a kid, at least not in the affection department. He loved his wife despite the fact that she didn't get this fundamental fact, which seemed so obvious. "She'll come around one of these days," he said. "You just need to be patient."

They swapped a few details about the calendar. She had realized there was a conference that weekend in Delaware that she wanted to attend. And then she had to get off the phone because she had to call Janet Grove, who wanted her opinion on the press kit for *From on Deep,* which Simon remembered was the show drenched in humanity, that apparently was going to take place after all. They hung up. By the time he made his way home, it was midnight. It was Jamie who was still awake when he entered the house. Her bedroom door was closed, but there was a band of light beneath it. She was playing the soundtrack to *Titanic.*

"Hey." He poked his head into her room. "I'm back."

Still dressed, she lay in bed on her back. In her hands, she held the liner notes from the CD. "Hey."

He tried a joke. "The boat still goes down?"

She rolled her head to the side, blinked at him, unsmiling. She was a funny mix, still a kid but with the edge of someone already wounded by the world. And then she could surprise you with an innocent question. "How old do you have to be to get a job?" she asked.

"I don't know. Sixteen? Eighteen? Why?" he asked. "You looking for work?"

"No."

He hovered in the doorway. "Don't you know anyone around? Like kids from school? Maybe you need to find some people, you know? Since you're going to be home for the summer."

"Were you serious about the wine? I went down to the basement, and I saw the stuff."

He let himself into her room and closed the door. "Shh. Keep it down, remember."

"Sor-*ree,*" she said, rolling her eyes.

"You saw it? It's great, isn't it?"

"You're serious about this one?"

"All we're waiting for are the grapes."

"So when?"

"Few weeks from now. End of summer?" he whispered. "I don't know when they'll get here."

"Fine," she said, turning back to the liner notes.

"But what about tomorrow?" he urged. "Do you have plans?"

"Nope."

"Maybe you could—"

"G'night. I'm going to sleep now."

"Well, I just wanted to say I'm back."

She just looked at him. That was it. No more. It was all the welcome he could have hoped for. All he cared to hear was that the idea of the wine kit had intrigued her and that she was on his side, after all.

He made his way down the darkened hall. Sitting on their bed, he watched his wife sleeping, wondering if he could wake her. Her shoulder jutted protectively; the strap of the eye mask hugged the back of her head. As he leaned over to kiss her hair, she rolled flat onto her stomach. In her deep breaths, he heard the sound of his loneliness, matter-of-fact and elusive and impossible to describe. *Lamentable,* he thought again.

At work the next morning, which was Friday, he had a mission. He set Julie McKinley to do the detective work, finding anything she could on the drug. "Sulmenamine, S-U-L-M," he directed. "Write it down. Go through all the drug books we have. Look up 'syncope,' fainting, drugs of the Old South. Whatever you need to do."

But an hour later she reappeared, having turned up nothing. "Are you sure it's not S-U-L-E?" she asked. "Or maybe there's some other variation?"

He fished the vial out of his pocket and squinted at the print. "S-U-L-M."

She narrowed her little eyes. "Why am I doing this, exactly? I mean, what's the goal?"

"It's not available through the pharmacy. I want to know what it is, what it's for."

"And then what?"

He looked at her. "Intellectual curiosity. Isn't that enough?" She didn't reply. "I'll take care of it myself. You can take these instead." He handed her a stack of folders. "It's about my father, if you want to know. I discovered that he's taking it, and I want to know what for."

"Fine, I'll do it," she said.

The edge in her voice surprised him, though he realized she'd been sulky since he'd been back.

He lowered his voice. "This isn't about what happened before, I hope. I tried to explain."

"I know," she said evenly. Her chin was high. He noticed again the unnatural texture of the foundation on her cheeks. It did not hide the ancient pitting. His stomach turned at the thought of having kissed her. What had he been thinking? That was it, he hadn't been thinking. He'd simply acted, and it had been exactly the wrong action.

He said, "I told you, it was unexpected. I shouldn't have done what I did."

"It's not that." She looked at him and then away.

"Then what's the problem?" he asked.

"It's that patient Maxi Bailey."

"Yeah?" he prompted when she didn't continue.

"Well, you were practically throwing narcotics at her."

He stared at her. "I was coming up with a solution."

"I was trained to watch out for that. To watch out for people who overprescribe narcotics. When there are a whole bunch of things that might be wrong with her. When she might be one of those people who just wants the drugs. I studied it."

"Is that so?" He was testy.

"She could be treated for depression, for instance."

"Of course she's depressed." A fleck of spit flew from his lip in an emphatic arc. "Pain is depressing. Not being able to participate in her life, that's depressing. When the burden of her pain is lifted, and she can enjoy what's around her, she'll feel better about everything."

He left the room to see another patient. But he couldn't worry about Julie's attitude or her overly traditional training. She'd have to get on-board with his philosophy if she wanted to be part of his practice. She'd have to learn that it was important to keep thinking of ways to improve treatment—and that it was important, no, essential, to listen to the patients above everything else. That was the cornerstone of his practice. He refused to be sidetracked by her doubts.

His best shot, he realized, was Ted Ebberly. He dialed Ted's lab at the medical school. The Bears and the Ebberlys had met years ago through a mutual acquaintance, Vera Bidgel, a retired physician whom Simon had known during his training. The two couples had known each other casually—or known of each other—but it was not until Vera was dying of breast cancer that they'd cemented a kind of friendship, running into each other in the hospital, swapping updates about her condition, admiring each other for having made what was the most difficult and awkward of social calls. After Vera was gone, the friendship persisted, something fortunate that endured out of all that dying. It was Betsy who would say from time to time, "I'll always remember how good you were to Vera at the end." Or she would say, "Vera was lucky to have you." Simon's answer to her always was, "She was lucky to have all of us," because in his mind all he'd done was show up, generate a little conversation. But he was pleased to be remembered for kindness, and he felt Betsy had something important to teach him—and everyone—for making a person feel good about the very little he'd been able to do. What he appreciated about the friendship with the Ebberlys was that it had begun in their earnest attempts to be their best selves.

Ted seemed happy to hear his voice. "Simon! I've been meaning to call. Betsy and I w-want to try out that new restaurant in Canton. H-how about we make an evening of it?"

"Suggest a weekend and I'll check with Emily," he said. "Ted, got a question for you. Ever heard of a compound called sulmenamine?"

"Nope. S-spell it f-for me."

Simon spelled. "Really, I've no clue about it. I came across it and I'm trying to figure out what it is, where it's from."

"Context?"

"A patient. Someone's taking it. I can't get any information about it."

"Gimme some more clues," he urged. Simon could hear that the stammer was gone.

"I don't have many. It's in formulation. Two percent. Liquid. Injectable. It's not currently in common use, I know that much. But what's the compound? What does it do?"

"You need a pharmacist," Ted suggested.

"I tried one, got nowhere."

Ted paused. "I'm having lunch with the chairman of pharmacology next week. I can ask him then."

"I can't wait that long. Any chance you can call today?"

"I'd like to, but I've got back-to-back meetings all afternoon."

"It's not just idle curiosity, you know. My father was in a car accident earlier this week."

"I hadn't heard," Ted said. "I'm sorry." Simon couldn't help appreciating the sympathy, at the same time feeling stung that Emily hadn't mentioned the event to Betsy. Or maybe she'd mentioned it to Betsy, who'd then neglected to pass the information along.

Simon described how his father had totaled the car. "But he's doing well. Anyway, it's his drug. I need to know everything I can about it."

Ted exhaled. "I can try to call over to the office, see if I can get a quick answer. Sulmenamide, you said?"

"Sulmenamine," he corrected. "See?" Julie lifted her head as he hung up, and he slapped his hand on the desk with satisfaction. "That's how you get things done! He's calling the chairman of pharmacology, and we'll have an answer in an hour."

Rita appeared in the doorway of the office. "Can you take a pain patient?"

"Who ya got?" Simon was back in a sporting mood.

"Jim Weaver."

"Ah." He signaled to Julie to follow him.

On principle, as his whole staff knew, he fit them into his routine, no matter how packed the schedule. Furthermore, he liked Jim Weaver, who was sixty-four, with a shock of white hair and a perpetual stubble that covered his chin like the first frost. He was an amputee, the result of an accident, and since losing his arm he'd had the bearing of a man who'd lost incentive to believe in his good looks. His eyes stared dolefully from beneath whitened brows, and his cheeks were slackening into jowls. The left plaid sleeve, rolled up, had been pinned just under the stump below his shoulder, and he walked with it twisted forward slightly as though he were protecting it from bumping into anything.

"I had to wheedle my way in here," he said as Simon entered the exam suite. He spoke in little gasps. "I couldn't wait another day."

"Gotten worse lately?" Simon asked him, rolling a stool close.

"Excruciating." His face contorted with the word, and his shoulders crimped, spine twisted forward.

"One of the greatest mysteries of the neurological system." Simon turned to Julie, who had followed him, and then he remembered to make an introduction. "This is Julie. She's my new star pupil. Tell her where it hurts."

"My arm," Jim said, then redirected her as she looked at the hand that gripped the edge of the exam table. "No, this one. The one that's gone."

"Phantom pain?" Julie murmured. "I've heard of that."

Simon urged, "Tell her how you lost your arm."

Jim Weaver grimaced again. "An accident with a circular saw. Lost my grip." He cracked a smile, showing a single row of teeth. "Figuratively, and then literally."

"It had to be amputated just below the shoulder, but in many ways, he's still living with it," Simon said.

They stared at the air underneath the pinned sleeve. "I know exactly where it is in space," Jim Weaver said in his tinny, breathy voice. "It's gone but not gone. You know how you can close your eyes and put your arm in the air and know where your hand is in relation to your body? I know where the missing arm is, its position, you know? It takes up as much room as it used to, and I'm conscious of it in the same way. The trouble with the missing arm is that I can't move it. It's like my fingers are curled over the thumb and the wrist is curled under. The tension is unbearable, and there's no release."

Jim shifted his torso, and the pinned sleeve waggled. They looked where the arm should have been. In sympathy, they became aware of its absent contours, and the knot of fingers that didn't exist and were thus impossible to disentangle. They looked and they were aware of it, but the arm was not there. The shoulder nudged forward, and the fabric of his shirt shifted. In the space where they looked, they could see straight across the room to the eye chart on the back of the door.

"Haven't you been to many doctors?" Simon asked.

"It gets embarrassing after a while," he admitted, "going on about something that you can't touch, you can't show anyone. You start to sound like a lunatic, even to yourself."

"Anyone you go to will tell you it's a real phenomenon," Simon said, "but nobody's quite sure what to do about it. Phantom pain can go on for years after an injury. We tried narcotics, but they didn't do much for you, did they?"

Jim Weaver cupped his present hand beneath the stump, without quite touching it. "It burns."

"They used to do cordotomy for that," Simon said. "Cut the nerves in the spinal pathway. The theory was that there were overexcited nerve endings feeding errant messages into the dorsal horns on the spinal cord. The solution? Sever the spinothalamic pathways leading to the brain." His voice rose as though he meant to impress upon them the ridiculousness of the procedure. "But they couldn't keep the pain from coming back. So where's the pain? The arm is gone, and so are the nerves in it. The message route from the injury to the brain has been severed, but patients are still in agony. Somewhere between the spine and the brain, there's a leak of information. The signal's still getting through."

Jim shook his head, sucked his breath in. He wiped his forehead with the crook of the good arm. "I've been considering that other procedure, the one the neurosurgeon suggested, where they burn the nerves, but I'm scared."

Simon nodded. "The dorsal root lesioning? It's dangerous, all right. They go into the cervical spine and burn or freeze out the nociceptive cells that are misfiring. Sure," Simon agreed, "it's like tossing a hand grenade when you need a sharpshooter. They have to hope they hit nerve cells and not motor cells. He could wind up paralyzed."

"We tried a therapy last time I was here," Jim ventured tentatively, as if he'd suddenly gone shy. "It worked for a while. I want to try again."

"Right," Simon said. "We gave you shots of saline—that simple—right below your shoulder. It's the absolute best noninvasive therapy there is for this kind of pain. Kind of a miracle therapy. Works wonders. I do it all the time. Happy to give it another go."

"And there was a cream you used," Jim Weaver reminded him.

Simon nodded gravely. "Ah yes. I'll get Rita to prepare that, too." He led Julie out of the room, and he instructed Gabi to prepare the injections.

When Julie spoke to him, her voice was almost a screech. "*Saline?*" She spun around and stomped.

"Fascinating, isn't it? Here's a man with no limb, and yet it hurts as if it were still there."

"You're giving him saline? How long does that work?"

He lowered his voice. "I'm not convinced it does. And unfortunately it hurts, too. I read about it in a book of therapies from the nineteen hundreds. Hypertonic saline injections, isn't that wild?"

"Are you *kidding*?" She looked at him like he was crazy.

"Nope. You give a mild ache to someone with pathological pain, and sometimes it manages to mask the larger problem. Who knows why it works? Maybe like a distraction, like pinching a kid so they don't feel a tooth being pulled. There were studies that suggested it might actually raise the pain threshold overall. But Jim believed it worked last time, so in my book, it's worth doing again."

Julie's mouth fell open. "But this is like before," she started, "with that patient Maxi Bailey! You're not giving him a cure. It's just like a Band-Aid."

He moved his body between her and the exam suites, and he lowered his head toward hers. "Keep your voice down," he grumbled. "I don't know if anyone has a cure. I certainly haven't seen one. The most important thing is to have something to offer. And it's essential to be enthusiastic— as much as you can. Skepticism does nothing for patients."

She put her hands on her hips. He could see the boniness of her arms. "So you're deceiving them?"

With a grip on her knobby elbow, he pulled her into his office. She stumbled against being yanked. "I'm not deceiving anybody!" he said when they were alone in his office. She crossed her arms and looked at him sullenly, but he didn't respond to her expression. "I'm giving hope. Know what the most powerful curative agent is? The mind. Do you have any idea what the efficacy rate is for placebos? Over thirty percent. They've seen placebos lower blood pressure and improve the immune system. Sugar pills have been known to cure kidney disease. It's not just wishful thinking, it's employing the body's most central, most powerful resource."

She lowered the lids of her eyes, as her whole face closed like a purse, and looked away. Was she for real? He was so surprised by her outburst, by her contrariness. Everything had been going so well. He wondered if her issue was about that other thing that had happened, the kiss that was a fluke. It was an accident. She'd said okay, as if she'd understood, and he'd believed her. He hadn't meant to do it, and she'd acknowledged, and they'd agreed it was over.

"What's the cream?" she wanted to know.

"Just something to soothe the skin."

She rubbed her elbow, looking at him in disbelief.

"You look mortified," he said, thunderstruck. "I'm telling you, I know what I'm doing. There's nothing deceptive here. Most important is to provide an option. Something to try. And know what? Sometimes it works. I've even given people dry injections. Nothing. Just a poke, moving the needle in and out of the part that hurts. Don't look so stunned. I didn't make these treatments up. I found them in medical texts. Some of them have been abandoned, but sometimes you find they work."

Her voice was almost a whisper, as though she hesitated to say the words out loud. "You just . . . poke them?" she asked.

"Nothing deceptive," he said again, with great exasperation. "I don't pretend to give one treatment and then give them something different. That'd be deceptive. I give them a complete record of what transpired during their visit, right? It's just that I'm willing to try therapies—even strange-sounding ones—when other doctors would throw up their hands and walk away. And I'm willing to let the patients determine what they need. They're the ones who guide me. One thing you have to learn about medicine is, if a patient believes something is going to help them, it probably can." He looked up to see Rita starting down the hall, and he halted the conversation because he didn't want it to look like they were discussing anything private. His hackles were raised to be challenged, that was all. He hadn't anticipated being second-guessed. "Did Ted Ebberly call?" he asked.

"Not since I've been here," she sang out.

"I'm expecting vital information from him," he informed her.

He turned back to Julie, but she was not looking at him. He stalked out to the exam room to give Jim Weaver the treatment. But he was not his best as he delivered it. Lifting the saline-filled syringe, his hand shook, an almost imperceptible quake. She'd rattled him. He turned his wrist quickly to hide the tremor, but he felt it, and he felt certain Jim Weaver must have noticed it. Julie had not accompanied him to see the treatment, and her decision not to follow him into the room also had unnerved him. She was young, he reminded himself, and her inexperience made her believe that medical journals were more real than people. But you couldn't treat human beings if you followed the texts like a recipe book. If you learned to listen to their voices, to everything they were telling you, if you learned to see with your own eyes, you'd know more than you'd ever learn from taking a class about a condition. She would come to understand, just as he had come to understand, that the point of a medical career was not to protect people from themselves, but to be as useful as possible in whatever way.

It was not an easy therapy. The shining, beveled edge of the needle dove into the meat of Jim Weaver's shoulder. Jim cried out, the stump writhing, as Simon plunged the saline solution into the blind-looking inversion of skin where the arm ended. Jim's lips pursed in acceptance of the pain, his eyes rolled back and then blinked wetly as he was unable to hold back the sound, *"Ohhhwwhh!"*

"You get a sharp pricking pain from the hypotonic solution, but it should counter some of the sensation in your arm," Simon explained, fighting against his own surge of nausea.

"I'm trying to keep it quiet," Jim Weaver apologized, with his one hand wiping the wetness that smeared his cheeks. "Oh. It's terrible." He sat hunched on the exam table, his eyes closed as if he were praying. *"Ohww."*

"Hope this does it," Simon said, jaw tight.

"Me too. Thank you. For trying." Jim's eyes filled with tears again. He said, whispering, "For taking me seriously."

Simon gave Jim a quick, soft squeeze on the good arm. "Keep me posted," he said, and left the room.

When he met with Julie in the hallway, she was leaning against the cabinet, scraping a spoon across the top of a cup of yogurt that was apparently frozen. Her pose was insolent and the sound of the scraping was punishing, a rake across pebbles.

He refused to look at her as he busied himself filling out an information sheet for Jim's folder. "You should get more experience before you go about formulating such strong opinions," he chastised. "You should wait and see. You'll be surprised what you learn."

She answered with a scrappy, scratchy noise, like the ripping of Velcro, stuttering the spoon across the surface of her yogurt.

"Is that lunch?" he asked with disgust, watching her shave channels through the yogurt.

She gave another coy scrape of the spoon. "I found your drug," she answered. "I called Boeker Pharmaceuticals. Sulmenamine is one of their drugs that's currently in Phase II trials. It's not available otherwise."

"It's currently being *tested*? For what?"

She stopped eating to push a scrap of paper across the counter with a single finger. "Here's their number, if you want more information." It was at that moment he realized he'd made a mistake. She was unkind and unfeeling, she had no internal sense of patients, no compass in her gut to make her understand them or why you sometimes had to put yourself on the line for them, and she probably had an eating disorder, he thought, as he watched the icy excavation she was performing on her so-called lunch. Oh, why had he kissed her? The blunder of all blunders. Now, if he fired her, she'd point to the kiss and say he was punishing her because she had turned him down. It had been a silly little outburst, a moment of emotion. She just happened to have been standing there.

In his mind, Emily's face chastised, and he wished he'd never seen Julie McKinley, that she'd never come into his office and that he'd never felt compelled to help her advance her career. She didn't like him, and she never would understand him. He picked up the number and, without another word to her, disappeared into his office. He closed the door and called the drug company.

The Boeker operator's voice, middle-aged, tired and unsmiling, made him instantly officious. "I'm a physician," he informed her.

"Are you participating in one of our trials?" she wanted to know.

"No. I'm looking for information."

"The sulmenamine trial is the one that's still open. Passed Phase I toxicity tests. Now, in Phase II, we're testing to see if the drug works. Next they'll do the Phase III double-blind placebo-controlled studies for efficacy. I can give you a phone number and you can listen to the prerecorded information."

So his father was involved in a drug test? Simon knew of physicians who were involved in conducting tests for pharm companies. He'd met a guy one time when he'd been on vacation with Emily in Colorado, Phil something, who'd been at the bar in the Regency Hotel as they both waited for their wives. He was good-looking, an internist with slicked hair, as if he were bringing back the old-school Vitalis sheen. Ekham Drugs, one of the big companies, was paying him to recruit patients for a study. He didn't even have to conduct the study, he bragged to Simon. All he had to do was refer patients along to the participating physicians and he was rewarded with a finder's fee. Like a guy with a used car he had to unload, he was telling everyone he could about the drug, a new asthma inhalant.

"I don't want a prerecorded message," he informed the operator. "I want to know about the drug. What's it for? What class is it?"

The Boeker operator said, "Let's see here." She sounded as though she were checking a chart. "Um-hm. Yes. That one is being tested for sexual dysfunction."

"No," Simon corrected her. "It's a drug for syncope."

"That's not what the trial is, though," she said. "It's for, you know, performance. Do you want me to read it to you?"

He snorted. "You must be making some kind of mistake," he insisted.

"I'm looking right at the information, sir," she stated. "It's right here in front of me."

"Okay," he said slowly, deciding on a different tack. "How do I find out about the trials? What if I want to participate?"

"Where are you calling from?"

"Baltimore. I'm an internist. Private practice. Big practice." There was a pause. "I was named one of *Baltimore Magazine*'s Top Docs," he added.

"We can have a rep come to you with a presentation. Greg's in charge of recruitment in the Mid-Atlantic. He can tell you about the drug and describe the study."

"How soon?"

"Next Friday?" she proposed.

"No sooner?"

"I have to let you know," she said, in a voice that would have offended him if he hadn't had other concerns, "that we're no longer offering incentives for recruiting patients."

"I don't want any money," Simon said quickly.

This response seemed to satisfy her. "Our rep Greg will be happy to come out for the presentation."

So his father had entered a trial for sexual dysfunction. He was relieved he hadn't told Emily. She'd probably say it was just another reason to stay out of Charles's business.

Of course, she would say, couldn't Simon see now why Charles had been so secretive in the first place? What business was it of theirs if Charles was trying to recapture his youth? Who wouldn't be afraid of dying, if not the old, when death was the next train station and the conductor was about to make the call? But Simon would have to protest: Maybe Charles had been recruited for the study of sulmenamine by some crank doctor, someone like the Vitalis-headed, used-car salesman Phil. Someone had pitched him the idea to participate in a trial, and Charles had agreed because he didn't know any better, because for all his skepticism and his talk-radio expertise about the world, when it came to health, he was really as gullible as an immigrant stepping off a boat, ready to hand over a life's savings for gum wrappers. Now he was giving himself injections of some unknown compound, some outdated, uninvestigated pharmaceutical from an ancient formulary. It was further proof the man needed a chaperone through his medical care: He needed Simon's help. What use does a man in his seventies have for a drug to give him a four-hour erection? He felt hatred for the doctor—a snake, no doubt—who had signed Charles up for a trial.

"Isn't that conflict of interest?" Simon had asked when Phil told him that he knew doctors who were going to make an extra half million just for signing patients up.

Phil must have already grappled with this. Or he'd already been fed a line. "How else do drugs get into the pipeline?" he argued. "Companies need patients, we got access."

When Simon hung up with Boeker, he dialed his parents' number. Lucille answered. Simon meant to sound breezy. He meant to sound like he was just calling to check in, but his voice brayed, the questions like karate chops. "What's the news? What do they say? How's he doing?"

"The same," she answered, sounding cheery. "Nothing to report."

He took a breath. "I know what that drug is, Mom," he said. "The one he was hiding away. It's being tested, did you know?" She said nothing. "Who signed him up for that? Did you know what he was getting into? Nobody knows anything about that stuff."

He waited, and he could see her stiff expression as she sat in silence. Then he heard the sound of a door closing. She lowered her voice, "It's his business, Simon. I'll thank you to stay out of it."

"Trust me, I don't want any part of it. Please," he groaned, "don't give me any details. But I have to know one thing. Did someone talk him into being part of a trial?"

She was quiet for a moment, and he knew that he'd hit on something. "I wondered about that, too. When he first brought it home, I thought, *Now, what's this?* It didn't have any effect that was noticeable, at least as far as the trial went—"

Simon closed his eyes. "Okay, already too much information. I don't want to know—"

She ignored his protest. "—but he did notice the medication made him feel better."

"What do you mean 'better'?" he demanded.

"His arthritis, for one. That felt better. Just his sense of things, better. I don't know, just better. So he kept it. When he ran out, he got more from the doctor. He doesn't need to take it that often, but it's really helped. His arthritis has been significantly better."

Simon struggled to put the pieces together, but then it began to make sense. "Is that why he felt fine after the accident? Was he taking it then?"

Her voice became light and aloof-sounding again. "I don't know why he felt what he did," she said. "All I know's what he said."

"I don't get it," he said. "Does anybody know he's still taking it? Is anybody supervising him?"

He wanted to ask Charles directly, but he remembered a moment in high school, a science project about weather, when he'd convinced pasty, encyclopedic Bruce Andrews that it would be possible to build a rain machine. Simon drew up the plans, which he insisted would require only a tank, a compression pump and a small generator. The night before the project was due, Bruce stayed over and the two of them worked all night, but all they'd managed was condensation on the walls of the tank. Bruce chewed pencils, then broke them in half, then kicked objects in Simon's bedroom, then cried when it was clear that the project was screwed.

Bruce sulked in his sleeping bag on Simon's floor until he eventually fell asleep, but Simon stayed up, writing by hand a rambling, very emphatic five pages of what the machine should have done—part technical explanation about what was wrong with the contraption, part scientific treatise about the difficulties of reproducing global phenomena, part diatribe for having too little time to build a real machine—and handed it in. The teacher gave them an A for concept, since they'd dared to undertake such an imaginative project, and an A for execution, not for the construction of the rain machine, but for not having backed out of a technical and intellectual challenge in order to whip together something simpler for a grade. Bruce, who cared only about grades, couldn't have been more astounded by their good fortune if they'd whipped up a tidal wave. But Simon had felt a righteousness about his effort, and indignant about what was possible given the confines of the assignment, and he accepted the grade as if it were a jacket sewn specially for him.

But that night, as he'd recounted the success, Charles had looked at him with no expression. "Let me get this," he'd said. "They're giving As these days for *not* completing science projects?"

"I thought up the whole thing," Simon responded. "It was my idea."

"It failed."

Simon shrugged. "I told her what happened."

"Thinking of something isn't the same as doing it. It isn't even the same as having the know-how to improvise. Know what that is in the real world? That right there's an A for going down with your ship. That's an A for being dead in the water."

No, he did not want to hear what Charles thought about the drug. He wanted information but he wasn't going to beg for it.

Then he heard a noise in the background, beyond Lucille's voice, and he was certain she was no longer alone. "It's not yours to worry about," she said quickly. "And that's all I can say." She was off the phone before he could inquire anything more.

Greg the drug rep appeared the following Friday. He wore a blue oxford and a tie that was lustrous purple, a color too flashy and too confident for a trustworthy man to use as business attire. Simon was accustomed to the reps, usually women, who were always overdressed, like stewardesses with evangelical intensity. Their manners were too smooth, their hair too perfect. You could smell how much they liked money. Greg's slacks were narrow, the crease down the front razor-thin. His combed hair appeared molded to his head like one of Jamie's old Ken dolls, from back in the day when she used to stage weddings for long-legged Barbies. He arrived with his laptop presentation strapped to a box on a dolly, and he wheeled the arrangement into Simon's little conference room.

Even though it seemed a risky proposal, Simon had suggested to Julie that she attend the meeting. "Want to know what I think? They might be testing this stuff for sexual whatnot, but I saw something in Florida that blew my mind. Here's my father in bed, banged up and acting like—like nothing happened. And there's no explanation for any of it, but then there's this drug that appears all of a sudden. There's something to this stuff, if I can trust my gut. It's got some other effect. So are you coming? You might even learn something new," he said glibly. He didn't specify, but he hoped she might learn a thing or two about *him*. That he was a man who cared, for instance. She sat in the conference room, picking at her nails below the table, which Simon noticed for the first time were ragged and gnawed. He had not been able to fire her. He wanted to, but he was trapped, which was both frustrating and inconceivable. His staff liked him. His patients adored him. Even Gabi, who seemed to like no one and who despised everything American, appreciated him. But Julie seemed disenchanted with him and his practice. She appeared daily and she performed her chores, but she scowled under the surface. And yet, he couldn't fire her because he'd made a mistake that looked like sexual harassment but was nothing like sexual harassment. When he thought about that moment in the basement, his stomach clenched. He couldn't even explain to himself what had happened. All he could do, he realized, was include her in his plans and hope to win her over. Otherwise, he'd just have to pray she'd decide to quit.

Greg unhooked the bungee cords that strapped the laptop to the box. "This your residence, too?" he asked as he began to set up the computer.

"Office on one side. Home on the other." Simon, intent not to reveal his nervousness, spoke too loudly for the small room. Julie refused to look at him, plucking at her cuticles.

"Gorgeous house," Greg said, managing to compliment in a way that sounded greedy.

"We like it," Simon said lightly. He had one eye on Julie, and he didn't want to say too much. She oozed disgust for him, and it startled him. But he was eager for this meeting, and he had a feeling—that trembling in the gut again—that something important was about to happen.

"No worry about the commute to work," Greg quipped.

"No, never." Simon coughed into his hand.

"Okay. So." Greg began his carefully rehearsed PowerPoint presentation with a computer-generated molecule, balls and ribbons in a three-dimensional structure like a Tinkertoy. "Sulmenamine's not a new drug. It was originally derived from pine bark and was used at the end of the nineteenth century, principally for fainting spells or to restore calm. As you might imagine, they prescribed it most often for the ladies." Simon noticed Julie staring back at Greg without changing her expression, but he could tell from her neck what she thought of the entire presentation. As Greg revealed the next image, a sketch of the pine tree, Julie didn't even look at the computer.

"It wasn't in widespread use," Greg went on with enthusiasm, "but there are accounts of doctors offering it in the South in small geographic pockets. Later, it was abandoned. We know the drug has no serious adverse effects and that it's nonaddictive. We know it stays in the system for a long time."

As Greg recounted the story, the Boeker research team had only just begun to explore the long-abandoned compound when they realized its structure resembled certain molecules in the brain. Simon glanced at Julie, who had folded her hands before her on the table and was sitting with impossibly straight posture. Her expression looked like someone waiting for a bus. Greg shifted to the next image, which revealed how the drug appeared to increase activity in certain areas of the brain. "This"—he pointed—"is where it's happening. We believe the drug targets the prefrontal cortex, though there are perhaps other areas within the limbic system where it's active."

"Prefrontal cortex, you said?" Simon interjected suddenly and with volume, as if he could make Julie agree that the region mattered.

Greg moved around the side of the table alongside the laptop. "The evidence of biochemical activity there makes sense, being a pleasure center and all. It's the brain's reward system. Reward and motivation. There's reason to presume the drug acts on neurotransmitters involved in sexual arousal, or at least provides the means to sustain feelings of pleasure."

"So," Simon began slyly, shifting sideways in his seat, "it's just being tested for sexual dysfunction?"

Greg nodded. "Because it's an old drug, it's on the books, we were able to skip ahead quickly to efficacy trials."

"But do you know exactly what's happening there?"

"Hasn't been determined yet," Greg acknowledged. "But actually we suspect the process is fairly simple. You know all about endorphins, right?" Without waiting for an answer, he continued as if he were giving a freshman lecture. "Small segments of protein molecules that give a person a sense of well-being. The brain makes them and then breaks them down. All happens naturally."

"So it ramps up endorphins?" Simon didn't mean to make his impatience obvious, but wanted to make sure Julie was taking it all in.

"We think the compound is interfering with the endorphin breakdown enzyme. The enzyme gets inhibited and doesn't do its job. Suddenly the brain is awash in an overflow of its own wonderful, naturally occurring chemicals. The drug doesn't create a sensation of arousal—we probably couldn't put it on the market if it did—we'd produce a society of horn-dogs." Greg smirked again. Simon distinctly did not look at Julie, who remained rigid in her seat. "But somehow, once a person begins to feel aroused—in other words, when another mental function is under way—the drug maintains the feeling of pleasure. It elevates and maintains interest."

Simon listened. Well, so what about this pleasure sustainer? They knew so little about the compound, it was likely they didn't know all it was capable of. His father's unusual state after the trauma of the car accident must have related to the drug as well. Endorphins served as part of the body's natural pain relief, just like opioids, attaching to specific receptors on the surface of a neuron and then transmitting a message to the inside of the cell. The broken rib, the bruises, certainly should have been painful, and yet Charles had hardly complained about anything. He found himself thinking about his father, and he felt certain that the medication had affected his father's ability to perceive what he ought to have been feeling. He also was becoming certain that the company had no inkling about any effects as a painkiller.

"Is that its only effect, sexual dysfunction?" Simon probed.

"Only effect!" Greg sounded insulted. "What more could you ask? It's what the world needs! So far, patients have reported the most minor side effects: dry mouth, frequent urination, sweaty palms. Other sexual dysfunction drugs on the market work by increasing blood flow to the penis. They work by widening the blood vessels. In other words, it's a mechanical process. Bottom line is, they can help you get it up, but they can't help you get in the game."

Simon couldn't help pressing again, just to make sure. "You're not testing it for anything else?"

The question did not seem to interest Greg in the least. He leaned forward, his fingertips against the table, as he said, "We think we could blow Viagra out of the water."

So Boeker Pharmaceuticals had no idea about the drug's potential as a pain medication. There was a heat under Simon's hair at the back of his neck, the prickle of secret knowledge. He was staring at untold potential. An answer. He'd witnessed the effects of the drug in his father's car accident. There was no doubt in his mind. With a broken rib, the man had wanted to get down on his knees to fix a cabinet.

"Are there contraindications?" Simon asked.

"We think patients taking psychotropic drugs shouldn't take it."

"What about women?" he asked.

"Seems to work for women too, though I admit with this study we've been targeting men."

"Any reason that women couldn't take it?" Simon pressed.

"None established. But they're not really part of our study."

"But no known side effects other than the ones you described?"

"Right."

Simon's heart was racing. He banged both hands on the table and exclaimed, "I'm in! How do I do the trial? How do I begin?"

Across the table, Greg slid a confidentiality agreement and a pen. Simon barely pretended to read before scribbling his signature, and then Greg produced the protocol, bound with a plastic cover, explaining as Simon flipped through: The drug was given by injection. Simon had the option of giving the vials to his patients and prescribing them hypodermic needles to give the shots to themselves at home, or he could administer the sulmenamine in his office. He would have to follow up with patients by having them fill out frequent questionnaires about their sexual habits and their moods. There were forms to keep track of the vials and more forms to record notes about the patients.

"Typical paperwork," Greg acknowledged. "First let me say, we know your time is precious. We want to compensate you for diverting attention from other things you need to do."

Simon put up one hand. "Whoever I spoke to on the phone said you don't do that anymore."

"Well, that's our official policy. Unofficially, we'd like the results as soon as possible. Our time's precious, too. I can reimburse you for your time and expenses, what we estimate will come to about five hundred dollars per patient enrolled in the study."

"I don't want any money," Simon said plainly. He glanced at Julie, hoping that she would take note.

Greg coughed into his fist. "Okay, then. Maybe we can work out some other form of compensation. I've never heard of someone not wanting to be paid—"

Simon interrupted, "How much of the drug can I have?"

Greg had a carton by his foot under the table. He set it on the desk and ripped back the cardboard flap, revealing small boxes lined with the tiny numbered vials, just like the ones that Charles had in his drawer. "How much? That depends. Truth is, we got a time crunch on our hands. This trial's been going on for almost fifteen months already. When we started, the protocol team determined we needed a hundred patients to make our case. So far we only got seventy-four who fit the demographic. In short, we got three months left to sign up twenty-six patients and get some results."

"Or what?" Simon wanted to know.

"They close down the trial. We move on. Company can't afford otherwise."

"What happens to the drug?"

"Shelved. Done."

"And nobody could get it then?"

"Got to be honest with you, this is my project. I believe in this stuff and I want to see it succeed." Greg pressed his two palms together in a gesture that looked like he was either imploring or about to dive. It turned out to be his special-deal pose. "Normally, we'd have you come in and go through training first, and then we'd deliver the drug to you. But I want to expedite. I have a case of the stuff in my car. We had a doctor go through all the paperwork and the training and back out yesterday, time pressure, yadda yadda. Anyway, because of the time constraints, I can bend the rules and leave that case with you. Do the training next week. You'll have the drug on hand so you can start immediately after that."

"I can get those patients," Simon stated. "If you want, you can leave me more."

Greg looked pleased. "That's what I was hoping you'd say. My car's parked on the street. I'll be right back."

When Greg stepped out, Simon turned to Julie. "They don't even know what they're sitting on here." Julie nodded, working hard on a stubborn cuticle. "I want a stash on hand in the office. If what I saw in Florida is an indication of what this drug can do, it's got incredible potential, this stuff."

She tore at the edges of her fingers. Finally she spoke, "How, exactly, are you going to do this?" Her voice flatlined with disinterest. "With all the notes you have to take for them? Shouldn't you just tell them what you think the stuff does?"

"These guys are all about making a buck. That's not what I'm in it for. When everything's said and done, I'd like to say I made the world a better place. Can't be done through their twisted system." He was already planning. "I'll design my own trial. I'll call all my patients, the ones with the most severe, intractable pain. I'll tell them I'm offering a new pain treatment. Maxi Bailey. Jim Weaver," he counted on his fingers enthusiastically. "I could come up with a whole list right off the top of my head."

Standing up, he began pacing the office. Julie regarded him without shifting, the only flicker of motion her nails working the reddened skin. He hated himself for that terrible, loathsome moment in the basement. His stomach turned. He was always on the edge of fucking everything up. Always teetering on the precipice of disaster. And now it mattered that he have her on board with this plan.

"Do you want to tell me why you're being like this?" he asked suddenly, turning and leaning toward her across the table.

"Like what?" she retorted.

He lowered his voice. "Like you're angry or something. Is it because of what happened—before? I told you I was sorry. It wasn't personal."

"Wasn't *personal*," she spat.

"Really, you should take it as a compliment, if anything."

"Puh-lease."

"Look, I realize there are things that shouldn't happen. And that was something I shouldn't have done. I don't know how to take it back. Can I possibly say sorry enough times?" Then something dawned on him. Maybe it wasn't that he'd kissed her, but that he'd stopped. Maybe she'd wanted something more to happen between them. "Oh," he said.

She read the idea taking form in his head and she slammed both palms down on the table. "You are so arrogant," she said. Her eyes blackened into slits.

"Me?" he asked, taken aback.

"So very arrogant."

He was genuinely surprised. "I don't think of myself that way."

"Case in point," she snapped.

Simon looked at her. He was so accustomed to feeling like he was in the doghouse, but so unaccustomed to being called on it. Emily did not engage him anymore. She'd simply stopped trying. And yet it felt good to be confronted. The heat of it felt real. He couldn't help appreciating this Julie McKinley, and he felt approval for the way her cheeks flushed and her eyes blazed at him and her hands were spread on the table as if she were about to spring over it and claw at him. The kiss in the basement didn't seem like such a big deal to him because he hadn't meant anything by it—it had just happened. It wasn't premeditated, for chrissake. He'd just felt—happy. But he couldn't dwell on this nonissue. Bigger, more important things were happening with this drug that Greg was about to wheel into the office. The drug was an opportunity. And if they could focus on it, they could move past this other trivia, which didn't have any substance and—no matter what she said—had nothing to do with arrogance.

"So are you going to help me with this?" he asked.

"With what? I still don't understand what there is to do."

"Look," he said impatiently. "They're testing this drug for sexual dysfunction or whatever. They have no clue what it can do for chronic pain. My gut's telling me otherwise. Instinct, I guess. If I tell them—if I call up Boeker and say, hey, and I wait for them to test it and take it through whatever channels, then it just means that my patients who are suffering have to suffer even longer. And if I tell Greg, by the way, have you tried it for this, I might not get a supply. Anyway, these companies are all about profit, and only secondarily about patients. If we dare to try, we might discover we have something amazing on our hands."

She looked at him, her lips narrowed into a line.

"It's nonnarcotic," he reminded her, "so all your gripes about overmedicating patients, all that stuff about overprescribing painkillers, would be resolved."

"I don't get it—you're going to do what?" she asked. "You're just going to give it to patients?"

"You heard him. It's safe."

Her head seemed to twitch momentarily, as though she were shaking against a noise she didn't want to hear. "I don't think I want to be a part of this," she said slowly. "I mean I don't know. I have my career to think about."

About then, he decided he'd heard enough skepticism. Emily provided plenty of doubt—that voice that was with him constantly—and he was tired of feeling torn. "If you're not interested in innovation," he said haughtily, "then this might not be the right practice for you. If I can't help my patients with treatments that are available, it's my job to find out what else I can do. And if you're not on board, then—" His voice dropped off.

"Then what," she goaded.

"Then that's that. I mean it. We're done."

"You're *firing* me?" Her eyes went wide.

"I'm sorry that's how it is," he said. "But we need to agree. My mission's to help my patients."

"Are you serious?" Her voice hit an uncomfortable pitch. "I've never been fired from anything. By *anybody*."

"I'll be happy to write you a recommendation," he pronounced curtly. "Wherever you decide to go."

A noise sounded in the hallway, the scuffle of footsteps and the sound of the dolly being drawn along, scraping against the wall as Greg dragged it around the corner. Julie McKinley stood up. Before Greg was close enough to hear, she leaned over the table toward Simon, her eyes scrunched again, and the look in them could not be mistaken. "I'd sue you for sexual harassment," she hissed, "but I know what would happen. It'd be my word against yours. So nothing."

Greg wrestled with the dolly, whose wheel was stuck on the edge of the door. "I told you I was sorry about that," Simon insisted to her, shaking his head, genuinely surprised that he had to keep restating it. "Why won't you believe me?"

Then the wheels of the dolly were freed, and Greg steered a box stamped BOEKER into the room. He'd thrown the purple tie over his shoulder to keep it out of his way, probably when he was leaning into the trunk of his car, and it still draped behind him like a flag.

"Here's a box," Greg said. "Keep it on hand to start as soon as you finish the training. I know you can get the patients we need. I can just tell about you. And you know your patient base better than anyone."

"I do, don't I," Simon said evenly, not looking at Julie.

She gathered the papers that were on the table in front of her and did not look at him again as she stalked out of the conference room. Took her things from the hall closet and walked right out of the office, her back stiff and her jaw jutted forward. She was good and gone by the time he escorted Greg to the door.

The first to try the medication was Jack Whitby. He wasn't exactly a current patient—he wasn't even Simon's patient—but he suffered from chronic pain and no physician had been able to determine its source or offer anything that helped. Simon dialed Whitby's number himself. He knew about Jack's pain because of what had happened eight months ago at the Frith holiday Christmas party. Jack Whitby was a partner and CFO of Emily's company, and in the middle of the black-tie affair at the Bethesda Hotel, he'd been seized by one of the hateful spasms.

They were all seated at a round table when it happened, the wife named Valerie, who wore a dress cut so low that it was clear at once she was his second marriage, then Jack Whitby, then Simon and then Emily, who had been busy the entire evening. Emily had presented the keynote speaker—what kind of Christmas party had a keynote speaker? Simon wondered—and she was flushed and, he thought, quite beautiful, despite being preoccupied and a little wooden in her manners. She was deep in conversation with the woman on her left, discussing what?—he couldn't quite hear, but it involved a merger between two companies, only one of which was repped by Frith, and how could they position themselves to keep the account? On his other side was Whitby, a man with a square jaw and a kind of silver-fox sultriness. Whitby was fawning over the low-cut wife, whose hair could not naturally, at her age, have been quite that shade of blond.

Simon could still recall the start of that evening because of how he'd managed to annoy Emily. On each of the tables in the ballroom was a small Christmas tree, a bonsai-sized centerpiece, decorated in miniature as if it belonged in a dollhouse. The ornaments were the size of earrings, and there were little *wrapped* matchbook-sized presents arranged on a puddle of felt beneath the bottom fronds. Simon studied the arrangement, wondering which secretary had spent the last two weeks wrapping miniature gifts for his benefit. Then, he noticed, next to each elaborate Christmas tree stood a plastic menorah, almost as tall, a nod to the Hanukkah season. Hanukkah had come early that year and was long past, and the menorahs themselves looked like afterthoughts, Simon decided. They were crappy plastic—as if they'd been popped out of a box from a dollar store and snapped apart by someone who'd had to bend them back and forth to separate them. As Emily remained engrossed on her other side, and the Whitby character had wrapped an arm around the preternaturally blond wife, Simon took the baby carrots off his plate and began fitting them into the menorah's candlestick holders.

"What are you doing?" Emily said through her teeth, suddenly taking note of his artistry. The way she'd said it, she seemed to be saying, What are you doing *to me?*

But, of course, he hadn't intended anything personally. He presented the menorah in front of her plate. The serving on his plate had provided only enough carrots to represent six nights of Hanukkah and the *shamash.* "It's a tribute to the Jews in the room." She glared at him, horrified. He shrugged and pointed at the display. "These weren't decorated, but look what they did with the Christmas trees. Someone somewhere spent a lot of time on those trees."

She might have reprimanded him, but suddenly on his other side they heard a gasp, a protracted sucking, like air drawn through a long straw. Jack Whitby stood frozen in a half-risen position, his hands clutching the edge of the table.

"Honey?" It came from the wife, its second syllable elevated into a shriek.

"What's happening?" Emily asked, because the wife had jumped to her feet and was leaning over the CFO, trying to help him. "Is he okay?"

"Is it happening again?" the wife asked.

The man answered with another sucking noise.

Simon had been uncertain what was happening. At first he thought the man might be choking—Simon had performed a successful Heimlich maneuver once in a crowded mall and he was ready to do another. But it was the look on Jack's face that made him realize something different was taking place.

"Back spasm," the wife explained. "He can't move."

But it looked more wrenching than that. Jack had turned a faint shade of green. Tiny beads of sweat stood on his upper lip, which trembled. He looked afraid to breathe too deeply.

"Simon," Emily whispered with a clenched jaw. "Do something."

Gripped so completely by the pain, Jack was caught between standing and sitting again. Instead of reaching a safer position, he leaned sideways and threw up. Chairs reared backward as the people across the table jolted upward. A woman—the wife of one of the district executives—put her napkin over her nose and mouth and turned away.

Emily, always confident in moments of crisis, jumped to Jack's elbow. "Help him get out of here," she directed in a low voice that no one would dare to question.

Simon clenched Whitby beneath the armpit and steered him out of the ballroom as Emily followed. Whitby seemed to be recovering in the lobby, at least he seemed to be breathing. His face was ashen, and he remained silent. The wife held his hand and said to Simon, "He fell off a ladder at our house in the summer. He was cleaning out a gutter. He was fine—at least he said he was fine—but ever since then, he's been having these episodes. We never know when they're coming."

"I need to go home," Jack mouthed.

"That'll be a trick and a half," the wife answered, realizing the predicament they faced. "We came in your car. You know I don't drive stick."

"Simon'll drive you," Emily announced. She said to him, "Then you can take a cab home."

His feelings about being excused were overcome by his delight at being useful. The valet brought around Jack's car, and Simon eased Jack into the backseat. The wife squeezed in next to him, and Simon took the keys. "Where to?" he said, settling into the front seat, and the wife gave him directions toward Chevy Chase. "What's he taking for this? Anything?" Simon had asked. "I'm a doctor, you know. I only sideline as a chauffeur."

"I had a prescription," Whitby said. It was the first utterance in a normal voice since he'd first let out that awful gasp. "But I'm out. Geez, what a night."

Instead of steering to Chevy Chase, Simon headed for the D.C. Beltway. "I'm taking you home by way of my office," he told them. "If you can just hang in there."

But they didn't have a choice. He drove all the way back to Baltimore, fifty minutes in the rather light traffic, and left the car running in the circular driveway as he dashed around the side of the house into the office to grab a prescription pad. "You can't phone in the best painkillers," he explained when he returned. "What were you taking?" He wrote a new prescription for OxyContin, handed it to the wife and then drove them all the way back to their home in Chevy Chase. He hadn't heard from the Whitbys since then, but Emily had told him how appreciative they'd been of his efforts.

But now he had sulmenamine, something unique to propose, and he was sure Emily would be pleased that he could make a difference to one of her colleagues. He called Jack Whitby at work. When the secretary patched him through, Simon said, "It's Dr. Bear." There was an awkward pause that prompted Simon to supply his first name and then, "I'm Emily's husband."

"Of course. How are you?"

"I was wondering how you're feeling." There was another pause. "Remember? I drove you across state lines last Christmas."

Jack coughed. "Mostly all right. From time to time, I have trouble. I try not to let it get in my way."

"Good," Simon said. "I mean, not *good*. I'm sorry for what you're going through. I have a new treatment for patients with chronic pain. People like you who've suffered for a long time."

"Oh?" Jack said, sounding like he had been called by a telemarketer and was about to insist on being taken off the phone list.

"It's an injection," Simon explained quickly. "A new substance. Well, it's old actually, but new in the treatment of pain. Nonaddictive. Safe. No significant side effects. You'd have to come into the office. I'm conducting a clinical trial. There'd be no cost to you," he added.

There was a pause on the other end that lasted so long, Simon asked, "Are you still there?"

"Yeah," Whitby said finally. "Let me talk it over with my wife tonight. Can I call you back? And"—his voice dropped—"can I give you my cell number? I don't like using the office line for personal kind of stuff."

Simon chafed at the response to his offer—what suffering person wouldn't jump at the chance to end the torment, whatever the chances? He wrote on his list, *Possible*. Rita had provided him with two full pages of names to call, and as soon as he hung up with Whitby, he began at the top. They were patients who had depended on him for years. Some he still saw regularly. Some he hadn't seen in quite some time and wasn't even sure if they were still suffering with chronic pain. A few were interested. Maxi Bailey told him she'd do anything, and she was even willing to go off the other meds she was taking in order to give the trial a fair try. She intended to come in for the therapy in a week. The next morning, Jack Whitby called back, and two days later, he became the first patient in the clinical trial of sulmenamine for the treatment of chronic pain.

The wife, whom Whitby called Vally, came with him to the office, stroking his hand and clutching his forearm and all but mopping his brow with a kerchief. Simon thought he might have to pry the woman

off Whitby in order to do a basic exam. But he appreciated their hopeful glances, the looks they cast at each other that were timid with anticipation, like two game show contestants presented with a triad of numbered doors.

"He's been having an attack at least every other week," Valerie said,
running her palm against the back of her husband's hand.

"That's not true, Vally. They're a lot less frequent," Jack said.

Her oddly blond hair was pulled into a floppy twist behind her head.
Whitby looked at her quickly as she protested, "Even if it's not often. It's
getting to be too much—for him, I mean. He's had every test under the
sun. The last doctor we saw told him he was under too much stress." She
eyed the tray Simon had prepared with a vial of the watery substance and
a sterile needle. "So, how does that stuff work?"

Simon snapped on a pair of latex gloves and then paused with his
hands in the air as though he were standing in a sterile zone, waiting for
an attendant. "The mechanism isn't known. But that's not an issue. We
use medications all the time, even when we don't know why they work.
Take aspirin, for instance. People who wanted to reduce fever were chewing on willow bark for centuries, as far back as Hippocrates. It wasn't
until the 1960s that anyone was able to say, That stuff's inhibiting an
inflammatory hormone and that's why it works as a fever reducer and
an analgesic. What they think about this medication, in simple terms, is
that it increases the positive molecules over the negative ones in exactly
the appropriate regions of the brain. But I think there's very good reason
to believe that it works, based on the locale it targets." He prepared the
injection. "So," he said, laying the needle against the vial, "you ready?"

His staff had been delighted, utterly supportive. Even Gabi, who had
complaints about typical procedures and then complaints when the procedures changed, was enthusiastic to hear about the clinical trial that he
was going to conduct with this new miraculous substance. She knew of
a woman, also from Jamaica, who was a housekeeper who was all but

crippled by her sciatica, and she was astounded that Simon could offer a promising treatment and not charge a penny for it. The gesture had all but reshaped her opinion of Americans. The staff had also been glad to hear that Julie was gone. ("Too young," Rita agreed, when he announced that he'd made a decision to let her go. "Too angry," he answered, and he hoped they did not suspect that unfortunate kiss, or anything else. It was done with.) His staff believed in him, they believed in his innovative vision in the service of his patients, and they were eager to see him succeed with a new treatment. Each of them could think of people with some form of chronic pain, and each of them was eager to begin making calls.

Jack Whitby shifted in the paper gown, revealing knobby arms.

"Intramuscularly is what we need, so the deltoid is the best spot," Simon said. "The shot itself won't hurt. I'll want you to sit here for half an hour, just to make sure you respond okay. Then you can go. Come back in a week, and we'll see how you're doing, but we'll talk in the meantime."

But before he even heard from the Whitbys at the end of a week, Simon had four additional patients interested in the treatment. Two were patients he'd called who were interested in trying it, but the other two were acquaintances of people on the list, who'd merely heard that something new had become available. All of them had run out of other options, but they hadn't run out of hope. They were ready to try it, as long as it wasn't addictive and didn't constipate them worse than the narcotics. Is it herbal? they wanted to know. Is it Asian? Is it available at the pharmacy? Why haven't we heard about it on the Internet? Can we get it from Canada if we need it? "What if it works?" one woman posed, as if the possibility of being released from her pain presented a range of other, untold threats.

He scheduled the four, and three had received the treatment by the time he reached Jack Whitby.

"I've been calling you for four days," Simon accused.

"We've been out, I guess."

"Well, that's good! So? How is it? How do you feel?"

"Okay, I think."

"Any spasms?"

"I haven't had any—but it's only been a few days and they can be infrequent. Hard to tell."

"And what about otherwise? Are you feeling—um—good?"

"I feel fine. I don't know. About the same, I guess."

"But better, you said," he urged.

"I don't know."

"Probably you should come in for another shot, just to make sure the spasms don't recur."

"I think—I'm not sure about this treatment. I mean, there's no literature on this stuff at all. I did a search."

"But if it seems to work," Simon reasoned.

"I just don't know," Jack sighed. "Maybe I could do another round. I'll talk to Valerie."

Simon was incredulous. "But if you haven't had spasms."

"It might be the drug. I've been changing my diet and doing yoga, so who knows."

But Simon knew better. Even if Whitby didn't want to credit sulmenamine with his improved state, Simon was convinced the drug had played a role. The following week, Maxi Bailey left the office with a hopeful face, her doleful eyes watery and her hands wringing a Kleenex. He called her a day later, just to check up, and she said, yes, it was hard to describe, but she thought she was feeling better. The pain in her back was a little less sharp, maybe, a little muted. It was still too soon to tell whether it was working, but she was going to try to go out for a little while, heading to the mall with her son. The Jamaican woman, Gabi's friend with sciatica, seemed to know the minute she hobbled into the office that the treatment, whatever it was, would do wonders. He didn't have to call her; she called him to say he was a miracle worker. But he was most hopeful about Whitby, particularly because he seemed most skeptical. And Whitby hadn't said he felt *worse*. Simon called Ted Ebberly, who listened patiently.

"I mean, I could be imagining it," Simon acknowledged. "But conceivably, couldn't there be something molecular—couldn't you imagine this as a plausible mechanism?"

"Sure, w-why not?" Ted said.

"No, I mean in the way of proof—could you run some kind of biochemical tests? In your lab? The company did fMRI studies. Something's happening in the brain. Can't you figure out what receptors are involved?"

"W-we'd have to grind up brain tissue—m-mice obviously—run it through a ligand binding test."

"Could that be done? Could you do it?" He knew he sounded too desperate, and he knew what Ted's answer would be.

"N-nope. D-don't have the manpower or the resources. Or the right m-mice. Got a lot of projects going on right now. But that's a fascinating finding, and I hope it works out. Aristotle postulated that pain was not a s-sensation but actually an emotion that's the opposite of pleasure. Maybe it'll turn out that they're directly linked through neurotransmitters. An erectile dysfunction drug would be a billion-dollar coup, but to have something for pain? Can you imagine? Hey, b-by the way, are we on for September? *La Bohème*?"

A laboratory study would have given him an ace in the hole, and he couldn't help feeling annoyed with Ted, who hadn't even entertained the notion of what it could mean to conduct experiments. The early results of his very small clinical study were promising but not quite as conclusive as he'd hoped. The Jamaican housekeeper with sciatica, a garrulous woman named Yolanda McBride, seemed delighted with her treatment and was insistent that her legs and back felt better than they had in months. Maxi Bailey said she felt "lighter" overall, and she would come in again and do another round. But there were others who wanted to go back on their regular meds. Simon kept telling patients that the nuances of individual pain were an order of magnitude simpler than the complexities of individual treatment. In medicine, he told them, even success has a range of meanings.

The question remained: What to do about the big picture? He considered the possibility of calling Boeker, not Greg but maybe one of the researchers. Perhaps he could interest someone in the industry in doing the work to prove the drug's efficacy as an analgesic. He knew a scientist in Boston who did computer modeling of molecules, but he wasn't sure how long a model of sulmenamine might take to create, and would it answer the question of what the treatment did to create feeling? Through the Groves, he knew of a researcher at an institute in Philadelphia who'd been reprimanded for giving brain injuries to chimps. Perhaps animal studies would help. But every time he listed the possibilities, he returned to the conviction that he couldn't wait for studies to take shape. It would take months and months just to plan them, not to mention get funding. He was convinced about the drug's potential, and he didn't feel he could keep it from his patients.

Then, amid all his reasoning, he picked up the phone and dialed his father. He wondered if he could get some corroboration. He hadn't spoken to Charles since he'd left Florida. His mother's voice, when she answered, was airy, like a person hosting a party.

"How is he?" she repeated in singsong tones. "No change. Nothing to report."

"So that's good." There was a brief silence. "We're fine here, too," he said.

Simon wanted to bring up the drug. He wondered what had precipitated Charles's involvement in the study—had Charles gone to someone

looking for treatment to maintain his verility? too terrible to think of it—
or was he the victim of someone else's greed? Either way, Simon found
himself unwilling to ask his mother about it. He got off the phone without
answers.

The only thing to do, Simon realized, was to recruit more patients, and
to find out whether he had stumbled upon a cure. No time to be wasted
if he intended to be of help. He went to the list that Rita and the staff had
compiled. Lewis Gimlet was a longtime patient who'd been crushed by a
tall book cart he'd been wheeling through a library and who continued to
suffer a pain he described as liquid heat. There was Evelyn Janers, whose
problems had begun long before she'd found her way to Simon, with
inexplicable pain in her pelvis during intercourse. With a gynecologist,
she'd undergone investigative endoscopy through a tiny dime-sized port
in her lower abdomen and was found to have minor patches of abnormal
uterine tissue growing in the pelvic cavity. The gyn had gone in surgi-
cally to remove the endometriosis, but the consequences of that invasive
procedure had been unbearable—damage to some nerve process that left
Evelyn Janers so pained she could barely stand up straight. Simon had
been helping her get by—just barely—with prescriptions of narcotics.
There was Sandy Undrsoll, a former pro football player who had suffered
knee pain twenty years earlier after a tackle, and even after total knee re-
placement surgery had continued to suffer, as though his old knee would
not be forgotten. There was Florence Rudolph, who had trigeminal nerve
pain, mysterious, sudden lightning-like bolts of pain that shot across her
face and made it almost impossible for her even to wear glasses. There
were others, too. Simon phoned them all, and they responded. They were
enthusiastic, and they marveled that the doctor remembered them. They
were touched to be called at home. Some were skeptical, but others were
eager to schedule an appointment.

"How soon can I start?" the former football player, Sandy Undrsoll,
asked. "I'll come over there now. It's only nine p.m."

Simon was stunned, but he agreed, and Sandy drove up to the house in the dark. Simon met him in the waiting room, flipping on the lights in the clinic. He gave Sandy the shot and then sat with him for the requisite twenty minutes to make sure the still-burly former athlete didn't have an allergic reaction to pine bark before driving back home.

All of this was happening—the patients, the anecdotal instances linking one to the next, all evolving into a possible solution to a horrific problem, and he wanted to tell Emily. She'd been distant since he'd returned from Florida, and busy with conferences.

Climbing into bed after Sandy Undrsoll's injection, he looked at his wife. Her arms were splayed over her head, the eerie mask covering her eyes. He dozed fitfully, with longing and with fragments of unfinished sentences. In disconnected sequences of dream, pained patients were roving outside the waiting room door, howling like wolves. One by one he let them in, reaching out to touch them, patting their shoulders with reassurance. *It works with enzymes in the brain,* he was explaining in the clinic. *It works with the body's natural capabilities for pain relief.* When they looked at him quizzically, he continued, *Long-term pain produces alterations in nerves, rearranges their normal activity and establishes new connections. You can't just step in and interfere with the process. That's like trying to put your finger on a bead of mercury. Just keeps breaking into more and more pieces and slithering away. You have to increase the body's ability to do its own job. You're not just subverting signals or trying to redirect them. You're enhancing the brain's ability to overcome pain at the highest level.* In his fingers, he held a syringe that glowed gold, and he was worried that he might drop it. Julie McKinley was standing next to him, naked to the waist, one hand on her wretched bony hip. Her breasts were the shape of the bell on the counter of a motel and they looked as hard. "A lot of good it did," she said. "Your being a doctor."

He woke, chilled by his own sweat, and turned toward Emily. In her night mask, she looked like she'd just stepped from a masquerade ball.

If he told her about the pain treatment, even with all the patients he'd already helped, she'd still be skeptical. She'd quiz him about whether he was imagining the results. *Wishful thinking,* she'd say. In any event, she'd think a trial was impractical. *Too time-consuming,* she'd argue. *It lacks good business sense. And how will you know, anyway, if the treatment's working?* That's what she'd press him on: *Where's your proof? Pain is subjective—you can't even calculate your results. You can't say, for instance, pain was decreased by twenty percent.* She'd be right. He couldn't know any exact measurement, but the effort was still worthwhile, wasn't it? You're doubting your results, the astounding evidence you've already seen, because you've arrived at the threshold of success, he reprimanded himself. You're about to reveal something significant to the entire world, and you're pulling back. Was it possible he was wrong? *No!* He had no doubt. He'd seen what sulmenamine could do. If he had any reason to hesitate, it wasn't because of the therapy. His own life mantra came back to him. They were words he'd used as long ago as medical school—no, maybe even before medical school: *You can't fear what you don't know. You have to go with your gut. Trust yourself.*

So what was it, then? He looked at the form of his wife's body as she slept beside him, mounds under the twisted sheet. Why was his heart beating so hard in the middle of the night? The truth was, she might think her criticisms, but she would never voice them. She'd never challenge him, and he was left to wrestle with his doubts on his own. What had happened to them? They'd buried Caleb at the Chevrei Emunah cemetery outside of Baltimore, and since the day of the funeral, he'd waited for Emily to blame him for what had happened. Waited and dreaded. *Why didn't you know?* He could ask the question of himself: *How could you have missed such an obvious diagnosis? Why didn't it cross your mind that he could die?* He wasn't sure if he'd been complacent, believing that since he was a doctor, nothing so terrible could possibly happen to them. Or maybe he'd just been too terrified to imagine the worst possible scenario. Or maybe, at the core, he really was a know-nothing with no skills, only puffery to offer. He glanced at Emily again. *How could you have let me down,* he imagined her saying. *How could you have let all of us down?* Even if she asked, he wouldn't know what to tell her. The symptoms had been all wrong. He'd been too busy. He'd been afraid. He had no idea how he'd missed every relevant, important sign, how he'd never even guessed about them, and he could only hope that if the question were put to him, he'd finally constitute an explanation that would make sense. But there was no doubt the longer she refused to talk about it, the longer he suffered. In a way, he had to acknowledge, her silence delivered a kind of justice. He had no choice but to accept it.

She stirred and turned over, and he sighed into the dark. There was a nervous, spidery feeling that had crept under his breastbone, and he shifted sideways to quell it, pulling the sheet up to his chin. He had to force himself to think about the present. *Think about the drug, the wonders it's capable of doing, how much it's going to help,* he told himself. *Think positive.* The uneasy feeling in his chest subsided. The new drug would not make amends for what had happened, he knew, but if he were successful with it, he might make Emily look at him differently. He rolled onto his back, closed his eyes and willed himself to sleep.

The one unfortunate thing happened two days later and was sheer coincidence, a matter of plain bad timing. He was making calls to patients, allowing Rita to double- and triple-schedule the slots for patients to receive a sulmenamine injection. The number of people in his drug trial had climbed to eight. He had begun to think about writing up a case study, beginning with his father's experience, and possibly including Jack Whitby. He'd undoubtedly include Maxi Bailey, whose results were perhaps the most dramatic so far. Her face had brightened, he saw immediately when she came in a week after treatment. She'd been out of the

house twice with her son, and she had the gleeful, self-hugging energy of
a girl with a crush. The other impressive case was the Jamaican housekeeper, who went on and on about his genius.

He figured he needed about twenty cases to make a persuasive argument for the drug. That many positive, unequivocal accounts of people
who'd been healed, and no one at any university would care that he'd
taken license with his research protocol. He was trying to decide on a
medical journal to send the account of the case series. His main goal, he
realized finally, was to get the academic community to take note. Only
through that route would he be able to get attention for the therapy and
establish himself as an expert on the topic. Take that, Guilford Medical
Associates! If you hammer away at a problem for long enough—and without fear—just see what can happen. But twenty case studies would take
time. Even getting a response from a journal would take time. All those
people who might be helped sooner would lose out. He put a phone call
in to the *Baltimore Sun* to see if he could get a health reporter to consider
doing a piece for the public. His regular patients were delayed, the appointments jammed. Even the sick contended with standing-room-only
around the koi pond. The waiting room sweltered like a sauna despite the
air-conditioning.

And that was when the unfortunate coincidence occurred. The grapes
he'd been waiting for arrived. They came in a white refrigerated truck
from a local distributor that parked in the circular driveway. The driver
hauled the coolers, stacked two at a time, into the waiting room on a two-
wheeled handtruck. "Where do you want these?" he wanted to know,
and he obligingly wheeled them through Simon's office to drop them off
in the basement to sit next to the waiting casks. He was young and awkward, with a long neck and hair that curled up at the back of his cap.

Simon pointed impatiently, directing. "Against the wall there." He
raked his hands through his hair, eager to get back to the clinic. Patients
were already angry, having been forced to wait. They needed him. And

this interruption was only a nuisance. Emily would have plenty of qualms about wine—and he'd have to persuade her about the mess and the investment of time and the space taken up in the basement. But the therapy, she'd acknowledge at once, was something different. It was an opportunity to make an impression on medicine as a whole. There was no telling how many patients' lives would be affected by his discovery. And now that the trial had begun, those patients needed him more than ever. He was sorry he'd initiated the wine-making project, which now seemed frivolous. "I didn't realize I'd ordered so much."

"Six more coolers in the truck," the delivery guy informed him. "Frozen. You got to keep 'em cold."

More? Bad timing, and he'd also overdone it, he realized with anguish. "Just fit them," Simon ordered with a loud, exasperated sigh. "I'll take care of it."

He turned to head back to the clinic when the door at the top of the basement stairs creaked open and light from the kitchen flooded the upper landing. Jamie must have heard the truck pull into the drive, he realized. She stepped down the first stairs. In her hand was a book she'd been reading, one finger holding open her page. She watched the driver unload, shifting the coolers sideways, fishtailing, to wedge them against the wall next to the oak casks. Then the driver wanted Simon to sign.

"Wow," she said, looking down at her father. "You got a lot."

She was waiting for him to say something. He looked from her to the delivery guy, who was struggling with the cooler. He raked his hair, feeling pulled back to the clinic where patients were waiting for him with serious concerns and where he was on the verge of what might be one of the biggest medical breakthroughs of the century. His focus had shifted. She couldn't possibly be expected to understand that. He made a noise that sounded like a grunt.

"When are we getting started?" she asked.

"Um," he began. "Why don't you empty out whatever's in the freezer down here. Make room. "

"The freezer?" she repeated. Then, as if he were an idiot and she had made exacting calculations with her eyes: "All that's not going to fit in the freezer."

"Just see how much you can get in there," he advised impatiently. He didn't have time for a side project. It wasn't that he wasn't interested—the idea of engaging Jamie in something still gnawed at him. The scheduling was simply off. He hadn't anticipated the discovery of sulmenamine, but now he had articles to write, reporters to call. Not to mention the fact that he still had to recruit more patients for the trial, and that if he didn't have results soon, he might find himself unable to get his hands on the drug.

"What about the rest?" she wanted to know.

"I don't know," he admitted.

She rocked on her heels. It was a gesture that he recognized—he rocked that way when he had something important to say—and it made his heart ache. "So maybe we should get started tonight."

But he had two appointments lined up for that evening, and there was no way he could get started. There were probably steps and steps of sterilizing wine equipment that had to happen.

"I wish I could explain this better," he said apologetically, "but something's come up. In the clinic. It's very important. It's almost too big to put into words. I'm onto something, a new treatment, and I can't just put it off. Not when it'll make a big difference in people's lives."

"Oh," she said.

"So I can't do the wine right now. I realize it may be a disappointment. And I know what you're going to say—I told you so. But it's really just a postponement. The grapes will keep. Most, at least. They're already chilled. No worries, see?"

"So when?" she pressed him.

But it was impossible for him to estimate. He was standing in front of the crates with the tubing and the siphons, the large, handmade casks.

"I can smell them," she said, her nose tilted upward.

He inhaled, but he detected nothing. "You can? I don't smell anything."

"Like summer, when you're really young." She breathed in deeply, her head tipping, her thin chest rising. "I think I'll remember that smell my whole life."

He smiled at her quizzically, apologetically.

"Your nose must be better than mine," he said. "I promise we'll do it. We're just postponing. We can always order more grapes. You understand, don't you?" She didn't say another word as she turned to go back upstairs. "Don't you?"

"I don't care."

There were patients ready for him in the exam rooms. Others had already grown bored with the magazines in the waiting room. The tension—the tug on his expertise—was palpable. That today would happen to be the day for the damn truck to arrive was unfortunate, but he would not be deterred. In fact, he took some satisfaction realizing the test of the new drug was the most important thing. He couldn't be distracted right now by starting a new hobby. All the avenues of his life seemed to lead to this one moment, and he felt he had no choice but to focus. He had to know, for certain, whether he had stumbled upon a cure. "I have a responsibility," he called after her, but she'd already shut the door at the top of the stairs.

Part Four

S he tucked her hair behind her ear, just once, as she checked her reflection in the dark sheen of the windows. The luxury Acela, according to the brochure in the seat-back pocket, hit rates as fast as one hundred fifty miles an hour in its glide along the eastern seaboard. The ride never seemed like what she imagined one-fifty should feel like. She always expected a rush, a burst of surprise, the outside world peeling away as it might from a space shuttle, the train itself as quiet and forceful as the interior of a bullet. Instead, in the dark, the Acela's speed felt about as fast as a train should be. The high-speed line shaved only about ten minutes off the time of the regular Metroliner. She had departed 30th Street Station in Philadelphia at 8:47 p.m. on her way back to Baltimore, and she glanced at the brochure to see how Amtrak's PR work had shaped up since Frith had allowed itself to be outbid in revamping the company's image.

She'd been seeing him for six weeks, since she'd come back from Florida. For the second half of July and all of August, she'd contrived appearances at conferences in Philadelphia, meetings in Trenton, Princeton, Long Island. After each, she ducked out as quickly as possible to meet Will at a hotel. In Philly, she was able to see his new two-bedroom apartment on the second story of a brick rowhouse on Pine Street. All of the quick excuses, the short, cryptic phone calls from work, the furtive plans, seemed as unremarkable as they were necessary.

The Acela raced on in the dark. Emily considered getting up and walking to the club car, but she stayed so she wouldn't lose her seat. She didn't marvel about any of the details of having an affair—except regarding the fact that in seeing him, she had stumbled upon a sense of relief that felt something like pleasure.

In many ways, Will was the same as he'd been years ago. That first meeting, Thursday afternoon, as scheduled at the unassuming, low-key café in Dupont Circle, he'd arrived in his khaki garb, appearing nervous, running his palm over his head-stubble. She wasn't sure yet what she thought of that gesture. He sat down at the table, and they ordered iced tea.

"So, twenty-four years," she said. She had that feeling again of being the older one, the mature one.

"Hard to believe, isn't it?"

"Where did you go?" she asked. "After."

After they'd split, he'd fled New York and traveled around the world. "I was a little wrecked, you know," he said with grim remembrance. *Is this what this meeting is all about?* she wondered with dread. *Does he want to make sure I know the damage I did? Is he after some kind of apology?* But he didn't stop speaking for her to interject. He had wandered from one country to the next, taken trains to cities whose names he couldn't pronounce, bunked in hostels with travelers who shared their wine but didn't speak a word of English. He had his camera with him, of course, and photographed people he met, a Mulam baker's family with whom he'd lived for a month in Mongolia. In Tibet, he watched young women carving flower sculptures out of butter for the festival of Chunga Choepa. But there was reason for everything, a destination in store for him. *So like him to put it that way,* she thought, *as if things happened* despite *him, as if the breeze could carry him around.* The first thing that happened, he said, was that the photographs, which became part of a show that hung in Amsterdam for a while, were reproduced in *Geo,* the German version of *National Geographic.* And then the second thing: In Morocco, he met Lindsay, who was teaching English, and with the money he'd made, they came back to the States together. They got married right away. She was a language instructor in the Philadelphia public school system. Their daughter, who was born soon after Will and Lindsay wed, was Rachel. Then came Anne. At home, he earned money as a designer of brochures and newsletters for nonprofits.

"You don't photograph for those publications?"

"Never." He grinned. "I still like to do my own thing." No, it was clear he wasn't after an apology. Here was a man who couldn't conceive of regrets.

He was curious about her husband, so she bragged about Simon. She told him about Simon's practice, located on the north side of the house, and how he'd been named among Baltimore's Top Docs. She didn't mention that he was still in Florida with his parents, too much detail, it seemed, but she painted him generously, describing his patients' admiration and the gifts they brought back and how he'd once saved a patient on a plane. Will marveled at all of it.

"So tell me about Lindsay," she said finally.

He cleared his throat. "Actually, we separated nine months ago."

"I'm sorry," Emily said, embarrassed to have presented her life with such a glow.

"It's okay. We've just gone different directions. There's only the paperwork now."

"Which direction did you go?" she asked.

"Wayward, I guess."

She stared at him in surprise. "You were unfaithful?"

"Oh no. At least not in practice. I just felt like I didn't understand anymore what our marriage was about," he explained. His hand, running over the stubble again, stopped in its thoughtful caress, and he sat forward. "I'd lost the thread, you know? When we sat down to talk about it, she didn't know what we were about, either. I wanted more intensity, I don't know, more gut-wrenching honesty about where we were in our lives, the changes we were facing. What things meant. She wanted more living, less processing, and it just didn't seem we were connecting. Or connected. I kept pushing, and she kept getting annoyed, and we just couldn't get along."

Emily felt again that shudder she'd felt years ago, when Will had seemed so startling and so dangerous. He could tell you about himself without worrying about judgment, ask a question that felt like it was tunneling right into your chest. And even though she had taken great pains to present herself, she could feel the way he looked at her, same as ever, with what felt like endless, bottomless admiration.

"How about you?" he asked. "It's clear you're at the top of your game. You're a partner. That's amazing."

"Mostly a matter of showing up every day."

"You and your Cal Ripken."

"I hardly compare." She laughed. "I did get to meet him though. Frith handled an account for a Maryland bank, and we wanted to use him as a spokesperson. He's charming."

"I got all misty when he broke Lou Gehrig's record."

She smiled. "You? Sports? I wouldn't have guessed."

"I don't follow the games. It's the pageantry I like. The symbols. Americana. How we have a weakness for streaks. For iron men."

It was so strange, sitting with the Will of now, imagining the Will of then. The core seemed the same, the iterations between their meetings impossible to fathom. "You used to hate all of that *Americana*. The commercialism, the consumerism. Remember how you wouldn't do the ad?"

He laughed. "I couldn't figure out how I fit in. I couldn't change any of it. And I didn't want to be part of helping it grow. I guess I've gained an appreciation. Anyway, Ms. Partner of the Firm, proud of your accomplishments? I'm sure your father would be."

"Ah." She smiled. "I'm sure he'd say I settled."

"He approved of success. Ambition. Pulling yourself up by your bootstraps."

Then, for some reason, the way she'd dared to present herself seemed false—even shameful. "I have a confession." She played with the nipped-off wrapper from her straw, rolling it into a ball between her fingers. "I wasn't exactly truthful the other day about how he died. He took his own life. I don't make a point of it with most people because it puts a damper on things. Who he was. But there it is."

Will seemed to take a long breath. "I didn't know."

"He was never diagnosed," she continued, "but I believe now he was bipolar. People back then said moody, but some days he was throwing parties and spending money and running off to Milan, or trying to phone Andy Warhol, and then sometimes he didn't want to see anybody, and then he was impossible to get along with. Didn't even seem to come out of his studio. There was nobody to keep up with all his swings after my mother died."

"Ah," Will sighed, and she was touched not by his tone, but that he knew so well where she came from. "Judith, too?"

"A bunch of years before him. That was a brain hemorrhage, which, thank God, was quick. A little while before Simon and I met. Her last years were—well, her priorities had sort of melted into my father's career, and she was a little, I don't know, lost? I'm glad she never knew about his suicide," she added, even more wryly than she intended. "She hated for things to go to waste."

"I'm surprised about Al," Will said, pensive. "That must've been hard. For Aileen, too."

Aileen. It was almost strange hearing her sister's name, realizing that they were still connected to each other. She'd grown up thinking of Aileen as the model for everything—what kind of music to like, how short a skirt should be, the tone of voice to use when answering the phone—and yet she'd always felt the threat, like a distant pulse, that Aileen would be moving away. Aileen was a tall girl, like Emily, with an intelligent face. People were always commenting on her brains, but she must have struggled to feel at ease, Emily realized later. Her hair was kinky and she spent hours blowing it dry to tame it. She battled acne, and she had an awkward, loud laugh that hit many registers like a bell's peal. What she possessed, ironically, was a singing voice that made music teachers swoon. Every year she was assigned leads in productions of Gilbert and Sullivan, and yet she had to be bribed and threatened by her parents to participate. She hated being part of anything mainstream. Emily sat in the dark of the community theaters, awed by the rippling melodic sounds her sister was able to produce, eager for the applause that would come, and hoping—just hoping—she might get to go backstage after the show. Emily just wanted to be included, but Aileen hated all the hoopla and got her revenge when she discovered her life's passion, joining antiwar protests and marching for women's rights and organizing demonstrations for Mayan communities in Guatemala. She fought with Al and Judith about their self-centered desire to rise in society and their shameful lack of social awareness, until Al threatened to cut her off financially. And through it all, Emily was aware of that drumbeat in her own chest, counting the moments until her sister's departure. "Aileen might still think it was a heart attack. I'm not sure. She's in South America somewhere. You could say we're out of touch."

"She needed to get away, huh?"

Emily sighed. "There are people in the world who believe they serve humankind. Like they have a higher calling to help the truly disenfranchised and dispossessed. They're not always able to be there in the simplest ways for the people closest to them. Ever noticed that?"

"Gandhi apparently neglected his wife. I read that somewhere."

She looked at him again, as if she couldn't imagine how the Will she knew might have information to cite. "Anyway, enough about all that. People don't know about the suicide, so please, um . . ." Her eyes implored. "The obits reported it as a heart attack."

"Loyal of you to keep his secret."

This was what she'd remembered about Will: He had a way of giving back to you your best even when you were most uncomfortable. She looked down again, rolling the paper between her fingers, thinking that she much preferred the version of the heart attack than the one of the man self-destructing, and that it was unfortunate that her mother was dead because parenting had turned out to be an inscrutable practice, and even poor advice now would be better than none at all. At that moment, she even missed Aileen and all of her sister's righteousness, though she couldn't possibly have said why. Glancing at Will, she remembered what it felt like, lying in his little New York apartment with the pipes crisscrossing over their heads, as he snapped pictures of her. A prickle crept up her neck and across her scalp, and she suspected then that she'd sleep with him again, not only that she'd want him, but that it would feel right, and that there would be no surprise. About as fast as a train should be. "I'm happy to see you," she blurted. "There. You've got my real confession."

"I've got one, actually," he said. "It wasn't really a coincidence that we ran into each other the other day." He was smiling. "I knew you worked there. I was just hoping I might see you."

"You did?"

"I wasn't anticipating a physical confrontation in front of the building, but I'm glad it was you I almost knocked over."

"You mean me and not somebody else?" She laughed. "You did almost take me out on the sidewalk."

"All these years, I've wondered where you were, if you were happy."

"I've wondered, too," she said, remembering how he'd almost been present as she pared the bottoms of candles. "About you."

He sat back, ran his hand over the stubble on his head. "My family's been my focus. Lindsay, my daughters." He looked out the window of the café. "My photography, the newsletters, even traveling, everything's been secondary to my home life. It's a bit of a shock to be getting divorced."

"I'm sorry," she said again.

He looked back at her, and he seemed to sigh. "You look beautiful, you know. Even more than I imagined. I wasn't sure if you'd have aged. I wasn't even sure I'd recognize you," he said. "You seem good."

She smiled in gratitude, another shy smile. "I'd say it's been hard, in its own way." The waiter dropped off their check and hovered, making it clear that the shift was ending and he was eager to get them out. Will reached for his wallet. She picked up the tab and waved him off. "You came all the way to find me," she said. "I'll get this one."

"No, let me. I almost knocked you down."

On the plane, traveling back from Florida, she had anticipated a quick return to the office after meeting him, but they lingered in front of the café, delaying the imminent good-bye. Shake hands? she wondered. Kiss on the cheek? She no longer remembered what it had been like to kiss him. It was sad how the mind erased what was once essential but left you with an image, something random, a trick with an orange. What did she need with that?

"I've missed you, Hemily." Of course he'd said "Emily," but it sounded like he'd named her himself.

"You too. This was nice."

"I'd ask you to walk back with me, but it might seem . . . unseemly," he apologized.

Men had hit on her over the years. There was a trainer at the gym who tended to touch her a little more than was necessary, and once, astoundingly, a reporter who followed her after a press conference whose "follow-up questions" included an out-and-out invitation back to his apartment. There was a drunken congressman who put his hand on her ass in a coatroom. She'd laughed at them and ignored their advances. She considered herself savvy enough to realize their interest satisfied her ego. Indulging any more than that would be—well, what would be the point? And yet she had a feeling that everything was different with Will, as they stood awkwardly in front of the café. Maybe it was that she already knew him or maybe it was the poignancy of the question he had posed—"Happily?"—that had made her take note of the stillness in her chest. She looked at him, that twinkling expression in his eyes.

"I'd walk you back," she had replied, "and I wouldn't be offended."

"Oh," he had said, just like the Will she'd known who didn't know anything and was always slow to understand.

"You came all this way." She had directed in a soft voice that left no ambiguity, "I'll walk there with you."

The Acela slowed though it didn't stop in Wilmington. Emily glanced up as travelers edged by her, apparently changing cars. A thirty-somethingish woman in a short gray skirt with a silk blouse wheeled a suitcase through the aisle. She had an air of self-importance that Emily keyed into at once. Then the woman turned and stood over the seat next to Emily.

"Anyone sitting here?"

With an upturned palm, Emily invited her to take the seat. The woman heaved her suitcase onto the overhead rack and settled herself. Emily turned to the window, absorbed in thought. On the way to Will's hotel, that first time, they'd barely spoken. And then upstairs. He released the lock with a magnetic card, flicked on a lamp, and she stepped into the room, barely breathing. The door clicked shut, and then he turned to her and held her face in his hands. So familiar: the feeling of his fingers on her cheeks, his palms on either side of her chin. When he looked into her eyes, she felt like she was very small, and for a moment, she thought she might cry. Her throat tightened, and she felt weak, all her bones fragile in his hands. Instead, she threw her arms around him and kissed him. Hard. He'd pulled back, surprised, and looked at her, but she kissed him again as if she could not take his tongue deep enough into her mouth, suck enough of the taste of him out of his lips.

She waited for the feeling that she was doing something she'd regret later, but it never came. In the hotel bed, the change in her life felt as welcome as an unraveling. She felt it: the yank on the exact thread in the knitting, rows of careful stitching coming undone one by one. Only when she left did her stomach surprise her, bounding in a loop-de-loop of uncertainty. He wanted to walk her downstairs to say good-bye, but she insisted she should leave the room alone. "People know me" were the words that came out of her mouth, and while they were true about a certain segment of D.C., and it was almost the dinner hour when that element would be leaving work, they couldn't account for the sensation in her belly, like the thrashing of a fish. In the descending elevator, she reached into her bag for her sunglasses, which seemed appropriate for anonymity, but her hand found her cell phone first. To her surprise, she called home. Jamie, who was alone, answered after several rings.

"I'm on my way home," Emily said, turning slightly toward the wall as a man wearing a gray pinstripe suit stepped into the elevator.

"Yeah?" Jamie replied, sounding bored. "All right."

Why had she bothered calling? It was clear Jamie couldn't care less. Emily stared into the wood-grain paneling of the elevator. Where did she belong? Home had become—there wasn't even a word for it. Simon wasn't due back from his parents' for at least another day. Jamie was probably having a grand old time entertaining herself in the house, maybe getting ready for full-body tattoos. Emily gripped the phone. Something had compelled her to call, and she groped to keep the conversation going. An idea occurred to her. "So I thought maybe I'd bring that rotisserie stuff you like. Boston Market?"

"If that's what you want," Jamie answered in a monotone. "I already ate."

"How about I bring it anyway. If you want some later." Jamie didn't respond with any kind of enthusiasm. In fact, she didn't respond at all. The elevator stopped at a floor, opened, but whoever had pushed the button had already chosen the stairs. The doors closed again. Emily still wasn't ready to hang up. "So whaddya do today?"

"Um, I don't know. Not much. Read a book. Watched TV."

Then, the elevator doors parted to reveal the lobby. "Okay," she said into the phone, stepping past the man who held the doors wide with one hand. She gripped the phone. She was trying, wasn't she? Would she have to keep trying until she got a real response? She ducked her head as she passed the main desk. "So yes to the chicken?"

As soon as she hung up, she reached into her bag and put on her sunglasses. It wasn't remorse she felt, she realized. It was the shock of having done something that needed defending. It rattled one's identity. She was standing on line at Boston Market, adding to her order a side of mashed potatoes, as she realized that what had happened with Will didn't feel like a betrayal of Simon. In fact, it felt separate from her marriage, connected to the past and to parts of herself that had once been—brighter, shinier, more filled with light. In a way she couldn't explain, what had happened with Will felt like she should have known it was coming. But there she was, heading home with her rotisserie offering, and what came to her were the words *Mean people suck.* She thought them in Jamie's voice, and when her own voice fought back, *You couldn't possibly understand,* she felt her stomach flip again.

What she hadn't anticipated was that the thing with Will would continue, but she discovered she was in its grip. He had stayed on in D.C.

for an additional week, and she'd left work early every day, like a person slightly crazed, to make love with him in his Dupont Circle hotel room. Then, in the following weeks, he'd driven back and forth between Philadelphia and wherever she'd arranged meetings, and she'd rushed off after her speaking engagements to meet him. He entered her slowly, watching every motion of her face, and she responded like a person wracked with hunger. Their bodies twisted up, their knees interlocked, his calf muscle fitting like a puzzle piece against the instep of her foot—all of it felt right. That admiring expression of his—God, it flipped a switch inside her. How long had it been since she'd just smiled and smiled? Wondrous, incredulous, she found herself where she'd never been, kneeling before him in the shower, the stream of water running over her face, feeling the water mat her hair and thinking that she had never, until that moment, so desperately wanted someone to receive what she had to give. And all of it seemed a matter of survival.

Now she was a woman on a train, coming back from a conference in Philadelphia with quickly showered legs and lips bruised from kissing. The Acela had not moved. The lights blinked for a moment, and the air-conditioning system sighed. Then the electricity revved up again and then slowed. An overhead announcement apologized for the delay, the result of a mechanical problem that would be fixed shortly. She smoothed her skirt. All the heaviness of her life with Simon seemed further away than ever. *Taking care of myself, that's what it is.*

The woman sitting next to her on the train was straining her neck and looking around for a conductor. "This isn't supposed to happen on the Acela," the woman complained. "We're supposed to get there sooner, not forty-five minutes late."

"They should reimburse us," Emily commented, "the difference between this and the Metroliner."

But the woman didn't stand up to demand her refund, and when the conductor passed through, she merely asked the projected time of their arrival. Once, long ago, Emily had chosen Simon because she imagined that life with him had a comprehensible trajectory. *Don't you get it? There are no assurances.* For once, she didn't mind the delay on the train. She was in no rush to be home.

When she was with Will, it felt like they'd tunneled back in time to the den of his old basement apartment. But they were also better than before, she thought. He was more knowledgeable, perhaps more confident. She was able to be more tolerant of him, appreciative of his rough edges and less judgmental. He still managed to suprise her. They were naked in bed in a hotel in Wilmington, Delaware, eating blueberries one by one out of a cardboard container. He told her that what he loved best about her was the sense of something childlike just under the surface. "Kind of careful and watching," he said. "You're checking out life's goodies, but you're not sure." *Goodies,* she thought. *What a word.* She considered herself someone who was careful, yes, but she didn't feel sorry for herself. She must have stared, because immediately he smoothed her hair away from her forehead, cajoling away the effects of his comment. "Did I say something bad? I didn't mean anything negative. Don't be mad. I didn't mean to make you mad. Are you mad?" He kissed her softly on the lips, taking back what he'd said, moving the carton of blueberries from between their bodies, asking forgiveness with his tongue.

But he was right, she knew. She was a careful watcher. She was still thinking of the comment when she left that afternoon to give a talk in the gilded second-story conference room of the fancy Hotel du Pont in downtown Wilmington. It was a presentation she'd delivered countless times, this afternoon to a gathering of young women inductees to the American Public Relations Council. "Believe in your clients," she advised. "Sounds simple, but the deeper your conviction the better you'll project them." She watched heads nod. "Know their strengths, but be

aware of their weaknesses," she said, and illustrated with the case study
of a public relations team that had attempted to glamorize a seafood dis-
tribution company as "eco-friendly" without first investigating its docu-
mented maritime infractions. "Know your audience," she told them. The
attendees (pert, eager communications majors; followers of at least one
daytime television soap opera; readers of at least one self-help book in
the last year; subscribers to at least one women's lifestyle magazine) took
furious notes. "Understand the reach and power of each media vehicle,"
she advised, watching the reaction, and launching into an anecdote about
a young mayoral candidate who'd based a creative, energetic and successful campaign solely on talk radio appearances. Last, she told them,
"Know exactly where you intend to head when you put your best foot
forward."

She made her final point with the example of a prominent restaurant
that had overshot its grand opening PR, instantly ruining its reputation
by being unable to fulfill demand, but her thoughts began to stray as she
recounted the story. In her own life, did she know where she was heading? She stammered as her gaze happened to fall on a redheaded woman
sitting in the front row wearing a black and white polka-dotted headband.
An impressive, daring choice, Emily thought, for someone with hair that
color. The woman's pen had paused, and she seemed to be smiling at
Emily. What was the goal Emily was aiming for? Did she need a plan?
The spots of the headband popped in Emily's field of vision, and she
revised her opinion about the style. *Cartoonish,* she thought, *indulgent.*
Was she missing out on life's goodies because she was so intent on having
a plan? Emily set her gaze beyond the red-haired woman and wondered
midsentence if she'd just misspoken in front of the entire audience. "And
that's all," she concluded shakily. "Welcome to the field."

There was a burst of pleased-sounding applause as Emily stepped
away from the microphone and began to collect her belongings. When
she looked up, the redheaded woman stood in her way. The dots of the

headband reminded her of a Lichtenstein from someone's apartment, from the era of her father's parties. Suddenly, she found them jarring and impetuous.

"Excuse me," the woman stammered, extending a slim hand. "I just had to say, that was great. I thought yours was the best presentation all day. Most useful, at least."

"Thanks," Emily replied, glancing toward the door. "I hope it helps."

"I remember you," the woman went on. "I used to work for Nestor and we contracted with Frith. You made a great impression. Even our CEO was, like, wow. That woman knows her stuff. Nestor was going under."

"After a lawsuit on behalf of the shareholders? I remember." Emily nodded. She realized she held the woman's headband as a strike against her. She wasn't even sure why. Then she checked her watch. "Well, thanks."

"Would it be possible—I'm changing fields—I was wondering whether I could sit down with you for an informational interview. Just to get your thoughts on the field and what I should be doing?"

"Sorry," Emily said. "Wish I could say yes, but it's an issue of time. If I sat down with everyone who wanted to . . . Don't you have an adviser who can help? A former boss? Someone who knows you and your particular skill set?"

"Well, I guess."

Emily hoisted her bag onto her shoulder. "Excuse me, I do apologize," she said. "There's somewhere I have to be." She liked to think there was a time she might have said yes, but she couldn't indulge the woman right now. For the first time in what seemed like forever, she was the one at the top of her own agenda. "I like your headband," she said, moving past the woman toward the door. She hailed a cab from the lobby and traveled back to Will for more.

When she was with him, she felt like she could see her life more clearly.

Her marriage, with all of its ill-defined distresses, gained lines around its edges. It also felt far away, like some other country, where there was another code of behavior and even her name sounded different. All the strife with Jamie seemed remote too, and she began to convince herself, thinking from a distance, that the adolescent furor might be general and nonspecific and not directed at *her*, merely one of those uncomfortable phases that humans have to pass through, like teething.

But their appetite for each other was almost insatiable. A week after Wilmington, they met in Annapolis. And then half a week later, they were lying together in a rumpled Hilton bed in Princeton, New Jersey, having just made love. Shortly, she would have to get up and get dressed and take a cab to the train station to head back to Baltimore. "Is he aware of where you are? Does he ask?" Will wondered. His hand rested on the inside of her naked thigh.

She propped her head on one hand, with her elbow dug into a pillow, and studied the lines of his face, the ridges at the corners of his eyes. They looked meaningful, she decided, even the color of his eyes, which were green flecked with brown. In another bed, in a different city, she had listened to him talk about Lindsay, and the strains that had led to their separation. Lindsay had become a vegetarian and gotten into Reiki and then began exploring a kind of ritual chanting. Each venture had seemed isolated and even intriguing until Will had begun to put them together and realized there was a pattern of retreat: Lindsay against the rest of the world. And then she had become short-tempered with Will and distracted and she didn't want to have sex, it seemed, ever. She worried about her body, but she wasn't interested in his declarations of approval or his reassurances. She didn't know what she was searching for or what she was struggling against, and she didn't talk with him about it, and so there was no room for him in her journey. Emily listened to all of this with wonder (laughing out loud at the image of the woman doing chants), but mostly she marveled at his ability to interpret even the smallest gestures.

She had not shared much about Simon or Jamie. "Funny how you can call him 'he' and I know exactly who you're talking about."

"Well?"

"Simon," she reflected, "is famous for his kindness. Great, mind-boggling acts of generosity. But it's pathological niceness."

Will seemed to think that was funny. "How's that?"

"Really. One time, the cleaning woman—I'm sorry, yes, don't hate me, we have a woman who comes and cleans once a week—anyway, it was her birthday. Her fiftieth. Simon went out for a gift and came back with a flat-screen TV."

"So?"

"So a picture frame would have sufficed. A nice robe from Macy's. The point is, it's all show. He's angry."

Will traced a shape along her naked leg with a single finger. "A flat-screen says he's angry? I don't get it. Did *you* want the TV?"

"It's hard to explain. Tons of energy, excessive, over-the-top generosity, all for strangers." Her gaze fell on the hotel TV. In its gray screen, she saw the reflection of their forms on the bed. She wasn't sure she could make Will understand. She wasn't even sure she understood. What she shared with Simon had the changeability of an Escher painting—was that a pattern of birds you were looking at or the heads of wizened men?

She knew deep in her core that Simon loved her. Loved her and needed her. And that they were bound by some shared image, however hazy, of what they'd intended when they'd gotten married in the marble, two-story hall of the Peabody Conservatory with four-foot candlesticks and garlands of roses and a veritable orchestra. Like it or not, they were also bound by what they'd suffered. There was an intimacy—maybe that wasn't the right word—a common understanding, even in the things that remained unspoken. But the fact of that love didn't make a relationship, it turned out. Something fundamental was missing. Every time she turned around, he was finding ingenious and devious ways to make her uncomfortable or inconvenienced, all the while orchestrating a show so that he managed to come off to everyone else as a nice guy. "It's kindness past the point of being appropriate," she said. "And all the time, it's like he's sticking it to me."

"Ah," Will said, nodding. With a single finger, he traced the shape of her kneecap, and then a long trail down the front of her shinbone. "What's he angry about?"

"Probably that I don't believe he's so nice," she said simply. "No, he doesn't know where I am."

Will, quiet and thoughtful, lifted her hand and pressed it to his lips. She wondered whether he was forming some sort of judgment, but when he spoke, he surprised her with a change of subject. "Want to meet Anne?" he asked.

"Anne?" she repeated.

"My daughter. The younger one. She's taking the year off from school, and she's leaving for California. I'd love it if you could meet her before she goes."

He wanted to introduce his daughter? To her, the married woman he was sleeping with? Typical Will Garth, she thought, suddenly annoyed. Will of the days of yore, who had a stirring of feeling and wanted to live it to the hilt. "I'm not sure we're ready for that," she said. As right as it felt to be with him, she continued to be prudent. She'd spent quite enough of her professional career salvaging the reputations of people caught mid-affair to know the wisdom of good judgment and timing. She'd person-ally advised countless powerful figures who suddenly found themselves in danger of becoming defined by their public trysts or doomed by their idiotic licentious text messages. Even as she counseled them about how to manage the press and how to rebuild their images, she believed, deep down, they must have craved some kind of relief from the lives they were living. What they wanted was for the world to take care of their choices for them. She was not about to be so careless. She insisted on being dis-

creet. Each hotel room she booked was a cab ride away from her conference. They never ate in restaurants, ordering room service instead.
They departed separately. But she realized that even more than being
concerned about having the relationship come to light, she wanted the
opportunity to digest what was happening between them.

"It's just that she's leaving."

Emily said nothing. Was he about to give her some speech about
throwing all caution to the wind? She wasn't ready. Then something occurred to her: "She knows about me?"

"I don't hide things from them." He lay back and his hand rubbed the
velvet stubble on his scalp. "My kids or Lindsay."

Emily felt stunned and suddenly embarrassed. "Lindsay knows?"

"I didn't give anybody a play-by-play, but it's been a month and a half.
I had to tell people where I kept running off to and why I was busy."

She said nothing. She hadn't been able to control the flow of information, what was said and to whom. And if she met his daughter, would she
eventually have to meet the ex-wife? And didn't that catapult them to the
question she knew was looming: Where was all of this headed?

"What does Lindsay say?" she asked. "Are you imagining we'll all play
Scrabble together, the guy, the new lover, the ex-wife, and everybody's
fine with it?"

He laughed and rolled on top of her, cupping her ass with his hands.
"First thing, you're not a new lover, you're an old lover. And to be honest,
I'm not sure Lindsay would be so comfortable hanging out. She knew I
always had a thing for you. But my daughters want me and Lindsay to
be happy, and they understand. And they're grown up enough to understand how we came to this decision together."

Grown up, she thought. Of course they were. They were all reasonable
and rational people with vocabularies that could pry loose and offer up
their feelings on silver platters. They were able to have sane conversations, and each of them cared what the other one was going through. If

she told Simon—well, there was no telling what he would do. Something drastic, she was sure, and she dreaded the melodrama. She dreaded having to explain his own behavior to him, what his actions said versus what he claimed he meant. And of course he'd refuse to own up to any of it. But telling Jamie—a nervous wave rolled through her stomach again. Explaining to Jamie would be another story altogether. She'd have to present herself properly, and of course, Jamie would never be able to fathom any fault in Simon. Emily would be culpable for yet another motherly transgression, and how would they ever manage between them to mend this one? She knew a woman who'd left a husband who *beat* her and the daughter still blamed the mother for the breakup of the marriage. "I can't meet your family," she stated.

"They understand what's going on," Will reassured her. "There's no pressure. It doesn't change anything between us."

"Exactly what *is* going on?" she asked. "I'm not even separated yet." But there it was. As she heard her own words, she knew she'd crossed over to the other side. The word "yet" hung there between them, with all of its hesitation, all of its promise. She shivered.

"No, that's true," he said.

They were silent for a moment. Then she demanded, "Doesn't it bother you?"

"A little bit, of course," he admitted. "But I can't help it. I want to see you."

She considered the flattery, but skepticism overtook her. "There's some thrill, is that what it is?" Her tone accused. "You're proving something?" She hadn't considered how she might play into his needs. She hadn't even thought about his needs, whether he had come to find her in order to mend the hurt from their breakup so many years before. Were they each experiencing a completely different relationship? Was she reevaluating her entire life while he was living out some trivial ego thing?

But leave it to Will to take a conversation seriously, to think over the

underlying impulses and own up. "I don't know. Maybe the tiniest little
bit. I'm human, aren't I? I certainly wasn't out to prove anything when I
came looking for you, but I'm sure, on some level, I was curious."

"Whether you could sweep me off my feet?"

"Whether you'd be even a little interested. But if it were only that, we
wouldn't still be here after so many weeks, right? So many hotels? We
wouldn't be in—" He looked around, feigning disorientation. "Where
are we again?"

She grinned. "Princeton."

"Yeah, Princeton. And there's this." He leaned into her, kissing her
neck, her jaw, her lips, and she let him until he pulled back to look at her.
"You tell me."

Well, so what, she thought, if the past threw various shadows on the
present. How could it not? They weren't new lovers. They were old lovers. And wasn't it bound to be complex? The point of it all, of figuring
out how to take care of herself, was to stop doing exactly what she'd been
doing, which wasn't working, and to seek something new.

"I might be, soon," she suggested, and she didn't have to choose a
word, "separated," "divorced," "out," to make him understand. "Then
I'd meet your family."

"Soon, then," he echoed.

Nobody met her at Baltimore Penn Station when she returned from
Princeton. She wouldn't have expected it, and she was relieved to slip
into an anonymous cab. The hour was pushing nine. As the cab pulled
into the circular drive on Greenway, she spotted the line of cars parked
alongside the north end of the house. Almost nine p.m. and he was still
seeing patients.

Once, a long time ago, when Jamie was a toddler, they'd talked about
cutting back their hours, making plans, having family meals. They'd both

agreed that it made sense and sounded important. But they had the conversation and, as if the acknowledgment of intent had been sufficient,
they proceeded with their routines as before. Simon, quite possibly, became even busier. Now they had developed terrible habits and they no
longer apologized. But letting herself into the house, she could hear the
muffled music of Jamie's stereo coming from the bedroom upstairs, and
she felt uneasy. Here's what an affair did to you: It made you feel like you
were intruding on your own space. Even the clanking of her keys felt like
a disturbance. She wondered about Jamie, hibernating upstairs, certain
that it would hardly matter that Emily was home.

What crept up on her, however, was the smell. So faint at first, she
couldn't tell whether she was imagining it, but with every breath there it
was, a vaguely perceptible sourness in the air. She opened the refrigerator, peeled back the foil on a dish that Lorraine had left, and sniffed it.
She opened the milk, wafting the air over its spout toward her face with
a few quick flutters of her hand. She took the tops off the juice bottles,
smelled them. She poked into the vegetable bin and, not knowing what
else to do, threw a questionable broccoli head into the garbage.

She turned as Jamie came tromping down the stairs.

"Where's your father?"

"Downstairs, I guess."

"This late? Have you left your laundry down here?"

"My laundry?"

She sniffed the dishrags, the sponge, the garbage. "Do you smell it?"

"Yeah," Jamie agreed, "it stinks."

She lifted the blue garbage can out from under the sink, tied the kitchen
bag closed and heaved it out in her fist, far from her body, as though she
were holding a feral animal by the neck. Reaching way back into the cabinet, emerging with a bottle of bleach, she took the blue can out on the
back patio and poured bleach directly into the bottom. She unwound the
patio hose with its firearm nozzle and fired it at the bleach. She came back

in, appearing satisfied, but after a few moments, the stench surrounded her again. She sniffed the garbage disposal. She dragged a broom against the bottom edge of the refrigerator and smelled against the wall. Getting down on her hands and knees, she took a sponge and scrubbed the baseboard of the cooking island, feeling for sticky spots where food might have dribbled.

"What are you doing?"

"It's like something died back here." She scrubbed, aware of Jamie watching her. The girl was just standing there, ogling, while she scoured on her knees. "You can help, you know. It wouldn't be completely beyond the pale for you to pitch in. Do you need an embossed invitation? The whole summer at home, and you barely even go outside. What do you do all the time? Holed up in your room like some kind of squirrel or something. Piercing your belly button. I mean, really. Don't you have friends around?" She looked up from her knees. "Do we need to be worried about you?"

"It's downstairs," Jamie said coolly.

"What's downstairs?"

"The smell. It's in the basement."

"How would you know?" But she could tell then that her daughter was right. The smell seemed to be rising through the floorboards. Even as she turned toward the basement door, the stench grew more pronounced. "What have you done down there?"

"Why do you always think it's me?"

"What's down there, Jamie?" Her voice became more threatening.

"You think I'm the problem. Don't deny it 'cause I know it's true."

"I don't know what problem you're talking about."

"You do," Jamie replied.

"Keep your voice down. Your father still has patients downstairs."

"'Keep your voice down,'" Jamie taunted in a high, nasal voice. Her head waggled. Her shoulders jutted up and down, mockingly, like a marionette.

"Don't be obnoxious."

"*'Don't you have friends around?'*"

"Enough!" Emily snarled. "That's it, or you're grounded." She'd never hit her daughter, but the sensation that flooded her felt like she'd touched a live wire, and she wanted to lash out at the small features, the straight-cut bangs, that taunting face. The anger rose right into her tooth pulp so that she could feel it, pulsating under the enamel of gritted teeth.

"*'Should I be worried about you?'* Hard to be *worried* when you aren't even ever here."

"That's it! To your room," Emily shouted, a rigid, wavering index pointing up the stairs.

Jamie glared, and then ran out of the room. Emily turned back to the kitchen, the open cabinet, the sponge on the floor, the bottle of bleach. She smoothed back a piece of hair that had fallen into her face, braced herself and reached for the door to the basement.

Of all sensory assaults, Emily most detested strong smells. She could not abide glaring lights, overly loud music, those cars with their woofers turned up so that you could feel the bass of their music in the small of your back, people who stood too close and couldn't modulate their voices. Eighteen inches of personal space, it was only fair. All of the senses, it was true, had limits. Beyond that limit, the input became offensive, uncomfortable. But above all, offensive smells were untenable.

As she stepped down the stairs to the basement, the smell accosted her. It seemed as though it reached through her nasal passages all the way into the back of her head. What had seemed sour in the air was cloyingly sweet as she descended into it, and dense, a confusing wave of sensations. On its tail was undeniable rot, a pungent smell with the cider of body odor. It was not healthy.

She held her breath as she passed through the basement, stepping past all of the shelves and their tidy Tupperwares. She didn't need to look to know that the bin marked "Baby" still sat on the shelf among all the other random bins. It made her cringe to remember it. Simon had packed it shortly after Caleb died, and only once in all the years since had she allowed herself into the basement to look at its contents. She'd been pregnant with Jamie at the time, and something—must have been hormones, she decided later—made her want to peek at Caleb's things again. But how miserable it had been, prying off the lid, catching sight of a few clothes she had once dressed him in and stuffed toys that had once nestled in his crib. There was his birth certificate with its tiny inked footprints, and there, a short rubber-banded pile of the few photos they'd managed to take in six weeks. She had thumbed through the pictures, Caleb in her arms at the hospital, and then in Simon's arms. She realized she no longer recognized Caleb's face, which flooded her with guilt. *Gone!* She couldn't even find in his features whatever she'd once found reminiscent of Aileen. Something made her pick up a little onesie jumpsuit and sniff it to see if a familiar baby scent was still in the threads. It didn't smell like anything, but suddenly—she remembered this distinctly—there was the kick in her belly, a resounding, insistent thump, as if the one on the way would not let itself be overlooked. She pressed her hand against the kick to quell it. Truly there was no point in rummaging through the past. Even the baby in her belly was telling her: It was her duty to move on with life. She had snapped the lid back in place and had never poked into the box again.

Now she did not look at the shelves, moving quickly past them. All at once she noticed the large, tarp-covered mounds lined against the far wall. One hand over her mouth and nose, she stood in front of the caterpillar-shaped mass. Lifting one corner of the drop cloth, she saw what looked like a wine barrel, round, bulbous, slatted, rose-colored wood. She lifted the cloth a little further, and she could see three of them. Another Simon adventure, she recognized immediately. Mere history could inform her, whatever the smell was, that she had encountered another one of his egregious hobbies gone awry. She was offended by the smell but the surprise angered her. She unlocked the door to the medical practice and walked into his office.

Simon was in the hallway, a syringe in his hand as he prepared a tray set up with several injections. There were still patients in the office, and he was wearing his white coat. Gabi stood next to him in scrubs and purple gloves as he adjusted the syringes.

"Hey!" His eyes were shining, a look as tender and energized as sex's afterglow. "You're back. You're not going to believe—it's amazing—there aren't even words to describe what we're seeing."

Between clenched teeth, she said, "What's rotting in our basement?"

"Oh, that. We were supposed to get everything started first. Fermenting, and all. Before you found out. They came all the way from Italy, actually, but I haven't had time."

"It *reeks*."

He peeled off the latex gloves. They made a quick, dismissive snap. "It's not that bad."

"It's coming up through the *floor*. All of upstairs."

"It's only grapes, and they're only a little outdated, and we can always order more. Emily, the most incredible thing's happened—"

"It makes me want to gag."

"C'mon, it's not so strong. They came a little while ago, and I haven't been able to get to them."

"I don't understand how you could do this to our house. It's like being mauled." Emily looked at Gabi, demanding corroboration. "How can you stand it?"

"We're just busy," Simon said. Was that a sheepish look on his face? "Emily, you'd never believe it. We're doing it. We've got a treatment. It's working."

"We done five this week," Gabi chimed in. "Two today. Two yesterday. One on Tuesday."

Emily looked into the waiting room. The two patients sitting near the koi pond each looked about as miserable as two human beings could look. One was an older woman with a walker, her face pinched. At her side sat a younger woman, possibly her daughter, who kept looking down the hallway with anticipation. Every few seconds the older woman emitted a soft moan, and the younger woman turned and adjusted something of her mother's clothes. The other was a man in his midforties, who sat with his head bowed, looking into his lap, or maybe at his shoes, breathing slowly and deliberately like a bellows for a fire. Emily was suddenly eager to get out of the office.

Simon followed her down the hallway into his office. "Wait." He caught her by the arm, a little too roughly. "I'm sorry I didn't tell you. I meant to. I should have."

"Get rid of the smell, Simon," she said slowly, "or I can't stay here tonight."

"Emily, you're not going to believe this." He was done apologizing. His eyes sparkled with some other fire. "I've come across something extraordinary. Remember when we were in Florida, and you and Jamie came back—"

"I'm just asking one thing of you. One thing."

"I can't do anything about it right now. I have two more patients I promised to see. I'll take care of it as soon as I'm done."

"Smells like that stick to the furniture," Emily said. "They get in the carpets. It'll never be gone."

"I'll get rid of it. Don't worry."

Emily put her hand on the door to the basement and hesitated for a split second as she considered her options: reentering the folds of the smell or walking through the waiting room to come through the front of the house—what a choice. She buried her face in the crook of her elbow, breathing into her sleeve, and strode as quickly as she could back through the basement.

————

The more convinced she became of the deeply buried seeds of Simon's un-
kindness, the more justified she felt about being with Will. She'd intended
to pass when she was invited to present at a college seminar the following
weekend in New Brunswick, New Jersey, because she was concerned her
many absences might begin to raise eyebrows at work. But at home the
air in the house still stank, and now Jamie was walking around refusing to
look at her. Even at the breakfast table, Jamie hunched behind the cereal
box, and she responded to Emily in grunts. Emily could have fretted, but
something new inside her had locked into gear and hummed with self-
determination. She refused to think about how she might explain herself
later. She made quick arrangements to be part of the seminar at Rutgers.

The hotel was plain on the outside, concrete blocks and steel, a vestige
of '60s architecture. Her room on the fourth floor contained multiple
tones of beige, as if its human inhabitants were intended to be the only
spots of color. She sat and waited for Will. She had been moderately
surprised that he was willing to drive all the way to New Brunswick at
last-minute's notice to meet her. She was pleased, of course, and flattered,
but it also occurred to her she knew no other adult who was less busy. She
wasn't sure how she felt about that. When he rapped on the door, two
hours had passed, and she had dozed off on the bed. He arrived holding
flowers, a bouquet of bright yarrow and proud daisies, and she almost
laughed because they seemed as unsophisticated as if they'd come from a
hardware store, but she also recognized that that particular pure, jubilant
yellow was the kind that could save a life.

She kissed him and she held a daisy under his chin, the way children
do with buttercups, pretending to study the petals' effects. "Let's go out
to eat," she announced.

"What about—don't you want to be careful—weren't you concerned
about—?"

"I'm reconsidering."

"Oh?" he said, looking not sure whether to be pleased.

She told him about the stink that crept up through the floor, the fetid grapes abandoned to their slow wasting. It had taken her a day to figure out from Simon that he was clamoring about a great breakthrough in the clinic, and that was the reason he hadn't been able to begin making wine as he'd planned. There were three handmade barrels sitting under a tarp and there were more than four hundred pounds of grapes from somewhere in Italy, but all of it was going to rot because at the same moment he'd come across some new medicine for his patients, he said, and he had to see what would happen. Four hundred pounds of grapes! Simon had apologized she'd found out the way she had about the wine-making. He'd wanted that to be a surprise and he still had every intention of following through the next season as soon as that particular varietal came available again. He was roundly apologetic for the smell, but also he kept saying sorry he hadn't told her about the new nurse he'd hired at the beginning of July and then had to fire—it was a gut thing, he said. He'd wanted to help her with the first step of her career, and he'd thought her youth, her inquisitiveness, would bring new energy to the office. Apologies on the backs of other apologies, and the smell of rotting fruit was still lingering in Emily's nose.

"Also," she said, "I'll meet your daughter. I'd be delighted. Before she leaves."

Will regarded her curiously.

"I've been thinking about what you said. About me. That I'm watching and waiting. I don't want that." Too much caution. She could see now how all of the rationalizing, the planning, the careful evaluating was a kind of fetter. "I can be in Philly next Thursday afternoon. And I can stay over. Will that work?"

"I'll ask her." He nodded. "We'll make it work."

They went to lunch in the hotel restaurant downstairs, and they would have looked just like friends or colleagues having lunch, she thought, except for the sparkle of admiration that was constant in Will's eyes. Then she departed to speak at the seminar, several blocks away. When she came back to the hotel room, Will was watching television, a reality show that followed a man who was trekking solo into the desert without provisions and had to eat scorched bugs and drink the evaporated condensation from urine to keep himself alive. How little she had in common with him—it was really a marvel.

"Next Thursday, with Anne," Will announced, clicking off the set. "Drinks and dinner."

"Drinks," Emily corrected.

"I'm her father. I can't not take her to dinner. We'll go to the Franklin Inn in Center City. You'll like it, it's swank. Good place to introduce my girlfriend."

She felt her heart skip. She put her bag on the desk. "I'm your girlfriend?"

"You prefer sex toy?" He reached out and pulled her down onto the bed. "Or maybe wench?"

She hesitated, wanting to make sure he was clear. "I'm not ready to tell Simon," she stated. "He'll be devastated."

"You're not ready to *see* the devastation is what you mean."

He made the comment flippantly, but he was right, of course. The damage was already done. But the thought of confronting Simon sickened her. She didn't answer. Instead, she saw Simon in her mind, the way he had paced in their bedroom like someone hyped up on caffeine. She said, "He believes he's onto something. At work. Some big breakthrough, and he wants my help."

She hadn't even been listening closely to Simon, who continued to gush about connections in the limbic system and receptor specificity and endogenous chemicals, wondering whether he should be promoting the therapy with some kind of campaign. He wanted to write an article for a medical journal but he was concerned how readers would receive a series of case studies if he had too few patients involved. "I need your expertise," he insisted.

"Campaign?" she had asked, confused. "What therapy?"

"I should give it a name, shouldn't I? I pretty much discovered it. Sulmenamine infusion therapy. S.I.T.?" he pondered. "I don't know, I kind of hate when they abbreviate everything. What do you think?"

Another one of his ridiculous projects? "What are you talking about? You *discovered* it?"

"It's been incredible so far. This one woman, Maxi Bailey"—he was talking so loudly she thought he might wake Jamie down the hall—"calls me a miracle worker. A month ago, she couldn't get off her couch because her back was killing her. Might've too, because she was practically suicidal. Two rounds of therapy with me, and now, no pain." He sat down on the edge of the bed, and she couldn't help thinking how distant she felt from him, how they seemed to have no language in common anymore. She felt a heaviness in her stomach knowing that changes were coming, and that there were things she needed to tell him, but she wasn't ready to find sentences to explain them. "I think I'm really onto something, Emily." And Ted had said the mechanism was plausible *(Ted Ebberly knows about this?)*, but wouldn't be able to conduct laboratory experiments for a while. But the hard science wasn't essential because the proof was in the pudding and now patients were calling him about the treatment, asking whether it was available, how soon they—or their husbands, or their mothers, or their friends—could make an appointment.

"I want to make sure the information that's out there is controlled, though," Simon went on. "I don't want people thinking that I'm compounding a drug in the basement, like I have some crystal meth factory down there. Can you imagine?" And he wanted to make sure that patients knew that it was still in experimental stages. He couldn't charge for the experimental treatment because he couldn't promise it as a cure. "Can't promise, of course, but I want people to know that I believe in it. Because

I do. I think it's the most promising thing that's come along in years,"
he said. "For people who are truly suffering, this could be the medical
breakthrough of our times." She knew she was supposed to provide some
kind of enthusiastic reaction, that he was waiting for wifely support, but
she had just stared at him, unable to say a thing.

Will looked amazed as she described it all. He had unbuttoned her
blouse, and he paused in his nibbling along the ridge of her shoulder to
ask, "What's the discovery? Is he for real?"

"I don't know," she admitted. "I assume it's real. He's not someone
who'd knowingly hurt people. He's very serious about his patients. They
really look up to him."

"How'd he find it?"

"Who knows."

"Are you going to help him promote it?" Will asked with such sincerity she had to smile. "Because I don't mind. If you need time. I promise
to do everything I can not to be jealous."

"You? Jealous?" The idea delighted her. She rolled over on top of him,
wrestling him to his back as she lost herself in the kisses she was giving.

She'd seen his daughters in pictures. One photo he'd showed her was
tucked in a fold of his wallet and the other sat alone in a silver frame on
the mantel of his new apartment. The framed photograph portrayed an
entire group of maybe twelve people sitting on, and standing behind, a
couch, and all the faces were small, so it was hard to discern anything
about them. The one who was Rachel, she could tell, looked somewhat
like him, the shape of her chin and her mouth, though her hair was wavy.
Anne, who was younger, was darker, more pointed.

"Tiny change of plans," Will said, when he picked Emily up the following week after her meeting with foundation trustees at a building on
Market Street. It was dark, and she slipped into the front seat of his little

Tercel. She'd taken the train straight from D.C., not even looking out the window as she passed the cityscape of Baltimore on the northbound trip. The gestures for the meeting were rote; she knew that world by heart. But for the rest of that Thursday night—she was nervous for the first time in what seemed like years.

"If it's not too terrible. Her friends are throwing her a small party before she leaves. It's at a gallery, her friend Maya owns it. I think it's really less of a party and more of an excuse to get people into the gallery, but it would mean a lot to me to stop by."

She straightened. "Isn't there protocol for meeting family?"

"It's my fault, I got confused about which day she'd said. I promise it won't last long. Then we can go to dinner as planned."

"I'm not sure about this," she said. "I thought this introduction would be kind of private, and kind of quick."

"It's a very small gallery," he reasoned. He stole a look at her as he drove.

"Things are different for you," she reminded him, without saying the obvious: *You're not the one who's still married,* and she worried again whether he was trying to push her into something she wasn't ready for.

"Okay, okay." He considered the options. "I could drop you at my apartment, just for a little while," he suggested. "Would that be better? I feel like I have to show up at the gallery, though. Even if it's just briefly."

She was aghast. "Wait in your apartment?"

He was struggling, she could tell. "I did promise, and it would mean a lot to Anne."

You promised me, she wanted to say, but didn't. That was the sort of thing that married people said to each other, and she wasn't ready for that kind of interaction, either. (She realized, moreover, she would not have made such a change in plans for Jamie. It wouldn't even have been an issue, and, guiltily, this bothered her, too.) Instead, making her disappointment clear, she said, "I needed this to be low-key."

"We won't stay. Fifteen minutes tops. And I swear I won't try to kiss you in public. I won't even hold your hand, unless you want me to."

What was wrong with her anyway, she chastised herself, that she felt she had to control everything that happened? And what did it matter if they hadn't put a name on the relationship, or whatever it was? And was she always going to be that kind of person who was, as he'd said, watching and waiting and judging and worrying about how everything looked—or was she going to learn how to live? *Stop thinking, Emily, just try to* experience the moment, *for chrissake.* "Just fifteen minutes," she agreed finally. "I want your word."

The gallery was on a side street in South Philadelphia. Ankle-high trash hugged the bricks of the building, old flyers, food wrappers, newspaper fragments. As she followed him into the gallery space—bloodred walls, white ceiling, large imposing pieces of art—he waved to a woman across the room. "Maya," he called. The woman, who was elflike, with spiky hair and giant hoop earrings, looked possibly twenty-five years old (it was getting more and more impossible to determine the ages of people younger than she was). She waved back to Will, but didn't make her way over. Emily could only imagine categorizing the crowd as suavely disheveled. The whole lot of them looked like displaced college students with unruly hair and long T-shirts and pants with *drawstrings.* She felt ancient. Waiters in black ties tooled around with little trays of food. Will snatched a glass of white wine as one of them passed. She would have preferred red, but she accepted it with a smile.

"Anne's been painting since she was a kid," Will told her. "Saturday art classes, afterschool clubs. It's her thing. She won't pursue it, probably because she's seen what the life of an artist is like, but I kept telling her she belongs in art school."

"Oh," Emily said. "You just said a gallery. You didn't say she was one of the artists."

"Go ahead," Will challenged. "See if you can guess."

Drinking the wine, she realized she hadn't eaten in hours. She glanced at the art on the walls. There were some rather ordinary nature paintings, puddles of water and barn doors in different kinds of light. There were Hopperesque imitations of street scenes and unimpressive collages with dull backgrounds and newspaper and shellac. Then she noticed the painting at the far end of the room, a large portrait of a man's torso, in all different shades of blue, some deep, some so faint they approximated a gray. To Emily, there was no doubt that Will was the subject, even though his features were blurred so that nothing of his face was exactly in place. She edged closer and stood squarely in front of it to look. His head was angled, a little to the side, a little downturned, and his eyes were closed, not quite flatteringly, but spontaneously, the way people sometimes found themselves caught in candid photographs. *A strange way to depict someone,* she thought. He appeared midlaugh or midthought, and somehow it conveyed exactly what she understood about Will, the unposed, easy motion, the self-effacing lack of sharpness. There was his scar, which she knew so intimately that she'd almost believed she was the only one who could see it. In the painting, he was not handsome—certainly not as attractive as he was in the flesh—but particular. The details were so right that the collection of them could not have been anyone else.

Will appeared at her elbow, staring up at the painting. "I don't know where she got it 'cause I can't draw a circle. Every now and then she sells something. This one's two grand. I'm really proud."

"You're here," a voice behind them said. Anne turned out to be taller than Emily had imagined, and astonishingly together-looking. She had presence, no denying that. Her dark hair was cut in an underturned bob, shorter in back than the pointed pieces that curved around her face. The brown of her eyes was so dark, the color was almost black. Lindsay must have been composed of sharp features and dominant genes because Anne had none of Will's soft angles, except for the gentleness of her expression, which Emily recognized immediately.

"I've heard a lot about you," Emily said, holding out her hand after Will introduced them. She hoped she sounded more than merely polite. "So nice to meet you." She gestured toward the painting with the hand holding her wine. "This is wonderful."

"It came out well, I think," Anne said (guardedly, Emily thought).

Emily wished they had started off with dinner. She worried that the evening would feel interminably long, but she cared about the impression she made. She looked at Will and then back at Anne. "Your father raves about you."

Grinning, Anne reached over and took her father's hand. "He's very sweet."

"I'll say it again," Will said, tucking Anne under his arm and giving her a squeeze, as though she were still a little girl, "I'm proud of you for going, but wow, I'm gonna miss you."

"Aw," she said again, letting herself be hugged. "I'll be back for Thanksgiving."

Emily felt herself regarding them as though they were a two-headed species she'd discovered on a tree branch through a magnifying glass. Where had she and Simon gone wrong with Jamie? Was it all their fault that Jamie was stormy, accusatory, impossible to get along with? Was it genetic? After her father died, she had wondered whether Jamie might have a touch of it too—some depression, some mania. Maybe she'd unwittingly passed some of it along. She didn't know how those things got diagnosed or what there was to do about it. Lithium, she supposed. That was all she knew. She didn't dislike her daughter. She just hadn't figured out how to love her.

"You have a real talent," Emily said. She was being honest, but she realized she needed this self-possessed, sharp-looking Anne to like her. Anne thanked her, smiling appreciatively with wide, white teeth, and then turned away as a friend tapped her on the shoulder to say he had to leave. Will suggested to Emily that they look around the rest of the gallery. She helped herself to another glass of wine.

"She's lovely," Emily whispered to him.

"Ah," Will said, closing his eyes and tipping his head as he sighed. She recognized the gesture then, the head tilt, from the painting. Anne might have rendered him well, but Emily recognized the painting for what it was: a love note. It was a message between the two of them that went back and forth. Anne told him she loved him by painting him. But she also showed him what he looked like as he was loving her, which let him know she knew she was loved. And as they stood in the gallery, admiring the painting with a group of strangers singing praises—including Emily—they basked in that love all over again. Emily began to suspect that she'd had too much wine already.

"Have you always gotten along?" she asked Will as they stood in front of a pedestal with a clay sculpture of half a head.

A waiter appeared, offering a shiny tray with speared cheese puffs in fluted cupcake foils. Will took one; Emily declined.

"We've had our moments," he acknowledged. "I told you about that boyfriend, didn't I? I've just loved them so much. Both daughters. When they were born, I just felt like—ah—this's what it's about. Life. What we're here for. My chest almost aches when I think of them too long."

All that sentiment. He was full to the brim with feeling. She stared at him. *Life's goodies.* She had tried so hard—with both children—how had she so thoroughly missed out? "You're a fool for love," she said, downing the rest of her glass.

"Here she is," he said, his face lighting up as Anne made her way through the crowd with her jacket. "She's ready for us."

They had a reservation at the Franklin Inn, but when they stepped into the dimly lit doorway, the maitre d' informed them they'd have a short wait. The party that was sitting at their table hadn't quite finished dessert. Emily looked around the Tudor-style entrance, terra-cotta tiles and wood beams and handblown glass windowpanes divided by lead into diamond shapes. She knew exactly what dinner would be like: the rolls in the basket would be a row of soft white bread; little pats of butter would come on pieces of cardboard with a rectangle of paper on top; the side vegetable would be a choice of cut green beans that would come too wet or buttered, or mashed potatoes.

"Let's hope it's not too long," Will said.

In the dim light, Emily felt bold. She reached over to straighten the collar of his shirt. " 'He that lives upon hope will die fasting,' " she said. "Ben Franklin. Get it? Franklin Inn?" Along with Einstein, Thoreau, Shakespeare and Mae West, good old Ben was quoted often in the world of PR. Will looked at her with a half-grin.

"No jokes," Anne cautioned. "He's very fond of this place."

Will offered to bring them drinks from the bar as they waited. Emily decided to switch over to red wine, requesting a Zinfandel, and winced privately as she remembered the fiasco in the basement of her home. The shipment of grapes—and the smell—was gone finally, all but a few pounds that Simon had insisted on keeping in the basement freezer. ("They fit," he insisted. "And they're not rotting, so why throw them away?") Anne ordered a martini. She was quite sophisticated, this Anne.

Emily sidled close to her and whispered loudly, "Are you twenty-one?"

"Shh," Anne replied.

"Change my order. I'll have one of those, too," she called to Will.

Will returned with their drinks and pointed out the art on the walls, which was nautical and historical, and didn't interest Emily. By the time they were seated, Emily felt not quite drunk but a little too loose. The bread arrived (she'd been right about the rolls and the butter), and an instant after she handed off the menu, she couldn't remember what she'd ordered.

"When do you fly?" Emily asked as a bottle of wine was opened for the table.

"Friday," Anne answered. "Did I tell you, Dad, Jen's picking me up at the airport, and the first thing we're going to do is see a cousin of hers in Oakland who makes parade floats for a living. She flies around the country, funded by corporations, and she conceptualizes and designs floats for events. Can you believe that?"

Emily looked over at Will and was startled to see him holding his table napkin to his face. At first she thought he was having a problem with the bread. She'd once bitten into a mussel that had turned out to be full of sand and had spit it into the napkin to show to the waiter. Then she thought—his eyes closed—he might be waiting to sneeze. It took several moments before she understood that he was wiping his eyes, actually crying at the table. Emily glanced at Anne and then looked down at the scalloped edges of her plate.

"Sorry," he sputtered, laughing at himself. "I couldn't help it."

"Can you believe him?" Anne asked. "It's not like I haven't been away before. It's just that there won't be a dorm and an R.A. and meal service. I promise I'll call."

"I'll pay your cell phone minutes," Will said. He dabbed at his face, which had turned bright pink. "You can even go over the limit."

"I'll stay in touch, Dad. I promise."

Emily cleared her throat. She hated herself for being uncomfortable, but she was not good at such displays. She didn't know what to do. "Have you spent time in California before?" she asked politely.

Then Will stood up, dabbing at his crimson cheeks all over again, laughing and coughing. "Excuse me, I need a minute." He started off in the direction of the restrooms.

Emily and Anne sat at the table in silence. Emily smoothed her napkin across her lap. The silverware was American colonial. The plates were French country. She finished off her wine. She didn't know people who lost composure like that. She smiled at the girl. "Have you chosen a major?"

"I'm still open. I've taken a bunch of English classes. I like reading. English and history are the main contenders. I'd like to go to law school. I thought I'd take a year and figure it out."

"But not art?"

"Oh no. I've seen what it can do to you, when it's not bringing in money."

Her first instinct was to commend Anne for being practical—it was her best career advice—but she realized what Will would probably tell his daughter. "If you follow your talent," she said, "you'll be successful. Figure out exactly what you do best, and give yourself to it. Your painting is wonderful, what I've seen so far."

Anne responded with a stiff smile. They indulged another silence. Then Emily remembered what Will had said, how they'd all discussed his private life. Best thing to do, she decided, was to own the situation.

"I hope this isn't too awkward for you," Emily said.

Anne gave a small shrug. "I just want him to be happy. That's about it."

The silence resumed. Emily looked toward the restroom. The waiter came around and poured more wine into Emily's glass. Emily drank.

"It's not that it's awkward," Anne said suddenly when the waiter had disappeared. "It's that it's hard to trust you. All the circumstances, and all."

Emily thought, *You mean, that I'm married, and a person who's married who's cheating may promise and promise to leave her husband, but may never come through. What's more, a person who's married and cheating may cheat again. I'm a real loose canon. Who knows what I'll do next?* "I can understand that," she said, and drank again.

"We're protective."

Emily presumed Anne meant herself and her sister, Rachel. She felt a weird heat, realizing that she'd been the topic of other people's conversation. Is this what they mean when they ask if your ears were ringing? she thought. Or was it that your ears burned when people talked about you? Maybe they were estimating risk based on the fact that she'd left Will once before. Sisters as a united front, what a concept. Emily tried to decide if there was a threat implied—*we're very close, so stay away from our father*—but there didn't seem to be anything harsh behind the statement, just concern.

"I imagine." She stole a look in the direction of the restroom. "He's an extraordinary person, your father. I knew he was, before. He still is." *Believe in your client,* she thought, suddenly remembering that she was representing herself. What arose in her, however, was a desire to spell it all out: *You'll find out someday. You're young now, but you'll encounter a moment someday when you'll realize how little you can control. Even if you take a precious year now to make the most careful decisions, things will happen to you that you never expected.* An image of Caleb came to her suddenly before she banished it. She didn't care to expose herself to Anne. *Know your audience,* she thought, composing herself. The wine had gone to her head. "Thanks for your honesty," she said.

From the corner of her eye, she saw Will turn the corner, weaving his way back through tables to where they sat. His head was tilted at that familiar, apologetic angle. She smoothed her napkin again and smiled as he pulled out his chair.

"Better?" she asked.

"It'll be easier in a week," Will said, smiling and seating himself. "I'm never good at saying good-bye to them."

"'We only part to meet again,'" Emily pronounced, and when Will looked at her blankly, added, "It's from a poem."

"'Change, as ye list, ye winds; my heart shall be, The faithful compass that still points to thee,'" Anne finished, victoriously. "John Gay. I studied him."

Will beamed at them, those eyes shining generously. "Lovely," he declared. "Both of you." He took a sip of wine, but he was only getting started on his drink. Emily's thoughts felt swishy. She should have stopped earlier. Now it was too late. They ate, and she could only wonder about the impression she'd made on Will's younger daughter. It would certainly matter to Will what his daughters thought of her. But those girls couldn't possibly understand what being with Will meant to her, how she had suddenly been presented with the opportunity to shift her life onto what felt like the right track. So much had gone astray for her, even though she'd done all she could to make everything appear trim and tidy. She consoled herself by remembering that the girl was leaving town at the end of the week.

When dinner ended, she excused herself to go to the ladies' room. Anne stood up too and followed. She heard Anne at an adjacent stall, rustling and unzipping, tearing toilet paper, flushing. They didn't speak a word until they were both done and were standing over the sinks. Anne washed her hands with what seemed to be great concentration.

"He loves you a lot," Emily said emphatically, hoping to reassure the girl that she, Emily, had no intention of edging his daughters out of the picture. She began stroking over her lips with a bricky brown color that had the effect of making her skin look paler and, she hoped, somewhat younger. She respected his relationship with his children. No, more than that, she realized, she envied it, wished she were capable of the same thing. "I've almost never seen a man love his daughters as much."

Anne dried her hands with a paper towel, looking at Emily without expression. "Be nice to him. He's vulnerable."

Emily paused, her mouth open, her lipstick poised on its way to reparations, and she nodded at Anne in the mirror. Tossing the crumpled towel in a metallic wastebin, Anne turned on her heel and left the ladies' room.

Drunk was not cute. It was passable in the cab on the way back to Will's apartment as they cuddled in the backseat. Anne had taken his car to move the last boxes of her packed apartment to a friend's house, and Emily and Will had clambered into a cab. She opened the window, and giggled and snuggled against his body. Her hair blew around her face. He put his hand on her knee under her skirt, and all of it felt like being in her twenties again, taking cabs around New York, skipping out on work, dodging her father's secretary. But she was in rare form by the time they reached his apartment in Society Hill. The cab pulled up along the colonial row houses with their short doors and their narrow windows, across the street from a cemetery with jagged, flinty tombstones that dated to the Revolutionary War—the *War of Independence*!—and Will had to drag her off the vinyl seat. He paid the cabbie, hooked an arm around her waist and hobbled with her up the steps of the house.

"Put your arm over my shoulder," he instructed. "That's it." They made their way together down a hall to the door of his apartment. He wasn't able to hold her and fish through his pockets at the same time, so he leaned her gently against the door frame. She accepted the spot like an abandoned doll. Simon, she thought, would have been able to hold her up and unlock a door at the same time. That was the sort of magic Simon was capable of. She felt sorry her husband had no idea where on earth she was. Slightly evil was how she felt. Earlier she'd felt rebellious, and even righteous, but now she just felt mean. He believed her to be speaking at another conference in Philly. ("Another one?" he asked. "By God, you're in demand these days.")

While she was home, Simon had babbled on about the treatment, the infusion therapy, or whatever he was calling it. A new wonder drug? Was her husband completely crocked? He needed more patients, he said, before he could make the medical community take note. "But the proof positives are still in the lead," he said.

She couldn't listen to Simon. Just couldn't listen. Here was his unproven treatment eclipsing everything. Why, he had no clue that she'd been away five of the last seven weekends and occasionally during the week. It was shit, her marriage. Will reached out his hand and helped her into his apartment. She stepped into the entryway, bumping into the coatrack inside the door.

"I need to sit down," she said.

"Here." Will led her by the hand to his couch. *Ikea,* she thought. *Well, here was bachelorhood revisited.*

He took off her shoes.

"I'll get water," he said. "You should drink."

She heard him opening and then closing a cabinet. She heard the tap running, the rising notes of the water filling the glass. She knew that the water would be just the right temperature, that it would be neither warm nor have ice. A man bringing a drink, not a cocktail, but a drink of water. Her throat was parched. A drink of water for the woman on the couch. Such a small, simple gesture, but so tender. The simplicity of it moved her. And here was Will appearing from out of nowhere, whose very way of being proved everything that was wrong with her life. And everything she had created with Simon—what had happened to them? When was the last time Simon had brought her a drink of water? Here she was, beginning something with Will, or was it consummating something with Will, everything was so unclear. The only truth that was evident Anne had so aptly pointed out: Emily came from a poisoned background—so much ill feeling—and could not be trusted. Sitting on the couch, she began to cry.

"Emily?"

Then it was pouring out of her. She was sobbing, her shoulders heaving, her mouth barely able to form words. "I've bungled everything. I don't know how it happened."

He sat next to her. "What have you bungled?"

"All my relationships." Her voice came out squeaky. This was terrible. She hadn't meant to lose it completely. "Every one I've ever had."

"Oh, sweetheart," he said. He smoothed her hair. His hand on her forehead felt like a salve.

She kept hearing Jamie's voice, taunting, seeing the hard look before she turned and ran up the stairs. "My daughter hates me."

"She's a teenager. You can't take it personally. She has to learn her own space."

"No, it's deeper than that." She cried. She did not want to be hated. She did not deserve to be hated. Yes, she did, another voice inside her answered. All of it was her own damn fault.

Will put his arms around her and sat silently, and she received his comfort. Finally he sat up, took a sip from her water and offered it to her. He had no tissues so he brought her a wad of toilet paper from the bathroom. Settling back down on the couch, he put his hand on her neck, under her hair. It seemed she'd never felt a human touch more supportive, that perhaps there was a secret to the back of the neck, that warm nook where sympathy could be imparted.

"When Rachel was sixteen," he said, "we all had a really hard time. She got in with the wrong kids. We knew she was experimenting with drugs and sex. I was out of my mind because I kept thinking about heroin and AIDS, and I was sure if we said anything, we'd inadvertently push her to do more of whatever she was doing. Maybe she'd go off the deep end, run away or something. But I did the scary thing. I took a risk and confronted her. I told her that I loved her too much to just watch. I also told her that I would drag her to rehab myself and I would handcuff myself to her wrist until she got her shit together. It got through."

She felt the tiniest bit pleased to hear that one of the Garth girls could have been said to have issues. But Will couldn't see that his anecdotes had no resonance in her life. "We've never—it's never been—" There wasn't even vocabulary to describe what was missing. She had never discussed any of this with anyone. Not Janet Grove with her five fabulous, high-achieving children. Not Betsy Ebberly, who came at parenting with her psychology degree and who also happened to be teeming with good-natured patience.

"I wasn't ready. When she was born." She knew it sounded like she was making excuses. Maybe she was making excuses. Something had to explain how it all got fouled up.

"Nobody ever is, sweetheart. You can't hold that against yourself."

She blew her nose. She'd stopped crying. Her eyes ached. "I was damaged. When she was born, I wasn't—I was broken."

He didn't say anything.

"I was watching you tonight. The way you look at Anne, the way she looks at you. You're her safest place."

"She was an easy kid to raise. Some kids are."

She had not planned to tell, not so soon, at least. She didn't need for him to know how deep the canyons of muck ran. But she realized, all of a sudden, that she wanted him to know she was capable of giving more, of being more. If she let him know what she'd been through, he might be able to guide her out of the place she'd gotten herself into. That was it: More than anything in the world, she wanted his help. She closed her eyes. "I didn't tell you this before. We had a son, Simon and I."

"Oh." He comprehended. This was how you could count on Will. At the right moments, he understood.

She was unable to look at him. She stared off toward the corner of the room, where he'd stacked his partially unpacked boxes. Clothes spilled out of the tops of some of them where he'd obviously gone pawing for a buried item. There were his khaki shirts, that odd color and mussed fabric he liked so much. It was comforting to see his things. She felt like telling because it seemed like the only way to explain herself, but how to begin? "He was a baby, a newborn really." She closed her eyes, feeling Will's chest against her, rising and retreating as he breathed.

"I didn't know."

Will didn't ask how her baby had died, but the desire to tell all about him swelled in her so strong, she could almost picture Caleb again. "He got sick," she said, staring again, barely breathing. "A bacterial infection that developed into meningitis. It happens in newborns. He was only six weeks. It took us by surprise."

"Oh, sweetheart."

And then she couldn't stop. She was back there on the late October afternoon. She was not the self-pitying type, but the instant she began to tell, all of it, even the dull sky, the wind picking up outside, was right there, waiting to be told. "The most terrible part"—she began sniffling again but the words were still coming—"was that he hardly even seemed sick. There was no way to know what was happening. In the afternoon, I remember"—her voice wavered, but then continued—"because he had just woken up from a nap, I was just changing his shirt, this little yellow thing with a bear on the front, and I happened to put my hand on his back, and I couldn't tell, was he warm or were my hands cold? I thought maybe he was a little fussy, but then I couldn't really tell about that, either. He'd been a colicky baby from the get-go. Colicky doesn't even describe it. For almost a whole month, he cried every day for three or four hours straight. There was nothing anyone could do. Then he woke up and cried during the night. No matter what I did or how I held him. So I couldn't tell if he was complaining for real or if it was just more of the same.

"All afternoon, I tried to hold him, I cuddled him, and still I couldn't really tell what was up, and I was just getting more and more frustrated. His face looked—I don't know—just *different,* except I couldn't even really describe what was different—and then again, he'd been crying for so long."

She sighed. "I wasn't really good at being a mother. From the beginning. Something about me just wasn't—I just didn't hit the ground running. And then he was not such an easy baby. And then that afternoon, I just couldn't tell. I took his temperature, ninety-eight point nine—what do you do with that? Even Simon said it wasn't really fever and we should just watch and wait. So I watched, and Caleb didn't seem any worse, but he didn't seem any better, either.

"We had this pediatrician at that time who had office hours in the evenings, and I called Simon, who was downstairs seeing patients, and said maybe I should call and take the baby in, you know, before night. Before the pediatrician's office closed. Simon said"—she swallowed—"he said, 'Ninety-eight point nine isn't really significant, but go if it'll make you feel better,' and I thought, well, better to ask. So I dressed Caleb, the wind was blowing and it was getting cold, and I took him. And then, the pediatrician, oh God, it was the most ridiculous thing. He just smiled, you know that smile? Where they look at you like—like you're overreacting—and they know ninety percent of their job is to look understanding while you're wasting their time. And I said, 'You can stop patronizing me. He's been crying all day.' The pediatrician just nodded, because at that point I could tell he thought I was overreacting and also annoying, and he did all the usual things, listened to his chest, looked in his ears, and said, 'No temperature.' He said, 'Don't worry. Babies can run a little warm. Especially if you overbundle them. Especially if they've been crying. And you can't trust most thermometers anyway.' He ordered a blood test, just to appease me, I think, because I don't think he thought anything would turn up, and sure enough, fifteen minutes later the results from the lab down the hall came back negative. Nothing. 'Probably gas,' he said. He gave me some drops to put into Caleb's mouth. And he said sometimes there are babies who just cry. 'Your husband's a doctor,' he said. 'So if anything changes, you'll know if it's real.'

"So I took Caleb back home, feeling frustrated with the doctor and frustrated with the baby. Caleb just cried and cried." Emily's eyes began to well up again as she suddenly could picture his red face, with his toothless, coral-colored mouth agape. "It'd been hours. Really, hours. The noise. Just the sound of it, not stopping. I started to lose my patience. Simon finished with his appointments and came back upstairs, and I just stuck Caleb in his arms and said, 'Here, you take him. I can't stand it anymore.' That's what I said, 'I can't stand it.'"

She dabbed her nose, which was running, with the wad of toilet paper. She could still remember the gesture: She had pressed the baby into Simon's chest—hard—along with an unfinished bottle of formula. Then she had gone into the bedroom and closed the door. After all the crying, all she could hold in her head was the thought she'd had in the hospital when Caleb was first born. Maybe she'd made a terrible mistake. Maybe she was not cut out for mothering. She didn't enjoy it. If there was some deep well of love she was supposed to draw from, it was shallow, and the bucket was tall. She was tired of Simon's absence—his practice had only just begun to boom—and she felt alone. *Bad mother,* she thought just as she began to picture running away. Just walking out the front door of the house and not coming back. But of course she couldn't do that. She would have to stay and endure it. Every thought in her head was an awful one and she had hated herself for every single one. Inside her bedroom, she'd felt better. The baby was out of earshot anyway. She was only vaguely aware when Simon finally came to bed, but she could tell he had put the baby into the crib in the nursery. And at about eleven at night, when she happened to awake, the crying had stopped.

"My first thought was just relief," she said, her voice a dull monotone. "I can't even believe I'm saying this out loud. But that's what I thought. Just—thank God for the quiet. It was so hard, you know? All that crying? The feeling that everything was going wrong, and that I was an awful person not to love the experience of it. I just woke up to a quiet house and my first thought was, Thank God.

"I got up just to pee, and I just happened to peek into his room. He was lying there in his crib, breathing harder than usual. I could tell he was awake. His eyes, they were just looking upward. And I knew right then—something was just wrong. Very, very wrong. I leaned closer to look. Very carefully, I picked him up, just scooped him out of the crib, and he"—her voice trailed into a whisper, "just went limp in my arms."

In the shadows, or possibly because of the unnatural yellow of the night-light, every motion had seemed bogged down, as if underwater. His head wagged to one side. She looked down and saw his skin was ashen, his lips bluing around the edges. And then there were no useful thoughts. Just her heart beating. Her tongue thick. Her peripheral vision gone and her focus quavering like the camera inside a race car. No words, but every one of her senses perceiving the occurrence of *that most terrible thing*. Then she was staggering with him, bumbling into the hallway, practically bumping against the opposite wall, as if she didn't have control of her feet. The braying noise she made did not sound human, but it woke Simon, who bounded from bed to her side, vaulting into action, looking at the baby and feeling for a pulse—still awake, still breathing—and rushing them downstairs, still in their nightclothes, and out the door into the backseat of the car. She was usually quick to act, but not this time. This time, she was a hulking mess, her arms gripping Caleb, uncertain which way to move, where to turn. Simon took over, was what he did. Suddenly they were in motion, heading toward help. She was wordless, knowing she'd be grateful—no, actually *indebted*—to him for the rest of her life, because otherwise she'd have been standing in the hallway of her house holding a lifeless child. What she feared but would never have said aloud was actually happening; she was about to lose her son, whom she would only realize later how much she loved. Simon drove like a demon through the streets, to the nearest emergency room less than half a mile away.

"They did all kinds of tests," she said. "They did everything. They really tried. And then—" She stopped.

His hands ceased in their rubbing and simply covered hers. "I'm so sorry."

She didn't mean to laugh, but she made another sound like a short bark. Then she said aloud, "I'm a very, very bad mother."

"Oh, Emily—"

"I'm not a natural. No, it's just the truth." It was the hardest thing in the world to confess, that she lacked a basic function. She lacked an inclination to nurture that all people—especially Will—possessed in abundance. But for some reason she now wanted to come clean. "I knew I wasn't good at it, but I was trying to get better. It was terrible, right after, I wanted to die. I didn't have any plan to die, but I thought maybe"—her voice changed again—"I don't know, I thought maybe something else would take me, and it would've been okay with me if it happened. If I'd turned up dead, it wouldn't have surprised me. And then—" Her voice trailed off again and then she remembered the resolve that she had summoned, the will to get over it. Deciding to move ahead had taken every power that she commanded. "We overcame it—we really did. Overcame it and moved on, but the truth was, I wasn't ready when Jamie came along. Somehow I thought I'd repair myself. The most terrible thing had happened, and it should have been a turning point. You'd expect it to be a turning point. But when Jamie came—I was still damaged. Maybe it was just too soon. She and I just never got off on the right foot, and I haven't been able to fix it."

"Oh, sweetheart," he said again. "I'm sure you're better than you think."

"No, I've never had the right stuff. Maybe my mother didn't either. There was some stigma or something to getting too close. Look at my sister."

"You can't say you're not a natural," Will protested, rubbing her hands. "You are! Even back then. You *knew* something wasn't right, that very night. Didn't you hear yourself? That's the instinct, don't you see? You were tuned in. *You're* the one who woke up in the night. That's the essence of it. Not whether you're tickled with joy."

She didn't respond. It felt good to be contradicted, even though she knew she was right.

"I'm bad for her."

"For Jamie?"

"We went shopping for shoes, the two of us. This was about a year ago.

She wanted some kind of Mary Janes so I took her. And all the way across the store a mother was yelling at her child, 'Caleb! Caleb, get over here!' I just pretended I didn't hear it but I could feel Jamie freeze, watching me, but not quite watching me. She knows about what happened, but it's not exactly dinner conversation. And then, she's testing me, Jamie decides she wants a pair of two-hundred-dollar shoes. Of course, I said no and picked out two very reasonable alternatives. I started shaking, just my hands, but I couldn't stop. And then, I was standing there insisting, almost yelling at her, 'This pair or this pair? Which one? Just pick one!' Completely irrational. And she wouldn't choose, so we walked out. I had to get out of there."

"Of course you did."

"No, you don't see. Jamie never even got her *shoes*. You'd think that a mother who"—the words had burrs, they caught in her throat, she couldn't say them—"would figure out how to do it right, if she were lucky enough to get a second chance. I got that second chance, but somehow—" Will continued to hold her hands, but he didn't speak. She wanted him to pull her close, to stroke her neck again. She wanted him to tell her he knew how to fix everything, but he didn't offer that. She sighed. "Do you have any tea?"

"Want me to make you some?" He departed for the kitchen again. She closed her eyes, feeling the rocking of the room, nauseating and comforting at the same time. She heard the kitchen cabinet doors and then the microwave.

When Will put the warm mug down in front of her, he asked, "He'd be how old this year?"

"Fifteen. Um, yeah." She did the math again. "Fifteen. Almost sixteen. Getting a driver's permit, probably. I'm lucky," she added, startled at the glibness she was capable of. "It might have been a very stressful year."

He smiled sympathetically, and she sat forward and put her hands on both sides of the mug. She felt sober, but she could tell she wasn't. Every-

thing in her head was clear, but she suspected the alcohol was still working its way through her system because she was still talking. "I want to
be better," she said, not caring that she sounded pathetic. "I see you and
Anne, and I don't want my daughter to hate me. I want what you have. I
need to be a better mother."

He smiled again. "So do," he said gently.

Easier said, she thought. Wasn't she already trying? No matter what
she did anymore, she was rebuffed. She had another vision of Jamie's
face, accusing eyes and tense mouth. She did not know the right words to
say to steer in a new direction. She could not go back in time. She cried
again, cried until her eyes felt like puffy slits, like cracks in risen dough,
and it took effort to open them.

The morning came, showering her with a sense of newness. It came with
the daylight, into Will's bedroom window, on a slant like driven rain. She
extended her hand into the shaft as if she could turn the light over, sifting
it between her fingers. She was sober now with only the faintest hangover.
Will was banging around in his little kitchen. He came in to say he'd
made scrambled eggs and toast to soak up the end of the alcohol.

She ate at the table. He sat with her, rocking a fork, one finger on the
tines.

"Do you mind?" she pleaded. "The noise?"

"Sorry. I was thinking about last night."

She felt not shame but a twang that reminded her she had not
acted like herself. She straightened in her chair. "I told a little too much,
didn't I?"

"No, not too much. I didn't know."

She nodded. "Sorry not to tell you sooner. About Caleb and everything. It's where it is, in the past."

Will was silent for a while. "Do you do anything to mourn him?"

"We're quiet about it, I guess."

"Ever go to the cemetery?" he asked.

"Oh no," she replied. "I couldn't." In truth, it was the thing in her life of which she was most ashamed. Reckless abandonment was what it was, but the thought of going to the cemetery made her catch her breath. A person couldn't be expected to go through that—it would be punishment all over again. Simon had suggested they go once, a long time ago, that same fall. The site wouldn't even have been caked dry under their feet. She hadn't even been able to *conceive* of the aching hardship of a graveside trip. No, she'd said. I can't. What she couldn't do—and it had made her bitter that it was expected of her—was share the grief. They'd left the hospital numb with exhaustion, tongue-tied with disbelief. Simon drove, and they didn't speak. What Emily craved more than anything was the opportunity to hole up in the quiet of home. She wanted to crawl into the familiar crevices of her own bed and drag the covers up to her eyes. When they arrived home, the hush in the house was more terrible than anything she'd ever experienced. It was a silence that roared. There was no distant mewling tugging at them, insistent, urging them to action. At night, she woke listening for noise, and lay still, both grateful for and oppressed by the sound of Simon's breathing.

The early days had the stickiness of a dream. Each moment she had the sense that there was something important to tend to, something that had just slipped her mind. Then, the reminder that, no, there was nothing to do. What she hated most was the sight of her own hands, holding a fork, reaching for soap in the shower. From every angle, they looked grotesque: the knobs of her knuckles, the webs between her fingers, her cuticles, fingertips, palms. They looked bony to her, and old, and confoundingly idle. She looked at Simon and she couldn't even ask. There was no helpful answer to the question: *Hey, look at my hands, don't they look wrong?*

Her breasts addressed the inattention with fury. Her flow had been low and she'd been using formula and pumping occasionally, and as soon as she stopped they became engorged with untapped milk, tough as footballs, unyielding. They itched and burned. Simon's tenderness toward her was excruciating, as he padded around in slippers, bringing her tea in bed, shielding her from phone calls. Having heard that cool cabbage could draw out the heat from her breasts, he brought a plate of detached leaves, like jade bowls. He carried them into the bedroom on a tray. They laughed their first, stilted laugh as she took the leaves and lay in bed with a cabbage-leaf bra covering her aching breasts.

But she didn't want to receive his attention. She knew he was hurting too—she wasn't completely insensitive—and yet she couldn't face returning the same comfort. She'd heard him crying in the shower, great, hacking sobs, and she wasn't able to go into the bathroom. She listened, and she sat frozen in the bay window of the bedroom, unable to move. Depleted, she didn't have it in her to be the source of help or understanding for anyone. And sharing the grief, she was certain, would allow it to take over like something living, like bacteria dividing itself and multiplying, becoming uncontainable.

Will tapped again pensively, until she reached out and took away the fork, grabbed it, the way one would from a child.

"Did your husband try to save him?" he asked. "I was thinking about it. Must've felt terrible. Being a doctor, losing his own kid."

"Even the pediatricians missed it," she contended.

Will said, "You must be a tremendously forgiving person. I think I'd have had expectations, if it happened to me. Even if I didn't want to acknowledge them."

"There was nothing to forgive," she insisted. "It wasn't anybody's fault. Caleb was sick in a way that nobody knew. It happened under the radar. There was no real fever or anything—none of the classic signs."

"You won't get mad at him for the one, most terrible thing he ever did to you. You've done a public relations job so good that even you believe your own spin."

"Nobody knew," she insisted with even more fervor. "The pediatricians, nobody. They didn't even know at the hospital. Not at first. They did tests. Anyway, it wasn't like he meant to. It could have happened to anybody."

"But he's a doctor, and he didn't save your son."

Emily raised her voice. "You don't know anything about it. It could have happened to anybody."

"Didn't though," Will persisted. His voice was gentle, but she still smarted. "It happened to him. And you."

"It wasn't his fault," she stated again. It was then, under Will's probing, that she felt for the first time that she had cheated on Simon. Cheated in a way that had really abused. It wasn't the sex, or the lying, or the sneaking, or the pretending, or even the audacious creation of a new image of herself, or the other thousand and one violations she had committed over the last two months. The gravest moment of her infidelity had just occurred. It happened when she exposed herself and Simon at their weakest and most vulnerable, when she allowed another human a glimpse of that night and what had followed. And here was Will—wanting to *analyze* it. She felt raw all over again, that clawed-earth feeling, sick to her stomach, and she wondered whether she might throw up. She wasn't seeing his face suddenly, just the bright-colored scar on his jaw where the dog had got him. It seemed to shine. "Are you trying to upset me?" she asked, frantic.

"No, but I'm understanding more. How come you're so afraid to talk about it?"

She remembered what he'd said about Lindsay. Gut-wrenching honesty was what he'd demanded, and she'd run away. Emily wanted to be worthy of Will's attention. She didn't want to be a woman who couldn't handle a conversation. But the words coming out of his mouth sliced at her. "I told you about it, didn't I? I told you everything." Her breath was hot.

"Not with me," Will said intently, "with him."

"There isn't anything to say. What would I say?"

He shrugged. "What you felt, for starters."

Will could pretend to comprehend them, but he couldn't know. She said, "I wanted to move on. I knew what I was doing, and I knew how I needed to get through it. I don't really want to talk about this anymore." Her teeth were beginning to ache.

"Because you can't."

"Because I don't want to." They were throbbing.

"It's just that I don't think you're being honest, Emily. You never closed a chapter of your life. You just walked off. And you can't. Just walk off from stuff. It comes after you."

She didn't say anything. She stood up and took her plate and her silverware to the sink. He didn't have a dishwasher, so she washed them by hand with one quick swipe. But she could not bring herself to sit down again. "I don't blame him," she protested, her back against the counter, her hand curled around the edge of the sink. "I don't blame anybody."

"You're punishing him, though."

"Me?" She was astounded. "He's the one who always finds something hurtful to do. He's the one who punishes me."

"Then what are you doing here with me?"

"You're insinuating I'm *using* you?" Her voice rose into a shriek. She shook her head as if he were crazy. "I'm here because I want to be here," she insisted. Just then, her cell phone sounded in the next room, and she was relieved for the intrusion. She left the table to find her purse. It was Suzanne, her secretary: Could she take a meeting that afternoon with Jack Whitby? He wanted her to come by his office.

"Did he say what about?" she asked, suddenly worried. Whitby almost never arranged personal appearances, and certainly never scheduled them through a secretary. "Tell him I have a few developments in the Niccorps account. I'll bring everything I have." But Jack hadn't left

Suzanne with a topic. "I'm wanted," she announced to Will—leaving him to wonder who wanted her—as she stood and began looking around for her things. He didn't offer an apology, and she was glad for an excuse to leave. "I have to get back."

Damn him. What right did he have to analyze her? He couldn't possibly understand what it was like to endure Simon's constant snubbing. With a shudder she recalled the face of the boy in the window, the hardened look of hatred as rigid as a mask. She wasn't lashing out, for God's sake—she was a victim. Her hands shook on the train from Philly to D.C., speeding south. She handed over her ticket, never looking into the conductor's face.

Did she blame Simon for not saving Caleb's life? She believed what she'd told Will: Nobody was at fault for the missed diagnosis. Even the pediatricians had missed it. Simon couldn't have done more than he did. But Will was right about one thing: She and Simon had never discussed it. They'd never shared a single word about it, which had seemed safe and reasonable and a fact of life. And there was a price for the way she and Simon had maneuvered through their tragedy, two people pushing off rocks in the rapids with pokes of their oars. Now they were whirling out of control. The event had tainted everything that had come after it, all of their conversations, their arguments, every one of their plans. But she had not sought Will as some kind of revenge. Her feelings for Will were—what were they? She wasn't sure, but it felt good to be with him, and didn't she deserve to feel good finally? She wasn't punishing Simon by seeing Will; she was taking care of herself.

The advice of a stranger, a loiterer in the supermarket from many years ago, came back to her. A woman in Eddie's Gourmet Market had stopped her in the produce aisle. It was shortly after Caleb died, during the time when people she knew were either avoiding her or were recounting

asinine stories about other dead babies or mourning parents they happened to know of. The woman had long braids, incorporating tiny gray
hairs, and a doll-like face, seeming old and young at the same time. Emily
was deciding between types of apples, organic or conventional, and the
woman rolled her cart close. She didn't introduce herself, but Emily immediately recognized her as someone who'd been pointed out to her, a
woman from Roland Park whose teenage daughter had been killed years
earlier in a car accident. "You'll be surprised," the woman said without so
much as an introduction, "but the pain will pass. Someday you'll think of
your baby, and it'll be like remembering a breakup. Your first boyfriend.
It'll be part of the fabric of your life, and you'll remember how deeply you
felt. It just won't hurt quite as much." Emily had said nothing, stunned
to have been addressed with such directness by a stranger, a stranger who
wanted her to know they had something in common. The woman merely
smiled and steered her cart away, leaving Emily staring, an apple in her
hand. *The nerve,* Emily had thought.

But fifteen years later, Emily wasn't sure whether the woman had been
right. Caleb was more than just a part of that long-stretching fabric, that
quilt of experiences. He continued to haunt her. She still felt the pain
of losing him, and she still suffered. She thought of Will, mopping his
face in the restaurant, the way his eyelids, and his eyelashes, and all the
creases around his eyes had shimmered with delight when he spotted
Anne through the crowd in the gallery. *Life,* as he'd said. Losing Caleb
had overshadowed her relationship with Jamie and imbued every moment that came after it with doubt. She didn't have delusions—she never
expected to become Jamie's hero. Instincts or no instincts, she knew she
didn't have superstar maternal qualities, but she also knew that she could
have done better. She could still do better yet.

She took a cab from Union Station, hurrying toward Bethesda, and
began to worry. Jack was going to ask her where she'd been. She'd spent
so much time out of the office in the last month; people must have begun

to notice. He'd want to know why she'd been attending so many conferences, seminars, speaking engagements, and she'd have to produce
answers. Was it possible, she wondered, that he knew they were only
excuses to be out and unobserved, to be having an affair? Had she been
spotted somewhere, in a hotel lobby? Were people whispering about her
behind her back? But maybe Jack would only mention her travel accounts
on behalf of the bean counters, taking stock of her expenses, and she'd
have to defend the talks she'd given for the benefit of the company. If he
suggested that she obtain prior approval for her speaking engagements
or her conferences or her travel, she'd—she'd—would she quit? No, of
course not. She'd worked too hard and too long to get where she was. She
wasn't going to throw it all away for the sake of a relationship.

No, Will was wrong. She wasn't angry. She didn't blame Simon for
what he hadn't predicted or for what he didn't know. And it was too late
now. Rushing into her building she cruised past Elmer, or whatever his
name was, who called after her to have a good day as the elevator door
closed behind her. She was out of breath as she reached the corner office,
and Jack's secretary admitted her immediately. Jack was seated behind
his desk. She had the thought that he looked better than he had in a long
time. His cheeks looked hearty, even plummy. He was going to ask her
where she'd been. She was prepared to act innocent. *Why, Philadelphia.*
Wide blink. *Speaking before one of the foundations. Didn't we say at the
last senior staff meeting that we'd like to enhance our nonprofit presence?*

"Sorry, Jack. Terrible trip back. I just got in, you know. I was in Philly."
She hoped she wasn't babbling.

"Emily."

"In Philly," she repeated, "as Suzanne must have mentioned. The
meetings went over well. I was pleased." She was determined to control
the conversation. "You're looking good, Jack. Are you tan? You look like
you've gotten sun."

"You think?" He stood up. "Tan, huh?"

"You look practically relaxed."

He came out from behind the desk and sat on the edge of it. "Emily, I'm not sure how to have this conversation."

Oh God, she thought, her stomach tightening. *He knows. He's going to call me out. I'm going to be* shamed *for having an affair. It's worse than I imagined.*

"I wasn't going to say anything, but I feel I have to."

They're going to fire *me,* and she felt the blood rising to her face. *For taking care of my own needs for one single minute. Men have affairs all the time. They have their cocks sucked in the Oval Office, and they don't lose their jobs. Goddamn double standards. The instant a woman even intimates doing something out of line, they're right there, ready to punish. I'll sue,* she thought. *I'll fucking sue every last one of them.* She began to rack her brains for a name she might call for legal action against sexual discrimination, and she came up with two.

"I think I can explain," she began.

"Let me give you my perspective first," he said. "You might know that I've been undergoing the—therapy."

"Um," she started, not comprehending.

"I asked Simon to be private about it, but I figured he'd mention it to you, being his wife and all, so I wanted to say something first."

"Simon?" she stammered.

"When he called me about the drug trial, I was so grateful to have another option. You probably don't know what Valerie and I have been through, but it's been nothing short of hell. When I heard Simon had something new, I was skeptical, but I also hoped. I've had pain ever since I fell, and I've done everything I can to put it aside and not let it bother me, but it's been a constant struggle."

She remembered the holiday party, the terrifying, sick look on his face. She cracked a small, hesitant smile. "You've been an inspiration, Jack."

"I was so grateful when Simon called, I didn't sleep that night. Not a wink. Like a kid on Christmas Eve. Eager and praying that this would be the thing."

"Of course." The smile was frozen on her face. She felt like she must look like a cartoon.

"I can only hope it lasts. I'm pain-free for two weeks, who knows why. I didn't know if I'd ever feel like myself again."

"That's wonderful."

"But I'm selfish, too. I have a reputation here, and I don't like to advertise how sick I've been. People see pain as weakness. They think I'm getting old, and they start wondering if I'm focused on my job. They question my leadership. And when they hear that I've gone in for an unproven, unapproved new treatment, well. I don't even know if it 'worked,' or if it was something else, but I have to be careful. I don't want anyone to think I was just making up how bad it was. My point is, I don't want pain to be the first thing people think of when my name comes up. I'm grateful to your husband, but I don't want to be a spokesperson for his treatment. Now that he's speaking to the press, I don't want my name used. I don't want to talk to anyone about it. I realize this might be a sticky issue, and I wanted to talk with you in person. There's no end to how grateful I am, but I hope you'll understand."

"Of course, Jack," she agreed solemnly. "You're well, and you need to move ahead."

"I don't mean to seem unappreciative."

"Of course not."

"I hope you're not offended."

"Not in the least."

"Vally and I would love to have you and Simon to dinner sometime."

"Certainly."

She smiled at Jack, and she congratulated him on his recovery, but under the surface of her skin, seismic rage rumbled. Her lips sealed in a tight line as she made her way back to her office. She had Suzanne

hold her calls and she shut her door, trembling. The traffic started and
stopped on Wisconsin Avenue and she banged her forehead against the
glass, the dull thuds rattling into her jaw. Here was Simon with another
one of those gestures, which looked like altruism to the world, but had
another message, a secret one, that was directed to her. He might insist it
was insignificant and trivial and utterly defensible. But she knew better.
She knew because it was his way of speaking to her. After a thousand or
so messages just like it, she knew she wasn't blowing a small thing out
of proportion. He was giving his made-up fantasy treatment not only to
patients, but to her CFO, as if he had no boundaries at all—it was his
way of reaching a long and meddlesome arm into her professional world,
threatening her and demanding that she pay attention to him.

And then, everything seemed obvious. Will was right. She'd never,
ever gotten angry. She'd been determined, reasonable, practical—but
never angry. (Wasn't that the best approach? Wasn't she putting forth the
best energy she possessed? She'd put everything into strength, persever-
ance, a stiff upper lip.) But Simon—after all these years, was making clear
that she'd come up short. As if she'd let *him* down by not pointing the
finger. And his way was to goad her with small threatening actions, denying all the while that he had anything but goodwill at heart. Everything
made sense, Emily realized. He'd done an excellent job. She *was* angry.
Moreover, it was clear: Not only had they not left the past behind, but as
they thrashed against each other, they'd become desperately tangled in it.
He would continue tormenting her with his small, damaging actions, to
make them live constantly with their tragedy. She wouldn't, couldn't, let
it happen.

She informed Suzanne she was leaving for the weekend, grabbed her
bag and walked out. At first she wasn't sure where she was heading. Not
home, that was for sure. *The gym,* she thought quickly. She wanted to be

alone, and far away. It was too early for spinning class, but she could bike
on her own. She needed, even for a few hours, to be out of touch with
everyone so that her mind could clear. She got into her car, turned onto
Wisconsin Avenue, shifting lanes with too much vigor, driving too aggres-
sively for the flow of afternoon traffic. Every car seemed to be moving as
if the drivers were looking sideways and ogling the scenery. She changed
lanes, cutting off a truck whose driver flipped her the finger. *Didn't that
just follow suit?* she thought as she banged the steering wheel with her
palm. She was getting it from all angles.

So maybe she was angry that Simon hadn't managed some kind of miracle with Caleb. But what was the use of that? Simon could go on about
this or that being a gut thing, but more important was how you handled
the emotion, what you accomplished with it. Right? She was proud of how
she'd gotten by. It was a kind of heroism in itself. What came to her, as
she stepped on the gas, was her father's face, rosy as an alcoholic, blustery
with arrogance. Must've been as he gabbed with a magazine writer: *Show
me a business model without grandiose delusions at the core.* You couldn't
pin a thing on that man. He made mental instability seem enviable. How
were you supposed to sift through the disappointments in one's life and
know who was at fault? And even if anyone were at fault—and nobody
was—what was there to do about it? Certain turns of fortune nobody
could control. *Sheer bad luck,* as Simon had said to Jamie when he picked
her up from camp. Or was bad luck just something people used as an
excuse? Random thoughts firing, Emily wove through traffic, danger-
ously, surprised as she happened to think of Aileen. Aileen, packing for
college. Aileen storming around the bedroom they shared, tearing shirts
off hangers and tossing them toward her trunk. She was fed up with their
parents and eager to be away from their poisonous pretensions, as she
announced with gritted teeth, *You make your own luck.* Crazy to think of
Aileen now, and whatever that conversation had been about. Emily didn't
even remember. In all the years since Aileen had moved away, they hadn't

seen each other for longer than a weekend, but Emily could still picture
the obsidian glint in her sister's eyes at the moment of that declaration.
She'd adored her sister (her favorite memory from all of childhood was
the night six months before that day of packing for college when Aileen,
at seventeen, had sneaked Emily, an impressively tall twelve-year-old, into
an R-rated movie, glaring at the cashier who was trying to guess their
ages). But she'd also been terrified of her sister, whose desire for drama
seemed destructive, and beneath it all, the rumblings that at any moment
Aileen was about to throw up her arms in disgust for the entire family. The
nugget of truth was that loss was always imminent; you had to be braced
for it. She'd spent a lifetime braced. And maybe it wasn't apprehension
she'd felt when Caleb was born, but the same threat of just-in-case. Just
in case the most terrible thing occurred and you faced a loss that couldn't
even fit inside the words for it. She felt nauseated, and she accelerated
with force that came not just from the ball of her foot but from the hip.
If you didn't give yourself to someone completely, you couldn't get hurt.
God, am I fucked up, she chastised herself, jamming on the brakes as the
car in front of her slowed. *Thinking of Aileen. Really.* Luck or no luck,
you couldn't plan, of course. That was the take-home message from all of
it. You could only figure how best to handle each situation.

But, God, did she *not* want to drive back to Baltimore. She wondered
what Will was doing, but calling would seem cloying. She wasn't using
him—she was certain of that. But perhaps he'd been right about the way
the anger simmered under the surface. It was impossible to see up close,
as you were living it, but it ate at you all the while anyway. Nearing the
Beltway, she glanced up as she approached a large, modern building of
steel and glass. Fancy-looking and impressive, it appeared anchored in
front by large concrete pillars. As she got closer, she could see that the
dazzling exterior had been constructed around an industrial-looking
structure. Now Open, advertised a billboard along its side, Luxury Living Quarters. She was a woman known as a careful decision-maker, but

she was also capable of taking swift action. She steered into the lot, and her heels clicked hard against the pavement as she strode into the business office. The manager, a woman named Monique who wore stilettos and carried a ring of jangling keys, led Emily up to the third floor, bragging about the square footage of the units in the Whitfield and the recent write-up in *Architectural Digest*. By Emily's count, she dropped the term "upmarket" four times. Emily followed, surveying without a word, thinking that she didn't give a damn what it looked like, but as soon as the door to the apartment swung open, she knew she had stumbled across exactly what she needed. She leased the apartment with an electronic check (never blinking at the steep cost of the rent, the first and last months' deposit that were required), and the manager handed over two keys and the code to an underground parking garage.

It was a two-bedroom, with an additional area described as a study that was separated by a pair of wide-open French doors. In the L-shaped bedroom, the sliding closets were covered with full-length mirrors, which she didn't like—a minor quibble. The ceilings throughout were vaulted, and vast windows provided a view of the leafy treetops of a nearby arboretum. The generous architecture made her feel like spreading out her arms. The entire building had been a factory, recently converted, and the units were wide and bright, designed to compel people keen on entertaining guests. She didn't have a single intention of entertaining, though. Quite the opposite, she realized. She needed that place for herself.

Even without a single piece of furniture or a single artistic embellishment, the apartment itself offered a kind of answer. The pale gray-blue of the carpet bestowed a sweeping, oceanic hue to the entire space. She stood at the top of three steps that led into the living room, and she realized that at one time she would have given herself to imagining furniture to suit the rooms, like Mies van der Rohe–style chairs with their clean lines and the illusion of suspension. But the idea of furniture seemed like clutter, and she realized there was comfort in the emptiness. She felt the swell and surge of her own decisiveness, her own heady, ingrained sense of self-preservation. She'd had that instinct in her youth. Good to know it was still in her. She had acquired a place to come and sit. To think. Far from home, away from the office, it was a hideaway to gain a little perspective. She would not reveal to Simon what she had done. She wouldn't even tell Will, she decided. She needed to figure out what was happening, and to put some name to what should happen next. She walked around the apartment, looking from various angles at the views outside. Then, for what must have been an hour, she seated herself on the steps, staring across the bare living room. She had to tear herself away to drive home.

"You must be overtired," Simon commented that evening when she responded curtly to his announcement of the latest inquiry into his pain treatment, a patient willing to travel all the way from New Jersey for a session. Jamie might have scowled at her, too, but Emily didn't take it to heart. She said nothing about the new space to which she had just laid claim. Her thoughts were elsewhere, but they were subdued and surprisingly peaceful, toned in part by the gray-blue of the carpet.

The Whitfield became a secret daily detour. Each day that week, on her way to work, she drove directly to the apartment, as if participating in a weird ritual. She savored the defiance of her new digression, and a sense that she'd finally done exactly the right thing for herself. *It's me versus the rest of the world,* she thought. (It took a while before she remembered she'd acquired the phrase from Will, and that it had signaled something rather uncomplimentary to him about Lindsay and her lack of communication skills. But it was possible, she decided, that some struggles were inherently personal and that you couldn't invite anyone to understand them.) Some afternoons, she stopped in again on her trip home. The strangest part was that she did nothing while she was there. Mostly she sat on the living room steps, looking out the windows. The tops of the trees had begun to change with the crisp September air, inflamed with a dramatic trickle-down of color, like brushes seeping dye. *Glorious,* she thought, as if they burned for her alone. The one clear thought she had was that she wanted a different kind of life from the one she was living— one that felt different from the inside. But she couldn't imagine what that other sensation would be or how a person achieved it. All she knew was she was missing what Will had described so crudely: *life's goodies.* And time was passing, wasn't it? What if you never figured out how to get to a place where you could enjoy them?

On Thursday, she talked to Will on her cell phone from the apartment; they were flirtatious, and she kept the chatter light. He tried to apologize for the conversation from the week before, but she wouldn't let him. "I've been wishing I could kiss you," he said. They began to plan the next time they'd meet at a hotel. "This weekend in Alexandria," he suggested, and she agreed she'd try to arrange a reason to be there. He wanted to photograph in some historic churchyard. She didn't mention the apartment, not wanting it to speak for her as any kind of promise, not sure how long she'd keep it. At home with Simon, when the urge arose in her to tell, she thought defiantly: *There's nothing to tell. Why shouldn't a person have a place to think?*

On Friday evening, a week after she'd rented the apartment, she was intending to stop in for a little while after work when she drove past an antiques shop in Bethesda. In the window she spotted an ornate rocking chair and a tall gumball machine, and above them hung a pair of worn ballet shoes. She pulled over, intrigued, thinking she might buy some kind of chair for the apartment, something to sit in front of the window. She wandered through the shop, and she didn't find a chair she liked but soon found herself paying for items she'd never imagined she would purchase. They weren't compatible with each other, and the combination of them didn't establish any sort of decorating statement. She took a floor lamp with a curved stem and a fluted shade, and a small three-legged table with a round, inlaid marble top. No rhyme or reason to her choices. Her apartment needed drapes of some sort, she thought. So many windows—they were fine for the view, but she preferred a little privacy. She had an idea about art she wanted on the large wall. And then, as she was imagining what she'd hang in the large bald space, she realized she was moving in. When she got to the apartment, she called to order a bed, the same type of bed she and Simon shared. "How soon can you deliver it?" she asked. The manager promised the drivers would call ahead to let her know they were coming. "And you'll assemble the wood frame?" she asked. "We do everything," he said. "All you have to do is let us in."

She hadn't fully considered the functionality of the space before, but now she began to plan and assign. The L-shaped room in the back, though longer and narrower, would serve as a main bedroom. The second room could be for Jamie, if she cared to have a bedroom there (the thought made her sigh out loud). Of course, Jamie would come there. Maybe not right away. But maybe in time. Jamie would be impressed by the factory-design elements that were still visible in the architecture, the pillars, in particular. The school year was around the corner, and she dared to imagine Jamie, hunched over a table, doing homework in the study. And then, on the days when Jamie wasn't there, the space was large enough for Will to stay over without either of them feeling crowded. All the travel back and forth on the highway and the trains was growing tiring. She didn't want to speculate where the relationship was going or what was developing between them. She wasn't sorry she'd told him about Caleb or that she'd broken down—she was well aware that the kind of changes she wanted in her life would be uncomfortable, and that some kind of discomfort was probably necessary in order to change. And slowly, as she parsed all the possibilities of the space she'd rented, she began to see what she had done. But things happened backward sometimes. She'd taken the first action, and her course was obvious now, she realized with a full-throttle head rush. She was leaving Simon.

But oh. How would she tell Jamie? Dread gnawed at her again, despite knowing she was doing the right thing. She'd have to explain in just the right way. She'd explain as slowly and as honestly as she could. And she'd be careful not to malign Simon in any way. No child needed that. No, Emily would be sensitive. Jamie would not react well, and might even be angry for a while, but Emily would be patient with her reaction. She'd weather the anger, accepting it. She wouldn't react to it. Emily couldn't go back in time and start over, but she could resolve to change, to be better. She'd tell Jamie that, Emily noted to herself. *I want to be a better mother to you,* she imagined herself saying. *I can do better.* Jamie would crack up, just laugh in her face. She remembered how Will had described confronting his older daughter, Rachel, during that tumultuous year of rebellion. He'd put his relationship with her on the line. She could withstand Jamie's response, whatever it would be. As far as Simon was concerned—she was ready to tell him. There was only to be honest now. Driving back to Baltimore, she was buoyed by a kind of giddy optimism, assuring herself the best she could do for both of them, to ease them out of suffering, was to leave.

On her own. *What a delicious prospect,* she thought as she drove. Of course, she wasn't entirely alone because she had Will. She felt open to learning about the world, and Will had so much to teach. She should have realized it about him years ago, she thought remorsefully, but she needed other things then. It was amazing to feel—after all this time, in this hardened state—that she was still capable of growing, of changing. Her instinct to take care of herself was still there, but it was seasoned with understanding. She was making decisions based on the realities of her life, the one she had lived until this moment.

When she arrived at the house on Greenway, it was a little after five o'clock, and she was half startled to discover Simon sitting at the dining room table. Spread before him was a mess of paper, half typed, half scribbled over with red pen. Upstairs, she could hear the long, melancholy song of the vacuum. She'd forgotten it was a Friday, and she realized she'd forgotten cash for Lorraine. She hoped Simon had remembered.

"Look at this," Simon said, showing the draft he was working on, crisscrossed lines and circles of red, the print sideways and diagonal. His hair was mussed, as if he'd been tearing at it. "I was up all night last night. Couldn't sleep at all. As soon as my last patient was done, I came right upstairs to try to finish. Journal article. I've got to get the word out."

Emily, thinking of the message she needed to deliver and wanting to speak with Simon alone, asked, "Where's Jamie?"

He gestured upstairs with his pen.

She stood at the edge of the room, barely moving. "Don't you wonder where I am anymore? Have you even noticed I've been in and out of town a dozen times in the last month?" she asked slowly.

He nodded. "Meetings, right?"

There was only to say it. She stood behind a dining room chair with both hands draped over the back as though she were giving it a massage. When she spoke, her voice came out low, as if she had pebbles in her mouth. "I don't want to do this anymore, Simon."

He tucked his red pen behind his ear, leaned back. "A lot of travel, huh? Sorry I've been distracted lately. This treatment is— Emily, it's going to be amazing. When people find out— did I tell you a reporter from the *Sun* was here today? I pitched the story and they sent a reporter out here to talk to me, to follow me and meet the patients."

"No, I mean, this." She indicated the space between them with a slow movement of her hand.

He grew silent. The skin under his eyes went lavender, and she felt her stomach clench. "You don't want to—"

"To be married anymore." As she finished his sentence, the expression in his eyes seemed to glaze over, as if he had ceased to see her. She remembered the moment with Will when she'd actually felt like a cheater, when she'd given them both away, and she felt herself falter. Like a hand in the dark, she groped for the decision she'd made—what was it?—a life that felt different—but what was it supposed to feel like?—she couldn't remember if she'd actually come to an image. Wasn't this for the best? Wasn't this going to save them both? *Yes,* that steely voice inside her said, *it was for the best.* She recognized that voice. It had once told Will that she wasn't going to India. It came from the place that took care of her, from the core that knew how to make critical changes. She had to take care of herself. And then she was strong again. And determined. "There, I've said it. That's what it is."

"Oh." He stood up, bent over, as though she'd just socked him and he couldn't straighten. The chair he'd been sitting on fell backward, banging dully on the rug. One hand went to his head, absently knocking the pen from behind his ear. It bounced and rolled under the table. "Really?"

He wasn't going to explode, she realized. At that moment she felt her strength turn a little bit brutal. *A matter of survival,* she thought. "I've rented a place. Near work, so I won't have to worry about the commute."

He began gathering up the papers. "This is not very good timing."

"I don't know what to tell you."

"It's a great treatment," he said in a voice that sounded like it came from a dream. "Noninvasive, nonaddictive. The only side effect seems to be a pervasive sense of well-being. You wouldn't believe the response. The phone's been ringing off the hook, people telling their relatives."

Could he not engage at all? "I want a few pieces of furniture. Nothing important. You can keep the dining room set. I know you cared a lot about the piano."

His voice dropped until it was almost a whisper. "It's the most important moment of my career. The most significant, hopeful thing I've ever been able to do. I'm flying to Salt Lake City tomorrow. There's a pain conference I just learned about. All pain people. Who treat pain, I mean. Who know how little there is to offer patients and how desperate most of them become when the therapies don't work."

"Did you hear me?" she continued like a robot. "I said I'm leaving."

"It's just—the timing," he said. Silent for a moment, he regarded her. "You believe me, don't you? You know I'm not imagining it, right? This treatment is for real."

"We can't just keep doing what we're doing."

"Right." Vindicated, he left the room, still holding his handful of papers, scratching his head. She looked around the room—would she miss any of it? Every item they'd acquired, every color in the room, seemed to have lost relevance to her. When he returned to the dining room, she hadn't moved. "You're sure about this? Because I think—I know if there's something I can do better, I'll try. Just let me."

But she'd already envisioned the end of the tunnel, and herself out the other side. Even if she began to list the things that had occurred that had bothered her, little things like the window washer, he'd never understand the link to other things, like calling Jack Whitby when there were a million and one people in pain he might have chosen. Simon would look at her the way he'd looked at her in the car on the way to the airport, as though she were the one who lacked understanding of social interactions as well as feeling for humanity. He could beat her over the head without ever acknowledging the cudgel.

"I've made up my mind."

"Really?" he repeated. "I don't get it." The fact that he hadn't seen such a change coming—and even worse, that he seemed not to be undone by her decision—made her more resolute.

"It's nobody's fault, but we ruined it. Both of us, a long time ago." He stared at her. "I don't think we ever healed." It was harder saying the words than she'd expected, and she had to force them out: "From Caleb."

"Right. Caleb."

She was reminded of standing in the shoe store, her son's name spoken in the wrong voice. Even hearing Simon utter it, somewhere between a statement and a question mark, was painful.

"We have to get out from under it."

He looked hard at her. "But we did, together."

She didn't respond. She considered telling him that she didn't blame him, that she knew what had happened hadn't been his fault. In her heart of hearts, she still believed it. She believed it as a fact, and she believed it with love. Even the pediatricians hadn't been able to save Caleb, she thought resoundingly. In certain ways, he was right, they had managed to protect each other all those years. But some other impulse kept her from uttering the words. If he was waiting for her to reassure him, she couldn't bring herself to say anything.

"I thought you needed space," he said. "I gave you space."

"It's still with us though."

"You didn't want space?"

"I don't know."

He ventured cautiously, "You don't love me?"

"This isn't about love," she said, both hands still gripping the back of the chair. Love wasn't the issue. You could love a person past the point that you could live with him. You could love him and need to start over, somewhere apart from your mutual wounds. She needed to look at a day without feeling like a person being swallowed by the past. "I'll have a phone by the end of the week." The sound of vacuuming ceased. She looked around in the stunning silence, having forgotten that they weren't alone. They listened to the machine being unplugged, Lorraine's foot-steps, the sound of the cord being sucked back into the bowels of the machine. "Where's Jamie?" Emily asked, more softly. "I should tell her myself. Or we can tell her together, however you think is best."

His stricken face pulsed with another wave of unease. "She wasn't feel-ing well. She went to bed early."

"It's only five," she said with concern. "She's sick?" She could see clearly, just then, how out of touch she'd been from the house all summer, how she'd floated through the space like a stranger. She was a terrible, terrible mother. She had to change.

"She's got some virus. She's not speaking to me lately. Since the wine. I told her—I promised we'd get to it, as soon as this treatment's on steady ground."

"She was counting on you," she said, watching him wince.

"It's consumed me, this treatment. You have to understand, it's monumental. It could change countless lives. I can't just pretend nothing's happened."

Emily took a deep breath. She'd imagined more emotion from him. Maybe she'd been hoping for histrionics. Instead, she felt deflated, all of it happening neither with a barrage of loud words nor with a weepy, hand-holding summit like Will had described with Lindsay. She had girded herself for the worst. Even more devastating, it was going to be too easy to split apart.

"I should be the one to tell Jamie," she said with determination. "We'll work something out, joint custody or something. I don't want to fight about anything."

He nodded, still processing. "Okay."

She walked steadily up the stairs, but the light was out in Jamie's room and she could hear her daughter breathing heavily from bed. She didn't have the heart to wake her—and it didn't seem the right way to do it. She wanted to sit down with Jamie and describe the situation, the whole complex and layered picture.

"I'll tell her tomorrow," she said as she returned to the dining room.

"Are you staying here tonight?" he asked.

"I don't know," she answered, realizing she hadn't thought that far ahead. She didn't want to stay, but she also didn't want to leave without explaining to Jamie what was going on. She wondered suddenly whether Simon would want her out of the house, but he didn't seem to be pushing her to leave. "I guess I'm staying. There isn't electricity yet. In the apartment. Or a bed actually."

"Okay," he said, not moving. After a moment, he added, "It would help, if you were here. I'm supposed to leave tomorrow for this conference, remember? Jamie, well, she'll probably be fine in the morning, but you should be here. I was supposed to leave early tomorrow. I tried to call you. But I just assumed—"

"I'll stay. Of course, I'll stay." She saw a chance to be with Jamie, alone. It would be a chance to begin rebuilding.

"The conference goes until Monday night. Three days." He looked bewildered. "Maybe we should tell Jamie together when I get back." And then so like a little boy that she was surprised to feel her first moment of sadness. "Can you wait? I'd really prefer to tell her together."

She swallowed. "We can tell her together."

He looked down at his papers. Then he looked back at her. She was glad he was leaving in the morning. She didn't want to defend her decision or explain. But apparently he wasn't going to ask her to. Instead, he changed the subject altogether. "I'm hungry," he said, as though he had just remembered the fact. "Lorraine made something. I'm not sure what it is, but it has potato. You coming?"

Then the strangest thing happened: As if it were any ordinary day, they went into the kitchen and ate together, some salami, potato and bean concoction and a green salad Lorraine had set aside earlier. They set forks and plates and sat at the table. Their postures were hunched, and they stared downward. They didn't speak for a long time. Sadness hung over the table, but a certain anxiety was gone, Emily observed, and just the way the vacuum cleaner had revealed itself when it shut off, the silence had crispness that was new.

Finally, Simon asked, "You sure about—this?"

"Yeah."

"My business is here. I'll have to buy you out."

"That's ridiculous. You'll change location."

"No, too much disruption."

"Your patients will follow. It'll be good for you to have the office far from the house. A little more breathing space."

That young, wistful look fluttered across his face. "You've always helped with the big decisions. We've always done these things together. You're sure this is what you want?" She didn't answer. "I was thinking maybe I shouldn't go. Tomorrow, you know? Because—" He paused, but in marital nuances it was clear he was talking about Jamie.

"No," she said quickly. "You go. It's important—as you said—the most important moment of your career. I'll wait for you to get back to say anything."

"This isn't a trivial cause," he said again. "These people are in pain. They can't get out of their houses. They're suffering and they're desperate. A lot of them have been hurting for years and nothing's helped them. Some of them lose the will to live because the pain's gone on so long."

What kind of pain had she been enduring? Something dull and tight and forced, imprinted under the skin like a watermark, and yet there were times when she'd convinced herself she had everything in order and she'd managed not to feel it at all. Why was it that he couldn't understand it in a way that could help her? "I'd like to get some sleep," she said finally, rising from the table and taking their plates.

"I'm back Monday night."

"I'll be with her."

They could hear Lorraine stowing cleaning equipment in the second-floor closet, and then descending the front stairs with her tired gait. Emily never liked the interaction at the end of the day, feeling something between guilt and embarrassment, as if Lorraine had too much dirt on them. ("It's her job!" Simon was always quick to point out.) Emily stayed in the kitchen as Simon went to the front to pay her. His voice sounded as energetic and exuberant as ever while he was thanking her and ushering her off. Emily listened to him close the door and then the sound of his footsteps returning to the kitchen. "I've got some things I need to look up," he said, as if he'd returned to business as usual. "Articles and such. I'll be up later." She watched him head down the basement stairs, and she waited for a feeling of unease or apprehension or dismay and felt nothing. No, she felt fine. She washed the dishes and wondered whether she would want any furniture from the house at a later date when she wasn't feeling quite as numb. Simon could have the piano that he'd lobbied so hard to buy with the house, the piano that Rachmaninoff had played at the music director's birthday. She might like to have a china cabinet that had belonged to her parents and the antique vanity that she'd bought at auction and that had turned out to be worth three times what she paid. She remembered two paintings in the house that Simon had acquired through connections, and she felt certain he would give them to her.

So she'd have the weekend alone with Jamie. As promised, she'd wait to explain the situation to her daughter, but it felt better to be saving the news for his return. It would be a family conversation.

She lay next to Simon that night, but she kept to herself inside her eye-shades, and she slept fitfully. She could hear his breathing, and she thought it strange how each person's breathing was as distinctive as a voice, even though there was nothing to hear. At some late hour, she thought she heard him say into the darkness, "Emily, my head's spinning." Was he talking in his sleep? (She noted smugly how different his pronunciation of her name was from the way Will said it. So plain and straightforward, no hidden musicality. *Hemily,* as funny as it sounded, was an unexpected gift.) She listened for more, but she didn't answer. Sometime later she heard him stirring, getting up, dressing, gathering his things for the airport. She didn't remove her eyeshades, and she didn't say good-bye. All night, she'd been trying to imagine how they'd tell Jamie when he returned. Delicately, she was sure, using vague adult expressions. *We've drifted in different directions.* She thought of Will, his face glowing with the thought of Anne, and she wanted that raw, bare-bulb emotion. *We had no choice but to . . .* and Jamie would say—what? Emily couldn't even picture it. They'd have to be smart to make Jamie understand.

When Emily came downstairs in the morning, Jamie was slumped on the leather sofa in the den, still in a nightshirt, long and pink with the word "Angel" in glitter across the front, and she was eating cereal out of a mug. She appeared zoned out, watching a cartoon, chewing with her mouth open and dribbling little drops of milk onto her lap. The cartoon featured a dorky man in a trench coat who seemed to have superhero qualities. Emily was tempted to say something about the mug on the leather sofa—there were house rules, after all. It took all her willpower to swallow the remonstration. She sat down and then reached out to put her hand against Jamie's forehead, but Jamie arched out of the way. Emily sighed and sat down on the sofa, staring at the TV.

"What's this?" she asked.

"Inspector Gadget."

"Is this new? I've never heard of it."

Jamie shrugged, eyes glued to the set. She had wrapped the afghan around her shoulders. Her skin had a weird greenish cast, and there were dark patches under her eyes. Typical virus, she thought. No more than that. It was astounding how you got to know your child's features, how you could see those color changes. "Feeling icky still?" Jamie shrugged again. "Dad left this morning for his conference. Did you hear him?" Jamie didn't answer, and Emily reached deep, deep inside for resolve. She could do this. "Can I get you anything? Want orange juice? Juice would be good for you."

Another shrug.

"You're not talking to me?" This was going to be a helluva weekend.

She watched the cartoon. Glancing at Jamie, she watched the girl's slow blinking stare. "You have a fever?" No response. Simon always took care of illnesses, and she always hung back, letting him. "Should we take your temperature?" Nothing. She stood up, decided. "I'll go look for a thermometer."

She rummaged through cabinets in two bathrooms before she located one. By the time she returned, Jamie had dozed off with her head on the arm of the sofa. The mug was on the coffee table, next to a water glass, and both were coasterless. Emily set the thermometer aside, found a soft, woven throw and covered Jamie's shoulder. She placed the water glass on top of a magazine, turned off the television and settled on the other end of the sofa, wondering grimly how long she'd be able to sit and wait.

Jamie slept for most of the day. Emily lingered and after a while busied herself, strolling through the house, taking mental inventory of their furniture. She found a small desk she wanted that she'd forgotten about. In the afternoon, she opened a can of tomato soup, heated it on the stove and set the bowl on a tray. Jamie had stretched out the length of the sofa, and Emily set the tray on the coffee table.

"Jamie, want soup? You really should eat something. Sit up, Jamie, and have some soup."

Lethargically, with glassy, unfocused eyes, Jamie lifted herself to a seated position and managed a mouthful.

"How's that? Want another bite? Have another bite of soup, Jamie. Make yourself wake up, Jamie. That's it. Open your eyes. You have to eat something. You have to drink. It'll help you feel better. How's that?"

Two spoonfuls, and Jamie lay back down. "Ugh," she grunted. "Not hungry."

Emily reached out and clamped a palm on Jamie's forehead, which she found warm before Jamie wriggled away again. "That's not enough soup, Jamie," Emily said helplessly.

"More sleep," she mumbled and snuggled down into the sofa again.

As night approached, Emily deliberated going upstairs to bed, but she thought Jamie might wake in the middle of the night. Instead of retreating, she kept Jamie company. She curled herself up in the leather lounger, feet up, head on the armrest. When she awoke in the morning, her back ached, and she gazed at the abandoned sofa, the afghan puddled on the floor. She heard noises coming from the kitchen. Jamie stood at the sink, downing a glass of water. Emily stared at the word "Angel" on her night-shirt, momentarily mesmerized by the glittery script.

"Feel better?" she asked. Jamie's cheeks were pinker, and Emily felt relief that she looked a little more alert.

"I feel sick," she said, sounding congested.

Emily tried to remember what Judith had done when she and Aileen were sick with the flu. She remembered a heavily stocked chicken soup loaded with garlic—or maybe it was jalapeño—that was supposed to be good for a cold, unwrenching the sinuses. She didn't have the recipe, and anyway, it would take too long to produce. She felt useless and despairing. She couldn't remember the last time Jamie had been sick, and she wished Simon were there to consult. Like a bird's flutter, some vibration under the skin made her wonder whether she should be more worried, whether this was something serious, and she quickly banished the thought. You had to let your kid have the flu without jumping out of your skin. "I have Motrin. You should take one." She looked around for her purse. She knew she had some in her little pillbox.

"I want to lie down."

Emily reached for the narrow patch of forehead and was relieved that Jamie stayed still long enough to let her head be felt. Under her palm, there was a palpable heat going. "I think you do have a fever."

"I just want to lie down." She headed out of the kitchen.

"Oh," Emily said, "okay." She knew she was being ridiculous, but she couldn't help being disappointed. She still had hopes of spending normal time with Jamie over the weekend, not having the truth-telling session that would come sometime later, but cooperating in something that would feel not particularly tense. It hadn't happened on Saturday, and it didn't look like it was going to happen on Sunday. She hadn't found her purse, and as she went to look for the Motrin, she realized that if she needed to, she could let herself into the clinic and look around for samples. Then, from the other room, she heard her cell phone ringing, and she hoped it was Will because suddenly she wanted advice from him. Not health advice, just support. Encouragement about how to handle her daughter: *Just stick with it.* But she knew better than to expect Will. He never called her cell phone when it was likely she'd be home. Instead, the call turned out to be Elegant Bed. Her new queen, said the dispatcher, was on its way to the Whitfield and would arrive by two in the afternoon.

"That won't do," she said quickly. "I need to cancel."

"There's a two-hundred-dollar cancellation fee, plus a fifteen percent restocking fee. Plus there's charges, I don't know what, to schedule a delivery the second time. You got to call the main number," cautioned the dispatcher. "You down with that?"

"But I'm not there," she said emphatically. "I'm not even in town. This is unacceptable. Who delivers a bed on Sunday anyway?"

"Can somebody else receive it? You got a building manager or something?"

"I'll call the manager," she said. "I'll call you back to confirm that someone'll be there."

She dialed the number she had for Monique in the office.

"Ah, I've been trying to reach you," Monique said. Emily was immediately annoyed. She'd disliked the woman's stilettos, the way her mouth had savored the word "upmarket," and now the suggestion that Emily had been inconveniently out of touch. "Did you get my messages? We received a large box here for you—hand-delivered—that was placed inside your apartment. Our office closes at noon on Sundays, and we can't be responsible for it. Policy, you know. We couldn't do that for all the tenants. There just isn't space."

Emily knew at once what it was, and she didn't care that they'd been inside the apartment, even though its sparseness would have made anyone wonder what on earth she did there. She understood also that there would be no building manager to let the deliverymen in that afternoon. She asked what the office's policy was, just in case, if someone, a friend, came to open the apartment for her. Would Monique hand over a key to such a friend before she closed? There was no one to ask, except Will, for such a favor. She remembered he was supposed to be in Alexandria over the weekend doing a photo shoot of some sort. Alexandria wasn't tremendously far from Bethesda. Perhaps he could take a break. She called his cell phone.

"I need help," she said. "I have no one else I can ask."

Her voice must have sounded despairing because he wanted to know at once, "Y'okay?"

Was she okay? She was trying to get a life in order. "I'm fine. I just need a favor. I remembered you're in Alexandria this weekend. Any chance you could make it to Bethesda?"

"Uh, this weekend?" he said, sounding surprised.

"Not for that. A favor." She whispered into the phone, turning her body away from the living room in case Jamie happened to be nearby. "I did it. I got my own place."

"Oh," he said, surprised. "Wow." The breathless catch in his voice gave her a tiny rush of pleasure. "That's not what I expected to hear."

"I did it for myself," she assured him, still in a whisper. "I wasn't even going to say anything until— I want you to know I'm sincere about— about what's happening between us. I'm not using you. You don't really think that, do you?"

"Emily—" he began.

She cut him off. "It's the right thing. It's healthy."

"I'm just surprised."

"Don't criticize," she insisted. "It's the only way. You have to believe me. It's a very nice place. Just let me show you. It's a very big step for me—after everything that's happened. I just can't get there today."

She explained that Simon was away and that Jamie had the flu and that she had no way to arrange to get the bed into the apartment because the office was going to close. Was there any chance he could make it to the

Whitfield office before noon to get the key and then perhaps hang around to meet the truck? Three-hundred-plus dollars in fines and fees seemed like a colossal waste. And, she realized, now that she'd decided to move, she wanted the bed set up so she could move as soon as Simon came back. She was ready to occupy the space. She apologized for intruding on Will's schedule and for interrupting his shoot. He stammered, but then he agreed. "I'll do my best to get there by noon," he said. She thanked him twice and gave him quick directions. It thrilled her that he would see the new space, empty and cocoonlike, and the collected fragments of her new experience, her odd lamp and her small table, her view of the arboretum leaves. They had hung up before she remembered about the package in the apartment, but she decided not to mention it.

She went into the living room and sat down on the leather lounger. She watched TV with her daughter, an inane program where a number of postadolescents were forced to live together and get along. They'd obviously been prodded and primed by producers, because the interviews provided staged comments and the young people—they couldn't have been more than twenty—were emotionally invested in every interaction. She managed not to utter any judgment or criticism of anything. Just being in the room and being silent as her daughter watched TV seemed like a small step toward a different kind of relationship. They watched two programs together without exchanging two words, and then she looked up and noticed that Jamie had fallen asleep again. She draped the woven blanket over her daughter again and muted the TV. She sat back and watched a cooking show where a long-haired woman was browning shrimp on toothpicks in a sauté pan. She jumped when her cell phone rang and answered in the kitchen.

"It's me," Will said, and from the static she could tell he was in the car. "Hate to tell you, but I'll never make it in time. I'm stuck in traffic."

"Now?" she asked. "It's the middle of the weekend!" She looked at the clock on the wall. It was twenty minutes to twelve. And in a beat, she had weighed all the details at hand: The essential arrival of the bed. That Jamie could simply go on sleeping. That Jamie didn't care whether Emily was home or not. What she had learned in her career was that it was often impossible to count on other people to perform eleventh-hour tasks as well as you wanted them done, and that ultimately you had to step up to the plate yourself. "I could still meet the truck," she murmured. "I'll make it work."

"I'm sorry. I did try." There was a pause.

"I would've liked for you to see the place," she pouted.

"Is there any chance I could see you?" She was reminded of the first day he'd bumped into her, when he couldn't hold back, when he wanted to walk her to her car, and she was flooded with warmth. All that good, generous energy. "I've driven all this way."

But she was gauging time: forty-five minutes (at the speed she usually drove) to the Whitfield, forty-five back, half an hour for the delivery guys to assemble the bed. Already, it was long to be out. "I can't," she said. "I'm not going to stay. I told you, Jamie's here and she's not feeling well. I want this to be in and out."

"Even if it's just briefly?"

She imagined showing him the view in her living room—perhaps while the deliverymen were doing their work. He'd just get a sense of it, and then she'd come straight back to Baltimore. "Just a hello"—she lowered her voice—"no more than that."

"No, no," he agreed, and she thought she heard him sigh. "I won't stay long."

"I do want you to see it. It's a great place."

"Okay," he said. Traffic was changing then, he told her, and he had to hang up.

She checked the clock again, refiguring the time. Jamie probably wouldn't even notice she was gone. She went to look for her purse. The problem, she realized, was the truck. What if it arrived late, what if the men had trouble assembling the bed frame? What if Jamie woke and found herself alone in the house? It just didn't feel right. She went into the living room where Jamie was curled on the sofa, the woven blanket under her chin. There was only one thing to do—and as she looked at her daughter, who was sleeping on her side, breathing strongly through her mouth, she decided she had to revise her plan. She'd take Jamie with her in the car. All Emily had to do, after all, was make sure the delivery-men could get into the apartment. Jamie could continue to sleep. And of course she'd tell Will not to come. She wouldn't explain the trip to Jamie in any detail. (That she decided instantly.) They would drive to Bethesda, meet the delivery truck. But she would keep her promise to Simon, and they'd explain the future to Jamie together. It was only fair. She waited until one o'clock and then she rocked Jamie's shoulder and whispered her name several times.

"We have to go somewhere," she said. "You have to get up. Can you put some clothes on? Sweetheart?"

"Where?" Jamie whimpered. "I don't want to."

"C'mon, I'll help you. We're going to do an errand. For a friend. You can sleep in the car if you want."

Jamie sat up and looked around. She blinked and her eyes were glassy. "Can't I just stay here?"

"I'm not leaving you."

Emily dug the Motrins out of her purse, and she handed Jamie the glass of water that had been on the coffee table. "We're in a little bit of a rush," she said, as Jamie downed the pills. "Ready now?" She stood and waited for Jamie, who just sat there, looking stupefied. "Can I help you?" She held out her hand. Already, she'd given up on the idea that Jamie would dress, or even change out of her pink slippers. "Here, put your arm over my shoulder," Emily directed, finding Jamie so heavy to lift from the couch that Emily began to wonder if her daughter was fak-ing the exhaustion. "We'll get this done efficiently, but I won't leave you here alone," she said again. Jamie stood on her own finally, and Emily guided her down the front steps of the house and into the front seat of the Sebring, buckling the seat belt around her. Jamie, snuggled into the seat, was hot on the insides of her elbows and her back. There was no other way to do it, Emily reasoned, and wouldn't a little fresh air do some good?

"I'm cold," Jamie complained. "I don't want to go." Clearly, she was going to make the trip as difficult as possible.

"I'll be right back." Emily raced into the house and brought the woven blanket from the sofa. She put it over Jamie, who sat in her "Angel" nightshirt and slippers, looking glazed and apathetic. "Very quick errand. You just relax." She began the drive to Bethesda. After a while, Jamie leaned her head toward the door. Emily couldn't tell whether she was sleeping or just avoiding conversation. She trailed a truck, reading the sticker on the back door that said HOW'S MY DRIVING? with the company telephone number. Someone had responded to the question, plowing the answer with a finger through caked-on dirt: SUX. Her heart pounded as she drove. She flipped open her cell phone, dialing Will to let him know the plans had to change. Jamie was with her now, and Emily was not about to make an introduction. "Hi," she said into his voice mail when he didn't answer. She chose the words of her message carefully, a kind of code, "I have Jamie with me. So. That's what I'm doing. I'll take care of this. I hope you understand. Yes, another time then. Okay," and she was absolutely sure he would understand.

It was a nonemergency last-minute trip, she fully acknowledged to herself as she headed south. It was indulgent and compulsive and slightly selfish, but this was a strange time, and she was caught this weekend in a strange limbo, having announced the end of her marriage and made provisions for her future and yet still having to hold back and pretend. She could have incurred the fees and the fines, but why? She began gripping and ungripping the steering wheel with white-knuckled fingers, and she was back to imagining the conversation that would take place when Simon returned. She glanced at her daughter, whose head had lolled drowsily toward the window, and in her head she rehearsed. *Your father and I have had many difficulties over the years, more than we can even explain, and they're the kind of subtle difficulties that only a couple can understand from the inside.* Too much information? Maybe just the plainer detail: *It's not working out between the two of us. Hasn't been for a long time.* She imagined beginning: *We respect each other, but we can't live together any longer,* which sounded, deplorably, like some press conference.

Jamie continued to sleep even as they drew close. Poor sick girl. Emily pulled up at the Whitfield into one of the guest parking spots, and she let the car idle for a while. Then she turned it off. She remembered the first time she had met Simon, the rum and Coke dripping over his hand. She remembered delight in his face as he watched her open an imaginative birthday present he'd dreamed up. Losing Caleb had ruined them—there was no denying it, she thought, and had made it impossible to enjoy even the pleasant things they'd shared. After a while, she caught sight of the Elegant Bed delivery truck pulling into the parking lot. She got out of her car momentarily and waved to the truck. "It's apartment 330," she told them, handing the driver the keys and pointing toward the east door of the building. "I want the bed in the L-shaped room." She gestured toward her vehicle. "I have to stay here. My daughter's in the car. Sleeping. Don't forget, the L-shaped room." She went back to the car and watched as the truck parked and the men hoisted up the rear door and began to unload the bed. Beside her, Jamie gave a quick spluttering cough.

"Just rest, sweetheart," Emily said. "You don't have to do anything."

The sleepy voice: "Okay."

They sat for forty minutes as the car idled and the air conditioner blew a chilly stream around their legs. She wadded a sweater and wedged it between Jamie's head and the door as a pillow. She was rehearsing again. *We changed.* Or reassurance: *This is not because of you.* This time she imagined, *It started before you were born. When Caleb—well, you know.* And then, despite herself, she found herself wondering. God, what would it have been like, if he'd lived? If she'd had the chance to know him? Certainly everything would have evolved differently. Jamie might have turned out softer, easier to be with. *And what,* Emily thought, *would have happened to me?* Her eyes welled up, startling her, and she had to blink to clear them because then the men were coming out of the apartment building. The tall one walked toward her, came to the window and returned her keys, and she signed a clipboard. "I suppose I should have looked at it first," she said.

"No worries," he said, sliding the pen into a groove on the clipboard. "Ain't nothing but a bed." And that was true, after all, it was just a bed.

She was going to leave then. The errand was complete, she had her keys, and it was time to take Jamie back home. Perhaps if she'd just stayed in the car and left, the rest wouldn't have happened. But she felt drawn to take a look at the new bed, and she felt another urge to check on where the building maintenance had placed the crate, and she had another compulsion to peek in again on the apartment, which was hers and which she hadn't seen in two days. At that same moment, Jamie half-opened her eyes and mumbled, "I have to pee," and Emily responded, "You do?" and decided that if they took two minutes to stop inside, it would not be the end of the world.

She hunched Jamie to her, gripping her across her shoulders, the woven blanket over Jamie's back like a shawl, and they made their way across the guest parking lot and into the building. "We've done our errand," Emily was saying just to fill in what seemed necessary information. "We'll just use the bathroom. Then we'll head back."

"Whose apartment?" Jamie asked, and even though Emily's heart stutter-skipped, Jamie didn't look like she cared.

"I don't know," Emily hedged, doing her best not to lie, and considering it a half-truth when she added, "Somebody new."

Inside the apartment, Emily escorted Jamie to the bathroom. They passed the paper-wrapped crate that the maintenance guys had dropped off just inside the doorway. It was tipped against the wall. Jamie was slow on the toilet, and there was only a travel packet of tissues from Emily's purse to use as toilet paper. But then when she was ready to leave, Jamie looked altogether out of it and wanted to lie down. "I don't want to sit in the car. My stomach hurts."

"Lie down here?" Emily asked.

"Please. Let me just lie down."

And that was how they wound up staying longer. Gently, Emily helped Jamie down the hallway and settled her on the bald, new-smelling bed in the L-shaped back room. She tucked the woven blanket around her. What she felt at that moment fluttered like something unexpected. Was it just the opportunity to be useful? Or was it being able to respond to a simple request with a *yes*? She brushed Jamie's bangs from her forehead, the skin beneath her hand as warm as before, and her heart felt so full of love for her daughter, she thought she might burst. This was what Will had brought her to, this moment, she thought as she looked into Jamie's flushed face. Why had she never felt this before, this ripped-apart feeling, for her little girl? Why not just let her sleep a little bit instead of marching her back to the car?

"I'll be right back, sweetheart," she said. "I promise."

As her daughter slept, she sat in the living room the way she had all week, except it felt different, more real and less like some kind of fantasy. She went to the wide living room window, pressing her hand against the glass, looking out over the trees embroiled in their red and orange transformations. Her phone rang then, and she turned away and knew that Will was calling her back. He'd be on the road back to his shoot or back home, but she was eager to tell him that she was taking steps in the right direction—all baby steps, she knew—but that she was going to be okay.

"I'm downstairs," he said, sounding tired. From all that driving, she thought.

Her skin prickled all along her arms. "You didn't get my message!" she exclaimed in a loud whisper. "I told you not to come. I have Jamie with me. She's sleeping."

"I didn't," he said, sounding disappointed. "I didn't hear the phone. And now I'm here."

"You can't stay," she said in a whisper.

"I really didn't get the message."

"Listen, I'm coming down to let you in so we can talk. But you can't come into the apartment. Okay?"

Leaving the apartment door unlocked, she ran down the stairs to let him into the building. At once, the sight of him filled her with pleasure. She waved and watched him cross the parking lot, his easy, loping walk, moving as if his hinges had been overoiled. He was wearing one of his rumpled shirts, a soft-colored plaid, wrinkled as if he'd never heard of hanging anything in a closet, let alone ironing. His shirt had come untucked, and she had the wonderful desire to tuck it in for him. How had she fallen for this person? It amazed her, and yet he'd managed to change her.

"It's the worst time," she told him, "but I'm so happy you're here. Jamie's sleeping, poor kid. Please, please come upstairs just for a few minutes. I want you to just peek inside the door." She refrained from taking his hand, but she led him up two quick flights. He looked slightly bedraggled, a little five o'clock shadow, a little tired around the eyes. All that driving, she thought. It wore on her, too. "I told Simon on Friday," she said, again in a whisper. "It was hard, and sad, but it went okay, I think."

She pushed open the door of the apartment, listening for Jamie. There was no sound from the bedroom. With a quick motion to him to wait a moment, she left Will in the doorway and went to check: Jamie was still asleep, lying on her side on the bed. She went back to where he stood with one hand against the doorjamb. She stood close to him, not daring to kiss him, but taking in the smell of him and thinking how that smell had so many meanings for her by now. It was connected to so many times in her life. "Isn't this beautiful?" She gestured so that he could see into the apartment all the way to the tremendous windows across the living room. "I wouldn't say I owe it all to you, but you did help me discover some things, and I'm—" She smiled with a full, unguarded smile. "What do you think?"

"It looks like a very nice place," he said. Was he tentative? She did not have any reservation. She'd made the right decision for herself. "Hemily—" he began.

"Listen," she said, leaning against the door, whispering. "I don't know where things are going between us, but I'm open to it. You've taught me a lot. Really." He looked embarrassed. She wouldn't let him interrupt. "And wait—don't say anything," she said. It was time for the surprise. "I wanted you to see this." She pointed to the large package, tipped against the wall just inside the apartment. She went to one end of it. "Look," she instructed.

She tore a single strip of paper away, ripped right down the side. The exposed area revealed a wooden crate, and beneath the protective wood slats there was a layer of filmy protective wrap. She tore through that too, so that he could see the many different shades of blue, the blurry image of himself, his eyes closed, his head tucked.

"I had to have it," she said. "She's very talented. Anne. I almost couldn't keep it a secret. I called Maya, and she arranged to have someone drive it down here, and then I almost called you and spilled the beans." Gushing, she didn't notice his face, which was still.

"Oh," he said slowly. "It was you. We had no idea."

She took his hand. His head was ducked, his eyelids shading her from seeing his expression. Was he going to cry? She was both nervous and eager for his emotion. She could handle it.

"Hemily," he began again. There was a tightness to his cheek, along his jaw. The scar of his old dog bite seemed to grow more complex for a moment, and just as she thought how well she knew that spot on his face, she knew what was coming. "I don't know how to say this—" he said. She steeled herself, not breathing, but she was a master of public relations. She knew a letdown from a mile away. "I had to come down here to tell you in person—there was no other way." Before he said another word, she realized he'd driven all the way from Philly and not from Alexandria, and that perhaps all along he'd intended to help her with her errand, but he'd also had more to say. "It's Lindsay. She just showed up at my door. We've been talking all weekend, and we think—I think—there's just too much history for us to walk away from. Our whole marriage, you know?"

Her pulse lulled. Finally, she let herself breathe. "But you've gone different directions," Emily reminded him.

"You're a wonderful woman, Hemily."

"Please stop saying my name." A swimming wall rose in front of her eyes, blinding her, but she was grateful not to have a view of the apology on his face.

"I think the world of you." Every word was another dagger. "You're smart, and you're strong, and I swear, you're in my heart forever. But Lindsay's my wife, and whatever reservations I've had, I feel we—she and I—have to work through it. Our daughters are growing up and leaving. We're having to discover ourselves again, you know? And we've probably done a bad job of it, and I'm sorry to have dragged you into something. I just didn't know."

"Oh, please." Despite herself, she was the one who had begun to cry.

"Hurting you was the last thing I wanted to do."

"Oh God." She smeared her hands across her cheeks, trying to hide the tears.

He reached out and rubbed a hand against her upper arm. "Y'okay?"

For some reason, it made her giggle. This long-winded speech. He'd probably rehearsed it. He'd probably been working on it for hours. Was she okay? Of course not. She wiped at her eyes again, but there was no hiding the fact that she was blubbering. Pointing at the painting, she asked helplessly, "What am I going to do with this?"

"I don't know. You can resell it—or return it? I'm sure Maya will take it back."

But they were beyond pondering its fate. She could not have formulated a plan anyway. Unable to stop crying, she wanted him gone, and she shook herself away from him, stepping inside the door, getting ready to shut it. "Good-bye," she said, as he continued to try to make sure she could cope. "Good-bye. I'm okay. It's all right." She shut the door against him, locked it and leaned against it. And then he was gone. She wasn't even sure why she was crying—except from the surprise, which was like being thrown into dark water. It wasn't as though they were in love. Or were they—madly, deeply—and she hadn't noticed until the moment he was leaving? Will had opened her up, like you open a fist, finger by finger. *Why are you crying, you idiot?* For all the changes at the eleventh hour. For the shock of being blindsided. For having imagined what it would be like to be released from the sorrow she'd been carrying around for so long and for not knowing what to do with herself in the world if she could be free of it. As though her spine gave out on her, she sagged, slumping down to the floor. She sat, unable to move, her legs splayed, and cried into the apartment's emptiness.

Then, gripped by an impulse, she looked at the package propped against the wall. She walked to the painting in its protective wrapping, and with a deft motion tore away all the rest of the brown paper. Grabbing through the wooden slats, she reached for the filmy protective plastic, shredding with clawlike fingers. Her teeth were gritted, and her hands were shaking, and she made little grunts as she ripped and tore. She grappled with clumsy fingers for her keys in her pocket and pulled them out. And then, with a fistful of them poking between her knuckles like a caveman's flints, she gouged at the canvas. She stabbed at it just once, and it ruptured like skin. Just once. That was all she would allow herself. But she'd ruined it. Her anger felt small and petty as an ember, almost adolescent, but it felt good, too, and she stepped back with satisfaction, breathing deeply, when the thing was destroyed. Then there was a sound from deep in the other room that made her halt. She'd almost forgotten about Jamie, lying on the bare bed, until she heard the plaintive voice calling her. It surprised her like a hand shaking a sleeping shoulder, and it stirred something that felt utterly primal—an instinctive alarm—that she hadn't felt, it seemed, since the night they'd rushed Caleb to the emergency room. She turned toward the voice, which rose from the dark of the bedroom, from the delirium of fever.

"Mommy? Mommy?"

PART FIVE

The sun vaulted high above the Wasatch Mountains, and Simon was sweating against the inside of his collar and under his arms. He wrestled the corners of his carry-on suitcase across the backseat of the taxi, lowering it onto the curb in front of the Salt Lake Hotel. Looking up, he noted a mounted sign for the pain conference. The Indian driver wore the blue turban of a Sikh. With a long, elegant neck, he turned around, his arm over the passenger headrest.

"I'm very sure you will impress them with your finding," the driver called over his shoulder, his buoyant accent like timpani notes. Since the airport, he'd listened to the story of Simon's father, the astounding car accident with no repercussions. He'd emitted a whistle when Simon described how Jack Whitby had left the office rubbing his hand against his back, blinking with disbelief. The cabbie said, "Ah yes, of course," when Simon reached the part about phoning a long list of chronic pain patients, beginning with the ones in the most pain of all.

Simon had described it all, aware of the way the driver was listening with more than passive attention. The more he narrated, suddenly in a setting far from his office, the more convinced he became about his discovery.

"This is a problem that has no nationality, no religion, no language of origin," the driver pondered philosophically as Simon dipped into his pocket for his wallet. It seemed he wanted to continue discussing it. "If there is one thing we all experience at some time, it is pain. It has the capacity to drive us, to instill us with motivation."

Simon glanced toward the mountains where the trees, like a welcome mat before the range, were just beginning to turn yellow and auburn. The driver said, "In my religion, it is mandatory to face tragedies in the world head-on and do whatever is possible within one's means. I have no doubt your news will be very well received."

Simon leaned into the cab with his fare, three bills together, fluted down the middle. "Keep the change," he said.

"Thank you," the driver responded, sounding as though he'd expected it.

"You'll hear about this stuff," Simon said enthusiastically. "I promise. It'll be in the papers and on the news."

"I have no doubt that I will."

Simon dragged his suitcase up the curb and into the lobby of the hotel. Inside, he blinked as his eyes grew accustomed to the lighting.

"I'm here for the pain conference," he said to the concierge, who pointed to a reception table in the corner and to a woman in a pink sweater who stood beside it, holding a clipboard.

"Dr. Simon Bear," he said to the woman—Bev, according to the tag pinned beside the V-neck of her pink sweater. She consulted page after page on her clipboard, peering through EZ-Read glasses that hung on a beaded string around her neck.

"I called," Simon insisted, rocking on his heels. "I spoke to someone. I paid. They said I could get on the list even though it was late."

"Your name again?" Bev asked.

It occurred to Simon then that he'd forgotten his ditty bag at home. The plaid nylon pouch, with his toothbrush, razor, shaving cream, styptic, was still sitting on the edge of the bathroom sink. He'd been packing it when he realized that Emily would be gone when he came back after the weekend, and he'd simply walked out of the room and left the bag, half packed and gaping open, on the sink. He marveled that his life had taken this turn, and that from here on in he would have to make a phone call to his wife, wherever it was she was staying, to orchestrate how they would take care of Jamie. Who was responsible for what, who got what. Divided up, the details became tedious and overbearing. He couldn't think about it. Not now. *Don't think about it.* There was too much he needed to do in Salt Lake City. He'd come this far to get the therapy into the public eye, to get knowledgeable, sophisticated people in the field to take note of it. This was an opportunity he couldn't allow to slip away. There was plenty of time for the rest of it. He'd immerse himself in the details of getting divorced—*don't think about it*—as soon as he was back in Baltimore.

As Bev flipped through the pages, squinting through the half-frames, he remembered also that he only had accommodations for one night of the two he intended to stay. By the time he'd called, the hotel nearest the conference center had been booked. An international gymnastics competition was occupying vast numbers of rooms at nearby hotels. He would have to hope another room opened up. He wasn't worried. Emily insisted on a written itinerary, every step mapped out when they traveled. He preferred to wing it. But he'd postponed booking anything because he hadn't determined a strategy for the conference, how he'd introduce the infusion therapy. What if he booked himself at one hotel and then found the best people to associate with were staying elsewhere? Location might make all the difference, and he wanted to be able to be flexible. But now it seemed he might have screwed himself by not taking care of the arrangements beforehand.

"Do you have a list of nearby hotels?" he asked Bev.

"One thing at a time." Still scouring her papers for his name. "I don't have you down here," she determined finally. She pointed with her pen to the other end of the marble hall. "You can use that phone to call the main conference number and pay your attendance fee. Then I can issue you a name tag."

"Look, I'm a little late as it is, and I flew all the way across the country to be here. I can assure you I've already paid."

"I can issue you a tag once I have your confirmation number." She was near his age, he estimated, maybe a little younger. Her face had the shape of a horse chestnut, and her eyes were made up to accentuate irises so blue they were almost teal.

Dutifully, he crossed the lobby, dragging his carry-on suitcase by the handle. He picked up the phone on the wall and glanced back in Bev's direction. He dialed the number she'd handed him, got a busy signal, hung up and dragged his suitcase back to where she was checking someone else in. He hung by her shoulder until she was finished.

"The line was busy, which I know is probably a matter of timing and the fact that it's a well-attended conference. It's amazing how many details you coordinators need to take care of. I'm amazed by what you do. As it is, I'm late. I'm bringing a new therapy, and it's important I get in. Can I trouble you for a tag and take care of the technicalities at the first break?" She was not unattractive. Her hair was shoulder-length and cut in feathery layers that all hung down, soft-looking. The eye makeup was overdone, but added drama. On the young side of forty, he decided now. Soothing face, athletic arms. The faint creases around her mouth and under her eyes suggested she'd spent considerable time in the wind and sun, and he revised his impression of her from a hard-nosed secretarial type to a grudgingly tough camp-counselor type, which appealed to him somewhat more. Stomach turning, he realized this was how it would be now: He could flirt with her. He was a man who was soon to be divorced. He ducked his head and conjured a boyish smile. "I'll get you all the right numbers. Soon as the session's over."

She twisted up her mouth as she considered this deviation from protocol. "Oookay. Just make sure you get back to me."

He explained ingenuously, "I'm here all the way from Baltimore. Bringing a new therapy. Absolutely new. I tested it out in my clinic back home, and it's done wonders. People who couldn't get off the couch because of pain have been able to walk."

"Well, you came to the right place," Bev declared. "We got everybody you'd want to meet here. All pain specialists. Seventeen states and six countries represented. Just make sure you get me your confirmation number, oookay?"

"Thanks, Bev." He turned in the direction of the session and hurried toward it.

As he was walking away, he remembered Emily, standing behind the chair in the dining room, coolly making her announcement. She'd taken him so by surprise, he hadn't even had a chance to respond. Hadn't even questioned her decision. Hadn't defended himself. He'd accepted it because he'd been expecting for the past fifteen years that she would leave him. He turned back to Bev, who was checking her clipboard. "Maybe I could tell you later about this treatment? Over coffee or something?"

"Just get me the number at the break," Bev said, not unkindly, "and we'll see then."

Dollying his suitcase down the hall, past an informational poster propped on an easel, he ducked into the first room on the left where the speaker—a neurosurgeon from Washington State—was already deep into a PowerPoint presentation on the benefits of a new implantable device that delivered electrical impulses to the spine. "So what we're doing is intercepting the pain signals, if you will," the clean-shaven speaker explained in a voice that was annoying for its pretend modesty. Simon knew the new treatment with its revolutionary electrode array was only a shot in the dark, nothing more impressive than sulmenamine, when the doctor added, "This system has shown efficacy for individuals with certain pain syndromes and particular constitutions. We've proved long-term success in sixty to seventy percent of those we've seen," the man went on, "and of course we choose patients selectively." The system he was proposing, Simon realized shortly, had a price tag of ten thousand dollars. Simon looked around to see if the audience of physicians seemed receptive.

"I don't get it," he called out, after waving his arm wildly as soon as the floor opened to questions. "Maybe I'm too practical, but ten thousand dollars for a therapy with no guarantee? Who's going to pay for this?" Simon had his suitcase wedged between his calves, and he was certain he saw other heads in the audience bobbing in agreement.

He was growing bolder. He sat through a presentation on trigeminal neuralgia and smiled smugly. It was a classic case, just like his patient Florence Rudolph, who had reached up to itch her nose and felt a burning flash across her cheek that was so severe, she thought she'd inadvertently cut herself with the edge of a fingernail. The condition was believed to be caused by the deterioration of the fatty coating around the facial nerve, which made the neuron short-circuit, sending scrambled messages into the brain. Florence was the one who refused to wear eyeglasses because of the sparks that would shoot through her cheeks and into her gums. The patient described in the case study finally had undergone surgery to separate the damaged nerve in her face from a cerebellar artery that had collapsed against it. But Simon had been treating Florence Rudolph with sulmenamine, and he was almost certain he was getting results. What he had brought to the conference would undoubtedly set the pain scholars afire.

He flipped through the program, reading the abstracts and the bios of the researchers. He wished he'd discussed the conference with Emily, formulated a plan about whom he would approach and how he would present his findings. He'd never met anyone who could deal so coolly with a multitude of people who were experts in their fields.

He decided the best tactic would be to introduce himself to individual researchers, a grassroots approach. He'd greet them first, casually describe the treatment and what he'd seen so far. That way, he'd generate buzz, a low-level undercurrent awareness of sulmenamine, and he'd wind his way slowly toward some of the more influential scientists. At the end of the second talk, he wheeled his suitcase back out to the hall. Toting it along behind him, he noticed another man leaving, heading toward the elevator. He positioned himself by the elevator, rocking on his heels.

"Simon Bear." He thrust forward his hand.

The hand that met his was strong, the grip competitive. "Bill Marlon." He had a shiny, ruddy complexion like a guy who golfed or sailed.

"Exciting stuff going on," Simon said, looking around. "You from around here?"

Bill named a teaching hospital in Virginia. "Interventional radiology. You?"

"Medicine. Private practice in Baltimore. You presenting? Yeah? What's your topic?"

"Percutaneous vertebroplasty. For compression fractures in the spine."

"Never heard of it," Simon said. "Is that for osteoporosis?"

"Or cancer. Osteolytic bone, older patients, seventy years old and so on. It's a relatively new procedure. I inject liquid cement into cracked vertebrae. Big syringe, X-ray guidance." He made a pumping motion with his fingers. "When the cement hardens, bye-bye pain."

"That works?"

"A fucking miracle. Stabilizes the collapsed bone, keeps it from breaking further. What's amazing is that it takes care of the pain, too. The exact mechanism isn't clear, but patients hobble in, have the therapy and walk right out."

"How about that."

"It came from Europe. I'm bringing it here."

Simon looked at him appreciatively. "Gluing them back together, huh?

All the king's horses, all the king's men. You're what Humpty-Dumpty was after. And the exact mechanism isn't known?"

"A couple theories, but nothing definitive. How about you?"

Simon patted the pocket of his jacket. "I have a new drug for chronic pain. Sulmenamine infusion therapy."

"Never heard of that, either."

"It's brand-new," Simon said. "I'm introducing it. Actually, it's an old pharmaceutical with new pain applications."

"You're a drug rep?"

"No, no!" Simon said, offended. "I'm a physician. I discovered the therapy."

"Ah, wow. So did you publish?"

"Not yet," Simon acknowledged. "I'm writing it up now. I just came to meet people, get some names behind it, see if I could spread the word some."

Bill Marlon glanced down the hall, looking to see who was coming. He looked at his watch.

Simon continued, "I've tested it on several patients so far, and the success rate has been remarkable. I have at least three cases of complete remission."

"Um-hm." He checked his watch. "I'm due upstairs, supposed to meet some people, old friends. Nice meeting you. Best of luck."

He thinks I'm a quack, Simon realized. *He can't get away fast enough.* It happened again later that morning when he tried to introduce himself to the head of a pain clinic in Minnesota. The guy—Fred Arbermore—shook his hand and listened with his face stretched into a smile. He nodded and stroked his beard. "If it's all you say it is, I'm sure we'll be hearing a lot about it," he said and turned to talk with someone else. Nobody asked for more details about sulmenamine infusion therapy, and nobody asked how he'd made the discovery. He'd flown all the way from Baltimore to be rebuffed by a tight community with its little in-groups and cliques and its hierarchy of publications. Dragging his luggage to the lobby, he decided to leave the conference center and head to his hotel. There was one other mogul he'd spotted: Adele Maples. She led a pain research center in Boston, and she had connections to Harvard and also to some spin-off companies that were developing therapeutics. If he could get to her, he might be able to make some headway, drop the name of the treatment, leave his card. He'd spotted her sitting to the side in one of the talks, but between sessions, she'd been flanked by other people and deep in conversation. He wanted face-to-face time with her in which he could explain himself fully.

In the morning, after taking a cab back to the conference center, toting his suitcase with him, he found Bev standing at the reception desk. Most of the name tags were gone from her reception table. She pointed at him with her pen. "We had a deal, Dr. Bear."

"I didn't call. I forgot. I'll phone right now."

"I meant coffee."

He smiled gratefully. "I could use some."

"There's a place down the block." She grinned and told him she'd gone ahead and phoned the conference headquarters for him. They'd found his name in the computer and she had the number she needed for her list. She dangled a ring of keys and offered to stash his suitcase in a closet in one of the main rooms. He declined.

"You pulling around gold in that thing?" she teased.

"Something like that."

She worked for the Pain Studies Council, which was hosting the event. A low-level administrator, he decided as they entered the wood-paneled coffee shop, adorned with dangling tangerine-colored lampshades. He thought maybe she'd be useful down the line getting names and numbers if he wanted to contact some of the scientists, but she didn't seem to have special access to anyone in particular, and unfortunately not to Adele Maples. In any event, it was helpful to have another human being to talk with. She ordered a decaffeinated latte with skim milk.

"Nonfat decaf?" he joked, standing behind her in line. "More aptly called 'nada latte.'"

She seemed amused. As they waited for her drink, she bopped slightly to the music coming out of an overhead speaker, and he couldn't remember the last time he felt like he was experiencing a moment exactly as it was taking place.

"What you're doing is amazing," she said, sipping her latte, after he'd told her the story of how he found sulmenamine. "All of you. Taking on this great black box. Trying to make sense of it. I was talking to a scientist who said it's as hard to pin down pain as it is to pin down consciousness. It's not a thing, it's not a place. It's not even a summation of experiences. I don't have a lot of scientific know-how. I just read about the nerve studies and type up what people are doing, but I'm amazed by all the ways you people approach it."

"I didn't go looking for the answer," he said. "It found me. All I did was question what I was seeing and connect the dots. I stumbled across this therapy."

"Chance favors the prepared mind," she said brightly. He watched her lift her coffee drink. Her maroon fingernails brought to mind the color of a scab.

"The trouble is, I can't get anyone to listen," he griped. "They want to hear from each other, not from some guy in private practice they've never heard of. They wouldn't care if it'd been handed to me from God."

"Why don't you just go to the drug company?"

"Because it would look like I'm after money. I could tell the company, but I don't want anyone to think I'm trying to capitalize on this cure. I'm not about the money. I just want to do something for these patients. Maybe I'll have to go to the company eventually, but I wanted to get the word out first."

"Maybe you need more evidence," she suggested. "Or maybe you could work with someone. You know, collaborate. Pick someone who's better connected than you are and work your way in like that."

"You can't even begin to imagine the joy of it," he said, almost bouncing on the seat. "You have a woman sitting in front of you in the office who's just a shell of a human being. Really, like a shell on the beach. It's like the pain has moved in and taken up all the space of her personality. Like her soul's been evicted. You give a shot of this stuff and she remembers she's capable of being in control. She's maybe not herself right away, but she's moving back in. She's the master of her fate, the captain of her soul."

She smiled and her almost-teal eyes sparkled. "I can tell the kind of person you are," she said. "Just from your face. I can tell all about you."

"How's that?" he asked.

"You got smile lines around your eyes. These ones." She pointed with a maroon-tipped finger without quite touching his face. "People have them who smile a lot. I always look for them when I meet someone new. Small thing, but they tell you a lot. I can tell you're for real."

He looked: She had them, too. Sitting with her in a coffee shop in Salt Lake City, Utah, could not have felt more otherworldly, more like a page borrowed from another person's life. But the feel of her genuine goodness was like slipping into someone's coat pocket, safe and warm.

"I think my wife left me," he croaked, looking down.

She put down her latte. "What do you mean, you think?"

He described what had happened just before he left for the conference. She listened, looking like she was weighing the facts he enumerated. For a few moments, from her expression, he thought she might say, "You completely misjudged what she was saying. She was just going out for a *walk,* just to cool her heels. You'll see when you go back home." But she pursed her lips in grave appreciation, and then she twisted up her mouth, just the way she had when he'd asked if he could report his confirmation number later.

"Our daughter, Jamie," he said, feeling weight against his chest. "She's

just a kid. This's gonna come as a blow." For a moment, his mind went
to his morning ritual, when he stopped on his way down the hall to peer
in her bedroom and watch her sleeping. The notion that he would not be
able to do that anymore, that the rhythm and the certainty of that habit
was halted forever, tightened like a string at his throat.

Bev tilted her head to one side knowingly. "Relationships have great
plasticity," she said. "Just like nerves. They can get injured, but they also
regrow." She gazed out the window of the coffee shop to the people passing on the street, and he thought that he liked that idea. He hoped she
might say more. "You probably want to get back to the conference," she
said finally.

The answer, he was convinced, was Adele Maples. The trick would be
arranging a private confrontation with her. At the end of the first morning session, she walked out of the room in animated conversation with
Fred Arbermore. Simon followed them down the hall, feeling hopeful,
and also like an idiot, wheeling his suitcase as if he were walking a dog.
She was older, with slightly stooped shoulders and a quick, determined
step. Then, they reached the lobby and were joined by two other people,
and Simon hesitated. He wanted to talk with her alone so that her response wouldn't be tainted by others listening, and he decided the moment wasn't right. He'd bide his time and approach her directly before
the end of the conference on Monday. He'd revised his opener: He would
ask her advice, as a pioneer in the field and a person who was capable of
taking discoveries and making them available to patients. He'd act more
circumspect. "What should my next step be?" he would say.

He plucked a map from a kiosk and brought it back to where Bev was
sitting at the front desk. He was growing tired and beginning to question
why he'd flown across the country. What had he believed would happen?
He'd thought maybe a Fred Arbermore would say, "Let's order some

of that stuff for the clinic and give it a try." Or an Adele Maples would say, "This is the most hopeful concept I've seen in years." But it wasn't about what anybody else said, he realized. He was telling the truth when he said he didn't want money. He wasn't interested in making a cent. Was he interested in the patients? He wished he could be the answer to their problems, but couldn't they all find another doctor somewhere else? What he feared was that the only thing he really wanted was to tell Emily about it. The glory, in its boiled-down form, was being able to describe it to her at the end of the day. Fired down further, as if in a crucible, the goal was to have something to say at all. He wanted to go back in time to the months before Caleb was born, when they were still reeling with a sense of their good luck. Hadn't they believed then that certain powers shined upon them—they had each other, they were skilled, they owned real estate. When they decided to make babies, they considered them-selves embarked on the most ambitious endeavor of all.

"How far's Ogden?" he asked, sinking into a chair next to Bev.

"What's in Ogden?"

"A hotel. Maybe."

"Ogden! That's ridiculous."

"Everything's booked." He confessed, "I didn't plan ahead exactly."

She narrowed her eyes. "I have a big room, and I'm all alone. You're welcome to stay with me, if you want. No funny stuff," she cautioned, "just a place to stay."

He actually blushed. "I couldn't trouble you."

"You won't find anything this late."

He looked at her, deeply appreciative. "Can I take you to dinner?"

"You can." Her smile reminded him of a commercial for a breath freshener.

It was something like a date, and he had to keep reminding himself that he was in Salt Lake City for the sake of the sulmenamine infusion therapy and for the patients who desperately needed it. But it was also relieving to leave the conference and to put off trying to present himself and explain what he'd observed in his office so far away. It was exhausting to try to pitch himself and his ideas to an audience that didn't want to hear from him, the kid on the schoolyard trying to get in the game. Under the suspended red lanterns of a Chinese restaurant down the block from the hotel, Bev Pinkney was lively, sweet and staggeringly uncomplicated. She lived with and took care of her mother, who had multiple sclerosis. She'd come close a few times, but she'd never married. "I liked them, but I didn't love them. Each time it seemed like I'd be settling," she said. He'd almost never met anyone with as little angst. "I like what I do," she said, "but at the end of the day, I don't take it home with me."

They went back to her hotel room. "You can have that one, if you want." She pointed to the far bed, the one near the window, tucked neatly with its mottled purple comforter, just like its twin closer to the door. "I don't care."

"I don't care either," he said. "Don't let me put you out."

Her pajamas were a set, a button-down top and baggy pants, like a man's, only pink. He got the theme, Pinkney, pink. Everything about her was simple and straightforward. It was relieving. He had only his boxers to wear and a T-shirt, and he got under the covers quickly, as unobtrusively as possible, in the far bed. So much kindness from a complete stranger—he felt gratitude that made him close his eyes and exhale. As his feet reached down in the covers, it seemed the sheets possessed an exponent of thread-count he'd never experienced before. They felt glorious along the hairs of his legs. The pillow received him. He felt the weight of his eyelids, and the heaviness of the skin on his cheeks, and he nestled into the bed, luxuriating in the feeling of being looked after. It was lovely. He waited for the sound of her turning off the light.

She'd said what she'd said about no funny stuff, but she was the one who sat on his bed instead of twisting the switch between them on the nightstand light, and she was the one who invited herself under his covers. The strange part was that he felt better in more ways than he could count, but as soon as they kissed, he knew he was going to be useless. His penis hunched like a timid hamster. His lips moved perfunctorily, but his tongue felt dry. His hands stroked the skin of her arms, trying to think of something, an image of Emily that might help. He was aware of Bev's breasts pressing against his chest, but he didn't feel desire. "Sorry," he said finally, pulling away from the kiss. She murmured reassurance, "It's okay, don't worry about it," and her hands worked with surprising and unusual industry. His thoughts strayed into his usual file of images, Emily's breast, that gentle, promising pink, which only made him sad, and then he considered the sulmenamine in his suitcase. Was it sexual dysfunction he was suffering from? He felt like laughing to consider taking the drug he'd brought as his trophy. But ultimately, he didn't want to sleep with Bev, as kind as she'd been, and there was no point in trying.

It seemed strangely like luck when his cell phone rang in the middle of the night. The blood was thick in his fingers as he picked it up and saw Emily's number. His first thought was that she was calling because she knew that he'd betrayed her, as Bev stirred next to him in her man-shaped pink sleepwear. His heart cringed and then thudded with hope. Perhaps she'd changed her mind. But the hope was tinged with panic: If he'd ever had any chance of changing Emily's mind, he'd now ruined it. Slowly, it occurred to him that if she was calling him, it wasn't because she knew he was lying in a bed in Salt Lake City with another woman. It was that something had happened.

"It's Jamie," Emily breathed. "We're at the hospital."

He was at the airport within an hour.

When Caleb was born, Simon became aware of a perceptible shift in the nature of time. At one point in his childhood there had been something unremarkable and true about how one minute became the next. The days dragged before summer vacation. In school, the minutes passed with syrupy slowness as he sat on the edge of his chair, waiting for the last bell to ring at the end of the day. But the day his son was born, time seemed to lose distinction, good or bad, tolerable or intolerable, memorable or lost forever. The minute-to-minute experience stretched in all directions at once, weaving and overlapping and, most frightfully, disappearing. The nights were long, and yet he could barely remember them in the morning. Each second felt precious, and yet he couldn't wait for them to pass.

It began with the panic at the office, Emily's labor and the process of sifting through the medical knowledge in his head and trying to listen to his wife at the same time.

"Do something," she'd insisted.

"Wait a moment," he'd responded, rushing to the cabinets to see what he had in stock to give her.

But how long was a moment? The time between contractions collapsed like a spring and then stretched as they counted the length of each one. And it was only half an hour, maybe forty minutes, from the instant she arrived at the office to the minute that Caleb appeared, slick with vernix, but it seemed like he lived through medical school all over again in that shard of time. The moments with emotional weight—the initial ecstasy of holding his son, the terror of dropping him—were pinned in the mind. The others just vaporized. How had Emily looked holding their son? He was sure they'd spoken to each other plenty those early days, but what had they said? The mind had a way of trimming what it considered unnecessary fat. But certain images seemed as though they must remain somewhere.

For instance, he didn't remember what his son looked like that first month. What he remembered was the wonder of such extreme fatigue, more thorough and more desperate than any exhaustion that he'd experienced during the call nights of his residency. He remembered one morning of great pride, walking down the street pushing Caleb's stroller in Sherwood Gardens near their home, and the feeling that he'd entered a brotherhood of men. But he did not remember Caleb the baby. With the exception of his son's shockingly flattened nose at the moment he emerged from the birth canal, he didn't remember what Caleb looked like.

A month and a half later, at the hospital, Simon was watching the stirrings under those same fragile eyelids, his own heart racing, his insides feeling like tin. The details of the death scene—those that he could remember—were stilled in his head like an ant in amber. He could look at those moments from every angle, if he chose to, and he didn't, but what about the others? It had begun with a fever. Emily picked Caleb up after a nap and thought he might be warm. But the baby was not febrile. Was Caleb lethargic? It was impossible to tell: He slept and he woke and he slept again. Was his cry distressed? Again: It sounded like the same ribbon-thin wail he'd made since he was born. Emily picked him up in the middle of the night, and then they panicked. Even dialing 911 seemed like it would take too much time. Emily cradled Caleb in her arms in the car, and Simon tried not to crash.

The triage nurse still had her mouth open when they were whisked to a secluded area in the ER. Simon pressed against the partition curtain, but Emily hung back at the periphery, biting her thumbnail, her arms close across her chest as if she were holding herself. The baby was feverish, and as they pulled away his clothes and then his diaper, there was a faint, purple rash dotting the crevice of his buttocks. There it was, the meningococcal hemorrhaging under the skin. How long had it been there, and why hadn't they seen it?

"We'll do everything right here," a nurse informed them as the medical team surrounded Caleb's body, and Simon crowded in with them, obedient, dry-mouthed, attentive. They gave Caleb oxygen. Another blood test. A spinal tap. The white blood count was nearly fifteen thousand, a doctor told them, and Simon had to think hard to remember normal would be under ten thousand. He wanted to know: which antibiotics? what doses?

Only gradually, like climbers in a slow rain, step by step losing footing, did Simon and Emily begin to realize the situation was desperate. They watched and they waited.

Then, all of a sudden, or maybe it was longer than that, they were in a free fall, and nobody could save him.

The nurse who appeared at Simon's elbow said, in the smallest of voices, "I'm sorry." *This is what they say when it hasn't gone right,* he thought, trying to make sense. Had they tried everything? Maybe there were other techniques that hadn't been considered? Other drugs that hadn't been used yet? He expected to hear the nurse say that they'd tried everything, to reason, to rationalize. He realized what he craved to hear from her more than anything in the world was something that sounded like an apology. *We've failed you, we've lost your son, we've failed you.*

Instead, she said, "Would you like the opportunity to hold him again?" She said many people did, in similar circumstances. She said studies had shown that having private time with the child, just the parents alone, could help the mourning process begin. *Begin?* he thought numbly. He was bobbing on the open sea, treading water, completely lost. He had to begin a mourning process, as if he could push off from somewhere solid, launch himself from a starting point? But where to? In which direction? How?

In the hallway, Emily resolutely said no: She didn't want to hold Caleb again. She didn't want to look at him, either. She didn't want the image of his body—like this—to be the final one of him in her mind, to carry that with her for the rest of her life. "Fuck the studies," she said. "I don't want to hear about any goddamn studies." She didn't like hospitals and sickness, blood and veins, in the first place, so he wasn't entirely surprised by her decision. Tears coursed down her cheeks, alongside her nose, as her shoulders shuddered. She sniffled into a ratted tissue, and she did not glance at Simon. "No, thank you," she said. And that was the only time he'd seen her crying.

But he believed the nurse, the studies, what others had learned from experience. What else could he believe in? He rocked on his heels for a moment, feeling stunned, and then stepped past Emily to reenter the room where the medical team had fought, valiantly he was sure, to keep his son alive. There were tiny marks on Caleb's skin where he'd been poked and stuck, where tubes had protruded into his tiny veins. His palms had begun to purple, finally, with the rash that might have helped if it had appeared sooner. He lay with his knees bent, vulnerable and pitiable, but almost comical, too. The bent legs reminded Simon of a dissection frog from his earliest biology class. The head, swollen from the meningitis, made him look more like a space creature than a newborn human. Simon had the macabre thought that if Caleb had been a cartoon, there would be x's now where his eyes used to be. His son's skin had already begun to lose its warmth, and its appealing pinkish color seemed more reminiscent of clay. He spent a few moments touching Caleb, stroking the wax-soft arms, covering the tiny cartilaginous feet with his hands, fingering the row of toes like corn on the cob, but, fearing that Emily might have a point about indelible images, he didn't lift his boy from the table.

They buried Caleb in a quick ceremony with as little pomp as possible. "There's nothing to say for a newborn that isn't a cliché," Emily said. They'd only recently purchased a membership at the Reform synagogue— and they'd only done so because a colleague of Simon's at Guilford Medical Associates had urged them to as a newly formed family—but joining turned out to be fortuitous. Their membership constituted a network, AAA roadside service for life's disasters. The middle-aged, soft-toned rabbi, Frank Berg, conducted the funeral with a few words and readings in English and Hebrew. The grass all around the baby's new grave was shockingly green, the vibrancy of the hue almost painful, even though it was October. "We can ask for meaning from God, but we can't always have an answer," Rabbi Berg said, which struck Simon as a way of using religion (actually *abusing* religion) to say nothing at all. He was reminded of how Charles's grandparents dumped God, unable to make sense of six million Jews annihilated in Europe. If there was any time to dump God, it was that moment, at the mockingly green gravesite of an infant son. But he could not formulate a philosophy—or an antiphilosophy—because either seemed to constitute involvement and Caleb's death seemed to have nothing to do with the Jewish people, or an age-old religion, or a set of practices that he only faintly recognized. Simon looked up during the service to see his parents in mute, polite attendance, his mother hanging on Charles's elbow. Al St. Bern, apparently in one of his funks, didn't make it.

Wordlessly, during a modified shiva at the house with a platter of garlic bagels, whitefish salad, half-inch-thick sliced tomatoes, and too-strong coffee, all of which stung at his senses with pungent offense, Simon let himself be hugged. His colleagues from Guilford Medical Associates gave powerful embraces with heavy back-slapping claps against his shoulder blades. He knew he should have felt comforted, but all he could think of was his father's comment at Caleb's birth, over and over again in his head like a taunt. A lot of good it had done, indeed. He should have known, he should have seen, he should have predicted, he should have understood the signs. He should have been on top of the information. How had he missed the diagnosis? But the fever had flickered like a candle and then disappeared. Caleb's mewing cries had sounded like they had on any other night. His muscle tone, appetite, diapers, everything had appeared unremarkable. The blood count had been unremarkable. The rash—where was the telltale rash? Simon's only solace was that he hadn't been the only one: Even the pediatricians had missed the diagnosis.

Simon wasn't able to get a flight from Salt Lake City until Monday morning. When his plane finally touched down in Baltimore, he felt numb. He directed the cab straight to Suburban Hospital in Bethesda. "Fast," he said. The driver did not ask, and he did not explain.

He made his way to a corridor decorated with paintings of blocky animals, crocodiles with squared-off snouts, turtles that looked like they were Jeeps. Emily was sitting by the bed in the pediatric ICU, holding Jamie's hand. He noticed his daughter's hair, stringy and matted on the pillow as she slept, and he was relieved that Emily had not straightened or combed it. He would have read grooming as indicative of a higher level of disaster. The tousled effects suggested that trouble was still fresh. A long time ago, when they'd first married, Emily had joked about his spousal responsibility to her in case she was ever in a terrible accident. She made him promise—swear up and down—if she ever wound up comatose, he'd come daily to the hospital to tweeze her facial hairs. "I'd come just to sit with you," he'd vowed, embarrassed by the darkness of the conversation. "No idle sitting," she warned. "Promise me you won't let my eyebrows meet in the middle." They'd had a good laugh over it, but he'd appreciated the responsibility, and any time he'd come across her in the bathroom, leaning into the mirror to pluck a hair, he'd remembered his pledge. At Jamie's bedside, Emily looked like she hadn't slept in days. Red, bloodshot eyes, hair disheveled. It was perhaps the worst he'd seen her since—when?—he couldn't even think.

"She's on antibiotics," Emily said, not standing up. "And fluids. They think she's going to be okay. No sign of kidney damage. The blood differential, or whatever that was, came back normal." She forced a grim smile. "No meningitis."

Simon sat at the edge of the bed, opposite Emily, and took his daughter's other hand. He bent over the bed and kissed her temple, that vulnerable patch. Her chest fluttered up and down, and she looked restful. He was thinking of all the things he'd fucked up in his life. He was thinking of a fight he'd gotten into with Emily. It was shortly after Caleb's death. He'd suggested going to the cemetery. Of course he should have known better, it was too soon. There were reasons you went for *yahrzeit,* one year later. But he wasn't religious, so what did the calendar matter? Emily had not blatantly resisted, but she'd conveniently made a list of other plans that needed to be taken care of first. They needed a hose for the backyard. A friend who was about to leave town needed to stop over. Who was this friend? Why did Emily need a hose that very day? The day had worn on, and he realized they were running out of daylight. Finally when the friend arrived he monopolized the conversation, giving medical advice and taking her down to the clinic for free samples. Emily had resisted his intrusion and so, in front of the friend, he'd made a cutting remark. What shocked him was the look in the friend's eyes. He and Emily could avoid talking about Caleb forever, but it was impossible to hide how they mishandled each other. And they continued to be unable to hide it even when Jamie arrived. They knew, children did. They didn't need words. You breathed your pain, and they breathed it with you.

He felt like he should look at Jamie's chart, in fact had the impulse to find it and rifle through it, but he didn't move. He just sat holding his daughter's hand, looking at the small seashell fingernails. Emily held her other hand. He thought how light the hand was, *like a leaf,* he thought. The torturous green of the cemetery came back to him, and he forced the thought away.

"I thought it was flu," Emily began. Her voice came out thick, as if warning of the danger of reading too much into her words. "She was feverish, you know? She slept a lot during the weekend. She was sick, re-member, before you left, but she seemed okay. Grumpy, but okay. I took her to—I took her to the new apartment. With me. I didn't tell her." She chewed the side of her lip, looking momentarily vulnerable, he thought. Was she daring him to get angry? He felt too numb to muster a response. "She slept in the car, and she slept once we got there. I made sure she ate. She slept, then she got up. She was shaking, and she wasn't making any sense. Just jabbering. Like another language." Emily's voice broke, and he could picture the apartment, and Emily taking care, and then the mo-ment of terror. The taste in his mouth was as wrong as a penny. "Like she was speaking in tongues. I couldn't understand a word, and I panicked. I didn't know what else to do. I called the doctor, and he said get her to an emergency room."

He listened, and for a moment, he discovered the urge to stand up, walk around the bed and fold her in his arms. He wanted to comfort her, but he was afraid that an embrace was exactly what she wouldn't want from him and he dreaded being denied. Instead, he remained still, holding Jamie's hand, gazing at her light fingers, imagining the way the wind would wrestle with such a leaf.

"She had a temperature of a hundred and five. They got her here immediately. They said it was the thing she did to herself—the piercing. She did it so long ago, I had no idea it could turn bad after so much time. Cellulitis, they said. The infection started on her skin and spread through her whole system."

He was thinking of porpoises. Sleek bodies arcing over the water as they hunted in small groups. He'd read a magazine article. They were shy of people, but for some reason, they didn't stick together well as a group. They got stranded easily. Well-meaning conservationists tried to help, but the worst thing for a stranded harbor porpoise, it turned out, was a human-built aquarium. He looked up and realized that Emily was staring at him. She had paused, and her face was mottled, and he wasn't sure how long he had been silent. But she looked more stricken than threatening as she implored, "Say something. Aren't you going to say anything?"

Emily wanted to stay on at the hospital. He offered to take over so that she could go home to sleep for a few hours, but she didn't want to leave. He fought her, until he decided the best way to win her respect would be to come back later. Plus, it was awkward. There was that ugliness hanging over them, the resolute cracking of that perfect egg, their marriage, which they'd managed so deftly for so long, running with two legs tied together as they balanced it on a spoon between them. There would be financial negotiations—*crack!*—arrangements involving the other apartment—*crack!*—a flurry of phone calls and legal consultations and a million details breaking all of it apart. They managed to keep the tense conversations away from Jamie's bedside, talking in the hallway, but it became clear, as each new conversation ran amok, that the best plan would be to split attendance at the hospital.

"How was your conference?" she asked. She might have been making conversation, but he presumed she was asking to underscore her annoyance that he'd been out of town when the crisis evolved.

When he wondered aloud, "Are all your clothes at your new place?" she presumed he was accusing her of callousness.

When she asked, "You presented the treatment?" he was certain she was mocking him.

And then when he queried, "Are you sure you want to stay overnight?" she took offense; did he think she wouldn't?

What they didn't discuss were the details of Jamie's piercing, what either of them had known or not known, said or not said. It wasn't clear which would be more culpable. He suspected guiltily that Jamie had been bored and that her boredom was his fault since she'd languished all summer with no plans, no desires, no other kids to hang out with. The wine kit, he realized, must have stood out for her as the first potential activity in months, and he'd dangled it in front of her and then summarily postponed it. He hadn't known that she'd entertained herself alone in the house, jabbing herself with a hooked suture needle that evidently had been pilfered from his office. It helped, he realized as Jamie awoke, to count on her illness to occupy them.

"Hi," Emily said softly, leaning onto her side of the hospital bed.

"We're here," Simon said, edging close on the other side and taking her hand.

"Let me get in there a sec." A nurse reached over to adjust the IV, and Simon leaned back.

"How do you feel?" Emily asked. "Can we get you anything?"

Jamie opened her mouth. "I'm thirsty," she answered in a whisper. "My mouth's all dry."

Simon turned to the nurse. "Can we have water, please?"

"She needs a sponge for her lips," Emily said.

"I'm sleepy," Jamie said with a small smile.

"You're pretty sick, little porpoise," Simon said. "You got a pretty good infection."

"I know," she said, sounding pleased.

A new doctor rounded in the late afternoon, explaining that the admitting physician, Dr. Baumgarten, had left for the holiday.

"What holiday?" Simon asked, annoyed. He had lost sense of the date, would have had to think to recall the day of the week.

"Um, Roshashawna?" the new doctor suggested with an apologetic shrug. "I think?"

"Right," Simon answered. September always sneaked up on him like that. Labor Day was starkly marked and widely observed, but then the Jewish new year arrived on tiptoe. In recent years, it was always too late by the time he realized they didn't have tickets to services. And he always considered the holidays a pair; if you missed the new year celebration, it seemed the height of hypocrisy to hop in ten days later for Yom Kippur.

He looked at his wife. They hadn't decided finally on the arrangements, what the bedside schedule would be. Simon had canceled his Monday appointments because of the conference, so he was in no rush to get back to Baltimore. It made sense, he pointed out, for him to stay with Jamie through the night. He'd have to go back in the morning to see patients, but then he could come back after work and do the night shift again.

"I'm here now," Emily said. "I'll stay tonight."

"Why don't you get some rest?"

The slightest shadow of annoyance crossed her face, and he realized he should let her take charge.

"Just tonight," she said. "You go. Come back tomorrow night after work."

"I'll see if I can get the schedule shortened. I can be here early."

"Good. Come early."

"You sure?"

"I want to be here with her."

So he agreed. He kissed Jamie's cheek, smoothed her hair away from her forehead. He hailed a cab to the train station. He returned to a house that was different than he had left it. Nothing was missing, all the decor was intact, and yet he felt the strangeness of the space, as if it had grown unfamiliar.

In the morning he called Emily, who reported that all signs were looking good: Jamie had eaten Jell-O. Emily encouraged him to go ahead and see the patients who were scheduled, not to cancel his appointments. She could stay on with Jamie at the hospital.

He hesitated, but then accepted. Getting back to the office felt like a relief. It took his mind off everything to work, to ask patients questions about their problems. Rita stepped into his office to tell him that two more people had called to ask about the sulmenamine infusion.

"You all right?" she asked. "You're in a daze."

The office was in full swing already. For a moment, he thought he might tell Rita that Jamie was in the hospital, that he might need to cancel the late appointments, but he decided not to.

"He's fine," Gabi answered from the hallway. "He got his head in the clouds. Ready to be important."

They had expectations. The patients and even his staff. They had expectations for him, and now they had expectations for his new therapy. He didn't want to admit it to anyone, but his resolve to explore sulmenamine was wavering. He'd begun to realize the therapy was going to be harder to promote than he'd imagined. He was faced with having to devise a PR strategy for it. He'd have to market it and send out fliers and think up catchy phrases and win over the press, all of which was less interesting to him than the investigative work in the clinic. And he didn't want to attend any more conferences until it was clear that he'd had enough undisputed successes to make other doctors sit up and take note.

But how many did he need? As it was, he had eleven patients who'd received shots. He'd turned down one person who wanted to try it, the friend of a friend of Maxi Bailey, because the man seemed odd. It was a snap judgment, but Simon found the man's manner too demanding, a bit too tetchy, and he didn't want his experiment dragged down by the type of person his mother would have called "a bad apple." He offered the man a heavily dosed prescription of Fentanyl instead, which turned out to be a fine solution for both of them.

When the first officer entered, Simon was in the hallway outside the exam suites, hunched over a patient chart. It was nine forty-five on Tuesday morning, and he'd already prescribed treatment for a thirty-two-year-old high-school teacher with uncontrolled acid reflux. He'd drained a tart-smelling abscess from the infected toe of a fifty-one-year-old plumber. The sore spot in the side of the sixty-five-year-old architect was most likely a hernia, he decided after careful palpation, and he was standing in the hallway, writing up a referral to a surgeon. That morning, before the routine appointments, he'd also seen a new patient, a twenty-eight-year-old woman named May Anderson, who'd come in with complaints about low back pain. There was nothing remarkable about her or the discomfort she described; she'd fallen on the ice the previous winter and jarred her tailbone. Her case sounded similar in many ways to several of the new pain patients he'd taken on in the last three weeks. She'd been forced to take days off work and she'd lost pay. She'd seen "like, ten other doctors," she said, and nobody could help her.

He asked where she hurt, and he asked what kinds of therapies she'd tried out. She said she'd been to the hospital, and the X-rays were normal and that she could have them sent.

"I'm testing a remarkable new treatment," he informed her. "It's an injection, a double dose of a drug called sulmenamine. It's safe, no side effects other than maybe dry mouth. For a lot of the patients I've seen, it completely blocks out pain."

He was tired, and he was aware that he was not presenting the treatment with his typical enthusiasm.

"I want something proven," she said quickly, leveling her gaze on his face. "I don't want to test anything."

"I'm very excited about this treatment," he reinforced, hoping the presentation didn't sound too rote. "It's been the answer for a lot of people."

"I'm no guinea pig," she insisted.

He, who usually felt such compassion for people who complained of pain that kept them awake, or from work, was vaguely aware of not liking her. Her hair was almost black, dyed over with an eggplantish shade of purple, and she'd pulled it back into a short, stubby ponytail. The look was severe and added to the repugnance of her cockiness. She kept her hand on her back, and she occasionally massaged the muscle with her thumb as if to ease it. Each time, she emitted a small grunt. Typically, he would have been inspired to puzzle through her symptoms and a wide variety of treatment options.

"What is it you'd prefer?" he asked with resignation.

"Like, how about Dilo—" She gave a stiff, slightly embarrassed laugh. "I'm not even sure what it's called."

"Have you been on Dilaudid before?" he asked.

"A while ago," she said with one of the little grunts. "It was the only thing that made a dent."

Later, he would think he should have asked more questions, as if knowing who'd prescribed it or how much would have made a difference in what came next. He would wonder if he'd been too tired to be vigilant because of lack of sleep, or if he'd been distracted because of everything that was going on with Jamie. He would wonder if he'd known—somehow—that the trap had been set for him and that all there was for him—for his own well-being—was to wander into it. What he decided, as he regarded her and the severe cap of bruise-colored hair, was whatever she wanted he was ready to give her. He didn't want to have to look at her any longer, let alone negotiate with her.

"I'll give you a prescription for Dilaudid," he told her. "We'll start with a small dosage, keep in touch and determine together how well it's working."

"Can I ask—would you—I was just wondering, can you give me more than a month's worth?" She cocked her head, pleading. "It's like a huge bother to have to keep going to the drugstore. And they're not that nice to me there, if you know what I mean."

"If you want, I'll send you to a pharmacy in Glenburnie. I know the guy, and it's a little bit off the beaten path. You won't feel you're under scrutiny."

She seemed satisfied. The appointment ended, and he went to the next patient. He was not particularly focused. The article by the *Sun* reporter Casey Rehem, which had appeared the day before, had not been flattering. After his experience in Salt Lake, he was hardly surprised. The world looked skeptically at people whose practices were not part of the mainstream and who dared to make claims that were too bold, too self-assured. If he'd been part of a university or a member of a pain cohort, his observations might have been taken more seriously from the start. And his conclusions might have quickly drawn attention and then might have been followed up by other researchers. As it was, he was labeled "an outlier," in the words of one neurologist who was quoted in the article. The neurologist was named Marvin Volk, and Simon had never heard of *him* either, but the writer had quoted Volk's caution to the public not to believe unsubstantiated claims about silver bullets for long-standing pain. "Unfortunately, as of today," Volk said, "we're still far from a cure."

With exacting detail, Casey Rehem had depicted how Simon had found the stash of sulmenamine in his father's bedroom. Casey had made finding vials in the drawer sound like stumbling upon loot, but Simon still felt the discovery had been a moment of intrepid shrewdness and investigative necessity, which he figured was probably impossible to convey in print. Dredging up past conflicts, Simon came off as eccentric and possibly unaccountable. Casey had interviewed partners at Guilford Medical Associates, who'd recalled how they'd asked Simon to leave after he'd disagreed with them about prescribing narcotics. "We had differences about how much to give patients, how often and for how long. We don't like using opioids as much as other therapies, and we determined it would be best to part ways," as good old Brad Neuworth apparently had told the reporter. There was even a line in the article about how Simon had received a cautionary reprimand from the State Medical Board for overstating the effectiveness of the Boardwalk Diet.

The strangest and most hurtful part of the article was the quote from Julie McKinley, described as a nurse who had recently "left" his practice. "There might be a method in the madness," she said, "but I couldn't defend most of the unorthodox practices I saw while I was working there. Patients deserve more than someone who looks like their advocate but whose ego drives him to unusual procedures."

Simon had read the article sitting at the kitchen table, occasionally looking out the bay window at the garden, the almost-finished gazebo at the edge of the lawn. Emily had often said, "No such thing as bad press." He'd heard her on the phone with clients, "It's all about how we handle it." She would know, and he was determined to move ahead and not let the article bother him. He knew what he was seeing in his patients. Jack Whitby was cured of the pains that had cramped him for over a year. The phantom pains had subsided in Jim Weaver. And the article, even in its uncharitable skepticism, only succeeded in getting the word out to greater numbers of people. He expected he'd be receiving even more calls from potential patients. He went down to the office and shot off e-mails. "How is your back???" he typed to one of them.

When the first officer entered, Rita was sitting at the reception desk with her hands-free headphones, assembling the paperwork to be filed for patients in the bear-embossed folders. In the back of the office, Gabi stocked a cabinet with paper towels, sterile plastic sample cups and tiny swollen packets of moist towelettes. Joyce was taking vitals from the patient in exam suite A, pumping the sphygmomanometer with her large hands. In the afternoon, he was due to perform two sulmenamine infusion therapies. One was for Maxi Bailey, whose pain had gone away for almost two weeks, but then had returned. She wanted another round. She believed in it—those days she'd been able to get out of the house had given her a glimpse of what remission would feel like—and she wanted him to give her another dose. The second was for a new patient, Ethel Vorhip, who happened to be the mother-in-law of the provost at the university. The route of information had been, of all people, Lorraine, his housekeeper, who was friends with the woman who cleaned for the provost. This, he believed, was a coup. The mother-in-law of the provost was the sort of connection that could get the treatment noticed by the right kind of people.

Writing up the hernia referral, he grew aware that something was happening in the front, out by the waiting room. The first officer was standing by the reception desk in a dark padded vest. Before he turned the corner, Simon heard Rita gasp.

"Police," the man said in an authoritative voice that was surprisingly calm. "Nobody move."

Someone in the waiting room emitted a high-pitched note, not quite a scream, but a sound pried wide with vowels of fear. He knew the officer's gun was drawn. There was an airy lightness to the moment. A breath.

Then he heard the door of the waiting room swinging wide and the sound of several people entering at once. The chaos of the next moments was excruciating. The police moved in, all in puffy bullet-proof jackets, like life vests. Four of them, six of them, ten officers. Simon glimpsed through the window the black and white cars on the street, their red and blue lights whirling. At first he thought he was looking at Baltimore City police, but after a moment he realized the yellow letters on the back of one officer's vest read "DEA." The patients in the waiting room were herded out the door to the side of the house. Lorne Williams, who'd had his prostate removed and who was bent over a walker, was shuffled outside along with them, an officer gripping him by the elbow.

"What's going on?" Simon said. "Don't touch him," he barked at the man holding Lorne Williams. "He's got nothing to do with anything."

"Are you Dr. Bear?" an officer asked, which seemed idiotic since he was the only person around in a white coat.

"Is this because of the article?" Simon asked loudly. "It's not a controlled substance. Call Boeker," he insisted. "Call Boeker. They'll tell you what it is."

Simon's first lucid thought was of Jamie: utter gratitude that she was supine in a bed far away in the hospital in Bethesda and not asleep upstairs. His second thought was that he wasn't going to be able to make it to the hospital to sit with her, and he'd be letting her—and Emily—down. He had the sense that he was supposed to defend his staff, first, and then the patients, like the patriarch of a clan, but he thought of Jamie and felt a surprising distance from what was happening around him. "Hey," was all he managed to say, as an agent rounded the corner and stepped into the hallway, parting the air in front of him with the nose of his gun.

"Quiet," the officer barked.

He still believed they would shortly announce they'd made a mistake. Sorry, wrong house, like a comedy routine. But the announcement didn't come. They had a search warrant that they handed to him. He glanced at it, noticing nothing but the address of his house at the top of the page. "Against the wall," the agent directed with his gun, and the other officers stepped past them and began to move into the exam rooms, ripping open the cabinets, flinging contents in all directions.

Simon felt the rush of fear and actually thought of the mechanics of his sympathetic nervous system, the sweat beginning at his scalp, under his arms. He took a breath, his heart pounding. The patient May Anderson came down the hallway; he recognized her by her purple hairline, except she was dressed differently than she had been less than an hour earlier. She was wearing a DEA vest and a holster with a weapon. "Hey," he greeted her, as if she might explain and clarify, as if they were passing on the street. Avoiding eye contact, she angled her shoulder away from him and edged down the hallway.

"Oookay," he said, in the unruffled, aloof way Bev would have said it, which seemed the only way to handle the moment. He turned and put his hands against the cranberry wall, a semigloss paint Emily had chosen several years earlier, with the explanation that it was dignified, serene and not at all ordinary for a doctor's office. It struck him as still a good color.

Despite everything that was happening around him, he continued to presume the warrant was because of the sulmenamine infusion therapy. Somebody, probably a Drug Enforcement bureaucrat, had read the article in the *Sun* and misunderstood the legality of the therapy. The charge against him would be a patent infringement—or, at worst, a medical investigation regarding the use of an outmoded pharmaceutical. Or maybe, he thought, the odd guy, the one he'd refused to treat, had called the cops to settle the score. The DEA probably believed that a seemingly miraculous new pain medication would be narcotic-based. *No such thing as bad press,* he reminded himself as the search continued, and he began to imagine how he'd parlay the experience of being arrested into an opportunity to get the word out about sulmenamine. He remained convinced everything would get straightened out, and he maintained his assurance that this was just another step in a long adventure. What came to him, in the din of it all, was the refrain of "Alice's Restaurant," *You can get anything you want,* and the mania of Officer Obie with his marked-up photographs as evidence, just because of a pile of garbage.

"Never been in the back of a po-lice car," he remarked rakishly to the cop who'd been assigned to keep an eye on him. The guy ignored him. The search of the office took place under brutal hands. Simon was temporarily held, his body quickly searched, but then the agent let him go as they ransacked the office. Simon paced, first nervously like a zoo tiger, then obligingly looking for keys and trying to explain the layout of the office, but the agents moved with speed, never quite looking at him as they directed him to open closets and unlock drawers.

"This?" Simon protested. "This?" Then he unlocked. "You're barking up the wrong tree," he warned them. "When you realize your mistake, you'll realize."

The brusqueness of their motions, the sweeping of an entire drawer of sterile syringes into a cardboard box, didn't reveal a shred of sensitivity that these rooms were healing spaces. This was where people found relief from misery, where the afflictions that threatened their lives were made less dire and sometimes even resolved. The agents ransacked cabinets, as if Simon harbored secrets that could take down a country, and their intent to protect a very innocent society was served by their seriousness and their intrusiveness. They insisted he unlock drawers in his desk. Simon's thoughts returned to Jamie, revisiting the relief that she wasn't home and the panic that he would not be available to leave Baltimore any time soon. His stomach dropped because his shift at the hospital was supposed to start when work ended, and he wanted to be at Jamie's bedside. He asked the man who seemed to be the lead agent, "How long do you think all of this is going to take?"

"Depends on how helpful you can be," came the steely response.

Rita, who along with the other staff members had spoken with the officers outside, stepped up to him. "Call Tory," she said quietly. "Right now. Don't say anything to these guys. Don't help them, don't clarify anything for them. Things you say can backfire later."

By the time Tory Beauregard arrived, the office was in disarray. The dark-haired attorney was tall and lean, a careful, distinguished dresser. Simon had encountered him once having his shoes polished at the shoe shine stand in the train station. He was neither old nor young and never married, and it was unclear whether his solitude suited him or saddened him, or whether he was simply a rather private person. He gave the impression of being concerned about nothing but work. He had a pensive stoop and a habit of focusing his gaze in the distance when he was thinking, but when he spoke he was bitingly direct, and that much was helpful.

"It's not looking good," he said.

"I didn't see this coming," Simon admitted. He had seated himself in the waiting room on the edge of the pond. The four koi lined up like battleships, but were otherwise still, as if they were watching.

"You know what it was?" Tory said. He'd already spoken to the U.S. Attorney's office. "Some nurse turned you in. Called the State Medical Board. McKinley? You know who that is? Said she used to work here. Didn't think you were prescribing within legal bounds."

Simon nodded dully, vaguely relieved. It seemed about right, considering the state Julie had been in when she left the office. He was glad that the rest of the staff—his long-standing employees and companions, whom he'd also diagnosed and treated over the years—had stood by him.

"They're going to review your records," Tory cautioned.

"Can they do that?"

"Or they can press charges now and work out the details later."

"I document everything," Simon attested. "Even the patients have copies. Just something that I do."

Tory rubbed the side of his face as if he were checking the state of his shave. "That'll serve you well," he said thoughtfully. "Anyway, you'll get an inventory of everything they take." He glanced off toward the window. Then he added, "There was a death, did you know that?"

Simon looked at him without speaking. The color green from the cemetery came back to him again. A haunting, glittering green, like plastic turf.

"A guy named Dane MacAllister?" Tory prompted.

But Simon shrugged. "I know the name," he said without emotion. "He was a patient. Months and months ago. I have nothing to do with his death."

"But you treated him?"

Simon had a sinking feeling. "A while ago. I'm not even sure what for, not off the top of my head. I haven't seen him since. Maybe even a year. What'd he die of?"

"Autopsy results said narcotics. He had a prescription of yours for methadone. The U.S. Attorney would probably love to pin the death on you. And add to that this Julie McKinley who says you've been pushing painkillers like they were Tic Tacs."

Simon sifted through his recollections of patients. He'd probably seen MacAllister a total of three times and remembered him mostly for his theatrical face, high cheekbones, teeth like a wind-wrestled picket fence. He remembered prescribing painkillers for him, but nothing remarkable. "He'd had X-rays done. I prescribed meds for him, methadone probably, and I knew how much he was supposed to be taking. I didn't overdose him." He remembered the maroon-headed agent. "They set me up this morning. An agent came in pretending to be a patient. She complained about her back."

"Whadja do?"

"What do you mean, what did I do? I gave her a prescription for Dilaudid." Tory rubbed the side of his face again, appearing to think.

Simon took the gesture as a sign that Tory didn't understand. He felt
he had to explain himself. "That's what she wanted. It's not my place to
talk patients out of pain medication. I can't see their pain, so I have to
believe what they tell me. People shouldn't be forced to suffer. I don't
believe they should be told to keep a stiff upper lip, or tough it out. Life
is hard enough, and long-term pain doesn't do any good for the person
who's experiencing it. Ask any doctor, any good doctor, any doctor telling
the *truth,* and they'll admit that opioids work best. They're the gold
standard for pain relief. And if the DEA wasn't breathing down everybody's neck, more doctors would prescribe them, and patients would get
better care."

From under his groomed brows, Tory's gaze had focused off in a far
corner of the room. "Well," he began slowly. "We'll have to prove that
this MacAllister was an addict and that you didn't know—or even suspect. That you prescribed an appropriate amount for whatever his com-
plaint was."

"It wouldn't have mattered," Simon said simply. "I probably prescribed what he asked for."

"C'mon, Simon," Tory groaned. "Work with me, would you? It doesn't
help your case for you to have some vendetta against the whole system."

Simon raked his fingers through his hair, realizing how disheveled he
must look. "I'm just being honest. I do what's right for my patients."

Tory jabbed at the air between them with a single finger. "You're going
to have to wise up, or you're going to see everything you've worked for,
your whole career, destroyed. This is a murder charge. It's September,
you realize."

"So?"

"Jesus, two months before elections? Time for the governor to let
everyone know he's serious about getting drugs off the streets. He's going
to want action."

Simon paced again. His voice was loud and high-pitched. "It's a witch hunt. It's because I'm out on my own in private practice. I'm the one who's going to burn at the stake."

"Did you think—I mean, you must have considered at some point there were risks for prescribing narcotics."

"I'm a good doctor," Simon stated.

"Know what the guys at the U.S. Attorney's office said? Doctors who overprescribe painkillers are one of the four D's. Either they're dated—they don't know what good treatments exist, or they're duped—they let addicts con them. They're disabled themselves—they're users who're suffering from their own addiction; or they're making a profit, and they're just plain dishonest. So which are you, and how are we going to convince everyone otherwise?"

Simon cracked a smile. "I just want to do what's right for my patients, and it's my policy to let them guide their care. I was just at a conference. I've seen a lot of the latest treatments and some are good, but nothing's a cure-all. I don't judge everybody who comes into my office, so maybe I get duped sometimes, but I also don't wind up turning away a guy who's got legitimate need. I don't do drugs, you can ask anybody. And I don't sell. I'm not profit-driven like that. I didn't even want to pursue money for the sulmenamine therapy I've been offering—"

"What's that?"

Simon's eyes flashed. "Didn't I tell you?" he said, animated. "I discovered a new treatment, still in its early stages, very promising, and I'm still testing it. It was in the *Sun,* though the article didn't mention I've already seen at least two patients cured, maybe three. It's nonnarcotic, in case you're worried about that. Nonaddictive. It's a legitimate drug." He paused. "What?"

Tory was looking off again to the far end of the room. Simon could see how, from the outside, the circumstances all seemed to slant in one direction. He looked like a vigilante, like someone who couldn't be bothered to follow rules. But he'd been careful, and everything he'd done was within the law. "I can understand this might not appear to add up right," he acknowledged. "The new thing's only happened very recently. I had to pursue it." When Tory didn't say anything, he added, "I'm not a criminal."

"You better hope the treatment that you're testing—this sulmenamine or whatever you call it—doesn't have any ill effects. You could be looking at a lawsuit. Or two."

Tory left then to check in with the U.S. Attorney and see if there was any new information about MacAllister that might be helpful. He reminded Simon they were still waiting to hear if an arrest would be issued, and he promised to be back in half an hour. When Tory stepped out, Simon dialed Emily's cell. His fingers shook, but he resolved not to let on what had happened.

"How's she doing?" he asked the instant he heard Emily's voice.

"Better, I think. They said they want a surgical consult to see if the sore needs debriding." She sighed. "I could use a break. So?" Her voice sounded flat. When they were first married, he'd been able to cajole her out of a dark mood, lift her spirits with a joke or a story or a plan for something wild and inventive that they could do together. How far they'd veered from that. A lump rose in his throat.

"I can't get there for a while," he said.

She was silent.

"Emily?"

Exasperated. "Now what?"

"It's out of my hands. I'll explain to you later." His voice grew hoarse, but he thought if he told her, he might break down. "But I can't get away." A pair of agents stood at the reception desk holding the enormous cartons he'd ordered with vials of sulmenamine. He held up one finger, *wait,* and called out to them, "There's no reason for that to go."

"Are you downstairs?" his wife was asking. When he didn't answer, she said, "I read the article in the paper."

"It wasn't exactly what I expected," he admitted.

"They never are," she said dryly.

"But no such thing as bad press, right? Right?" Wasn't that what she'd always insisted? He called across the room to the agents. He didn't want to have to describe to Emily what was going on in the office, but the agents were taking his only supply of the Boeker drug. "Excuse me, there's no reason to take those," he yelped. "They have nothing to do with this. Wait. Excuse me."

"Simon," she interrupted.

"I can't believe this," he groaned.

She was pressing him. "I need to know when you'll be here."

He wanted to explain, but he couldn't. "I'm not sure I'll be able to make it until late. Tell Jamie to hang in there."

Emily grew silent again. The agents headed out to the fleet of police cars. Tell her or don't tell her, he couldn't decide. He wanted her to know, but he couldn't handle a reaction from her, an analysis of his business mistakes.

"It's not easy being here," Emily said finally, in a voice that suggested she was changing the topic. He felt his heart quicken. "She's demanding."

"She's thirteen." Two agents began to load patient charts into a cardboard box. He watched them note the segment of the alphabet in black marker on the side of the carton.

"We haven't been good parents. We've been shitty, shitty parents. You know, she told me about camp finally."

"Camp?"

"The whole thing with the knife. She said she was borrowing it, and she had no intention of doing anything with it, no plan at least, but that whittling thing wasn't—it wasn't true. She says she might have decided to—to hurt herself. If she'd stayed. She was thinking about it."

"What?" He felt his breath squeeze away.

"Like, hurting herself. Like—" She paused, as though she was having trouble saying the words. "Cutting herself. Did you know people do that?"

"Is that what she said?" he asked nervously. Once he'd seen a TV show in which a contortionist had folded his body into a two-foot-by-two-foot box and submerged himself underwater. The man was a reasonable height, maybe five-nine, and he'd consciously had to slow his breathing and his heart rate in order to survive in the container. He watched the agents outside moving with officious strides, consulting clipboards and calling into walkie-talkies. He imagined Jamie in the hospital bed, her lips parched. It seemed a long time later that he felt himself exhale again.

"She didn't," Emily continued, "but she said she might have."

"Shouldn't someone at the camp have told us that?" His voice cracked.

"She hadn't done anything, so they couldn't accuse her of anything other than stealing. But they were suspicious. I asked her finally. I said, 'What was it for? Why'd you borrow the knife?' You know what she said? 'It seemed like I needed it.'" Emily sighed. "You know, it's hard here." He knew she meant at the hospital. "She's no easy patient. Each time I think we're doing okay, she's insensitive, and bitter. I'm sitting at her bedside and she barks, 'Get me a magazine.' Not, Can I please have a magazine? Or, Would you mind getting me a magazine? 'Get me the nurse. Turn the light out. Close the curtain, will you? Why do you always have to have the curtains open?' Then she looks at me with this horrible expression on her face, and she says, 'Why are you staying so long?' I want to have a relationship with her. I'm trying, but she's making it hard."

Ordinarily, he liked to believe, he would have said something reassuring. He would have said, *We might not win a Nobel Prize for parenting, but we're doing our best, just like everybody else.* Or he might have said, *Well, teenagers, what'd you expect.* But it was difficult to make pronouncements as his daughter lay waiting for the opinion of a surgeon and he was unable to be near her, unable to participate, and there was clearly so much they didn't know. Stacks of patient files, cartons of medication, prescription pads and supplies, were heading out of the office in the arms of federal agents who marched like ants to a waiting van on the street. Piece by piece they were dismantling what he'd built, what he'd made of himself. One of the officers had even knelt at the edge of the koi pond to run a latex-gloved hand along its bottom, no doubt feeling for hidden compartments, ingenious places to stash drugs. ("Are you kidding?" Simon had barked at him.) He held the phone, not answering his wife, and looked outside to the police cars, still flashing their lights. The entire front and side of the house had been roped off with forbidding yellow tape, and the quiet Guilford corner near Sherwood Gardens had become a spectacle like a carnival. He was still waiting to learn whether he was going to be charged with killing a man he'd only tried to help; he dreaded what would possibly be the next phone call to Emily, the one from jail, in which he would face not only her inability to help him but her complete uninterest. At that point, he figured, she would be done with him, and it seemed to him that Jamie's desire to fight for attention, to inflict torment on them, was the best news he'd heard in a long while.

His throat swelled as he thought about how he feared, even more than Emily's criticism, her indifference. He said, "We're lucky she wants to punish us."

The good news was that, by nightfall, no charges had been pressed. "At least not yet," Tory said in the darkened waiting room. He took another call on his cell phone as Simon began to wander through the office, picking up stray papers, screw tops for medicine vials, overturned jars of cotton swabs. The agents had finished and left with whatever they'd construed was going to be evidence. Rita had lingered longer than the rest of the staff, but she was eager to leave. Her husband wanted her home. She hugged Simon, throwing her large, maternal arms around his torso and pressing herself to his body.

"They'll see they were wrong," she said to him. "Everything will get cleared up. They'll see."

When she pulled back, Simon saw that her face was red. "I'm sorry for the mess," he said, pointing to the debris—the splayed innards of the filing cabinets—littering the floor.

"You do what's right for the patients," she said, patting his chest. "That's all there is. If you weren't there for them, who would they have?"

"Go on home," he said. "I'll call you when I know anything."

"We all believe in you," she said. "We'll help you through this."

"I know," he answered. "Now get."

She left, the screen banging behind her, her large ring of keys like bells in her hand.

Tory ended his call and slipped the cell phone into his briefcase. "Can't promise what will happen tomorrow or the next day, but apparently there isn't enough evidence yet. That MacAllister guy had all kinds of other drugs in his system, so they might be worried whether they could nail the methadone. The bad news," Tory continued, "is that the State Medical Board is suspending your license." Simon would remain on suspension until the matter could be thoroughly investigated and the prescribing patterns deemed within reasonable limits. Additionally, the DEA had revoked his registration, rendering him unable to prescribe until further notice, and there was no telling how long that action might take to clear up.

"We can fight them both," Tory assured him, "but legally you can't practice until you've settled the issue with the Board."

"So, what, a disciplinary hearing?" Simon asked. "How soon? We have to get this straightened out. People depend on me. It's not just the inconvenience or the financial burden of time off. Or my staff, who I just realized will have to start looking for other jobs. I have patients whose pain is so severe they want to kill themselves. What are they going to do, travel to some other doctor somewhere who might or might not take them seriously? What's going to happen to them?"

Tory smoothed the jacket of his suit. "You send out a letter to them, explain you can't see them and try to think of who you can refer them to," he said. "You know, I've heard of cases where patients come to the doctor's support. They write letters to the Board. Your patients might speak up on your behalf." An idea seemed to dawn on him. "How credible is this nurse who acted as an informant—this Julie McKinley—?"

Simon's thoughts went back to that first interview, when she sat rigidly in front of his desk with her too-large pearls and a hopeful expression on her face. He had imagined he would teach her—and hadn't it seemed she was going to be a good study?—but everything had soured so quickly. He thought of the kiss, that terrible mistake. What had happened to him? How had he managed to lose control? His large fingers went to his hair, tearing at it. "She was a negative presence, I couldn't have her around. Can't we prove that she's got a personal grudge?"

"Apparently she's got a whole list of medical issues she saw that she found questionable, beyond the narcotic thing. The DEA won't care about that, but the Board might."

"You mean my research?"

Tory responded with a grimace and a half-shrug. "All I can say is, I hope what's an earnest effort on your part doesn't backfire."

"I'll tell you," Simon said. He was trembling, his large hands, his knees. He felt a queerness in his joints. He knew what he was about to say was true, even though it wouldn't come out with a polite measure of humility. "There aren't many doctors anywhere who are as good at doing what I do."

"I'm sure of it," Tory said, smiling.

Simon looked around at the disarray, the litter. Entire cabinets gaped open, their shelves cleared. The agents had left with nearly three hundred patients' files, all of whom had at some point been prescribed a schedule II substance. Had he anticipated this? Had he known this was coming? Was there some part of him that wanted the cabinets emptied, all the responsibility lifted? "I'm starving," he announced. He intended to leave for Bethesda, but he realized he couldn't face the emptiness of the house alone. "Can I get you something?" he urged Tory. "A cup of coffee? Something to eat? Our housekeeper usually makes some kind of casserole dish. You've been here for hours."

"Wouldn't mind something for my throat. I'm parched."

Simon led the way past the waiting rooms, through his office. As he pushed against the mahogany door, he realized that the agents had continued their search inside the house. "Are they allowed to do that?" he asked.

"If the warrant is for this address," Tory answered with a woeful bob of his carefully groomed head, "they can do a sweep of upstairs."

But as they entered the basement, they saw the wine casks. The copper bands had been pried from the barrels, the oak snapped. Splintered staves littered the floor, like the aftermath of a hurricane. The crates with the wine equipment had been wrested open, the interior packing plumbed. Simon reached into the yawning holes. They'd taken the siphon tubing, the sugar refractor.

"They must have thought you were hiding something. This might have been your secret stash." Tory looked around. "What is all this?"

"Wine," Simon murmured, pushing a tuft of haylike stuffing back into one of the crates. "Just a hobby. Just for fun."

"They're beautiful. Were—beautiful. Sorry," Tory said slowly. Surveying the mess, he added, "They must've cost you a bundle."

"Tory," Simon said, as they stood there staring at the wreckage. The busted wood told the destruction of everything fine in his life, the end of his marriage, the rodeo ride of his creative instinct. Gut instinct was another expression for what you didn't have words for, what you lived by but didn't understand. There was nothing precious about it. "You ever do divorce law? My wife wants out."

"I don't," Tory said. "But I've got a name of someone."

Tory didn't stay long. Simon poured him a seltzer; there was little to talk about, and Simon had to leave for Bethesda anyway. Tory intimidated him a little, the weird gentlemanly habits, like the way he took off his suit jacket and folded it inside out before resting it on a chair. He wondered at the man's mysterious solitude, and he worried that he himself was headed toward a similar ghostly existence. Was that what happened when your family was dismantled and your practice disassembled and you were alone? Here was a lawyer who made housecalls. The doorbell rang then, and Tory stood up obligingly, like someone who'd just awakened. Simon went to answer it, harboring the vague hope it might be Emily, though he knew it wouldn't be. He knew she'd use her keys. Ted and Betsy Ebberly stood on the stoop, peering in tentatively, like two shy children.

Tory had opened his jacket and put it on. "I'll be in touch as soon as I hear anything," Tory said, squeezing by Simon and then past the Ebberlys. "Hello, good-bye, hello." He trotted down the steps, the fine leather undersoles of his expensive shoes smacking against the bricks.

From the Ebberlys' sympathetic faces, Simon could tell they already knew. "It's not as bad as it looks," he insisted. "How did you hear?"

Betsy pointed to the side of the house. "The Do Not Cross tape was a pretty good sign something was up."

"It's a temporary setback. As soon as everything gets cleared up," he stammered. "I'm not worried about me, I'm worried about my patients, is all. What'll they do? They're the ones who really get punished in all of this. They're the ones who suffer."

"Sure they do," Betsy said. "How's Emily taking it? I'm sure she's got a strategy for you."

When Simon didn't respond and didn't move aside, Ted asked, "Can we c-come in?"

But Simon blocked the doorway with his body. The last thing he needed was the Ebberlys looking around. He'd have to explain how things stood with Emily. "Actually, I'm on my way out. Jamie—have you heard? She's in the hospital."

"Oh no," Betsy exclaimed, instantly motherly. "Is she okay?"

He explained the pierced navel, and they shook their heads. Betsy put her hand over her mouth as she listened, her eyes wide. Their sympathy felt good. Simon even mentally forgave Ted for not offering to do a sulmenamine study, a little basic science project that would have given Simon's clinical results more backing, a Petri dish worth of proof. Even a small project from the laboratory would have underscored the importance of what he was doing and would have given him more data to bring to Salt Lake City. He wouldn't have sounded like he was some nutcase. But too late now. There was no way to continue with the study in the clinic, at least not legally, and there were no grudges. "It's been a long couple days," he said. "It's almost too late for me to drive down to Bethesda."

"W-what happened t-today?" Ted asked. "We got a call from the Groves." He looked over his shoulder toward Rick and Janet's house. The porch light glimmered, but the rest of the house was dark. He realized, of all people, he should have heard from them, and he realized then that he probably wouldn't. Janet's exhibit was about to launch, and they were people who were concerned about whom they were connected to. They would stay away until his name was cleared and it was safe to associate with him again.

"Just your basic raid," Simon answered. "The feds didn't like the way I've been handling my pain patients. Apparently it's a crime when you see people hurting to try to do something about it."

"We came as soon as we could," Betsy said.

Simon took a deep breath. The night air was soft and faintly sweet. Summer was ending. "The short of it is, they closed me down."

Ted whistled. "Wow."

"I'll have to appeal to have my license reinstated. Emily doesn't know yet," Simon admitted with a sigh. "She's been at the hospital all day. I didn't have the heart to tell her."

As they stood there, he realized he should tell them that Emily wasn't living there anymore, that she had a new place she was calling home, even though he had no idea where it was. He owed it to the Ebberlys to tell them. People needed to figure out where their alliances fell when their friends split up. They needed to poise themselves to take sides. But his throat grew tight as he thought about having to utter the word "divorce" and surprise tears prickled against his eyes.

"What are you going to do?" Ted asked.

"Nothing. She decided it all," he answered before he realized Ted was inquiring about the practice.

"Simon, can we come in? Please?" Betsy pleaded. "We're worried about you."

"I'm fine. Really. I have to go down to Bethesda." He looked down the street at the streetlights and their domed orbs of lemonade-colored light. The street looked absolutely picturesque.

"Y-you don't look like you should be on the road," Ted said.

"No, you look terrible," Betsy agreed.

"I'm a scapegoat," Simon said. "That's basically it. It's like attacking a sheep apart from the herd. No one can say what I was doing or wasn't doing, so they'll assume the worst and pick through my records to see if they can make it stick. Thank God I kept records. Can you imagine? What will I do—I'll fight. What else? My lawyer thinks I'll be able to be reinstated within a year. I'll rebuild. Bigger and better than before. Add another exam suite. Maybe I'll even hire another doctor." Something dawned on him. "It'll be a good lesson for Jamie. She should learn from this too, right? A thing is how you handle it. I know I'm in the right because I know what I've done. My patients know. My staff knows. But the rest of the world? People find out about things like this and they shy away. You know who I really feel bad for? My patients. Especially the ones who had appointments tomorrow or the next day or the day after that. They're going to have to go knocking on doors to find someone to treat them. I've heard of patients getting turned away from doctors who don't want a paper trail from someone like me leading to someone like them. Those doctors don't want the *stink* on them."

"As soon as you're reinstated, Emily will polish up your reputation," Betsy declared.

Simon looked at his shoes. He realized he was still wearing his white coat. Standing on the front step of the house, he saw it as a costume.

"We don't think you stink," she added tenderly.

"You were nice to come over." He couldn't say it, but it was like a drink of water, their kindness. He could not recall anything like it except the feeling of being refreshed. He didn't want it to end, but he couldn't invite them in. He had to get his clothes together, go to the bathroom, get ready to drive to the hospital.

"Anything we can d-do for you?" Ted offered.

"I'll be fine," he said. "Maybe down the line. Maybe I'll need you to write something on my behalf. A testimonial to my character." He grinned. "Something to show the Board."

"Sure," Ted said.

"On a side note," Betsy said with a kind change of topic, "if you all want to come over next week to break the fast. If Jamie's feeling better, of course. We're having people as soon as services end. Not a big gathering this year, just a few families. Light meal, you know, the usual, Aunt Ethel's kugel, unless someone comes up with another recipe."

"I've always liked Aunt Ethel's recipe." He squinted. "What day is Yom Kippur?" Some years he and Emily and Jamie dropped in on the end of the event at the Ebberlys, even though they hadn't fasted themselves. The Ebberly children typically came home for the holiday. It was a quick evening of bagels and cream cheese, roughly tradition.

"Next Wednesday," Ted answered.

"So we're in it now," Simon said mildly, "the ten holiest days of the year? Am I right?"

"You're invited to break the fast," Betsy said again, "just so you know. I'll keep telling you, if you want. I'll remind Emily."

He nodded sadly, saying no more. Betsy reached out and squeezed his arm and they left then. He watched them as they descended to the street.

Even after he had closed the door, he watched them from the window. Ted put his hand on Betsy's back as they headed down the curve of the brick steps, and when they reached the sidewalk, he glanced back at the house. Then, as they made their way toward their car, he drew his wife close into the crook of his arm.

Simon awoke on the couch in the living room, still in his clothes, with the sticky tongue of cotton mouth and a mental fog. In his head, a eustacian roar prickled like radio static, incessant background noise. He held his nose and swallowed purposefully, trying to clear the waterfall sound in his ear, then palpated his glands. Definitely, he was getting sick.

The jumpiness wasn't all in his head, either. He found himself unable to sit still, bouncing his knees, drumming fingers on the surfaces of tables. He was suffering from a little twitching around the edge of his eye—myokymia, he thought, putting a name to the quick ripple under the skin. Was it visible from the outside, or was he just feeling it? He leaned into the bathroom mirror, inspecting. It was a minor distraction, not terribly uncomfortable, but a sign that he was not handling the stress. He had become a jerking heap of involuntary impulses.

Time had passed since the raid, but he wasn't sure how long. It was Wednesday. Maybe Thursday. He had not managed to drive to Bethesda on the night after the raid. The Ebberlys departed and he'd sat on the couch, only intending to rest a moment, fortify himself for the drive. Even he was surprised by the toll the events had taken on him. He woke in daylight from a sleep so encompassing, he was not sure where he was and he wondered for a moment whether he'd imagined some or all of what had happened. The phone rang with a tone he somehow knew was insistent. The details settled back into place all at once, the ripped-apart office, the quiet house, Jamie, in trouble. He heard Emily's voice, a *hello* with edgy reverberation.

"I fell asleep," he explained, feeling frantic. "I didn't mean to. I'm coming right now." He began looking for his shoes.

"Don't tell it to me, tell it to her," she responded coldly, righteously. "She's the one waiting for you."

He kept his voice steady, but he felt like crying. "Emily, I'm sorry I didn't make it. I was going to get in the car, but I sat down. Kind of blacked out, maybe. You should have called me. I'm coming now." There was an interruptive note of call-waiting and he remembered that Tory was intending to call as soon as there was news. To Emily he insisted, "Hold on a second. Just don't go anywhere."

"Simon," Tory began as soon as he clicked over.

Then he had to ask Tory to wait. "It's the other line," he explained to Emily. "I have to take it. Don't hang up."

"Goddammit, Simon," she said, and he knew exactly what her face looked like, her mouth slightly pulled down at the corners, her lips curled in. His heart ached.

He clicked back to Tory, who said, "I want to know of any other pa-tients who've died. Anyone else that might raise flags. They're combing through files with the forensic pathologist, but I need to know if you've got other cases that maybe you haven't mentioned."

"None that I can think of," Simon said earnestly.

"Any accidental overdoses? Suicides?"

Simon recalled a woman named Helen Frieden, an older woman with an unenviable case of fibromyalgia, who suffered daily and who got only modest relief from the narcotics he offered. She was lovely, and he wished he'd known her before she was sick. By the time he met her, she'd ar-ranged to have many forms of therapy in place. She meditated and did hypnosis, and counseling, and she still, somehow, was unable to keep the pain at bay. After some time, she didn't want to fight anymore. "A long time ago, maybe ten years, I had a patient who helped herself to a lot of pills and died. I'd followed her carefully. Frieden, her name was. She suffered horribly, but I wasn't her only doctor. She had a shrink even. Her death came as a complete surprise to everyone. Is it my fault if my patients exercise free will?"

"Her name was on their list. I need to know about absolutely everyone."

"That's it. I mean, I've had patients with cancer who've died and who were taking all sorts of pain medication at the end. Does that count too?"

"Listen, here's what we need to do—"

"Um, Tory—" Simon interrupted, "Emily's on the other line and my daughter's in the hospital, and I've got to get to Bethesda."

"I talked to the U.S. Attorney's office—"

He was impatient all of a sudden. "Are they arresting me today?"

"No, but—"

"Then whatever it is can wait," Simon said. "I gotta go." He clicked back to Emily. He could hear her breathing. "You there?" He wanted to tell Emily everything, but he felt he didn't deserve to. It was impossible to know where to begin.

Her voice had urgency, a kind of belligerence even. "Can't you focus on us? Right here? Even for five minutes?" Emily demanded. "Are you getting ready to see patients already?"

"I'm not," he insisted. "I'm coming now."

"*I'm* here now," Emily said. "I'm thinking she doesn't need the drama. Our whole drama. She's recovering. Maybe you should come this evening instead."

"Let me talk to her," he urged.

He heard Emily negotiating with Jamie, trying to hand over the phone. He began to feel more panicky. The myokymia flickered under his lower lashes, twitching and undermining, the wings of a little moth trapped next to light.

"Hi," the little voice said. It was a little voice, but he was certain it had an edge of resentment, too.

"How are you feeling, little porpoise? I've been trying to get to you, but it's been hard."

"It's okay," she said. "I mean, let's be honest. I'm almost better."

"I was there on Monday night. Do you remember?"

"Yep." She was shutting him out. He could feel it. It was like a door creaking shut that he had to jam with his foot.

He thought of all that had happened since he'd been standing at her bedside in the hospital. It seemed like weeks ago. "I think I've messed up, sweetheart," he said.

"Yep," she answered.

Her curtness irked him. Who was she to blame him? What did she know about the stresses he was facing? He responded, "What were you doing piercing yourself?"

"I wanted it," she said.

"But you didn't think it might get infected, did you?"

"Nope. I just wanted it," she said again.

"Put your mother back on the phone," he directed, and when he had Emily back, he announced, "I'm driving down there, Emily. I'm leaving the house now."

"Come tonight," Emily replied. "We'll have a proper Changing of the Guard."

But Tory called in the afternoon, saying that nobody had filed charges, and that the best thing to do would be to begin to formulate the appeal to the State Medical Board. That way, they'd be ready to address the suspension the very instant the charges were dropped, and he stood a better chance of reinstating his practice, possibly without too much interruption. They were entering patient names onto Tory's laptop in the early hours of the evening. "Don't stop, Simon," Tory urged. "We're going to be ready for them."

When Simon called Emily to inform her he'd be just a little bit later, she said, her voice like ice, "I heard. Yes. From Betsy. Did you think you just wouldn't mention anything?"

"Ah," he sighed. "There wasn't ever a good time," and then confessed, "I didn't know how to tell you."

"Is it that treatment of yours?" she demanded. "Is that why you lost your license?"

He felt anger at her that she could simplify it so easily, but he didn't feel like arguing with her. "Narcotics, actually," he said with a sigh. "There was a man who died. It wasn't my fault, though. Really had nothing to do with me—I hadn't seen him for a long time. Sort of a bad coincidence. But there it is."

"How could you have gotten yourself into this?" she asked quietly. "How is this happening?"

Julie McKinley, he thought quickly. If he hadn't hired that nervous little girl, none of this would be happening. But then there were other answers. If he'd refused, like most of his colleagues, to give patients the medication they needed, he wouldn't be in the same mess. Or if he'd just shrugged and referred patients to a pain specialist—or a psychiatrist. Or if he happened to be the type of person who wasn't driven to find solutions. Or if he happened not to care. If he'd been a little less available to his patients. If he'd been busy. If she'd responded to the fact that he loved her and that he still wanted her more than he'd ever wanted any woman. If he'd been making wine or growing orchids with his daughter instead of trying to be a hero. If he'd let someone else play the role of David to the Goliath of the great unknown. If he'd managed to recognize in time how sick Caleb was. If he'd managed to get his baby to the hospital earlier. If he'd chosen a different hospital. It was impossible to know where to begin.

They sat on the phone in silence. He had his head in his hands, and vaguely he wished she could see him like that, bent over, his head fallen. There was a time, right after Caleb died, when he'd felt like he couldn't stand the pressure of every approaching minute, when he didn't know what to do with himself or what to say. He'd entered their bedroom and sat on the edge of the bed with his elbows on his knees, his face sunk into the basket of his palms. He'd already cried; he was done crying. He was wasted from crying. She came out of the bathroom and she saw him. He knew she had entered the room, and he could feel her standing there, knowing all of it without uttering a single word as she stepped toward him. Unable to look at her, he opened his eyes and saw her feet on the floor in front of him, bony and sculpted, the color of sunbleached stone. He saw all of their contours, the magnificent arches, the crook of her big toe, the wide flat nail. Bare and vulnerable, rawly human, they were also sturdy and reassuring. He felt lost in the architecture of her feet. He stared at her feet, planted before him, unmoving, before she touched him. He didn't move, didn't breathe, and she put her fingers into his hair. Lightly at first, then deep, against his scalp, and then holding his head with kindness, her hands poised in a kind of priestly blessing of benevolence, and maybe even forgiveness.

He remembered that moment, and he yearned for it again. But she could not see him now. Probably she would not have guessed that his head was in his hands because she said something that he didn't quite hear. What he thought she said was, "You brought this on yourself," but he wasn't sure and he didn't want to ask her to repeat it. He smarted from the sound of it. "I don't know how," he stammered, his voice barely audible.

But he did know, and he did not go to the hospital that night because he was afraid to see them, his wife, his daughter, because all of the ruin around him pointed back to that night fifteen years earlier when the nurse at his side said, "I'm sorry." Emily called later to say that Jamie was being discharged, that the antibiotics had worked, the wound did not need cleaning, and that she was taking Jamie back to her apartment. He answered the phone and heard the news as if from a stupor, and he felt relieved without quite knowing why. He didn't ask the kind of medical questions he felt he should ask, and there was relief in that, too. There was mail on the floor in the hallway. He sifted through it with his feet, mostly bills, and he would not read them. Among the envelopes, he spotted a red one and recognized the jerky loops and triangulated curves of his mother's handwriting. He took it to the living room where he ripped it open. "Simon," began the letter in her spindly cursive, even more ragged than he remembered, and strangely, he felt his heart beating,

> I hardly know where to begin. I'm so astounded by your actions, I feel I do not recognize you. How dare you, is all I can say. How dare you? We raised you to respect other people's property and especially privacy. We did not raise you to behave in such a reprehensible manner as you did in July when you went uninvited into your father's things. I'm still angry when I remember how we caught you with the medication in your hand. All of that might have been forgivable, however. It might have been possible for me to understand your actions as a form of concern for your Father, who has done so much for you all of your life. I was sensitive to the fact that we might have done something dangerous not mentioning the medication to the doctors at the hospital. But regard for your Father did not ultimately seem to be your central concern.
>
> I cannot understand your decision to write about him in the newspaper. Our friends in Baltimore were kind enough to send it to us, but when we read it we were wounded to the core. Isn't there such a thing as patient confidentiality? Doesn't your Father deserve at least that much respect? It is a terrible thing to open up the paper and see your personal matters laid out for everyone in the world.
>
> I cannot imagine how such behavior makes you a responsible doctor. But even worse, I cannot respect your sense of what it means to be someone's son. I do not understand why you subjected your Father and me to this public and very undeserved disgrace.
>
> Your Mother
>
> P.S. If anyone can be said to have "discovered" any sort of cure, the credit should go to Charles.

He couldn't remember the last time he'd been on the receiving end of one of his mother's famous missives, other than the occasional postcard. The last one might have been during his internship when he'd announced he wouldn't come home unless she and Charles paid for his train ticket— and the familiar rambling weirdness charged him with a bizarre sense of delight. Emily would have gotten a good kick out of this one. His mother hadn't called in months, but she'd taken the time to write an entire letter? *How dare you,* he read again, and tasted in his mouth the rising ire, that rage of being poked with a stick. He'd gone all the way down to Florida to *help* them, and they hadn't appreciated a single ounce of the effort. His trip had only proved how dysfunctional his relationship with them was. They'd *deserved* his interference. They'd deserved their public disgrace.

But one line in the letter wounded him more than the others. *I cannot imagine,* he dared to read again, *how such behavior makes you a responsible doctor.* So it was true, then. People were looking, judging not just the self he put into the world, the self that dressed, went out to dinner, greeted neighbors on the street. People expected more of him just because he was a doctor. Who could live up to such standards? He'd acted in such good faith, tried desperately to make people more comfortable. He'd done everything he could to make them know their suffering was legitimate and assure them their needs were heard. And yet, after all of it, everything he'd done had been so wildly misunderstood. Where was the person in his corner? Who was watching his back as he'd been so concertedly watching everyone else's? He put the letter on the coffee table and watched as it missed and drifted to the floor. He curled up on the sofa in a fetal ball and dozed.

He remained on the couch, disappearing deeply into caverns of sleep as though he were making up for years of exhaustion. Daylight turned into night, turned into a shale-gray dawn. He rose to go to the bathroom with the seam of the couch's leather panels imprinted in a line down his cheek. The phone rang and he spoke to Tory, and except for being aware that he wasn't going to jail that very day, he didn't remember what they'd said. At one point he lifted his head from a pillow to the sound of a low rumbling. The noise seemed to be inside his head, and then he realized that the vacuum cleaner was running upstairs. It must have been Friday; Lorraine had let herself into the house. She must have passed him on her way upstairs. He was embarrassed at the state of the house, but he couldn't bring himself to get up. He was filled with a vague hunger, and he wondered whether she'd made anything that was waiting for him in the refrigerator. He wasn't sure whether Emily typically left instructions about what to cook. Finally, he heard her padding down the stairs, and he lifted his head when she seemed to be standing in the doorway of the living room.

She was a large woman with limp, straggly hair. The colorless, tough-ness of her skin, like caulk, made her look much older than she was, which was probably only thirty-five. She wore a T-shirt and wide black jeans while she cleaned. "Doctor," she ventured politely, "I didn't do this here room because I didn't want to wake you. But I gotta be going. I got another job, and I have to get the bus."

He sat up and squinted at her. "It's Friday, isn't it?"

"All day."

"I don't have cash. My wife—she's—"

She was rushed, exasperated. "I can take a check, but just this once."

He could tell by her tone that she knew, and he was surprised to feel embarrassed. She must have heard that Emily was leaving. And here he was sleeping in disheveled clothes on the couch when he should have been seeing patients. He rummaged through the dining room sideboard to get a checkbook. She'd been coming to clean their house every week for more years than he could remember, and he had no idea where she lived or that she had another job or that she took the bus to get from one place to the next. She had cooked for them, folded their underwear, wiped flecks of their spittle from the bathroom mirror. And yet he knew nothing about her. How was this possible? He flipped through the check-book until he found a blank one, and he considered telling her that she didn't need to come anymore, and yet he couldn't find a way to say it. Instead he said, "How much do we owe you?" and he added twenty dollars to the fee she announced.

When she was gone, he felt strangely infused with a new sense of what needed to happen, realizing that what he'd needed was sleep, a chance to let the body rest and sort through the tumult. He was refreshed, and he decided he would not succumb to the DEA's charges. He would not be a victim. He would fight the medical board, maybe even write a book about the persecution of innocent doctors. Ravenously, he shoveled cereal into his mouth. He drank milk straight from the carton, finishing it off. He dialed Tory and left a message: "We've gotta talk. I'm not going to let this get me down. You're right, I've worked too hard to play dead now." When he didn't hear back from Tory, he left another. "Call me, we need to talk strategy. I need to know what's next."

What's next? he asked himself. *What's next?* He went down to the basement and surveyed the disarray of the shelves, the battered wine-making kit. He bolted up the stairs and found a cardboard box in a closet, and dumping out the clothes that had been stored in it, decided it would do for trash. He picked up the broken pieces of the casks, swept the splinters. He'd heard about people like this, whose day-to-day lives careened like a car around blind curves. Mishap after mishap happened to them and they could no more get out from under the downward pull of events than they could escape gravity. He would not succumb to it. He would pick up the pieces, address the problems head-on and continue to do the right thing.

Throwing away the wine casks was not as melancholy a task as he'd feared. They could buy more, he reasoned. If Jamie wanted to do the project, maybe they'd invest again. Then he began to consider the effects of the divorce and the future of the space. He did not want to stay in the house. There were too many memories. At the bottom of a kitchen drawer, he dug up the business card of a realtor, a woman named Irma Franken, and he called her. If he was getting divorced, he ought to know what they could get for the house. He'd just intended to get some figures, but she arrived, all business, with a three-ring notebook with a photograph of the house on the cover and, inside, sections that compared neighborhoods and instructed how to improve a property's curb appeal.

"Ixnay the offices," she said as they walked through the clinic space and he explained what he'd been through in the last week. She had a heavy accent that sounded like it might be Russian, dragging through the *v*'s and the *r*'s, and for a second he wasn't entirely sure if she'd spoken in pig Latin or some other language. "You'll move your practice first. Can't sell it with the commercial space. Unless we sell to another doctor. But given your circumstances, I'm not sure someone would want, you know what I mean?"

"Okay," he said, still stuck on the way she had pronounced *shirkumshtances*. He was imagining the timing. He'd have to get his license back first, so that he'd have income to open a practice at a new location. Quite possibly, he'd have to take out a large loan. Would he be able to get a loan, he wondered?

"I mean, let's be honest, and let's not take offense," she said. "Somebody's going to think twice about picking up where you left off." He nodded. *What's next,* he kept repeating to himself, a new mantra. *What's next?*

Upstairs, she stopped in front of the piano and surveyed the ballroom. "Lovely. A perfect ten. Beautiful, large room. Lots of space."

"The piano's staying," he insisted, regarding the svelte curves of its body. As long as they'd lived there, he'd felt proud of having it, and having fought to keep together the pieces of a long-lost past. "I told you about the history of the house, right? It belonged to one of the early directors of the Peabody Conservatory. Caruso sang in front of that fireplace. Rachmaninoff played on that very piano at a birthday party that was held right here. The piano was here when we bought the house, and I negotiated long and hard to make sure the piano was part of the deal. It should stay."

She walked over to the piano and laid a finger on a key. A sole, melancholy note sounded, and even Simon, who did not have a single musical sensibility, could tell that it was out of tune. "It's a lovely piano," she pronounced, "but Rachmaninoff did not play on it."

"Oh yes," he insisted. "It's archived at the Conservatory." He knew exactly where he would find documentation. He would dig up proof of that music that had once filled the house, auspicious concerts by musical luminaries who did not need words to speak the reverence they experienced in the world, who could say it all in chords and notes.

"Not on this one, I hate to inform you. My father built and restored pianos," she said. "He gave estimates. I grew up knowing all of them. This piano was built in the mid-1940s—you can tell because of the type of wood used during the war. Sergei Rachmaninoff was dead by then."

Some time ago, he would have felt indignant. He would have charged to the library—he would have *driven* her to the library—intending to prove her wrong. But after everything that had happened, he suddenly didn't doubt that she was right. He would never have anticipated it, but the information imparted by Irma Franken made him laugh. He laughed out loud, his eyes watering as his body quaked. He held his belly as the laughter rattled through him and did not stop laughing, or even try to control the outburst, until he began to wheeze, holding the edge of the piano as he tried to catch his breath. Irma Franken stared at him, looking sorry, then amused, then concerned.

He knew from his patients—especially those with chronic pain—that a person could only take so much. They'd talked with him frankly about considering suicide, what it felt like to hit the breaking point. After a

while, the fight to endure became too much effort. It was not overwhelming at first. The torment became a kind of friend, not necessarily a welcome one, but a companion of sorts, a houseguest with staying power. At
first you resisted, but then you adjusted yourself to a compromised existence. You hoped for the return of what you considered normal life. You
blamed yourself. You blamed other people. If you were desperate, maybe
you prayed. You carried on, but more and more you acknowledged the
damage to yourself. And then after time, maybe after a long time, you
entertained the treasonous notion of letting the enemy win. What was
the point of an existence that was all suffering? You played with the idea
of not suffering as if you were holding a coin in your pocket, turning it
over and over, knowing, even when you took your finger away, it was still
there. The possibility of release became a surprisingly tantalizing prospect. Eventually you might acknowledge that the fight to overcome was
as wearying a burden as the pain itself.

He was not suicidal, he decided. But he was not himself, either. He
experienced spurts of optimism and ambition and cleaned out a closet or
unloaded a box of old hiking gear. And then he would try to imagine himself in a new space, a new office, surrounded by new people, and across
town in a new apartment, some other woman who was his new partner
in life (cutting and pasting in his brain, he fit Bev's face into the newly
blank space, then tried out Betsy's, then Rita's), and he couldn't picture
any of it. He had to keep reminding himself who he'd been. It had been
a week since the office had been closed, and he went down to the clinic.
He fed the koi, who appeared unfazed by all the changes, and he stood in
exam room A and read the clipping on the wall from *Baltimore Magazine*
where his very own name and the address of his office was listed with the
other Top Docs.

He tried to imagine himself beginning sentences with, "My ex-wife . . ."
and he found his eyes smarting. In a week, he had spoken to Emily once.
After leaving the hospital, Jamie had gone home to Emily's new apart-

ment. With a criminal case hanging over Simon's head, Emily argued that maybe Jamie should begin the school year in Bethesda. Reluctantly, he agreed. She'd bought Jamie a whole closet of clothes, and she hadn't said a word, letting Jamie select the new outfits. They'd gone to see a shrink together, the two of them.

"What's that like?" Simon asked Jamie on the phone. He could barely imagine.

"Not as bad as you'd think," she replied. He could see her twisted-up little mouth, the bright eyes under the straight cut of the bangs. "You could come sometime."

"We'll see," he said.

"When do you think you'll know about the charges?" she asked. Emily had obviously filled her in, and he felt a seeping of shame.

But it was important to be honest. "I don't know," he said.

"Do you miss it?"

"Seeing patients?" he asked, and then realized the truth: "Not as much as you'd think."

He got off the phone quickly. What he remembered was Bev's comments about the plasticity of relationships. The thought of Bev in her pink pajamas, her wide smiles of reassurance, brought no comfort and instilled a vague queasiness, but the unexpected wisdom she'd offered returned to him. He missed Jamie and he wanted desperately to see her, but he couldn't bring himself to suggest plans. He couldn't bring himself to make the drive to Bethesda, even though he thought it might make him feel better. In the week since the raid, he hadn't eaten much. If he was hungry, he couldn't feel it, and he only realized how little he had taken in when his pants began to sag, the material at the waistline pinching and gathering when he tightened his belt. The few dishes he'd used were piled in the sink. The mail remained on the floor. He'd left clothing strewn around the house, socks in the living room, his oxford shirt on the floor of the bathroom.

Rita called the house and left messages. "I'm changing the outgoing message for the office," she said into the machine. "I thought patients should know." The Ebberlys called. He didn't answer the phone. Betsy stopped by and left a container of homemade chicken soup in a bag on his doorstep. He would have left the bag sitting there, but he didn't want her to drive by and think he was unappreciative of her friendship. He carried the bag inside and rested the whole thing in the kitchen sink and left it there. *And this too shall pass,* he told himself.

He was partly right. He was not a long-suffering Job. At the end of a week, Tory called to say the U.S. Attorney's office was dropping the investigation altogether. "No criminal charges," he crowed into the phone. "They didn't have a good case with that MacAllister guy. Too many question marks. They've got bigger fish to fry, is my guess. Anyway, it's the best scenario we could've hoped for. Now we just have to work on the appeal for the Board, get your license reinstated and get you back in business."

He appreciated Tory's energy, but he could not match it, and he told Tory he'd call later to schedule a meeting. He looked around the house where nothing seemed familiar, and it occurred to him for the first time that he was not ready for an appeal. The phone rang again. He could see that it was the Ebberlys again, and he listened as the machine picked up the call.

"It's us," Betsy's voice entered the room. "We wanted to remind you about breaking the fast tomorrow. Sundown. Our house. Don't bring anything. Just yourself. Might be good for you to get out."

For a moment, he wondered if maybe they were scheming. They'd been unusually persistent. Maybe they had invited Emily, too, with the intent of bringing them together again. But Emily didn't care for religious events, and the chances of her attending a post–Yom Kippur event with its sanctimonious overtones, the guests buzzing with the tremors of having gone holy with noneating and repetitive prayer, were next to zero. The

Ebberlys were just looking out for him because he had not left the house in a week or returned calls and because they were hopelessly kind. There was no one he wanted to see, and it was clear from the way the Groves had disappeared that his welcome was not assured. What would they do if they saw him? Would they stop to talk? He walked to the front door and opened it, looking down the block in the direction of their house.

The colors of the day had begun to shift and wane. Simon stood in the doorway, waiting for something, not quite sure what. He turned to go back inside and was suddenly overcome by the quiet of the house. It hummed. It suffocated. For the first time, he thought he could not be alone. He needed help getting through this. He looked at the phone and thought of Tory, eager to set a date and move ahead. He considered dialing Bev in Salt Lake City, just to hear her voice. He thought of the Ebberlys, and he wanted suddenly just to be near them. He wanted to be with people who cared about him. Grabbing his gray wool coat from the hall closet, he left the house. It was better to be outside, he realized as he gulped in lungfuls of fall air, invigorating to have a destination.

Not until he was in the car, well on the way to the temple they attended, Beth Shalom, did he look down at the coat. It was the one with a deep ink stain, like a bullet hole, over the left breast pocket where he'd once forgotten a capless Bic. Emily had urged him to get rid of the coat, throw it away or donate it to one of the associations that were always calling, asking for bags to be set curbside for pickup, but he'd held on to it, arguing that he might be able to locate a solvent for the ink. He'd called several pen manufacturers, dry cleaning businesses, and even tried to reach a columnist at *Good Housekeeping* (that was Rita's suggestion) who gave tips on stain removal. Then he'd gotten the idea that it might be possible to cut the stain out with scissors and darn the material, just like a sock, and he bought thread and set aside a surgical needle and was waiting for a day when he had enough time to focus on it. He'd managed to pursue none of the options, much to Emily's continued annoyance.

"Clothes are clothes," he'd retorted when she'd badgered. Though he'd known she was right, he'd continued to defend the coat. As if it deserved to be salvaged. "Entropy dictates that eventually you'll have stains." Remembering that conversation embarrassed him. Poetic justice had been served: His wife had left and he remained with a bullet-sized stain over the heart.

Shyly touring the packed lot at Beth Shalom, he realized he didn't have tickets for services. Did God forgive you for sneaking in on Yom Kippur? he wondered. Maybe, if your need to be there was great. A benevolent God would know that Simon had nowhere else in the world to be. He was wanted by no one, needed by no one. He parked on the street and trotted through the cool evening air toward the temple.

As he stepped inside, he could hear that the service had begun. The ushers were nowhere in sight, and no one was standing watch at the door. Inside, he helped himself to a yarmulke from a box in the hallway and entered the sanctuary, still trying to locate the one angle at which the black silk would cup his head without sliding. Only a few solo seats remained in the back of the auditorium. Several rows ahead, he could see the Ebberlys and two of their children turning pages in their prayer books. Their youngest had come home from college for the holiday, and he wondered, suddenly, what Jamie was doing. She'd roll her eyes if he were to tell her that, with nothing to do, he'd wound up at Kol Nidre services. Him! He was pathetic. He didn't read Hebrew, he only knew a few of the prayers by humming along. Reaching for a prayer book, heavy and solid as a brick, he held it in his lap without opening it.

The service of Kol Nidre was the evening service that led into the holy day of Yom Kippur. He'd attended years ago with Emily, but only because a friend of theirs was going. He remembered that they'd discussed it afterward as if it were a cultural event where the focus was the music, not the day of the year in which the Book of Life was opened before it was summarily sealed. Parts of Kol Nidre echoed the Yom Kippur service, but its purpose was different, the cantor was explaining as Simon leaned back in the seat. Kol Nidre offered the annulment of the year's vows between people and God, or between the individual and one's sense of the holy. "In other words, tonight the formula we recite is restricted to those vows which concern only the relation of the individual to his conscience or to his Heavenly Judge. For those vows we've made in the last year, all bets are off," explained the cantor, who was young with Coke-bottle glasses. "Tonight we ask for forgiveness for forsaking God."

"We now stand," said the cantor, so Simon rose along with the people seated around him. He gazed up at the stained glass towering above the Ark where the Torah scrolls were kept, joyous points of light catching the dipping sun. There were reasons that sanctuaries of mankind were great and lofty, and he felt eased by the sense of being small and insignificant. He'd never been good at praying, in any language. He was easily distracted by the sights around him. His mind strayed to his patients, his little concerns, return e-mails, the phone calls he needed to make, and he was never able to get into a holier state. He questioned the prayers as he read them, and he said "God," because the prayer on the page said "God," but in his mind supplied skeptically, *Or whatever higher power that we imagine we need,* because he didn't believe rationally in God. Two of the congregants, one of whom he recognized from the crowd that attended the opera, opened the Ark and lifted out the Torah scroll in its velvet sheath. They raised it and began the procession around and down the aisles of the congregation.

He raised a hand in a small wave at the Ebberlys. Betsy returned the greeting with a smile, nudging Ted, who turned around and nodded. The service of Kol Nidre asked forgiveness and annulled the vows between humans and the divine. *What's next?* he thought as the procession edged around the synagogue. He would call Tory and schedule a meeting. He'd get back on track. He'd appeal to the Board. But did he want that? The congregants took their seats and a woman with a pillbox-shaped yarmulke stepped to the center of the stage. Her voice lifted and wound in a melancholy, ancient melody that throbbed like a pulse. He read along in English as she asked on behalf of all of them sitting there, as if they all were seated in court, for a pardon.

He looked around, the people seated in front of him and on his sides. What sins could these people possibly have wrought? They'd taken God's name in vain when the garbage bag ripped on the haul down the driveway? Or they'd promised to be kinder human beings? The woman on his right had a protruding chin and slightly bulging eyes that looked like she had a thyroid disorder. The man on his left sat with a thumb-sucking kindergarten-aged child on his lap. Was he, Simon, so arrogant that he imagined his own transgressions were worse than any perpetrations of the people sitting around him? But they were. He was certain of it. He could chant along with them, but his circumstances were so singular, only he could know. And what could he make of all of it? He felt like he held pieces of a torn map that didn't come together cleanly at the edges. The information he felt he needed was exactly at the tear.

One detail he had never told Emily was that he had visited the cemetery after Caleb died. He'd gone alone. The weather had not been pleasant, the sky measureless and dull as the inside of a jar. The wind whipped at him, and he first realized he was underdressed for the cold and then thought he was deserving of the discomfort. As he walked to the gravesite from the car, the chill began to punish. The weather was forbidding, keeping other visitors from walking the paths or tending the grounds, and he was relieved not to encounter anyone. It took time to find the site, and he grew anxious as he stepped along the plots, looking for the little gray stone. But there it was. The rectangle in the ground bore only his son's name, Caleb Joseph Bear, and the digits of the year, no month, no day, and Simon was relieved they'd decided to leave the information off, because reading the brevity of that short lifespan would have been too painful.

He had wanted to say to Caleb that he wouldn't forget him. He had a new daughter, with a scraggle of dark hair, who was healthy, feeding voraciously, and he knew to appreciate that fact. But he wanted to say out loud, in the way of a promise, that he would always remember those weeks of being Caleb's father. On the drive to the cemetery, he had imagined that when he stood before the grave, he'd find a voice to say some words aloud. Not as long as a speech, exactly, or as overbearing as a vow. Just a short communication. *Hey there, it's me, Daddy.* But the reality of standing there was not as comfortable or as freeing as he'd imagined. He stood, peeking at the stone, feeling almost shy. With hands jammed in the pockets of his slacks, he rocked on his feet, tried to form sentences in his head, hoping the dead did not need a message all spelled out word for word. He wished Emily had come with him to visit the grave because they might have talked to each other there. They might have said, "Do you remember the—?" and "Wasn't it funny when—?" Caleb, overhearing, might have been able to understand something in the sentences they said to each other. But Simon stared at the little gray stone, rough at the edges, polished smooth across the flat top where flecks of quartz twinkled merrily. His hands were balled in his pockets. His mouth was dry. His tongue had gone still.

In the cold, a hesitant drizzle prickled at him, enough to make him realize that he would not be able to stay long. He would not sit down. *I hope you know,* the thought formed in his head. But that was all that came. He did not have an image of heaven in mind, but he pictured his son hovering somewhere above him, not below him in the ground. And he imagined the words he was thinking—actually *squeezing* with forceful intent out of the language center of his brain—floating upward, too. His sense of upwardness, the pull of his attention, seemed proof of something, not necessarily of the existence of God, but of something eternal and undying in human need.

Simon looked up at the ceiling of the synagogue. It was a modern-styled chapel. Rosy wooden beams flanked either side, like the walls of a barn, toward a flat section in the middle. Crossbeams divided the central area into rectangles. For the sake of acoustics, dropped, slanted panels hung a foot or two from the ceiling, suspended by dark chains. Humans were small creatures with good intentions. They did the best they could with physics, constructing buildings that would remain standing, channeling sound waves that could be heard. There was a science to such buildings. Since the beginning of time, people had struggled to build space in which they could hear. They did the best they could, striving, striving. It was a comforting thought.

The woman with the pillbox-shaped head-covering led a chorus of responsive reading. Simon struggled to find the page. He caught up as the congregation chanted:

> Thou knowest the mysteries of the universe and the hidden secrets of all living. Thou searchest out the heart of man and probest all our thoughts and aspirations. Naught escapeth Thee, neither is anything concealed from Thy sight.

Standing at the grave, he had imagined the spiritual Caleb, more animated, fuller, rosier than he'd been as a newborn—Pre-Raphaelite in color, rounded and dimpled with the succulence of infancy. Little stinging pins of rain had dotted his hands and his shirt, prompting his sense of urgency, and yet hastening his conviction of futility and waste. He stubbed around in the grass with the toe of his shoe until he saw a small pebble, which he knew, from Jewish funerals he'd attended, to place on the corner of the headstone, simply to say that someone had been there. That was all that had happened at the cemetery: He'd moved a pebble. Then he departed, and on the drive home he'd gotten a ticket for running a red light. (At another time, he might have tried to talk his way out of a fine, but he'd sat, tongue-tied, unable to look up at the trooper, certain that if he looked into the face of punishment, he'd cry.) He'd not mentioned the ticket to

Emily and then not paid it, and then forgotten about it, as it accrued fines and additional fees and finally came to Emily's attention because she was unable to renew the registration. And it was with this long chain of fuck-ups that he'd tried to tell her the simplest thing: I went to look for Caleb. There were reasons to atone yearly, he realized, but in his case, they never changed. He was the same story over and over again.

He wasn't sure what he might have done differently when Caleb got sick, but he should not have stopped thinking about it after his son had died. He should have continued to wonder. Around him, the congregants closed their hands into fists and knocked on their chests as they recited a long list of sins. It was a list of sins that they acknowledged they'd done willingly and unwillingly, knowingly and deceitfully, falsely, fraudulently, violently, irreverently, plottingly, arrogantly and distractedly. The words were rote and repetitious. *And arrogant,* Simon thought. We have trespassed, they said, we have dealt treacherously. *I haven't, though,* Simon took issue. *I haven't dealt treacherously with anyone.* But he chanted along with the people sitting on his sides.

> We have robbed, we have spoken slander, we have acted perversely, and we have wrought wickedness; we have been presumptuous, we have done violence, we have framed lies, we have counseled evil, and we have spoken falsely. We have scoffed, we have revolted, we have provoked, we have rebelled, we have committed iniquity, and we have transgressed.

It was all so archaic—but where in the list was his sin? Were there words in the prayers to acknowledge that he had failed his newborn son? Or that, after that, with everything he hadn't done, he had failed Emily, too? He longed to start over fresh—but they could not start over. All he and Emily could do was acknowledge the damage they'd wrought by trying to move away from their pain as quickly as they could. He curled his hand into a fist, and he rapped it against his chest. He knocked against his sternum, in a rhythm that matched the thumping around him. He looked at the man on his left. The child had closed her eyes, leaning against her father. She sucked at her thumb as though she would devour it. The man held his child in his left arm, balancing his prayer book in front of him, the knuckles of his right hand thudding against his chest. Simon was looking—staring—when the child's eyelids fluttered open and regarded him evenly, observing without judgment.

They listed their sins, one by one, but they were communal sins, he understood at once, and they accepted responsibility all together. He didn't feel like one of them. He felt his separateness, like a stone set aside. People came to *him* for help. He guided them through their pain. But it was a relief to think he was one of them, just another transgressor. At that moment, he happened to look down into the text, and his glance caught the words as though they were meant for him alone. "May my soul be humble and forgiving unto all." *Unto all,* he thought and a wave rose in him that felt like hope: *And not me too?* Before he could check himself, tears had sprung to the surface, forged from a hidden source. One betrayer rolled down to his chin. He glanced toward the man with the child to see if he had been noticed. A chant had begun, the collective voice of the congregation reverberating in melancholy tones. The words of the prayer came to him from some long-lost memory, some pattern etched in his core, and following the motions of the congregants around him, he rapped his knuckles against his chest—not a separate solitary breast beating beneath a cage of ribs, but part of a great organism that hummed and moaned in repentance. Another fat tear dribbled to the end of his nose and he wiped at it furiously and sniffled.

He heard the little girl then. "That man's *crying,*" she exclaimed, pointing at Simon with a hand slick with drool.

"Shh," her father answered, keeping his head bent, though several people in rows ahead had turned around to see.

But the child persisted. "Why, Daddy?" she asked. "Why's he crying?"

The father didn't answer, but instead nervously shifted the child to his right arm, facing her away from Simon. She would not be diverted, though, and craned her neck around her father's arm to get a good look at the spectacle.

Simon, eyes blurred, had lost his page again. He flipped ahead, trying to find where the cantor read, and it was then he happened to see the words in English, at the beginning of a paragraph. *Open Thou my lips.* It was the beginning of a prayer. Here was age-old proof the words didn't come easily. It took help to get them started. He could not atone for his sins against Emily until he'd sought her forgiveness, but would she forgive?

He picked up his coat, with its punctuation over the heart, and he clutched it under his arm. Hurrying down the synagogue steps, he felt the crisp air on his still dewy face, and he knew what there was to do. He would find Emily, and he would hold her by the shoulders and look into her eyes, implore her to look back at him. It was not clear to him which words to use to begin, and he realized the futility of trying to plan, but he would start somewhere, perhaps as far back as he could reach in memory, and he would feel his way forward to that very moment of atonement. When he opened his mouth, he felt certain he would know what to say.

ACKNOWLEDGMENTS

My deep gratitude to editor and publisher Amy Einhorn, who went over this book with a keen eye and an exquisitely sensitive heart, and to literary agent Lisa Bankoff, who believed in Simon Bear and who is ever a generous and kind source of wisdom and advice.

When you take ten years to write a book, as I did, the well of indebtedness runs deep. I'm especially grateful for the sage advice I received from talented writers Becky Hagenston, Oren Uziel, J. Robert Lennon and Julie Kimmel. Thank you to my brother, Gabriel Ledger, and lifelong friend, Miriam Laufer, who cheered me on with all their hearts and tirelessly answered questions about doctors and medical conditions, even when I wasn't quite sure what information I was seeking. Thanks to the writers I met at the Wesleyan Writers Conference, and also friends Jonathan Brody, Ute Eberle, Nicole Sorger, Rebecca Caine, Abby Weinberg, Julie Weissman (who gave me a key to her house and let me write a chunk of the book at her dining room table), Ben and Lisa Sachs, Boo Hill, Jennifer Tilton and Laura Goldblum. They all listened to me babble as my ideas about Simon and Emily were taking shape, and were sweet enough to indulge me as though we were talking about real people. From the core of my being, I thank two wonderful women, Barbara J. Tower and Rebecca Barth, each of whom took loving care of my children so that I had time to write. Thanks, too, to my children, who amaze me every day.

Forever and ever I will be grateful for the love and support (and I'm summarizing here because both were bestowed in a breathtaking multitude of ways) that I received from my parents, Martha and Marshall Ledger, and my parents-in-law, Merle and Murray Sachs. This book, and a whole long list of life dreams, would not have been possible without them.

At long last, I stumble to find words for the gratitude and love I feel for my husband, Jonathan Sachs. He is wise beyond compare, fierce and stubborn and a dreamer of the highest order. He didn't flinch as I spent years writing about a troubled marriage. All along, he pushed me to make important self-maintenance decisions that would enable me to finish the book. He urged me to draw on good material, asked challenging questions and, when I floundered, Scotch-taped on the wall above my desk two vital, loving words: "What's next?"